CROWNS

WAR QUEEN

NICOLA TYCHE

COLUMBIA RIVER
PUBLISHING

COLUMBIA RIVER PUBLISHING
Vancouver, WA 98685

First published in the United States

ISBN: PB: 978-1-959615-09-5; eBook: 978-1-959615-08-8
HC: 978-1-959615-10-1; Audio: 978-1-959615-11-8

Cover design by Saint Jupiter
Edited by Kate Studer
Edited by Hanna Richards
Proofread by Lauren Riebs

This is a work of fiction. Names, characters, places, and situations either are the product of the author's imagination or are used fictitiously, and any resemblance to actual persons, living or dead, business establishments, events, or locales is entirely coincidental.

For Everly and Rosemary

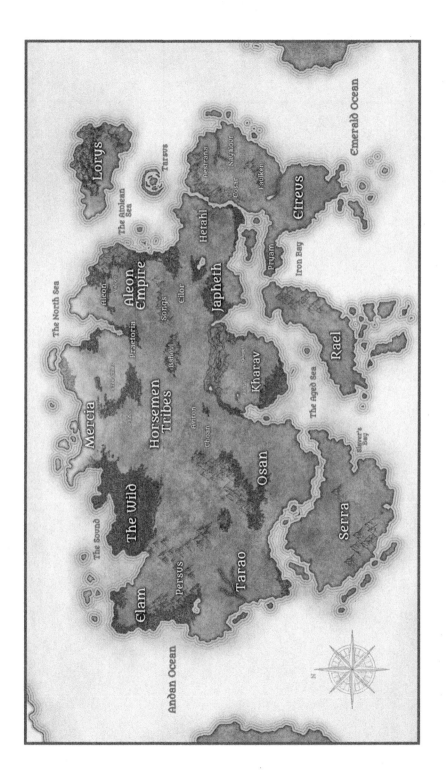

WAR QUEEN

CHAPTER ONE

Again. They were here again.

Norah's eyes drifted around the empty Kharavian throne room. It wouldn't be empty in a few moments. She sat in her chair on the dais and tried to push down the unease creeping in as Mikael took his own seat. She watched her husband and the calm that sat over him—not the calm of peace, but the calm that comes before battle.

"I hate this room," she muttered.

He turned to her. "Why?"

So many reasons. It was the coldest room in the castle; even in the warmth of summer, she practically needed a cloak. It was the room where they received bad news. And it was where the Kharavian nobles incessantly judged them, judged Mikael. She didn't say those things, not when they were about to face another slew of judgments—judgments that threatened Mikael's crown—and not when he worked so hard to protect her from the worry of it all.

"Because you're too far." She reached out her arm, unable to stretch even half the distance between them. It wasn't a petty complaint. They could face anything together, but here it didn't feel like they were together. She couldn't touch him, couldn't get strength from simply putting her hand in his. When he faced challenges from his nobles, she couldn't put her hand on his arm to help settle him as she usually would, to remind him he wasn't alone.

Norah looked down at the bottom of her chair. "And these gods-damned things were built into the floor. I can't even scooch over."

He raised a brow. "Scooch?"

"Yes." She frowned. "I can't move to come closer."

The corners of his mouth turned up ever so slightly. "Ah. Well, scooch just your body here then."

"What?"

"Come here."

She glanced at the closed double doors at the end of the hall. The nobles would arrive soon, but she rose and moved to him anyway. He reached out his hand, and she took it, and they threaded their fingers together as he pulled her closer. His lips held a smile she hadn't seen in months.

"Why are you smiling?" she asked. He shouldn't be smiling with what was coming in the next moments.

He brought her hand up and kissed the backs of her fingers. "Because I have you."

His words brought a wave of emotion as she caressed the side of his cheek. "I love you."

"I know," he whispered. "And I love you." He pulled her into his lap, and she laughed.

"This is a good compromise," she said, grinning. "Yes, I like this much better."

Mikael shrugged. "This is how we'll sit, then."

She laughed again. "You can't address your nobles with me sitting on your lap."

"Why not?"

Norah drew her brows together. "It's not... kingly."

"I don't care about being kingly; I care about making my salara happy." He pursed his lips through a small smile. "Which also makes me happy."

"Well, I don't want them seeing me like this—they already view me as a distraction to you."

"The most beautiful of distractions."

His body responded underneath her, and she swatted him. "Stop it!" she warned with a grin. Then she rested her hand on his chest. "I should start my journey back to my chair now if I'm going to make it there by nightfall. I'll miss you." And she kissed him deeply.

His body hardened more, and she smiled as she pulled away and walked back to her throne. He protested with a rumble in his chest.

Norah took her chair just as Salara-Mae entered. As soon as she saw the woman, the smile fell from her lips. For a fleeting moment, she'd forgotten what they were facing, and the woman's hard countenance pulled her back to the reality of their situation. Mikael's mother rarely joined them in the throne room, but she did now, no doubt to support her son.

The nobles were displeased. More than displeased. Kharav's alliance with Japheth was broken, and a new enemy—Rael—was on the horizon, an enemy they felt Mikael had underestimated. He had. They all had. Who would have thought a kingdom of freed slaves would be such a threat?

As if that weren't enough cause for concern, Kharav's alliance with Mercia had crumbled—an alliance the nobles had always doubted. If Mercia united once again with their old ally, Aleon, they'd have the advantage if they attacked.

With no allies, Kharav stood alone.

And now another had a claim to the Kharavian throne—one who held the respect and loyalty of their great armies as much as Mikael did, one that no longer stood by Mikael's side. Soren. After learning he was Mikael's half brother, he'd disappeared, and his absence was a gaping void.

Mikael was alone.

Norah glanced at him as he set his eyes on the heavy ashen doors, all traces of play now gone from his face. He wasn't Mikael now. He was salar. And this was the fight for his throne.

On her right, her Crest guard Bhastian stepped between their thrones, his spear in one hand and his other hand resting on the hilt of the sword around his waist. The Crest protected the king and royal family. Bhastian's place was to Mikael's right, on the side of the dais, but Mikael had wanted him closer to Norah. She caught movement to her left out of the corner of her eye and looked to see Adrian beside her as well. She hadn't noticed when either of them had entered, but she was glad they were there now. Her stomach turned at the thought that she might need them.

The doors swung open with a deep boom, startling her, and she forced herself to settle. She always forgot they did that—another reason she hated this room.

The nobles filed in. She lost count as they came through the doors. There were perhaps a hundred. Or a little less? And although they were nobles, they still embodied every aspect of Kharav's essence. These weren't like the nobles of Mercia—elevated and fattened solely on the backs of others. They were warriors, protectors of their people. Some of them were warlords with vast lands and armies of their own.

They had called for an audience to show their continued concern over the increasing threats to Kharav and press for Soren's return—neither of which Mikael had control over. She folded her clammy hands in her lap to keep from wringing them together. She wanted to look at Mikael, to draw in some of the power that radiated from him as he sat so calmly looking out across the nobles, but she didn't dare look away. Instead, she did her best to fake the same.

"Salar," Lord Narsing greeted, polite yet cold. "This is an unfortunate state in which we continue to find ourselves."

Norah hated this man. He reminded her of Edward, the elder Mercian councilman who'd no doubt been the one to orchestrate the coup against her—only he was a larger, more intimidating version of Edward. Unlike the other Kharavian nobles, there was an air of scheming about him, and when he spoke, he spoke only in challenge.

"It is," Mikael replied.

The noble's eyes narrowed. "We'd like to understand your plans to salvage the alliance with Japheth."

"There isn't one," Mikael replied, matter-of-factly.

Murmurs rippled through the nobles. Narsing puffed a small breath of incredulity.

Another noble stepped forward. Unlike most of the nobles, he covered his face like a warrior. But Norah knew who he was. Lord Jarik. This was a man who could plant seeds of fear in even the bravest of men. He was an influential lord, not just in status but by his pure embodiment of blood and battle. Jarik was a man of war, and the markings of his bravery covered almost his whole body. He was one of the few nobles to lead battle charges from the front. And he looked like he might lead a charge against Mikael now. "You plan for Kharav to stand alone?" he asked.

But Mikael wasn't shaken. "And what would you propose otherwise?"

"Gregor—"

Mikael cut him off. "Gregor is now an enemy of Kharav and has allied himself with Rael's King Cyrus."

"Is he an enemy of Kharav, or an enemy of Salara?" Narsing pressed.

Gregor. Norah tried to hold her repulsive shudder at the sound of his name. She knew they'd use her previous confrontation with Japheth's king against Mikael. They saw it as a deliberate attempt by her to fracture the alliance between Japheth and Kharav, with Mikael doing nothing to mend it. Heat radiated from Mikael, and her pulse quickened. He couldn't let his anger drive him. Not here. Not now. But she was too far to touch him, too far to pull him back.

"When will the lord commander be returning?" Narsing asked—a question with an indirect threat.

Mikael continued to sit on his throne, calm on the outside. "Why?"

"Would you not expect Kharavian nobles to want to keep track of those with a claim to the throne?" Jarik said.

"We must continue to assess options for Kharav," Narsing added, clearly emboldened by Jarik. A direct threat.

Another ripple of whispers moved through the crowd.

Mikael rose, and the murmurs in the room fell silent. He slowly stepped down the stairs.

Bhastian and Adrian shifted even closer to Norah. Her other Crest guard, Kiran, made his presence known as well. She gripped the arms of her chair, her fingernails biting into the ornately carved wood.

Mikael stopped in the center of the hall, in the center of what looked like a potential battlefield, only a few paces from Narsing. It was a move of challenge, daring them to act against him. Norah's heart pounded in her chest. She breathed prayers to every god she could remember for Mikael not to react with blood. The Crest and Adrian would be focused on her protection and wouldn't be able to help him, not with the nobles now surrounding him.

Salara-Mae stood to the right of the dais like a statue, but Norah knew she was beside herself. Soren's bloodline had been a secret the woman had harbored for so long, and in her moment of anger, she'd released it. Salara-Mae had brought this added threat to Mikael, and no doubt she blamed herself. As she should.

"Where is the lord commander now?" Lord Narsing asked.

"He's not here," Mikael replied stiffly.

"When will he return?"

"Again, why?" Mikael demanded. "*I* am salar. If you have a grievance, you'll address it with me, not the commander of *my* armies that he leads with the power given *by me*." He loomed closer to Narsing, daring the noble to challenge him further.

Narsing's eyes flicked to Jarik. The large warlord put his hand on the hilt of his sword. Faster than Norah could blink, Narsing whipped his hand to his own sword. But Mikael was faster. Before Narsing had fully drawn his blade from the scabbard, Mikael had buried his own blade in the lord, to the hilt—so clean that blood had yet to spill.

Norah jumped to her feet. Adrian and Bhastian bumped against her shoulders on either side, their swords out. But no one else moved. The hall was silent.

Mikael leaned even closer to Narsing, who still hung on his sword. "I accept your challenge," he snarled. Then he shoved Narsing back off his blade. The lord fell to the floor of the hall and didn't get up. Blood pooled under his body, spidering along the lines where the patterned stone joined together.

Mikael roved his eyes over the nobles around him. "Anyone else?" His stare landed on Jarik, who stared back. The warlord's hand was still curled around the hilt of the sword at his side.

The air in the room was suffocating. Norah couldn't breathe. She had no doubt of Mikael's ability to fight, especially in defending what was his. But Jarik wasn't a man she wanted to see against him. He was a man even Soren respected. That meant he was dangerous.

"Anyone else?" Mikael pressed again, not taking his eyes from Jarik.

Norah couldn't see his face under his head wrap, but Jarik's eyes held enough of a message that one didn't need to see his face to understand—a warning.

Finally, after an eternity, the lord said, "No, Salar." But he didn't drop his hand from the hilt of his sword.

Norah didn't dare let relief settle her. This wasn't over.

Mikael looked around the room. "We're done here," he said. Then he turned his back—another invitation for violence that made bile rise in the back of Norah's throat—as he strode and took the stairs back to his throne.

It was perhaps the shortest, although seemingly the longest, exchange with the nobles Norah had seen. She shakily lowered herself back to her seat as Mikael took his own chair, and they watched everyone start to filter out. Two men grabbed Narsing's body and carried him from the room, leaving a trail of blood along the stone.

They waited until the last of the nobles had departed and the doors had closed. Even Salara-Mae wordlessly disappeared into the wings and down the side hall from where she'd come.

When they were alone, Norah turned to him. But she couldn't speak. Her heart still hadn't slowed.

He held out his hand for her. "Come, journey back to me from that ridiculously far chair." His words were said in jest, but there was no happiness in them, no play in his voice. Still, she was too eager to be back to him and moved quickly to his side. He caught her hand in his and brought her palm to his lips, planting a reassuring kiss. Whether he was reassuring himself or her, she wasn't sure.

"Are you all right?" he asked.

She nodded. "Are you?"

Heat still pulsed off him. He didn't answer.

She threaded her fingers into his hair, messing up the tie that bound it back, but she didn't care. She drew her fingertips gently across the back of his head, as she often did to help him relax.

"I need to appoint someone." His voice was empty. Hollow.

"For what?"

He didn't answer.

Norah cupped his cheek and pulled his face to look at her. "Appoint someone for what?" she asked again.

"Lord commander," he said finally.

She swallowed. "You have a lord commander."

He said nothing in reply.

She tightened her fingers against his skin. "Mikael, you have a lord commander."

"And he left me!" he raged suddenly.

But she didn't react to his explosion of hurt. It had been over three months since Soren had left, and his absence was felt every day, by both of them. Norah softened her touch but still held his face as she moved to his front and stepped between his knees. She pulled him to look at her again.

His brows dipped in sadness as he sucked in a heavy breath. "He left me," he said hoarsely. Emotion filled his face, and she pulled him to her, wrapping her arms around him.

"He'll be back," she tried to assure him.

"He's not welcome back."

She pulled back so that his eyes met hers again. "Don't say that."

"He's supposed to be by my side. But he left me when I need him most."

"No," she countered. "Did you not hear Narsing and Jarik? Soren knows he's seen as a threat to you—he would have wanted to remove that threat."

"He could have rejected his right. He didn't need to leave."

She shook her head. "You know it wouldn't have been that simple, not with the nobles. They're not happy. They'd use him to pressure you."

"And did he fear he'd so easily allow them?"

Norah sighed. He knew the answer to that foolish question. She ran her nails gently through his short-cut beard. "The news about your father—his father—had to have hurt him. Deeply. And to reconcile the feelings he had... around you... These things aren't easy."

"Why not? We would have been what we've always called each other—brothers—what I've always felt we were." He shook his head. "But I was wrong. He's not my brother."

"Mikael," she breathed. "You can't mean that."

"I mean it," he said coldly, his emotion gone. "Don't speak to me about him again. I no longer know him."

It was his pain talking. But she couldn't deny the deep, aching worry that seeped into her heart.

Chapter Two

The sun had started to sink under the horizon, and the sound of Salara-Mae's teacup clinking as she set it on the saucer echoed through the dining hall. Norah chewed her food slowly. That probably echoed too. Hardly any words were spoken as they ate, much like the last two days had been since the confrontation with the nobles. Mikael took drinks from his chalice, staring blankly at his plate of untouched food.

She knew what was on his mind. Her eyes drifted to Soren's empty chair, as they did every meal since he'd left. But Mikael never looked at the chair, or his mother. He had raged at Salara-Mae after first learning the secret that had rocked their kingdom. Now he only simmered in silent anger.

Norah had blamed her too, for a time, but as the months passed, she found her anger fading. Despite the turmoil it had caused, there was a relief to be living in truth, no matter the challenges it presented or how raw it rubbed the heart.

But she didn't like this, the way they were now. This wasn't how they healed—by not talking. But she couldn't force a conversation about Soren. Not with either of them. Not yet.

"I was going to take a walk in the gardens in the morning," Norah said in an effort to break the perpetual silence. "To try to take advantage of what's left of summer."

Mikael lifted his eyes to hers, and he nodded. "You should."

She shifted her gaze to the king's mother. "Will you join me, Salara-Mae?"

The woman paused her chewing, then swallowed. "Very well."

Norah had expected to have to work harder to convince her and was pleasantly surprised. "All right then," she said with a small smile.

Salara-Mae put her dinner cloth on her plate and rose with a nod. "But for tonight, I'll retire."

"Good night," Norah told her.

Mikael remained silent.

Salara-Mae left the dining hall, and Norah looked back to Mikael to find him watching her.

"You can't stay angry at her forever," she said softly.

He took another drink from his chalice.

Norah rose and moved to the chair beside him, then reached across the corner of the table and took his hand. "Mikael. She spoke in a moment of anger that she's deeply regretted ever since."

"I'm not angry with her for speaking the truth. I'm angry with her for not speaking it sooner."

"And when would she have done that? The longer you carry a secret, the harder it is to tell."

"It should never have been a secret!"

Norah sighed. She didn't disagree, but these things were never that simple. "It's a mother's job to protect her children. To love them." She squeezed his hand. "And she loves you fiercely. Whether what she did was right, whether you agree with her choices, she made those choices with your well-being in her heart."

His continued objection flashed in his eyes but remained unspoken on his lips. He pushed out a breath and covered her hand with his. "We don't need to talk about me. You've endured so much more."

"It's not a competition."

The muscle tightened along his jaw. "I haven't even asked you how you've been. I'm sorry."

She shook her head. "It's okay."

"No, it's not." He rested his weight on his elbows and cupped her hand in his. "Tell me how you are."

How she was—such a simple question, yet so complicated. She wanted to smile and tell him she was all right, mainly because if she spoke of what she was really feeling, it would bring a wave of emotion she couldn't control.

"Tell me," he said softly.

They had spoken of Mercia before, speculating on what might have happened after the coup, but only to a point and only of best-case scenarios—assuming that her grandmother was unharmed and that Alexander was all right.

Alexander.

Her heart still dropped like a rock every time she thought of him. Despite the harsh words between them when they last spoke, he would have never stood idle while Norah was attacked. And unlike her grandmother, an aged royal of Mercia easily overpowered, Alexander was a soldier. He would have fought. He would have come for her.

But he didn't.

"I'm scared," she whispered.

14

He nodded but didn't speak. He only waited for her to continue.

"We know nothing. The council has surely crowned my cousin, Evangeline, logically. But I know nothing of my grandmother, if she's well." She paused as her voice caught in her throat. "If she's even alive. And..." Her voice dropped off. She didn't want to raise her fears for Alexander. Of course Mikael would know she had them, but she didn't want to so openly lay them out before him.

He squeezed her hand tighter. "The Bear is alive," he said, as if reading her mind, "and he'll watch over your grandmother."

"But what if he can't?" Even if he hadn't been killed in the coup, he was only one man, and a man in danger at that. He might be lord justice, but the balance of power had shifted. The council was in control now. Even if he'd made it through the takeover alive, he wouldn't have stayed silent. He would have acted, with devastating consequences. The fact that she hadn't heard from him made that scenario all the more likely.

"If the Bear had fallen, we would have heard," Mikael said, trying to reassure her.

She'd like to think that, but her mind wouldn't let her take comfort so easily. Instead, it lingered on the worst-case scenario—the most likely scenario.

Something had happened to him.

Norah swallowed. "I was thinking of writing to King Phillip." She paused and waited for the reaction she knew was coming.

Mikael shifted his weight back.

"He would know what happened," she added. "The council would have written him."

"Salara, you cannot write the Aleon king."

"Why not? Phillip hasn't shown himself to be an enemy."

15

"He hasn't shown himself to be a friend," he argued. "He doesn't come to your aid against treason, and he still occupies Bahoul."

That was mostly true. She hadn't heard from him after the coup, and the forces of Aleon still remained in Bahoul, the Kharavian stronghold that Phillip had occupied without her consent first. But they'd come to what she thought were friendly terms in the months leading to the council overthrowing her. She thought he *had* shown himself to be a friend. "True, he has no duty to me; he's not an official ally. But he didn't recall his forces when I sent them to aid you against the threat of Japheth and Rael. And he did warn you to close your ports, saving Kharav from fever."

"That was when he thought the North was united with Kharav," he argued, "which quite obviously isn't the case anymore."

She pushed out a frustrated breath. "It's worth a try."

"Salara. Do *not* write the Aleon king," he warned. "If you haven't heard from him yet, he stands with your council. Don't show them your weakness."

Dearest Alexander.

Norah drew her bottom lip between her teeth, biting it raw. She crumpled the parchment into a ball and tossed it into the fire. Tapping the pen into the inkwell again, she brought the tip to another blank parchment.

Dear Alexander.

She stared at the words. His name. She'd started this letter a hundred times over the months, but she could never get past his name. What would she say? Their last words to each other had been harsh. She wanted to say she was sorry—sorry for the distance between them, sorry for the state in which they now found themselves. How did he find himself? Was he safe? Was he well?

The chamber door opened and closed, and Mikael's footfalls traveled around the hanging panel and into the room. Her breath hitched. She didn't move. His warmth seeped into her back as he came behind her, but she didn't try to hide what she was doing. His hand rested on her shoulder.

Norah swallowed. "I'm not going to send anything. I just..." Heat rushed to her cheeks. She was just what? Writing to the man she still deeply cared for? Writing to the man who was still foretold to bring her husband's end, wishing him unharmed and well?

Mikael's left hand came to her other shoulder, and he squeezed gently as he leaned forward to see. She held her breath.

"Tell him not to die," he said.

Her head jerked back to look up at him. "What?"

"Tell him not to die."

It took a moment for her words to come. "W-Why?"

"Because he listens to you."

She looked back at the parchment, bewildered. "But I'm not going to send it."

He gave her shoulders another light squeeze. "Just write it, and he'll know." He placed a kiss on top of her head, releasing her, then withdrew and stepped out of the chamber.

Norah looked back at the parchment and drew her fingertip across Alexander's name.

Don't die, she wrote.

The mornings were turning colder, and Norah pulled her wrap tighter around her as she walked beside Salara-Mae through the late-summer gardens. Most of the flowers were spent now and had been trimmed back, but the evergreen topiaries still made for an impressive sight.

Their morning walk had started as quiet as their breakfast had been with Mikael, and their dinner the evening before. Salara-Mae walked with a stoic countenance. While Salara-Mae was still the model of regal poise, Norah knew below the surface she was tormented by what she'd done. And she felt for the woman in her silent suffering.

"He won't be angry forever," Norah said—no use avoiding the topic. "He just needs time."

"I know you talk to him."

Norah nibbled the inside of her lip. As in good talk or bad talk? The woman wasn't scowling. That was a good sign.

"You're the only one he listens to," Salara-Mae said, "and I know you try to talk reason into him."

Norah breathed out, smiling. *Progress.* She raised a brow and dipped her head. "Well, he's actually quite reasonable. He's just hurt. And matters of the heart aren't as simple as alliances and battle plans."

To her astonishment, the king's mother actually laughed. It occurred to her she had never heard Salara-Mae laugh. It was beautiful.

"No truer words have ever been spoken," the woman told her.

The morning was starting to warm, and Norah welcomed it.

"I'm glad that you invited me on your walk this morning," Salara-Mae said. "There's something I've been meaning to raise with you."

Oh. Her stomach started to tumble. No doubt there was something that needed correction, or it was perhaps again about a child. Salara-Mae hadn't broached the topic in a few months. Norah had thought she'd given up, but now that seemed foolish. Salara-Mae wasn't a woman who gave up easily. Would a child even matter anymore? Now that Norah was without a kingdom and Kharav was on the brink of rebellion, perhaps it was better she wasn't with child. All the easier when she and Mikael had to fight for their thrones, and possibly their lives. Or run. She wrinkled her nose. Mikael would never run. And she would never leave him to face it alone. It would be a fight, and if Mikael didn't make it through, she wouldn't either.

"Salara." Salara-Mae's voice brought her back to the present, and she turned to see the woman had stopped a few paces back, where Norah had simply continued on.

"Oh, I'm sorry," she said quickly.

"What were you thinking about?"

What had she been thinking about? "Oh, um... not being with child and hopefully not dying." She grimaced as she said the words. Sometimes her mind failed her. As she saw Salara-Mae's face, she knew this was clearly one of those times.

"I'd rather not follow that thought process," Salara-Mae said slowly.

Norah nodded, heat beginning to flush her cheeks.

Salara-Mae stepped to her side once again. "I don't always understand you."

Not unexpected. "Well..." Norah tilted her head slightly to the side. "In fairness, I don't always understand myself."

"But I have come to respect you."

Norah stopped. Now *that* was unexpected.

"I used to think Kharav was the only kingdom with great warriors. But you, North Queen, have rivaled them all." She looked down at her hand as she pulled a ring from the center finger on her left hand. "My mother gave me this ring. It was given to her by her mother before, and her mother before. It's a ring passed down generations, from a line of strong women. I had planned to give it to my own daughter one day. Fate took that opportunity from me."

A wave of sadness ran through her. Mikael's sister had passed from an illness. Norah had never met her, but Mikael had told her that his sister was a lot like him, and Norah knew she would have loved her.

"But fate has given me a new opportunity," Salara-Mae said. "Another daughter."

Norah locked eyes with her in surprise.

"You're a strong woman, a strong salara, and I want you to have this ring." She took Norah's hand and pushed the ring over her center finger. Then she reached up and clasped Norah's cheek, her eyes glistening. Norah's own emotion choked back any words that may have been in her throat. She glanced down at her hand, stretching her fingers out and admiring the smooth-cut black stone set deep in silver. Norah had never been one for jewelry, but this meant something. And that made it even more beautiful. All she could do was nod.

Salara-Mae let out a long breath. "Now I think I'd like to go sit and read awhile," she said, as if the short emotional exchange had completely drained her.

"Of course," Norah said.

The king's mother turned to leave, but Norah caught her.

"Salara-Mae, thank you. This means a lot to me."

The woman nodded. "Me too." Then she turned and walked back toward the castle.

Norah watched her go before heading to the strip of garden between the parallel windowed halls leading to the library. Breathing in the late-summer air, she closed her eyes as the sun kissed her face. Hope stirred within her. This was what she needed—light, warmth, healing.

She *was* a strong queen, she told herself. She wasn't perfect, but she forgave herself for that. And she wasn't without a kingdom, as she'd felt only moments ago. It had been temporarily taken from her, and she would take it back and see those she loved were safe.

Norah reached into the pocket of her gown and clutched the folded parchment inside—a letter she'd written but battled whether to send.

A letter to Phillip.

She turned on her heel and strode inside. She needed to find Adrian. As she stepped through the doors, she almost collided with a woman coming from the hall of the Circle's chamber. The Circle was Kharav's council.

"Forgive me, Salara," the woman said.

Norah stared at her for a moment. The woman's long, black hair hung loose over her shoulders, and her face was one Norah had seen uncovered only a couple of times. "Katya," she said in surprise. "I didn't recognize you for a moment. I hardly ever see you."

The Kharavian captain was rarely at the castle and rarely without her face wrap.

Katya smiled. "You'll likely see me a bit more, now that I've been assigned to matters at home. Until the child comes."

Child? Norah looked down to see her swelling belly and grinned with a gasp. "Katya! I didn't know you were with child!" She didn't even know she was married. Was she married? She supposed it didn't matter. Not in Kharav.

The captain nodded. "It was a surprise, but a welcome one."

"I'm so happy for you!" Norah meant it. To be blessed with a child was nothing short of a gift from the gods.

Katya's smile widened. "Thank you, Salara. It means a lot that you'd find joy for me in times like this."

"How soon are you expecting?" Just looking at her, it couldn't be terribly long now.

"Only a couple more months."

Children were a blessing. "If you need anything," Norah said, "anything at all."

The captain nodded appreciatively. "Thank you, Salara."

Norah watched as she disappeared down the adjoining hall, and pushed down the pang of jealousy. This was a good thing, and she was happy for Katya. She wondered if she'd see the child around the castle—she'd like that. Surely Adrian and Sevina were tired of her constant doting over their little boy, Theisen, and would welcome another child to occupy her attention. Thoughts of Adrian pulled her mind back to her task at hand, and she continued her course to find him.

Adrian had been in Kharav during the Mercian council's takeover and had stayed with Norah since. She knew he had to be sick with worry for Alexander—his brother was the person he loved most in the world. And Soren's absence had hit him hard as well, but he didn't show it. He always wore a brave face, for her benefit, no doubt.

She made her way through the castle, out the east door, and across the courtyard, and he was at the first place she'd guessed—the sparring field with Cohen. Adrian had become close with Calla and Cohen, the young siblings that had helped Norah travel to the seer, and whom she'd brought to Kharav to formally train. She watched as they worked through their movements. Fast. Precise. Deadly. Yet poetic.

Adrian and Cohen had become master swordsmen. Their dance was beautiful, their ease of movement deceiving. When Cohen noticed her, he signaled them to stop.

Adrian turned, and a grin spread across his face. "Norah."

Salara, Cohen greeted with his hands. Norah hadn't picked up the silent language entirely, but she could follow most of what the deaf boy said.

"Adrian, Cohen," she greeted back. "Where's Calla?"

Adrian smirked. "Where do you think?"

The archery field, Cohen answered. Where the girl always was.

Norah smiled. "Of course."

Cohen gave a small bow of his head, then signed, *I'll leave you.* He was always so perceptive, reading people like a book, and he left her and Adrian to speak privately.

"What do you need?" Adrian asked.

Glancing around, she pulled the letter from her pocket. "I need to get this to Phillip. In Bahoul."

Adrian shifted as the muscle tightened along his jaw. "Do you think that's wise?"

"I have to know what's happened in Mercia. What's happened to Grandmother, to Alexander. I'm calling on Phillip's friendship that he himself has proclaimed. And I'll see where he stands."

He stood taller at the mention of Alexander. She knew he was as desperate as she was to know how he fared. "And you think he'll tell you?"

She shook her head slowly. "I don't know, but I have to try." She put the letter in his hands.

Kharavian forces patrolled the border at the eastern pass. She couldn't send just any Northman without exposing her intention, but Adrian had influence with the Kharavian army. She needed him to help get her letter past them and to the stronghold, where she hoped Phillip still remained.

"All right," he said as he nodded in support. As she knew he would.

CHAPTER THREE

Mikael took another drink from his chalice. He leaned back in the desk chair of his study, staring at the parchments in front of him. War was coming. The armies of Japheth and Rael had been ravaged by fever, but they were rebuilding and growing stronger than before and faster than expected.

News flooded in that slaves from kingdoms all over the world were escaping to join Rael's cause, even slaves from Kharav. It was a compelling purpose—the fight for freedom. This Raelean king, Cyrus, had grown quite a name for himself. He had an impressive story, even to Mikael. He had been a blood sport fighter, his origins unknown. It was said that he started the slave rebellion by attacking the onlooking Raelean king directly during a blood sport match in the grand arena.

Rael was famed for their blood games. There would have been thousands of fighters—thousands of men to join him, and blood sport fighters were the ultimate warriors. They rivaled even the warriors of Kharav. These men were raised in blood and battled for their lives daily.

Once he'd taken Rael, Cyrus turned to those who had enslaved him—the neighboring slaver kingdom of Serra. Within four days, he had taken all the port cities, and by the sixth, he had taken the kingdom.

Six days to take a kingdom.

It was an accomplishment unheard of. While Serra was primarily a wasteland island kingdom, it was larger than Kharav, and it would have required a large army to overtake it. Cyrus took it merely with the slaves from within.

Mikael took another drink of wine. It was rumored Cyrus had his sights on Kharav now. This puzzled him. *Why?* Yes, Kharav had slaves, but many other kingdoms did as well. Perhaps it was Kharav's proximity. Mikael's only consolation was that he wasn't the only enemy. With Rael allied with Japheth, Japheth's enemies were Rael's enemies. And Phillip, king of Aleon, was Japheth's greatest enemy. Japheth's King Gregor had tried to overtake his brother many times. No doubt it still consumed him.

So, the question was, would a united Japheth and Rael attack Aleon, which was Japheth's obsession? Or would they go after Kharav, which was Rael's target?

Rael's focus on Kharav didn't seem like a circumstance of convenience. Yes, the kingdoms were close, with only the Aged Sea between them, and yes, Kharav was a kingdom that had slaves. But it felt more personal, somehow.

Salara had tried to change the slaving norms in Kharav, but that change wasn't easy. Not one of his nobles would approve, and he couldn't risk even more of their dissatisfaction. Tensions were rising, as was the risk to his crown, especially since the confrontation with Narsing and Jarik. His anger surfaced again. Did they really think they could threaten him with Soren? His lord commander wouldn't usurp him. Soren didn't want power, but that wasn't enough to stop the nobles from taking dangerous action. And he was weak without Soren by his side.

Soren had left him weak.

His mind shifted back to Salara. It wouldn't be long before Kharav was no longer safe for her, but he had nowhere to send her, no place to keep her from harm. Soren's leaving stung. Not only had he abandoned his friend and brother in his time of need but he'd abandoned Salara, to whom he was sworn.

And Mikael would not forgive him.

Norah walked through the courtyard, a book in her hand. She'd thought she'd sit in the garden and read a bit, but she couldn't focus her mind. It had been two weeks since she'd sent Phillip her letter, and he still hadn't responded. With each day that passed, her worry grew. Was Phillip allied with Mercia? Had he been involved in her removal? Had he told her council of her letter? If not, why hadn't he answered?

She'd give anything to go for a ride on Sephir—to clear her mind—but she hadn't been able to get the mare before fleeing from Mercia. What had happened to her? Like all of those she loved and had left, the question remained. Adrian fell in step casually beside her, and she forced a smile. "Adrian," she greeted. She had stopped asking every other moment if news had come, resigned that he would tell her when it did. It was hard to hold back the question yet again.

"Nothing has come," he told her, as if reading her mind.

She pulled her bottom lip in between her teeth.

"Don't think the worst," he said.

"How can I not?" How could *he* not?

"There are many reasons you might not have heard. Maybe the message didn't reach him."

"Did the messenger not confirm he delivered it to Bahoul?"

"But not to Phillip's own hand," he countered. "We don't know if it made it to him. Maybe Phillip's not in Bahoul."

She took little comfort in that. A message from the queen of Mercia, even the overthrown queen, would have been treated urgently.

"And I'm sure he has his own worries," he added. "I hear Japheth and Rael are rebuilding their armies at a surprising rate."

More news that wasn't favorable for Kharav—as everything seemed to be. And what could she do? What could anyone do?

"I wish Soren were here," she found herself saying.

"Me too," he answered softly. Loss peppered his voice, and she glanced to see it written on his face as well. But he quickly stowed his emotion and straightened.

Her heart broke for him. She almost forgot sometimes how much this affected him too. Soren didn't just train him, he believed in Adrian, cared for him. Soren secured Adrian's marriage to a Kharavian nobleman's daughter with his own name and his own seal, as the head of a family would do. That was what Soren was to Adrian—family. Like he was to her and Mikael.

"I'll let you know if I hear of anything else," Adrian said.

"Thank you."

He nodded, and she watched him disappear toward the stables.

Norah made her way past the garden topiaries, trying to breathe calmness back into her body. But calmness wouldn't come. Day after day they remained in this hold. When would it end?

The flutter of a small bird drew her gaze. It lighted close by on a manicured laurel, looking at her curiously. She smiled.

Then the hair on the back of her neck stood on end.

She knew this kind of bird. A small brown bird with black eyes, watching. Watching her. And on its head—a smeared marking.

It was *him*. The man who had sent the assassins. The man who wanted her dead.

"Have you returned?" she called bitterly. She always knew he would. Eventually. "What do you want?" How long had he been watching her, waiting? Why now, after so long? He was obviously sending her a message in letting her see him. Did he think himself clever? Dangerous?

Well, she was dangerous too. "Have the courage to come yourself, coward!" she yelled as she hurled the book at him. He took flight and disappeared into the gardens.

Norah turned on her heel and stormed toward the armory. As she walked briskly through the courtyard, Kiran fell in close behind her.

"Is everything all right, Salara?" he asked.

Everything was not all right.

The guards bowed their heads as she entered the armory and swept past them. She had been here enough times with Soren; she knew exactly what she was looking for.

Norah tore open the cabinets lining the far wall and pulled a crossbow from its pegs. Soren's words echoed in her mind. She'd show this man how the Shadow Queen welcomed him.

29

Norah swung open the door to Mikael's study, followed closely by Calla and Kiran. In her hand, she held the shaft of an arrow that was speared through a small brown bird. Breathlessly, she smacked it on the desk in front of Mikael.

"He's back."

Mikael looked at the bird a moment before lifting his eyes to hers. His brows drew together in question. "Who?"

"*Him*," she said.

His face darkened. "The one who sent the assassins?"

"This is his bird. Look at the blood on its head." In the time that had passed since the assassination attempt against her, since her suspecting of being spied on by a bird, she'd almost convinced herself she'd imagined that detail, or misremembered. It sounded like lunacy—being watched by animals with blood markings. But lunacy or not, here it was in front of her, and she was sure now. The blood had to be part of his sorcery somehow.

Mikael stood and picked up the arrow, staring at the dead bird impaled on the end. "So, he's returned."

He didn't even question her mind. He believed her, no matter how absurd it sounded, and she loved him for it.

His brow dipped. "Did *you* hit this bird?"

Calla snorted behind her. "Are you serious?"

Mikael looked at the girl.

"Apologies, Salar," Calla said quickly.

Norah shot her a chastising glance to hide her own smile. For a moment, the air lightened. "I might have made a fool of myself with a crossbow before Calla stepped in," she admitted.

"With a longbow?" he asked.

"Yes, Salar," Calla answered.

He looked back at the bird and frowned. "An impressive shot."

She gave an appreciative bow of her head. "Thank you, Salar."

Mikael looked back to Norah. "I know you're not going to like this, but I'm going to double your guard."

He was right. She didn't like it, but she nodded.

Mikael turned to Kiran. "Find Bhastian." Of course, he'd rely on Soren's most trusted man.

Kiran bowed. "Yes, Salar." And he left to his task.

"I want him with you," he told her. "Always."

She wanted to object, but she didn't. This man unnerved her, whoever and whatever he was. What was this power? Was he a sorcerer? She hadn't thought sorcery or magic were real, but what does one call embodying another person using blood? Watching through birds—what was that if not magic?

Mikael looked back to Calla. "Take down every bird you see."

Norah held up her hand. "We're not going to start shooting all the birds from the sky."

"Perhaps just the birds that aren't of Kharav," Calla suggested.

Mikael paused. "What do you know about these birds?"

Calla shrugged. "Nothing, only they aren't native to Kharav."

"Where are they from?"

"I just said I don't know anything about them."

"Calla," Norah whispered.

"I'm sorry," the girl said quickly. "I mean, I don't know. *Again.*"

Norah shot her another daggered look. Despite being at the castle for over a year now, the girl was still oblivious to courtesies and societal norms. Mikael tolerated her, for Norah's benefit, but she had less desire to push his patience lately. "Wait for me in the hall," she said to Calla.

"Yes, Salara." The girl turned and stepped into the hall.

Norah looked back to Mikael. "She's young."

"It's not an excuse, but it's not the girl I'm concerned about right now." He tossed the arrow with the dead bird back onto his desk. "I'll find who's behind this," he promised.

She knew he already felt the sting of failure for not finding who was responsible for the assassins. Every path he'd chased led to a dead end. And things had quieted for a time—it was as if her enemy had forgotten about her, or no longer cared. Until today. She didn't want this to be yet another thing for him to worry about, but here they were.

And in the spirit of additional unpleasant things to deal with—

"There's something else I wanted to talk to you about," she told him. Something else that made her stomach knot.

"And what's that?"

"I've written Phillip for news," she confessed abruptly, and not as smoothly as she would have liked. She waited for his anger.

The line of his jaw tightened. "I told you not to do that." His voice came low and calm—the voice that made her squirm the most.

Yes, he had. He had told her. She said nothing.

"He stands with the North," he said as he stepped even closer.

"You don't know that," she countered.

His voice came more pressing now. "You shouldn't have written him."

"I have to know," she argued. "I have to know if my grandmother's all right." She stopped herself from the mention of Alexander. "I have to know where Phillip stands."

"You show your weakness."

"It's not weak to ask about those I love! And if it is, I don't care. I would ask my council directly if I could. I have to know."

"It's no longer your council! They're your enemy. And if they know what you care about, they'll use it against you."

"I think it's quite obvious I would care about my grandmother," she cut back, her own anger rising.

"And what about those not as obvious to them?"

Norah stopped. *Alexander*. She swallowed.

His voice dropped lower. "Did you ask about the Bear, Salara?"

A chill ran up her spine. "I asked Phillip if he'd heard from him," she answered finally.

"And?" he pressed. "What else did you ask?"

"If he knew whether Alexander was all right."

"Your grandmother and the Bear. That's all you asked about?"

She nodded.

Mikael pushed out a long breath as his jaw tightened again. "They'll be working to find those still loyal to you. Your actions put him in danger."

Her heart seized in her chest. She hadn't thought of that. If she was inquiring about Alexander, it would show she worried for him. If the council didn't know before, they'd know now—if Phillip told them. Would Phillip tell them, though? She felt like such a fool. She hadn't even realized.

Her lip trembled. "I didn't think. I was so desperate to know. I needed to know." What had she done?

Mikael sighed as he pulled her close and put his arms around her, but it brought little comfort now.

Chapter Four

Dear Alexander,
Please live.
I command it.
Do not have died. Do not die.
Be well. Be strong. Be safe.

"Salara?"

Norah snapped her attention to the maid that had been calling her. How many times had she said her name? Had she asked something? "I'm sorry, what?"

"Would you like me to make up the bed?"

Norah realized she had the quilt from the bed wrapped around her as she sat at the small table by the window. She wasn't ready to give it up yet. "No, I might... need to crawl back into it and hide." Her worry over her letter to Phillip still sat like a weight in her stomach.

Her maid smiled warmly. Salara-Mae had assigned her to Norah—not as a slave—when Norah returned from Mercia without Vitalia, and the girl had taken kindly to her. Amara was her name. She was no Vitalia, but Norah liked her. She was quiet but friendly, and reminded her a bit of her Mercian maid, Serene.

"You haven't even had breakfast yet," Amara said, "and it's getting late. You might feel better after you eat."

That was true. Mikael had risen early to tend some things. She knew he wouldn't take his breakfast in the dining hall, and she'd skipped it herself, but a little food might help, or just getting out and walking, perhaps. *Fine.*

Norah gave her maid a yielding smile and reluctantly gave up the quilt. She took the parchment and walked to the fireplace. Lighting the corner, she watched the flame eat her words until she could no longer hold on to it. Then she released it into the fire, willing the Aether to carry her words to Alexander. Or at least to Samuel, the Mercian seer who could paint them for him.

That wasn't how it worked, she told herself. Still, she wished it all the same.

Washed and dressed, Norah stepped out into the hall. Bhastian picked up behind her but gave her space. He was vigilant under the new threat of the blood-bird assassin.

The chill in the air reminded her that the last of summer was fading—gone too soon, just like everything else. The days came long and endless, but the months were gone in an instant.

Suddenly, Norah found herself at Soren's chamber door. She hadn't been paying attention to where she was walking in her blind thoughts.

She pushed it open.

After Soren had left, she'd put the room back together herself. She had set the furniture back in place, swept up the broken glass, and had the mirrors replaced. Clean linens covered the bed. It was ready for his return, whenever he decided to return. *If* he ever decided to return. The worrisome thought tried to snake its way into her mind, but she pushed it back. Soren *would* return. He wouldn't abandon them.

Norah imagined him sitting inside, angry at her disturbance. And she smiled. She came here a lot. Her best thinking, calm thinking, seemed to come here.

She let herself fall backward onto the bed, and she stared up at the ceiling as her mind took over. She worried for Mikael—not whether he could stay strong in the face of mounting threats, but for his heart and his happiness. Soren's leaving crushed him. It wasn't that Mikael needed his presence. He'd managed quite well without him when Norah had taken the commander to Mercia. But Mikael felt abandoned now, betrayed by the one closest to him, and it was eroding his spirit. She couldn't talk to him about it. She couldn't talk to anyone.

Norah missed Vitalia. She'd been a true friend and deserved so much more than what fate had given her. What had been done with her body? She didn't even know what Vitalia believed. Would she have wanted to be buried, as they did in Kharav? Or be sent by fire to the next life? Did Vitalia even believe in the next life? Norah cursed herself—how did she not know? Not that it would have changed anything, but she should know. Vitalia was her friend. Her eyes welled.

Her mind turned to Catherine. Had they killed her too? Surely not. The council had the authority to strip her of the regency, unlike with Norah and the crown. They wouldn't have needed to kill her grandmother, but that alone didn't ensure her safety. Catherine wouldn't have gone quietly, and she wasn't sure how much patience the council would have with her. Norah's stomach twisted.

And Alexander. What had her letter done to him? She tried to push it from her mind—it was breaking her.

The door of the chamber opened, and her heart nearly leapt out of her chest as she bolted upright. Then Norah let out a sigh of relief as she recognized Adrian. "Hammel's hell," she said breathlessly. "You scared me."

"I saw Bhastian and knew you must be in here."

She had forgotten about Bhastian. He must think it strange she'd be in Soren's room. She frowned.

Adrian looked around the room. "What *are* you doing in here?"

Heat rose in her cheeks. "I just come here to think sometimes," she confessed.

He eyed her skeptically. "Does it help?"

She paused for a moment, and shrugged. Then she let herself fall back on the bed again and reached over and patted the space beside her. She felt his hesitancy but smiled as his weight fell beside her, shaking the frame of the bed. They lay quietly, looking up at the ceiling.

"Mikael thinks I've put Alexander in danger by writing Phillip, by asking about his welfare." She turned her head to face him. "I fear he's right. I've shown he's important to me."

"Of course your lord justice would be important to you. It doesn't take a letter to know that." He turned his head toward her and met her eyes. "You don't need to worry about Alec. They won't kill him. They can't." He smiled. "Better men have tried and failed."

She wished she had his optimism. Perhaps they wouldn't kill him, but there were things worse than death. *No*—she couldn't think like that. Adrian was right. Alexander was no stranger to peril. And better men *had* stood against him—Mikael. And Soren. She gave a small laugh.

Adrian's brow creased. "What?"

"Soren *really* tried."

He smiled. "I know. But Alec holds the gods' favor. If the lord commander can't kill him, no one can."

Gods, she loved him for saying that, and for settling the gnawing worry in her stomach. She felt herself favored by the gods to have a friend like Adrian. He was the only one she could truly talk to now.

"What if Soren doesn't return?" she whispered. "I'm scared, Adrian. I can't lose him too."

"You won't," he promised. He rocked up to sit, then rose from the bed. "I have to go. Katya will be expecting me." Since Soren's departure, Katya had stepped in to fill a lot of his responsibilities, including monitoring the development of the earlies, the men in training for the Crest.

Norah sat up and raised a brow. "Don't keep her waiting, then."

He turned but stopped. "Oh, and, uh, I'd appreciate if you didn't tell the lord commander I was on his bed. When he does come back. Because he will."

She smiled as he winked and slipped out the door. Then she rose and straightened the furs and linens. She didn't want Soren knowing *she'd* lain on his bed either. Norah gave the room a final check, ensuring everything looked in its place, and then stepped back out into the hall. Bhastian acted like nothing was unusual, and she was appreciative. He missed the lord commander too.

Her stomach grumbled. She supposed she should get something to eat.

The sound of birds chirping gave the morning a song, but her spirit fell as they reminded her of *him*. Her unknown enemy. The man who wanted her dead. Was he watching her? What if he was? She tried not to dwell on it. She couldn't be paranoid. And surely a possessed bird wouldn't be singing. She glanced back at Bhastian, who followed at a respectful distance, and he nodded to her.

As she turned the corner into the mainway, she caught sight of Mikael at the end of the hall leading to the throne room. He was talking to a man—not a soldier or an adviser—a man in working clothes, uncommon around the castle. He nodded to the man, who bowed back and departed. Mikael held a smile on his lips as she approached, so whatever he was tending hadn't added to his burdens. That was good.

"Where are you headed?" he asked her.

"Just going to get some breakfast."

His brow dipped. "You haven't eaten yet?"

She shook her head. "I wasn't very hungry."

"I haven't had anything either. I'll eat with you." He held out his hand, and a light gleamed in the darks of his eyes. "But first, walk with me."

He seemed to be in a good mood, and she smiled. "All right." She put her hand in his, and he led her down the hall, toward the throne room. "Where are we going?" she asked.

"I just feel like walking with my wife."

Very suspicious. "Hmm," she said through a pursed smile as she looked up at him out of the corners of her eyes.

When they reached the throne room, he stopped. And waited.

She looked at him quizzically, then glanced around. The room was empty. No one was there...

Then she saw it. Her mouth fell open.

"What have you done?" she whispered.

Norah stared at the ornately carved thrones that had been cut from their foundations and placed side by side. While the old bases had been sanded down to be even with the stone floor, the remnants still showed where the chairs had spent many generations.

"What... Why... Mikael..." She stood, speechless.

"Now, perhaps you won't hate this room so much."

"I was joking!" *Kind of.* "I didn't think you'd rip up your throne room."

He smiled as he pulled her closer. "I didn't rip it up. I made improvements."

As much as she absolutely loved him right now, she shook her head. "Mikael, people are going to be upset by this. Those chairs were beautiful."

He shrugged. "They still are."

"But you've changed something that's been a certain way for generations. Like it was nothing."

"It wasn't nothing. It was a problem—a problem I've solved."

She tried to purse back her smile. "Your mother's going to die."

"Well, she's selected where she means to be buried, so I feel prepared."

She shouldn't have, but she laughed. "I'm serious! When she finds out..." Norah covered her mouth and then glanced at her hand. "I'll tell you what she's going to do, she's going to rip this ring back off my finger. She was just starting to *like* me."

He clasped her chin and forced her to look up at him. "Stop," he said softly. "I'm the first salar to have a salara that loves him so much that even the distance between our thrones is too great. Having to... resolve this issue... makes me proud. And anyone who objects, well..." He tilted his head in indifference.

She shook her head, grinning. "I love you."

He smiled back. "And I love you," he replied, and he kissed her.

Days passed slowly. Two, or three. Or four. Norah forgot how many.

"Another one," Calla said as she held up an arrow with a small dead bird pierced on the end.

Norah's attention popped back to the present, and her jaw tightened. *Another one.*

"What on earth?" Salara-Mae gasped.

They stood in the gardens where Norah and Salara-Mae had picked up a regular cadence after breakfast. It had been a challenge to explain the increased guard without alarming the king's mother. They hadn't told her about *him*—how the blood-bird man had returned. She rolled her eyes in her mind. She had to think of a better name.

Blood-bird man. Sender of her assassins. The birdman. Blood sorcerer. Everything she thought to call him sounded too silly or too reverent of his power—whatever inexplicable power he had. He was back, and he was watching her.

"Diseased birds," Norah said quickly. "We've been culling them to stop the spread."

Salara-Mae winced and gave a disgusted frown.

Norah picked up their walk again. They'd have to tell his mother at some point. Mikael had said he didn't want to worry her. More likely, he didn't want to face questions he couldn't answer from a person he was trying not to speak to. She silently chastised herself. She should give him the benefit of the doubt. It was true that burdening her wouldn't be of any benefit. They didn't know who was behind the birds, or what he would do next. The information would likely only make Salara-Mae paranoid of every bird she saw, as it did Norah. Or Salara-Mae would think they'd gone mad, which also wouldn't be helpful. They needed to find out more.

"Have you stopped trying for a child?" Salara-Mae asked as they continued.

Norah stopped, speechless for a moment. She'd raise this topic now? Now, of all times? "Ummm... now's perhaps not the best time for a child."

"On the contrary, it's the perfect time."

Perhaps it was Salara-Mae who had gone mad.

"My council has usurped my throne. We're on the brink of war with Japheth and Rael, perhaps Mercia and Aleon as well. How is this the perfect time?"

"So you *aren't* trying."

"It's not a choice!" she cut back, sharper than she'd intended. She drew in a deep breath to calm her anger. "It's not a choice," she said again, softer.

It wasn't that they hadn't been trying. They just hadn't come to expect anything. At least, not Mikael. He seemed happy without, as if Norah alone were enough. He placed the fault on himself, which might be true. Or perhaps it was her failure. There was no way to know for sure. Either way, something died a little more inside her every time her blood cycle came.

"We should get back," Norah said. She couldn't have this conversation again.

Salara-Mae didn't object, but as they turned toward the castle, a servant ran to meet them.

"Salara!" he called before he even reached them. "There's a messenger from the North."

Her breath caught in her throat, and she struggled to pull a breath. "A messenger?"

"They've escorted him through the western pass," he said, breathless. "They're bringing him to the castle now. Salar waits for you in the throne room."

Norah glanced at Salara-Mae, who held an equally shocked expression on her face. Norah turned back to the servant. "Send for Adrian as well. Have him meet me there." Then both she and Salara-Mae picked up quickly toward the throne room.

A messenger from Mercia—what news would he bring? Would Alexander have sent him? Or her council? What could they possibly have to say?

Mikael stood in the center of the room, waiting. They didn't spend much time in the throne room, but he always waited for her before taking his seat. He held out his hand as she walked toward him, and she took it. His warmth thawed her icy fingers, seeping up her arm and calming her racing heart. She forced a smile. He'd stood solid beside her through Mercia's betrayal. She feared he would waver with the pressures of his own kingdom, but when she needed him, he was there, as if nothing else mattered.

"What has happened in here?" Salara-Mae gasped.

Norah followed her horrified gaze to the two thrones cut from their elevated bases and set side by side. She bit her lip; she'd forgotten about that. Norah glanced at Mikael, and he shrugged.

"I like them better this way," he said.

And she loved him even more.

They took their seats. Norah waited impatiently. Months had passed since she'd fled Mercia. It felt like years and days at the same time. So much could have happened by now. What *had* happened? Now she would know. Suddenly, she didn't want to know. She glanced around. Where was Adrian?

Mikael's hand wrapped around hers, and she looked up at him. He brought her fingers to his lips and kissed her skin, and a calm returned.

"You settle me so easily," she told him.

He smiled. "You do the same. I didn't move these chairs together only for you, you know."

Gods, she loved this man.

Finally, the doors to the throne room swung open, and a small army of the Crest entered with a Northman at their center. Her heart pulsed so hard in her throat that she thought she might choke on it.

He stopped before her and bowed. "Queen Norah," he said as he pulled off his helm. He was younger than she'd expected. She didn't recognize him and glanced around again for Adrian, but he was strangely still absent.

"I bring a message from the lord justice," he said.

She froze. *Alexander.* Slowly, she stood. "Alexander sent you?" She didn't feel steady on her feet. "He's alive?"

He stood with his mouth open, as if confused. What was confusing about her question?

"He's alive, and he's well?" she asked again, more urgently this time.

He bobbed his head. "Yes, Regal High. Alive, anyway. *Well* is relative, yeah?"

What did *that* mean?

"And he sends me," the man added.

She clenched her hands to keep them from shaking. "You have a letter?"

He bowed his head again. "No, not a letter. Only his words." And he stood.

It was all she could do to not clamber down the steps and shake him. "Well, what does he say?" she pressed.

The soldier looked around uneasily. "Um, I'm to deliver it to the Destroyer."

"What?" *What?* Alexander would send a message to Soren and not her? "What's the message?" Her patience was now gone.

He hesitated.

Mikael rose from his throne and stepped beside her. "What is the message?" he demanded.

The soldier shifted back. "To prepare for war."

Her heart leapt into her throat. She couldn't breathe. "Alexander sends a threat?"

"No," the Mercian soldier said quickly as he eyed Mikael. "Not war against him. To join him in taking back Mercia. The lord justice holds the loyalty of the North in the queen's name."

"So why a call to war?" Mikael asked him shortly. "If the lord justice commands the army of the North, why doesn't he just give it back?"

"Well, because he's not lord justice anymore, I guess."

Norah's heart stopped. The council had removed him.

"And even if he was," the soldier continued, "the council holds control with mercenaries. He can't take the kingdom back alone, and so he's been waiting in silent opposition."

"And what of Aleon?" Mikael asked.

The soldier shook his head. "I don't know. I'm not privy to such information."

Norah narrowed her eyes at the man. "Yet you've been sent here with this message. Why would Alexander send someone I don't know?" And why to Soren?

"He and those close to you are watched by the council. And... he said the Destroyer would know I come truly."

"How would he know?"

"I don't know. I don't ask questions. I only come with the message."

"What of my grandmother?"

"She's well." Then his face twisted slightly. "Well, maybe not *well*. She's confined to the castle, and angry. All the time. She yells a lot. We can hear her over the wall."

Her body shook with relief. She looked at Mikael and could see the doubt on his face. "What's your name?" she asked the man.

"Colb, Regal High. Colb Matheson."

Norah let her eyes run over the man. He was dressed in Mercian armor, but he was missing the polish of a trained soldier, both in stance and in words. *Strange*. "You don't seem like a soldier."

"Because I'm not a soldier, Regal High. I work the mines."

Very strange indeed.

"The Bear sends a miner?" Mikael's voice was edged with skepticism.

The young man shifted again.

"Does Alexander say anything else?" Norah asked.

He shook his head. "No, Regal High. Only to bring the Shadow army, and he'll be waiting."

Mikael gave a slight wave of his hand, and the Crest ushered the man back out, leaving him and Norah alone. She watched him as he sank down on his throne and crossed his arms, bringing his fist to his lips. Her heart still thrummed in her throat. Was this her opportunity to take back Mercia?

"It could be a trick," he said, as if reading her thoughts. "If we marched on the North and Aleon was waiting with them, we'd be easily taken."

"It's possible," she admitted, "although if the council was trying to trick us, I don't think they'd send a miner to do it."

"Or it's exactly who they'd send. A disarming cover. And someone you wouldn't be familiar with. Perhaps they don't know who in your army is loyal to you."

"I can't help but be inclined to believe him. His knees were practically knocking together."

"A scared man isn't necessarily an innocent man. Or perhaps he does believe he comes with a message from the Bear, but he's been fooled himself."

True. Norah sighed. It was a very real possibility that the council was trying to trick her into marching to war. And Mikael was right. Together with Aleon, the council would be able to overtake Kharav. But if it wasn't a trick, then this was perhaps her only opportunity to take back Mercia—to take back what was rightfully hers.

She looked at Mikael. Could she really ask this of him now?

CHAPTER FIVE

The dining hall was quiet. Shocking. Norah kept herself from rolling her eyes as she chewed her food slowly. She shifted her gaze between Mikael and Salara-Mae, wagering which topic would first be broached—the call to war from Mercia or Mikael's choice to redecorate the throne room. One she was desperate to talk about, and one she wasn't.

Mikael mulled over a small stack of parchments as he ate, which wasn't unusual. He sometimes brought work to the dining hall instead of taking breakfast in his study. While it annoyed Salara-Mae, Norah didn't mind. He'd drop it in an instant if she mentioned it.

Mikael paused, perplexed at one letter in particular.

"What is it?" she asked.

"Outsiders. Possibly."

A chill ran down her spine. Could it be *him*, the man who'd sent the assassins? Had he sent more? She had been bolder in facing the blood birds, but now that he might be back, she couldn't shake the pang of fear that turned her stomach. "Possibly?"

"There are signs inside the Canyonlands, but no outsiders have been seen." His eyes met hers. "I don't want you to worry. You're safe."

"I know," she said quickly. But did she really believe that?

Mikael put down the letters. She pushed her breakfast across her plate with her fork.

"Salara," he said, calling her attention back to him. "I'll get to the bottom of this."

She nodded.

The hall grew quiet again. They ate the rest of their breakfast in silence, and Mikael left his remaining letters unread. She felt his eyes on her.

"Are we going to pretend there's nothing else to discuss?" Salara-Mae said as they neared finishing. "That you didn't uproot a keystone of this castle?"

Norah pursed her lips. She should have wagered more than a glass of wine in the bathtub that *that* would be the topic Salara-Mae broached. She motioned to the servant, who refilled her chalice—she'd take that wine right now.

"The throne room isn't a keystone," he replied calmly.

"Of course it is. It's what everyone sees. It represents your strength, your legacy, your family's legacy."

"A legacy of lies?" he cut back. "Secrets?"

"Oh, Mikael," Salara-Mae said with a sigh. It was the first time Norah had heard her call him by his name. And it was the call of a worried mother. "Now you're going to host your nobles to discuss this matter of the North, and they'll see how you focus your attention."

Norah knew what she meant, that he focused his attention on her more than his own kingdom. True or not, this was how the nobles felt.

"Are you not already under enough scrutiny?" Salara-Mae asked him. He didn't answer.

"And I fear your answer for them," she added. "You know they won't support marching against the North." Her face turned bitter. "Even your commander didn't support it. *Publicly.* You know his voice will still be in their ears."

Slowly, he took a drink from his chalice. "They have a right to be concerned," he said finally. "It's a great risk."

She huffed a small breath. "Of course it's a great risk! Japheth and Rael are at our door, waiting for the moment to strike, and you would leave to go to war with the North? With no allies? No one by your side?"

Still, he said nothing. He only rested his gaze on Norah. She twisted inside.

"And don't be a fool to think the North is alone," Salara-Mae stressed. "Aleon will be lying in wait. This would be it—the vision of your end. The Bear lures you to it."

Mikael's eyes turned to his mother. "My fate comes when Salara rides beside the king of Aleon. Now is not my time." He looked at Norah. "And the Bear wouldn't betray his queen. The question is, did *he* send the messenger? Or is this a plot from the council?"

Salara-Mae gaped at Norah. "Talk him out of this madness."

But Norah wasn't sure she could do that. This could very well be an opportunity to take back Mercia. Perhaps the *only* opportunity.

Salara-Mae's voice came more urgently now, pleading Norah. "You would let him walk right into a trap?"

Of course she wouldn't. But was it a trap? The miner had been believable. A skilled deceiver, if that's what he was. But if Alexander *was* alive, he'd be working to take back her throne. If he wasn't and this was a trick from the council, she'd lose more than what she already had. But could they afford to do nothing? If they didn't win back Mercia, they'd have to stand alone against Rael and Japheth. She wasn't sure they'd survive that either.

It was a gamble of life and death, and she didn't know what to do.

Damn Adrian. Where was he? Norah stalked out of the army field office and toward the castle. He was nowhere to be found. Calla and Cohen hadn't seen him. She'd even checked with Katya, who'd told her she hadn't seen him in days and was livid about it. So was Norah, although perhaps she was more worried than livid. She just wanted to make sure he was all right. And she wanted to ask him about this Colb Matheson. Adrian would be able to help decipher anything suspicious and give her his thoughts on marching on Mercia. How would he feel about it? If he believed Alexander called them, no doubt he'd go. But to march against one's home, it was hard. Even for Norah.

Yells from soldiers on the sparring field caught her attention, and she turned. Men on the north side waved their arms toward her, signaling... something. She stood, staring at them. What were they saying? She swept her eyes around her but saw nothing. What did they see? She looked back to them and caught a man pointing north. Her gaze followed.

She squinted her eyes against the horizon. To the movement.

The ripple of white and silver.

And she gasped.

Tears sprang to her eyes, and she let out an emotional laugh. *Sephir.*

The mare galloped straight toward her. Norah ran to meet her, not able to wait for the animal to reach her.

Sephir skidded to a stop in front of her and reared before tossing her head with a squeal. Norah threw her arms around her neck. Her laughs turned to cries as she clung to the mare, her tears falling into the animal's thick mane. She smelled like mountain air and fresh forest pine.

The last time she'd seen Sephir, she'd been queen of Mercia. She'd had Alexander and Soren and her grandmother. And Vitalia. She'd had Cusco and Cavaatsa. Sephir smelled like family, like happiness and rich memories lost.

Norah cried.

The heartache turned to joy that she'd gotten something back. And she cried some more. Not just for Sephir's return, but for everything. All of it. It all came to the surface—her fear, her hope, her exhaustion, her loss. And now her joy.

And she needed this joy.

Norah held on to the mare until her tears ran dry. Then she held her longer. The animal's warmth seeped into her skin, the Wild spirit feeding her own. She'd known she needed Sephir back. She just hadn't known how much. It was like the gods had given her back a piece of herself.

Norah wiped her cheeks before stepping back. "You missed me, did you?" She smiled at the mare as she wiped her eyes again and patted the animal's neck.

Sephir snorted and tossed her head again.

Norah laughed. "Gods, I've missed you too." She grew more serious. "I was so worried something had happened to you."

Bhastian's voice came from behind her. "She's returned!"

She grinned back at him but didn't take her hand from the mare for fear it was only a dream.

Kiran came forward, his eyes smiling under his wrap. "She escaped the North and traveled all the way to Kharav to find you."

Norah hugged the mare again. "Maybe she heard my heart calling to her."

Kiran shook his head, still in disbelief. "The men can take her back to the stables, give her a good rub down and feed."

The stables. Right. Norah longed to jump atop the mare and feel the wind of a gallop again, but she had to find Mikael and talk to him about Adrian. Not to mention, galloping off alone with rumors of intruders wasn't the wisest idea.

Norah hugged the mare once more, scratching her neck affectionately. "You've journeyed a long way to get home, friend. How does a brush down and a bucket full of grain sound?"

The mare tossed her head, and Norah laughed. "All right then, go with them, and I'll come visit you later." She gave Sephir a pat, and the animal let two approaching stable hands lead her toward the stables.

"I almost thought you were going to jump on her and take off," Bhastian told her as she watched Sephir be led away.

"You know she thought about it," Calla added, coming up behind them.

Kiran and Bhastian chuckled.

"Of course she did," Kiran said.

Norah smiled at them both. They knew her well. "But I have something more important," she added as she turned her mind back to Adrian. She needed to find Mikael. "Where's my husband?"

Bhastian nodded toward the castle. "I last saw him in his study."

He was likely still there. She nodded and picked up her pace toward the castle. As expected, Mikael *was* in his study, where he'd been spending more and more of his time. *Plotting* is what Norah usually told him he was doing, but she knew it was more like thinking, and worrying, and searching for solutions.

He looked up from where he sat at his desk as she entered.

"What are you doing?" she asked as she moved behind him and wrapped her arms around his neck.

"Plotting," he said, putting his hand over hers and leaning back against her.

Her lips pulled into a smile. *Plotting.* She bent and nestled into his warmth and brushed her lips across his cheek. "You're always plotting."

"Well, that's how one becomes a master plotter."

Or it was how one lost their mind. "Sephir's returned."

He straightened and pulled her around in front of him. His eyes were large with surprise, and bright. "That's good news."

She nodded. "I'm so relieved and glad to have her back. I can't believe it, that she traveled all that way on her own to find me again."

"She's a special horse, Salara."

That she was.

His brows dipped. "But something's wrong?"

Yes. Something was wrong. "Have you sent Adrian on a task?"

He frowned and then shook his head. "No, why?"

She pushed out a breath, her worry returning. "He's gone. And no one knows where. Not Cohen or Calla. Not anyone. It's as if he's disappeared."

"Well, I'm sure he'll turn up."

"This isn't like him. I'm really worried. You were just talking about possible intruders again. What if something happened to him? What if he needs help? What if he's needed help and we've just been—"

"Hey," he said, pulling her closer and quieting her. "Adrian's a warrior. One of the best there is. And he's smart. He's fine. He'll show up."

"How do you know?" She could hear the desperation in her own voice.

"My master plotting senses."

That almost made her laugh. *Almost.*

He pulled her between his knees and looked up at her from his chair. "I'll send men out. We'll find him."

She nodded, feeling a little better.

His eyes lingered on her, and she knew his mind had drifted back to Mercia.

Norah held his face with her hands, lightly grazing his short-cut beard with her fingertips. "Talk to me," she whispered. "What are you in here thinking about?"

"Do you believe the Bear sends this miner?"

Such a difficult question. "I don't know."

"Not what you know. What do you *believe*?"

She swallowed. Such a subtle change of words, yet so significantly different. What did she believe? "I believe that if Alexander's well—even if he's not well, if he's simply alive—he'll stop at nothing to give me back my throne. He will have been... plotting himself." Despite the risks, despite the odds—any odds—Alexander would try. More than try. He would be compelled. And her lord justice compelled was a powerful thing.

"I don't believe the miner lies," she added. Then she swallowed again. "And I believe that if what he says is true, it may be our only opportunity to take back Mercia. And to gain back an alliance. To not stand alone."

Mikael drew in a long breath and then let it out slowly. He settled his arms around her more firmly, then nodded.

"Then tomorrow I'll tell the nobles we go to war," he said. "We'll march to join the Bear. And take back the North."

CHAPTER SIX

Kharavian nobles filled the throne room. There were more than Norah expected. More than last time. Their eyes shifted between her and Mikael as murmurs rippled through them. Their whispers and judgments, she'd expected that, but something was different today.

Kharavian nobles of the court bore the markings of fighting men, but unlike warriors of the army, they generally wore more clothing. Not substantially more—maybe a wrap of fine silk over a shoulder; an open, sleeveless tunic; or other accents and pieces that displayed their wealth. But today brought a throne room of bare chests and prominent battle markings. A message.

Norah's heart beat faster as her eyes traveled over their bodies laden with weapons. True, Kharavians loved their blades, and many wore them when they came before Mikael. But today, there seemed to be more. *Were* there more? More swords? More daggers?

Would there be more blood?

The prior confrontation between Mikael and the nobles that had left Narsing dead was still fresh in her mind. As it was for them all, she was sure. Did this display mean that they were well prepared to challenge the crown now?

And they didn't even know yet about Mikael's news.

Bile rose in the back of her throat.

The nobles wouldn't support a march to war with Mercia, especially to reseat a queen they didn't want from a kingdom they had warred with for ten years—a queen who'd failed to bring a true alliance with the marriage and who failed to give an heir. And judging from their stares, now a queen who influenced unwanted changes to their throne room.

The air hung heavy, leaving her lungs unfed despite her breaths. Sweat beaded across the nape of her neck. With no room now between the thrones, Bhastian stood to her left, close, where Adrian normally stood. Adrian still hadn't returned.

Kiran stood to Mikael's right, and the rest of the Crest lined the wall behind them. On the surface, they looked prepared for a confrontation. But truly, if a battle for the crown broke out, the Crest would take her and flee.

Norah's argument with Mikael had gone late into the night before, but it did nothing to change his position. She had refused to leave him, but it wasn't a choice anymore. Bhastian had his orders, and he'd follow them—if the nobles rose against them, he and the Crest would take her to the only place safe for her in the world now. Back to the Wild.

But Norah had no intention of going back to the Wild. The dagger strapped to her calf chafed her skin as she crossed her ankles, but she wanted the reminder it was there. She refused to lose two kingdoms. She refused to lose her king. There would be no leaving this throne room unless it was to march to take back Mercia.

She shifted in her chair as she cast a quick glance at Mikael. He sat calmly, his face giving no indication of worry, but his eyes held the threat of blood if things went poorly with his nobles. Mikael was a formidable man and a strong king, but even he couldn't stand alone against them—not all of them, and not without Soren. But the gods have mercy on the first man to oppose him.

Bhastian beat the floor with the butt of his spear, and a hush fell over the room. Norah's stomach turned.

"I've gathered you on the matter of the North," Mikael started. "We've received word that the Bear prepares to retake the throne in Salara's name and calls us to join him."

Yasir, an imposing lord, stepped forward. "You mean you have received word from a man who claims to be sent by the Bear." Several nobles were members of the Circle. Yasir was one of them and, as such, had already been briefed on the circumstance and all its details.

"Yes," Mikael answered.

"So, the North would draw us out from the protections of the Canyonlands to take back the throne of the queen they unseated?"

Norah hated how he spun the story.

"The council took the throne by mercenaries, not with the Northern army," Mikael countered.

Jarik stepped forward now. The sight of the warlord made Norah shudder. He was definitely wearing more blades than he had before. Her heart hammered against her chest.

"The time for the Northern army to have fought would have been during the coup," Yasir said.

"The attack came suddenly," Norah interjected. "No one knew it was happening. You know this."

Yasir ignored her, as did Jarik. Their eyes stayed leveled on Mikael.

Despite the cold of autumn creeping in, the air was suddenly stifling. Whether it was from her own anger or Mikael's as his patience started to burn to ash, she didn't know.

"How do we know Aleon hasn't joined the North and isn't merely lying in wait?" Jarik asked. "How do we know this isn't a trick?"

Mikael was silent for a moment. "We don't," he said finally.

A wave of murmurs bubbled through the hall again.

"And how will you respond to this call, Salar?" Yasir and the Circle had been pressing for an answer for days—an answer Mikael would not give.

Until now.

All eyes were on Mikael, and he answered, "We march."

Immediate objections rang through the hall, voices of disbelief and condemnation, calls for refusal, questions of intent. But Mikael sat firmly, unwavering.

Bhastian struck the floor with the butt of his spear again, bringing quiet back to the room.

"This is my decision," Mikael boomed out.

"And we should so blindly follow?" Jarik challenged. "Kharav is already weakened against our enemies, and you would bring us closer to fall?"

"Even the lord commander didn't support war," another noble spoke up angrily. Lord Arminar—another member of Mikael's Circle. It was true; Mikael had sought war after Norah fled Mercia, and Soren had spoken against it. In front of the nobles, it was the equivalent of denying him. And now the nobles knew of his blood right. As a bastard son, Soren held a weaker claim to the throne, but it was a claim nonetheless.

And now he had the power to deny Mikael so much more than war—he had the power to deny him everything.

Mikael's gaze shifted to Lord Arminar. "Circumstances have changed, and the lord commander's not here."

"You don't know circumstances have changed," Jarik challenged.

The nobles crowded closer, and from the corner of her eye, Norah saw Bhastian step closer too, his hand clenching his spear. The hair on her arms stood on end, and her breaths came faster.

The nobles couldn't petition the Circle to override Mikael because the Circle couldn't veto a regal decision like Mercia's council. A noble could challenge him. Or they could collectively remove him. They would have to do it by force, and it was becoming increasingly likely they would try now.

Norah reached out and rested her hand on Mikael's arm. The fight of rage radiated from his skin, but he needed to calm. Violence would solve nothing here. She desperately searched her mind for anything that could sway them to see this was the only way to strengthen Kharav. They needed to take back Mercia. The kingdoms needed to be united again.

"Once again," Arminar said, still needling, "you put the North Queen before Kharav. And I see it comes on the heels of your decision to uproot our throne room at her whim."

"*My* throne room. Your *salara*," Mikael snarled as he rose. Norah still held on to him. "And would you rather our chairs parted?" he added. "As her hand on mine is the only thing keeping me from striking your head from your shoulders."

Jarik's hand moved to the hilt of his sword. "You continue to threaten your nobles?"

"Warn," Mikael corrected him.

Yasir stiffened. "A warning for you, Salar—when the lord commander returns, there will be much you'll be held accountable for."

Mikael laughed. "You'll challenge me? You think you can so easily give my crown to another? You think you can take it from me?" He bared his teeth and ripped his arm from Norah's grip as he pulled his sword. "If any man thinks he can, come forward!" he bellowed.

The hall fell silent, and all eyes were locked on Mikael. Then their gazes shifted to Jarik. In a challenge, the warlord was perhaps the only one who could rival Mikael; he was almost equal in size and covered in markings, noting his skill. If it would be a collective takedown, the nobles would look to Jarik to lead the effort.

Norah clenched her hands so tight her nails dug into her palms. Jarik pulled his sword, and Bhastian's hand wrapped around her arm.

Just then, the ash wood doors of the throne room swung open, booming an echo through the hall. All heads jerked toward the sound. Norah's heart leapt into her throat, and she staggered up from her chair.

Gods' mercy.

Through the threshold stepped Soren, axe in one hand, his sword in the other.

Norah's heartbeat pulsed loud in her ears, so loud she could hear nothing else. She glanced at Mikael, but he stood, unmoving. The muscle corded under his skin as he clutched his sword tighter—he was ready to use it.

The air hung thick with tension. The nobles on either side of the hall bounced their gazes between Jarik and Mikael, then Jarik and Soren. But no one spoke.

Soren's gaze swept over the room. His eyes held the night, darker than she'd ever seen, and they locked on Mikael as he strode forward.

Heat pulsed through Soren's veins. He kept his eyes on Mikael. He saw it now—the likeness between them. The same darkness. The same fire.

They had the same blood—the blood of salar.

The eyes of the nobles followed him down the center of the hall and toward the throne. They were eager to have him back, their disapproval of Mikael rich on their faces.

And they waited. They waited for him to make his claim. He had their support. His gaze shifted to Jarik, and their stares locked. The warlord had followed him into battle countless times. Jarik gave a small bow of his head. He'd follow Soren as salar.

But Soren wasn't salar. Salar of war, yes. But there was only one true salar of Kharav, and Soren had returned to make sure it stayed that way. He'd kill every man in this room if he had to, and by the looks of how the nobles were armed, he might just have to. But first, a message for them...

He strode to the edge of the dais, where Mikael stood with his sword ready. And Soren dropped to his knees, his head hung low.

This was his brother. His salar. Husband to the woman who had wormed her way into his heart. This was his family that he loved and would give anything for. He'd let there be no doubt of where his loyalties sat. He'd left because he was a threat to Mikael's crown, but then he realized—with some help—he didn't weaken Mikael's power. He made him stronger by standing at his side.

He felt his brother's eyes on him, but he didn't raise his gaze. Mikael would be upset by his leaving, hurt even, as Soren himself had been. But he would understand.

Mikael stepped down the stairs.

The cold steel of a sword pricked his chin as Mikael used its tip to draw up his face to look at him. Soren let his head fall back, offering his neck. Out of the corner of his eye, he saw Salara draw closer. How he missed that annoying woman.

"You've returned," Mikael said.

"I should have never left."

"But you did." Mikael's words were dipped in venom, each one delivering a sting. He was angry. Soren knew he would be.

Mikael stepped slowly to his right shoulder, his eyes burning into Soren. Soren knew his gaze was on the matching ink marking they both bore, the sun encircled by a ring of mountains—the marking of how they'd become brothers.

Suddenly, Mikael sliced his blade through the encircled sun, and the warmth of blood poured down Soren's arm. Soren gritted his teeth through the pain, but he didn't move.

"You are no longer lord commander," Mikael said.

A weight crushed him. He couldn't breathe. He knew Mikael would be upset, hurt at his leaving, but he never thought he would strip him of his place. The pain stung more than any pain of the flesh.

"Mikael," Salara whispered with a faint breath.

Mikael held his arms wide. "I asked you before, is there a challenge?" he bellowed across the hall. He looked directly at Jarik and pointed his sword. The warlord stood for a moment, his eyes moving to Soren, then back to Mikael. Then he sheathed his sword and bowed his head.

Soren's submission carried a message for the rest of the nobles as well. Now to remove Mikael, they'd face Soren too. They'd be victorious with their numbers, yes, but how many would live? Soren and Mikael together would spill the blood of at least half. Would they wager their lives? As the nobles drew back, Soren knew the answer.

"We march in a week's time," Mikael thundered, seizing control of the moment and keeping control of the crown. "Now get out."

Soren didn't move as the nobles shuffled out of the throne room. He didn't rise to his feet. He only waited for Mikael. He waited for him to say something—perhaps when the nobles all departed. But Mikael didn't wait. He left Soren on his knees and strode from the throne room himself. Soren's heart fell to his stomach.

Only Salara remained. He didn't look up, but he knew her eyes were on him. Did she feel he'd betrayed her too? She stepped in front of him, but he still couldn't look at her. He couldn't bear it.

She reached a hand and brought her fingers to his chin, pulling his face up to look at her. There were tears in her eyes, and it broke him. He sucked in an emotional breath, ready for her anger, her hatred for him now.

But she only dropped down and threw her arms around his neck, hugging him tightly. She clung to him, stripping him of the rest of his composure. Soren let himself fall apart. He wrapped his left arm around her and held her close as the emotion took over.

They stayed on the floor for a long time, until Soren could breathe again.

As they broke, she smiled through her tears. "You came back," she whispered.

It took a moment for him to answer. "I didn't have a choice. Adrian found me. Told me I had to come." Adrian had tracked him down all the way to the Stone Forest, talked some sense into him, told him he was needed. Of course he had to come.

"Adrian!" She let out a breath. "I've been worried sick about him. Gods, I'm going to kill him." She gave him a tear-filled smile. "But, Soren, I'm so glad you're home."

He was glad to be home. Even under the current circumstances.

"We have so much to catch up on." She stood and pulled him to rise. "But first, let's get you to the healer."

She led him to the healer's chamber, but the old man was gone. Soren moved to a narrow hutch with thin stacked drawers against the wall. He knew where to find what he needed and pulled a curved needle from a small dish and a string of silk from a separate drawer.

"Here, let me," Salara said as she moved to take it from him.

He pulled back. "I've seen your needlepoint."

She pursed her lips at him with an angry brow, but he shook his head. He did allow her to help thread the needle and clip the silk length, but he sat and stitched his skin together himself, as he'd done so many times before.

Except this time, it was different.

He paused on the last stitch, his breath catching on the broken image of the sun.

Salara put her hand on his knee. "Give him time, Soren," she said softly. "He loves you. He just needs time."

CHAPTER SEVEN

Hope came with the sun. Norah lay awake in bed but didn't move to rise. Soren had returned. Yes, the reunion wasn't quite as she had hoped—slightly more soul crushing. But still, he was home, and she had Sephir back, and Adrian was safe. That reminded her: she still needed to kill him for worrying her as he did, although he had brought Soren home, so he might escape with a mild bodily injury and a hug. A smile came to her lips as she nestled against Mikael under the quilts and furs.

"Come closer," he murmured.

Her smile grew as she wriggled nearer to him, soaking in his warmth.

"Closer," he said, and pulled her on top of him.

Norah laughed.

They lay in the quiet of the morning, her head on his chest. She felt the thrum of his heart under her cheek, in time with her own.

"Will you talk to him today?" she whispered.

His chest tightened underneath her, but he didn't answer. She couldn't feel his heart anymore, but she knew it was there. Angry, hurting, hiding.

Norah crossed her arms over his chest and rested her chin on them. "Will you not talk to me?"

She didn't think he'd answer her, but finally he said, "Not yet." But the anger in him was fading. *Progress.*

"Okay," she said softly, and gave him a small smile. The air became lighter with her acceptance, and he relaxed again.

She swirled her fingertips over his chest. "Will you eat breakfast with me?"

Mikael brushed her cheek, and a mischievousness came to his eyes. He drew her up and closer. "I want breakfast in bed," he said with a smirk, and pulled her to meet his kiss.

Norah laughed as he twisted and turned them, moving her underneath him. It wasn't unusual for him to wake with a hunger, one she was happy to satiate.

Morning Mikael, she called this side of him.

She loved Morning Mikael.

Norah frowned. Everything in Soren's chamber remained untouched. He hadn't been there. If he hadn't returned to his chamber, where had he stayed? She rolled her eyes. If this was some gods-damned humble acceptance of his discharge, she'd scream.

She turned on her heel and stalked out of the castle and toward the sparring fields. When she spotted him, anger rippled through her. He was on the field with the warriors, calling moves, as he usually did. Except now he was among them, participating. What in the nine hells?

She stormed onto the field toward him. He stopped when he saw her. They all stopped.

"What are you doing?" she demanded when she reached him.

Soren's brows creased in confusion. "What?"

She waved her hand at the field. "This. What's this? And why didn't you sleep in your chamber?"

"It's no longer my chamber."

What? "What do you mean it's no longer your chamber?"

"I'm no longer lord commander."

What complete and utter nonsense. "Wasn't it your chamber before you were lord commander?"

He shifted. "Kind of."

"What does that mean?"

He said nothing.

"Well?" she pressed.

"Well, we were like brothers then. I had more privilege."

"You're still brothers, dummy. It's still your chamber." She pulled the spear from his hands. "And you're still commander." Norah shoved the shaft of the spear against the warrior he'd been sparring with, who clasped on to it in surprise. "Take this," she said angrily.

She grabbed Soren's arm and pulled him toward the castle. "Come on." This was absolutely not the way things would be now. "He's still commander!" she shouted back to the men over her shoulder.

Norah practically dragged him into the castle and down the halls. He was a heavy beast, but her anger fueled her. Gods-damned men and their gods-damned sensitivity. And who did Soren think he was with his drivel of assumptions? He was the gods-damned lord commander of Kharav. She pulled him along as she cursed the gods for not having more curse words.

When she reached his chamber door, she swung it open. "Go on, then."

"What are you doing?"

"I'm reminding you of your place. *Someone* has to. And at least compliment me on your chamber not being the complete wreck you left it."

He snorted, then looked around. "It looks very nice," he said finally, but too forced for her taste, and she narrowed her eyes at him.

"Good," she snapped. "Glad you like it. Settle in."

"You can't just say it and have everything return to normal."

Norah pursed her lips. "Why not? I'm salara."

He paused, and the crease between his brow eased. "That you are," he said softly. He drew in a breath as he looked around.

Her anger dissipated and was replaced by the happiness in just having him home again. Gods, she'd missed him. She really wanted to hug him again, but they were past all the emotional homecoming energy that had allowed her to get away with it in the throne room.

"Have you been in my chamber often?" he asked her.

Norah raised a brow. "Oh, *now* it's your chamber?"

His eyes darkened.

"Maybe." She shifted. "Why?"

"It smells like you."

She frowned. "You say that like it's bad."

"Not bad," he said quickly. "Just... woman-y."

Whatever *that* meant.

He sat down on the bed. There was still a sadness in him. It would pass, she told herself. They'd get past this. She took a seat beside him, and they sat in the quiet.

"Where did you go?" she asked after a time.

"The Stone Forest of Khalakhan."

She hadn't heard of it before. "Is it in Kharav?"

"It is."

Norah waited, but that was all he said. She pursed her lips. "You're as bad as Caspian in telling a story. What is Khalakhan? Why did you go there? What have you been doing? How did Adrian find you?"

He grumbled at all her questions. "It's the place of dead gods. Back when Kharav had gods."

"Kharav had gods?"

He nodded. "Many generations ago, Kharav had many gods. There are ruins in Khalakhan, with their symbols still carved in the stone. It's where the gods were born. And where they died."

She stared at him. "So, they just all... died?"

Soren shrugged. "Well, that's what happens when men stop believing in gods. They die."

Norah drew her brows together. That made no sense. "Or... they continue living, because what do they care? They're gods."

"You wanted me to tell the story, and I'm telling it," he said between his teeth.

She shifted. "Fine. Sorry."

Soren set his eyes forward again but didn't pick back up. She squirmed inside. She hadn't meant to shut him down.

"Did you go to ask for wisdom from these gods?" she jested with a smile, trying to stir some lightness. "Because you obviously didn't have any of it when you left."

His brows dipped. "Why would I ask them for anything? I just said they were dead."

"Oh. Right."

He gave a faint shake of his head. "I went there because I was sad, and I wanted to be with dead things."

That wasn't the admission she was expecting, and she stilled. "Oh," she said softly.

"And I knew it was a place no one goes," he added. "No one would bother me."

"Except Adrian?"

"I should have known," he grumbled in agreement. "I thought if it was anyone it would be you, but I forgot how annoyingly persistent he can be too."

Her smile returned.

His brow creased again. "Did you lay on my bed?"

"No." She bit her bottom lip. *Not today.*

He pulled a long hair from the side of the bed as he glared at her. Then another.

Norah swayed as she looked around the room innocently. "I would come in here to think," she confessed. She grew more serious and turned back to him. "I missed you, Soren."

Surprisingly, she wasn't met with a snarky reply. He only looked at her. He wouldn't say it back, but his silence spoke for him.

"You're the only one," he said finally.

"Mikael's missed you too. Your leaving hurt him, but he'll come around." She reached out and clasped his forearm and gave him a reassuring squeeze.

Soren ran his fingers over the scabbed gash on his shoulder.

"It'll heal," she told him.

"But there will always be a scar."

In more ways than one, she knew. "Life is like the supreme Salta Tau," she told him, thinking of the ink mastera. "And scars are the markings of your story. They're a testament to what you've survived. You'll heal. *Both* of you."

CHAPTER EIGHT

The rump of Mikael's horse was quite large, like the rest of the beast. Dust faded the midnight-black coat that lay underneath. Why was she watching a horse's rump? They'd been riding for two days, having departed Kharav for Mercia with the full army, and her mind was all over the place. They were holding on to the nobles by a thread, headed toward a battle where they weren't sure whether they'd find an ally or a foe, and praying their other enemies wouldn't notice and take advantage of an undefended Kharav while they were gone. And then there was Soren's return. Norah blew out a breath and urged Sephir up beside her husband.

He rode quietly.

"You have to talk to him at some point, you know," she said.

He kept his eyes forward. "No, I don't."

She looked back over her shoulder at Soren riding at the end of their company. His wrap covered his face, and he was too far for her to see his eyes, but she knew he still wasn't himself.

"Yes, you do," she pressed. She smiled wryly. "It's not possible for you to hate him. I know—I've tried."

But his face held no reaction. "He betrayed us."

Norah stiffened and cast all joking aside now. "He didn't betray us. Knock it off with that absurdity."

"It's not absurd, he—"

"No more!" she snapped in a sudden flash of anger.

His head jerked toward her, and his eyes blazed. "You can't be serious."

She'd never been more serious. She'd tried continuously to help him move forward with Soren. She'd tried in all the ways of kindness, but her patience was gone, replaced by a sudden defensiveness. "I mean it," she hissed. "That is your brother, both of blood and heart. You need to sort out the mess between you two." She was done with this conversation and done with this ridiculousness altogether. Norah urged Sephir forward and away. "And don't come back to me until you do," she called over her shoulder.

Time passed slowly. They reached the eastern pass of the Canyonlands and then wove west, toward the Uru. It was a longer route, but easier and faster to navigate the whole of the Kharavian army through. The ride already felt like an eternity, and Mercia still seemed lifetimes away, especially with Mikael keeping his distance. As he should. She'd been serious—she was done with him until he mended things with Soren. He needed to do it soon, though. She missed him, especially at night alone in their tent, which he respectfully stayed out of.

They neared the Uru lands toward early evening on the fifth day, and she slipped down from Sephir with an exaggerated slump. They weren't quite to the village, but walking would breathe some life back into her.

Strange—Tahla hadn't come to greet her yet, but she would see her at the village. Norah was excited. She hadn't seen Tahla since fleeing Mercia so many months before, and even that time was a blur. Norah chided herself—she should have visited, or at least written. Why hadn't she? She'd been so caught up in her own wallowing. She hoped her friend had stayed well. They had a lot to catch up on.

They reached the ridge, and Norah smiled at the beautiful view of the sprawling terraced stone houses of the Uru. It had been too long since she'd been there.

"This sight never ceases to amaze me," Adrian said, drawing up and dismounting beside her.

She loved how he saw its beauty too. "Same." And she was happy he was with her again. Norah glanced at him. She had given him a good berating for the worry he'd caused when he left to find Soren without telling her, and she threw in a couple of threats for good measure before breaking down in tears of thanks. Now that he was by her side again, as was Soren and Sephir, and now that Mercia was potentially so close to being retaken, things seemed like they could be set right.

As she neared the center house leading Sephir, she stopped.

Tahla emerged from inside, smiling.

With a very swollen belly.

Mikael chuckled as he shifted in his saddle. Seeing Tahla with child was the last thing he'd expected. She was a woman who'd just as soon cut off one's manhood than allow herself to be wooed.

"Tahla!" Salara exclaimed, and Mikael watched as his wife swept forward and pulled the chief's daughter into a warm embrace. "What a surprise—congratulations!"

A pain daggered his heart. Salara put on a brave face, but she had to be thinking of their own failure for a child. Of his failure to give her one. He desperately wanted to put his arms around her now, to hold her. She'd want his touch. It comforted her like hers comforted him. But he wasn't allowed to do that. Not yet.

Mikael slid down from his destrier and made his way toward them. "Tahla," he greeted with a smile, putting on a brave face of his own.

She bowed her head with a grin. "Salar."

He glanced around the village. "Do you have a man tied up around here, or have you properly chosen a mate?"

She laughed.

"Good luck getting an answer from her," Coca Otay said in the Urun tongue, coming out of the center house. "She won't speak of him. I don't know if I'm welcoming a son or need to bury a body."

Mikael smiled at the Urun chief as the old man stepped to him and clasped his shoulder.

"It's good to see you," Coca said, but his eyes held concern. "You bring your army. And your anger."

"I go to war."

Coca nodded as he looked at Salara. "You go to put the North Queen back on the North throne?"

"Of course."

"You are a very different man now."

Yes. Yes, he was. He watched his wife fondly as she still talked with Tahla. His heart swelled. "She's made me a different man."

Coca nodded. "It suits you."

Mikael chuckled.

"Go settle, get food to eat. Rest, my son. You have quite a task ahead of you."

Mikael nodded as Coca left him to settle in. He glanced around. Tahla had led Salara away in a rush of conversation. It was good to see them together again, and happy.

Coca had been right. Salara had changed him—had changed how he saw the world, what he wanted. She was kind and smart and brave. She was compassionate and forgiving. She was strong, and she made him strong. And she was right. He needed to mend things with Soren. Not simply so he could go back to her, but because she knew what he needed. And he needed his brother.

Adrian approached. "The army's settled, Salar. I'll be with them."

Mikael nodded. "Where's Soren?"

"He's checking rations and weapons."

"Have him come."

"Yes, Salar." And the young bear turned on his heel and headed back to the army outside the village.

Mikael took a seat on a log by the large fire. He had always loved this about the Uru—that they grouped around the fire. Dancing. Celebrating. Celebrating wins, even in the face of loss. Celebrating life.

Obeweta brought him a large bowl of stew. He'd known the elder woman since he was a boy, and he smiled appreciatively at her. Coca was very much like a father figure to him, and the Uru were his family. And he was fortunate for his family.

All of them.

A silent presence stepped beside him.

"Salar," Soren said quietly.

They hadn't spoken since Mikael had stripped him of his title nearly a week and a half ago. The heat of anger at his betrayal came rushing back, but also the pain of loss. Soren's leaving had hurt him, more than he had thought he could ever be hurt. Yet there was still something that hurt worse. Missing him. Without Soren by his side, a piece was gone from him. And he needed to be whole again.

"Sit."

Soren took a seat on the log beside him.

Mikael handed him his bowl of stew. "Eat, brother. We've wounds to mend and battles to win."

Their eyes locked.

"Lord Commander," Mikael added.

Soren took it slowly, and his eyes glistened in the firelight.

They sat in silence. Soren pulled down his head wrap and drained the bowl before setting it down beside him.

Then Mikael held out his dagger.

Soren stared at him as his brows dipped in question.

"They need to match," Mikael said. The story of their brotherhood, the markings they both bore—except for the coloring of the sun, they were the same, and they needed to remain the same.

Soren was a little too accepting of the task, but at least he made it quick as he ripped a slice across Mikael's shoulder.

Mikael gritted his teeth. "Fuck, I didn't cut you that deep," he said angrily. He'd cut Soren only deep enough to leave a scar.

"Fuck, you did," Soren growled back. "Deeper. You got me with a damned sword."

Mikael gripped his shoulder as blood streamed down his arm. Well, now they'd both certainly have a scar.

Soren eyed him a moment. "Are you all right?" he asked finally.

He pushed out a breath between his teeth. "I'll have Salara stitch it."

"I'll stitch it."

Mikael nodded. "That would be better. Have you seen her needlework?"

Soren snorted. "Why do you think I didn't let her stitch mine?"

And just like that, they were well again.

With a stitched and aching arm, Mikael made his way toward the house where he knew Salara would be. He pushed open the door and stepped inside. She sat on the edge of the bed but rose when he entered.

She pursed her lips. "I told you not to come until you've settled things with Soren."

"We're settled," he said.

Her eyes narrowed at him.

He showed her his shoulder. Her mouth opened but no words came out. "We're settled," he said again.

"Oh." Then her eyes narrowed again. "Wait, did you really just willingly injure yourself to the point of stitches right before we walk into battle?"

He frowned. He hadn't thought of that, but no matter. "I'll be healed enough by the time we reach the North."

She eyed him skeptically.

He could only look at her, all beautiful in her admonition, but there was something more. Something else that troubled her.

She smiled. "I'm glad, then. I needed the two of you back." But it wasn't an easy smile.

He stepped closer. "Are you all right, Salara?"

She shook her head. "I'm fine."

But she wasn't fine, and he knew why. "Salara."

"Really," she insisted.

Ever so gently, he pulled her to him and drew his hand to her stomach, where there was no child and likely never would be. She sucked in a breath.

"I'm sorry," he said softly.

"I'm happy for her, I really am," she said, her voice tinged with emotion.

He nodded. "I know."

"I just—"

"You don't need to explain yourself. You can long for something and be sad when you're reminded of it." He pulled her chin up to make her look at him. "And I'll be here, sad with you."

She wrapped her arms around him and smiled with the most beautiful of sad smiles. "I love you."

"I love you." And nothing had ever been more true.

Chapter Nine

The Kharavian army reached the borders of the North, silently and undetected. As expected. They hadn't earned the name of Shadowmen without merit. Now the challenge would be making it to the capital.

Soren had ridden mostly in silence, his mind not entirely focused, which frustrated him. It was good to be back where he belonged, fighting for those he loved. Salar's forgiveness brought a joy that he struggled to push aside to keep his mind on the task at hand—the North.

Adrian rode beside him. He eyed the young bear. How strange it must feel to lead an army against one's home kingdom, but Salara was the North's true queen. Adrian believed this, and Soren had faith in him. And Adrian would see his brother again, a day Soren knew he longed for.

Salara worried for the Bear, and if he was honest with himself, Soren did too. The Bear would never stand idle as his kingdom was overthrown. And he'd certainly never stand for his queen being attacked. He'd die first. Soren prayed it hadn't come to that. He wasn't sure what he'd do if something had happened to the Bear—an enemy he'd fought for so long, yet a man he could never imagine himself without. So, he told himself what he told Salara time and time again—the bastard prick wouldn't die.

And Soren worried for Caspian. If he didn't deliver the Northman back to Tahla alive, back to his child that he knew nothing of yet, Tahla would never forgive him. Before departing the Uru, Soren had promised her. He needed to keep that promise.

The task before them was a dangerous gamble. For the first time, Soren wasn't completely confident in the outcome. If this was a ruse, if something had happened to the Bear and it was Aleon that awaited them, united with the North, the Kharavian army would be overtaken. Not easily, or so Soren preferred to think, but Aleon had one of the largest armies in the world, and the North not only had their own forces but mercenary armies as well.

And these were no ordinary mercenaries the council had obtained. The Holy Knights were the most sought after of mercenaries and came at the greatest cost, but unlike ordinary mercenaries, they didn't fight for gold alone. They fought only what they considered to be holy wars—battles of good and evil—and the council would have definitely made this a holy war.

Men fought most fiercely for that which they believed, and the Holy Knights fought only for what they believed. It made them near invincible.

The Kharavian army made their way through the outer reaches, spreading ranks out and weaving in and out of villages, using every tool of stealth to pass through the Northern lands in secret. The army had now made it farther than they ever had before. Soren would have liked to boast it as skill, but in truth, in their years of war, the Bear would have never let them get this far. He would have known the moment they stepped inside the borders. Someone was letting them draw near, but whether it was the Bear who called them to join him, or the North and Aleon luring them into a trap, he didn't know.

When they reached the midlands, Soren called for a group to break off, mitigating the risk if they were, in fact, walking into a trap. He and Mikael would covertly lead a smaller army through the mainland toward the isle, assessing possible routes across the channel to the castle and ensuring Aleon was not in wait. If all went well, they'd cross the channel and launch a surprise attack to divert attention. If the Northmen were on their side, they'd open the gates of the main bridge, where Adrian would lead the army across to join them. It was a solid plan.

That was, if the Northmen were loyal to Salara.

And if they weren't, if it was a trap, the army would retreat and get Salara to safety. Despite her vehement objections, he and Mikael were able to convince her to stay with the broader army. Soren ordered Adrian to keep behind as well, to make sure she followed the plan.

Night hung heavy over the mainland, the perfect cover, and the Kharavian army slipped quietly through the darkness. They followed the messenger who had brought the news to Kharav. Soren could practically hear the man shaking in his boots, and he gritted his teeth in annoyance.

Cohen followed after the messenger. Soren was glad to once again have him in his service. He watched the boy closely. Cohen's eyes and mind were sharp; he saw things others missed. If there were warnings to see, he'd be the one to catch them. But all was quiet, and Cohen motioned the small army forward.

There was no sign of Aleon—no sign that anyone knew they were there.

Good.

Or bad.

They slipped through the dark alleys of the city, and when they reached the channel, they scanned the banks, looking for the best way across. In all his time in Mercia, crossing the water to the capital isle was the one challenge Soren still didn't have a solution for. He knew there was a tunnel that ran underneath, one that Caspian had led him through when he'd fled with Salara. But his mind had been on escaping and keeping Salara safe. He couldn't remember his way back to it, and they didn't have time to find it.

The bridge was the only way across, although with summer now gone and winter approaching, the forming ice provided a possible alternative.

"There," Soren said to Mikael as he pointed to a strip of ice stretching across the still water between the mainland and the castle isle.

"It hasn't hardened enough to carry the weight of a man," the messenger said, his voice still lacking confidence. "And if you fall into the water, that cold will have you dead within moments."

"Then how do we get across?" Mikael asked.

The man shook his head. "The only way I know is the main bridge. But I'm supposed to bring you to the Narrows—the market stall side streets."

Soren snorted. "That sounds exactly like what we're *not* going to do."

"What's there?" Mikael asked him. "Why the side streets?"

The Northman shook his head. "I don't know. It's just what I was told."

"By the lord justice?"

"Yes," the Northman said nervously.

Mikael frowned. "And how does that get us to the castle?"

"I-I don't know."

"What *do* you know about the castle?" Soren growled impatiently.

"I've never even been in the castle. So nothing."

Soren forced himself to not dagger the man in the throat as he ripped an annoyed gaze toward Mikael.

Mikael cast his eyes out across the channel and over the castle, thinking. "We'll go to the side streets," he said finally.

"You can't be serious," Soren hissed. "Does a back alley not scream 'trap' to you?"

"We'll go," Mikael said again.

Soren clutched the messenger by the collar of his jacket. "If you're lying—"

"I know, you'll kill me," he finished quickly.

"No," Soren snarled. "You'll wish I would've killed you." He shoved the man forward, and they followed him into the dark.

The Narrows were just as their name implied—narrow market streets made even smaller by the covered merchant stalls. The men weaved in between the stations and carts, taking cover from shadow to shadow.

The messenger walked down the center. Like an idiot.

When he reached the end, he stopped.

They all stopped.

Soren scanned the street. All was quiet. They lifted their eyes to rooftops, searching for movement. But there was nothing. Soren looked at Mikael, who only looked back at him. They waited.

"We're here!" the man called.

Soren winced and gritted his teeth again. He'd kill him. This was definitely a trap.

A side door swung open from the end building, and Northmen poured out. The Kharavian soldiers fell back, surrounding Mikael, and Soren brought up his axe to strike.

"It *is* a trap," Mikael hissed beside him.

But then Soren stopped. His eyes trailed the person who stepped out behind the Northmen, and he snorted as he shook his head. He knew that frigid grace. "No. It's not. It's the grandmother."

"Destroyer," the foul woman said icily as she stood in the center of the street. "What took you so long?"

Irritation rippled through him. "We marched the entire Kharavian army across the Tribelands and through the North, in just over two weeks' time."

"Did anyone see you?"

Was she serious? "Of course not." *Insulting.* Curse the North gods, he hated this woman.

Her gaze moved past him to Mikael, and she stiffened. "Shadow King," she said. It was the first time they'd met.

"Lady Catherine," Mikael greeted her back, as politely as Soren had ever heard him speak—trying to make a good impression, no doubt.

Soren rolled his eyes. "What are you doing here?" he asked her.

"What do you mean *what am I doing here?* How do you think you're going to get in?"

"Across the bridge."

"I thought you Shadowmen were smarter at this battle thing."

Soren scowled at her.

"Come," she called to them, and stepped through the door from which she'd come. Soren snorted—she was taking them through the tunnel. He glanced at Mikael, who looked back at him with the flat want of refusal written all over his face. But Soren gave him an encouraging nod, and they followed after.

She led them down a steep staircase, into darkness that was dark even for the Shadowmen. Their way was lit only by the lantern the old woman carried.

"Are you sure about this?" Mikael said quietly to Soren.

"The old woman's annoying," Soren said, "but she's loyal to her granddaughter."

"This annoying old woman can hear you," she called out in front of them.

They poured into a larger tunnel, and she took them through a series of turns to a staircase leading upward, which Soren guessed came out somewhere in the main castle.

"This will bring you out inside the temple," she told them. "It's as close as I can get you to the bridge."

"Where's the Bear?" Mikael asked.

"He waits by the keep, at the north end, where the council will seek refuge when the battle starts."

The Bear was alive. A small wave a relief passed through Soren, and he thought he might have seen the same from Mikael. Likely not. But maybe.

"He plans to cut them off?" Mikael asked.

The old woman nodded in the lantern light. "But the mercenaries will be with them. It won't be an easy task."

Mikael looked at Soren. "I'll take half the men, clear the bridge for our army to enter. You join the Bear."

Soren nodded.

"There's a young girl, Norah's cousin, Evangeline," the grandmother told them. "She's a pawn in all of this. She's not to be harmed. Do you understand?"

Mikael nodded.

"But the council—show them no mercy," she said. "I want them destroyed for what they have done."

Soren snorted. "Do you not know who I am?"

And for the first time, the old woman smiled at him. "Then the gods go with you, Destroyer."

CHAPTER TEN

Soren ascended the staircase in the darkness, into the castle he'd dreamed of taking since he was a boy. But never had he imagined taking it in the name of the North Queen, who he was now sworn to, and never by the Bear's side. Five hundred of his men followed behind him—men who had followed him into the hells of battle again and again. And they would yet again. Not all of them would make it through this night, and if they died, then they died for the North's cause. Surely, they, too, had never dreamed this was their path, but still they followed him.

They silently spilled out into the darkness of the sleeping temple. Mikael split off and headed toward the bridge, taking Cohen and half their men with him, and Soren drove for the north side, toward the keep. He'd memorized the isle from his time before—every building, every structure, especially the keep—and knew exactly where he was going.

He thought about Mikael making his way toward the bridge, and he quickened his pace. He wanted to reach the Bear before—

Shouts rang out, and a horn sounded. The mercenaries knew they were there, and the night came alive.

Too late.

He pushed faster. Torches sprang up down the mainways, lighting up the night. As he rounded the corner of the massive library, almost to the keep, Soren spotted him.

The Bear.

The justice fought in his signature battle dress with the head of the great Northern bear on his shoulder. Flames from the torchlit city gleamed off his armor. Soren hated it—the Bear always looking so fucking majestic.

A small group of Northmen fought by his side against a troupe of mercenary Holy Knights as even more mercenaries poured out of the keep. Curse the North gods—they'd be slaughtered. Soren and his men surged toward them. These hired swords were the best there were, and the Northmen were no match.

A mercenary lunged at a Northman with his spear, and the soldier spun sideways, using the momentum to grab it and arc around, ripping it from the mercenary's hands.

Soren snorted. *Not bad.* Quite good, actually. Better than he'd remembered. Training in Kharav had turned the Northmen into respectable soldiers. Perhaps they'd last a little longer than he'd thought.

But now the Northmen were outnumbered and falling one by one. Three mercenaries swept around, attacking the Bear at all sides and knocking him to the ground. One advanced and swung his sword over his head to deliver a deathly blow. Soren let out a snarl as he barreled through, cleaving his massive battle-axe into the man's back and felling him midswing. The two Kharavian warriors by his side took up the others.

The Bear lay on his back, and Soren held out his hand. The justice gaped up at him for a moment before clasping his forearm and letting Soren pull him to his feet.

"What took you so long?" the Bear panted.

Soren cursed. "As I told the old woman, I got here in just over two weeks' time, with my *entire* army."

More mercenaries joined the ranks against them, and the two men defensively positioned themselves back-to-back.

"And we weren't sure the message wasn't a ruse," Soren added.

A mercenary attacked with a series of maneuvers that pushed Soren back, against the Bear. These soldiers were good—too good.

"What do you mean a ruse?" Alexander snapped over his shoulder as he worked his own defense. "I sent you a miner, so you'd know it was from me."

What? Why? Soren snorted in utter confusion. "Why would you send a *miner*?"

Alexander ran a man through on his sword and paused. "Are you serious?" he asked incredulously before kicking the dead man off his blade. "You told me Northmen soldiers were shit, that you'd rather have our miners because you'd only trust a man who could properly swing an axe." He panted between swings. "I sent you a miner."

Soren landed a fatal wound on the mercenary in front of him. "I never said that," he argued.

"You definitely said that."

And suddenly, he did remember telling the Bear those words. "Am I supposed to remember everything I say?" He kicked back another soldier. "And there was nothing else you could send? You know—a letter with a seal, something meaningful, other than a stupid reference to a comment I might have made years ago?"

"Something the council would have traced back to me should they have caught him?" the Bear cut back through labored breaths. "And it wasn't years ago. It was right before you left Mercia. You were supposed to know what it meant."

"Well, I didn't," Soren spat. "You should have sent something meaningful to Salara."

Alexander stopped. "But I needed *you*. The message was for *you*."

Soren spilled the entrails of another man and paused. The Bear had needed him. "Oh." He should have gotten the reference. He should have driven the army to the North faster. "Well, it was a stupid fucking message."

Soren glanced across the city, which was now lit up in battle. He could see that the tall gates of the bridge were open, which meant the Kharavian army was in. He looked back to Alexander. "Your brother leads my army across the bridge. Your queen comes for her throne."

The faintest of smiles pulled at the corners of the Bear's mouth. "To the keep, then? The council's there."

Soren gave a nod. "To the keep."

The clang of sword strikes rang through the air as she charged over the bridge atop Sephir. Norah held her own sword in her hand, although she hardly needed it. The Shadow army protectively surrounded her like a thick fog—she could barely see through them. It wasn't entirely as she'd imagined when she thought of herself riding into battle to take back her kingdom. Not that she wanted to fight, or kill, but she'd been prepared to.

In the distance, she heard Mikael's booming voice, giving orders to his army in the Kharavian tongue. Somewhere just ahead of her, Adrian echoed, and the ranks around her pushed forward.

Her eyes combed the sea of battling men... Where was Alexander?

As they pressed deeper into the capital and through the courtyard, more men flocked around her, and she noticed it wasn't just her Kharavian warriors. The gleam of silver armor blended into the black of shadows—her loyal Northmen, joining her at her side.

But this would not be an easy win. The castle was filled with mercenaries—the best in the world—and their numbers were greater than she'd imagined.

A *sip* flew past her, and she didn't need to see it to know it was an arrow. Her gaze shot to the turret's walls, where mercenaries fired down on them.

Bhastian grabbed her, pulling her off Sephir. "Keep down, Salara," he ordered as he raised his shield over her. Kiran pressed close on her other side.

She kept herself smartly under Bhastian's shield but still scanned the battle-strewn courtyard around them. "I have to find Alexander."

"He'll be going after the council, who are likely in the keep," Bhastian said. "But, Salara, the fighting will be strongest there."

"I have to find him," she insisted. She had to see him, see him with her own eyes, and know he was all right. Then they would face her council together.

The corners of her Crest guard's eyes creased with objection.

"Bhastian. I have to find him. Please."

Reluctantly, he nodded. Then he and Kiran shouldered closer, and they moved with her army as a unit toward the keep.

The ranks thinned as more mercenaries flooded them, and the fighting pressed closer. How were there so many of them? The Kharavian warriors and her Northmen fought shoulder to shoulder, working tirelessly to push them back.

Suddenly, to her right, the gleam of a sword caught her eye. Kiran spun and struck it to the side with his own blade before sinking his second short sword into the mercenary.

Bhastian swore. "Salara, we should fall back. It's not safe."

She hadn't come for safety. "We keep going," she said.

Another onslaught of arrows rained from the sky, taking some of the men down around her. Kiran and Bhastian pressed her between them with their shields held high. She glanced up at the walls lined with mercenaries, and her heart fell. There were so many of them.

Then she noticed a darkness snaking in from both ends, pressing the mercenaries toward the center, and hope sprang within her. The Kharavian army was closing in—her men were gaining ground. The arrows falling from the wall turned into falling bodies of the enemy.

She urged her men on toward the keep.

The fighting thickened, and the smell of blood filled her nose. Kiran drove back another attack to the right, and Bhastian felled a man who broke through on the left.

Norah heard her name, but she couldn't place where it had come from or who called it. The clang of battle was near deafening now, drowning out everything around her. Bhastian yelled something, but she couldn't make out what it was.

A mercenary broke through in front of her and drove a sharp swing from above. She countered with her own blade and then followed with a quick series of defensive moves. But he was good—too good—and pressed her back. He let out a roar as he launched a lethal sequence and swung again for her neck. But both Kiran and Bhastian crossed their swords to block him, and Kiran followed with a thrust to the mercenary's gut with his short sword. The man fell to his knees, and Bhastian took his head.

A hand grabbed her arm from behind, and she twisted, whipping her dagger from her waist and driving it into the man's side. It was a punishing blow, but his armor kept it from being a kill strike.

And Norah gasped.

Caspian stared back at her, still holding her arm, with a dagger jutting from his side.

He was alive. Or, he was...

No!

"Caspian!" She let go of the dagger.

He winced. "Queen Norah," he managed between his teeth. They both looked down at the hilt protruding from between his plates of armor just above his hip.

"Caspian!" she cried again.

"It's not a fatal wound," Bhastian said. "He'll live. But we can't just stand here."

Caspian curled his hand around the dagger and pulled the bloody blade from his side.

"Oh gods, Caspian! I'm so sorry!"

"No, it's all right. I'm all right." He grimaced through panting breaths. He didn't look all right. "We have to get you away from here until this is all over," he said. "It's not safe for you here."

She shook her head; she wasn't going anywhere. "I have to find Alexander."

"He's going after the council now," he told her.

"He's here?"

He nodded, still panting. "Yes, with the lord commander."

"Soren's with him?" Her eyes welled.

"They really work quite well together when they're not trying to kill each other."

She laughed through her emotion.

Swords rang behind her, and she glanced back to see Kiran and her Northmen fighting off another wave of mercenaries.

"Salara," Bhastian pressed. "You see? He says the Bear is well. We should fall back until the commander takes the council and secures the castle."

She shook her head again. "I can't *fall back* in the fight for my own kingdom."

Caspian wavered and dropped to a knee. Norah and Kiran both jumped forward and caught him.

She raked her eyes around them. "We need to get him somewhere safe."

"This way," Bhastian said, and they fell back toward the library.

Away from the thick of the fighting, Caspian sank to the ground along the arched stone. Their men formed a protective wall around them under the direction of Bhastian and Kiran.

"We'll get you a healer," Norah said as she dropped down beside him. "Just rest for a moment. You'll be okay."

"It's not feeling that way," Caspian said between labored breaths. He gripped his side tightly and grimaced again.

Her heart beat faster. "What do you mean? You said you were all right."

"Help me hold the bleeding," he said.

Norah's hands shook as she fumbled along the ridges of where the armor split. The tunic was stained with blood underneath, but she wasn't exactly sure where she had hurt him.

"It's a side wound," Bhastian said, "he's perfectly fine. He's not even bleeding that much."

"Shut up, Bhash," Kiran said.

She paused and glanced back at Bhastian, then at Kiran. "Wait, is this your way to keep me out of the battle?" she asked.

Kiran puffed an angry snort and cut Bhastian a glare. Bhastian shifted, just catching on.

She scowled back at Caspian and swatted him. "I can't believe you! I was actually worried!"

"Ow!" He winced. "In fairness, I didn't expect to get stabbed. I'm just trying to make it worth it. And it really does hurt."

"I should stab you again."

He gave a slight smile. "Welcome home, Norah."

Soren cut through the battle at Alexander's side as they raced toward the keep, with the Kharavian warriors at their heels. The mercenaries grew thick as they drew closer, but the Kharavian men were skilled swordsmen, and they kept the small team moving forward. Alexander and Soren charged the hold at the doors, bringing down the defense and bursting inside. Both men took the stairs at a run. Mercenaries met them in force, but Soren and Alexander shouldered them over the railing or cut them down. Bodies on the stairs slowed their advance, but they battled through. The sting of a blade ripped across Soren's arm, but it was only a surface wound, and he delivered a deadly blow back, ripping open his opponent's neck and sending him tumbling down the staircase.

The councilmen had already fallen back, deeper into the keep.

"We have to catch them before they reach the tunnels," Alexander told him.

They raced by a large hall and skidded to a stop. Inside stood a man with a dagger in his hand. Soren recognized him as a councilman—the one called James. He was thinner than Soren remembered, his frame now gaunt and his eyes, hollow.

The Bear held up his hand as he approached slowly. "James," he said, but instead of the warning or threat Soren expected, there was a pleading in his voice.

"I knew it was only a matter of time," the old councilman said, clutching the dagger and bringing the tip to his own chest. "The gods send their judgment for our sins. I'm sorry, Alexander. I've failed you."

The Bear shook his head. "James, don't do this."

Soren glared at Alexander. "That's exactly what you want him to do."

"Shut up," Alexander snapped back. "James," he called to the man. "Put the dagger down."

"I've failed you," the councilman said again. "I've failed Norah. But most of all I've failed Mercia."

Soren clenched his jaw. They didn't have time for this.

James plunged the dagger into his stomach.

Soren rolled his eyes. *Finally.*

"No!" Alexander shouted as the councilman fell forward to his knees. He caught the old man and eased him down. "No! James!"

"I'm sorry, Alexander. Forgive me."

"James!"

"Forgive me," he said as his last breath left him.

The Bear sat clutching the councilman.

Soren gaped at him. "Are you going to be able to do this? We have"—he counted on his fingers—"five more to go." Or more... He didn't remember how many councilmen there were. No matter—everyone in a robe would die today.

Alexander stood slowly. "James was like a father to me."

"Yeah, well, a coward, traitor father who tried to kill Salara. Come on."

The Bear grabbed Soren's arm. "It's not my intention to kill the council. These men need to be brought to trial for their crimes against the crown."

Soren stopped, speechless. He shook his head in confusion. "Trial?"

"This is the way things are done in Mercia."

Was it? "Are you not literally called the justice of the queen? Is it not you who judges their innocence?"

The Bear shifted his weight back on his heel. There was a pause before he said, "I am, and I do."

Soren stepped closer, his eyes burning into the Bear's. "Have you personally not witnessed their treason?"

Alexander's eyes burned back. "I have."

Soren gripped his breastplate. "And how do you find them?"

The Bear's breath deepened, and Soren soaked up the fury radiating from his armor. "I find them guilty," Alexander said.

He pounded his fist against the Bear's breastplate in solidarity. "Consider this your trial, then. Come the fuck on."

But Alexander grabbed him. "They *will* die for what they've done. But they'll stand before their queen and answer, after they've watched her retake her throne. I won't take that away from her."

Noble shit. Soren growled his protest. "Fine," he said between his teeth.

"Now come the fuck on," Alexander said to him, and Soren smiled.

They made it to the back of the keep. Despite the skill of the Holy Knights, there was now only a small group of soldiers providing a final defense. The rest of the mercenaries had made for the bridge to meet the Kharavian army coming through.

An elder Mercian councilman clutched a small satchel and cowered behind several men. Yes... Soren remembered this one. *Edward.*

"Attack!" Edward screamed at the mercenaries as he backed toward the wall. "Think of your souls. You would let this darkness defeat you?"

A knight rushed forward, and Alexander threw his dagger, catching him squarely in the base of the neck. The man fell backward, choking on his blood.

"The tunnels!" Alexander shouted at Soren, and he turned to see another councilman hurrying through a side door and down a stairwell.

Soren took after him. Austair? Alastair? He couldn't remember, and he didn't really care. As he caught up with him, the councilman pulled a vial from his pocket.

What—

His eyes widened as the old man quickly pulled off its topper and swallowed the contents. *Poison.* "No!" Soren shouted, springing forward. He grabbed the councilman by his robes, holding him against the wall, but within moments, foam sprang from the man's mouth, and his legs gave out from under him. There was nothing Soren could do, and he let the dying man sink to the ground.

Another one dead. Soren swore.

He took the stairs back to the keep, cursing himself again. Alexander would be angry with him for losing another councilman, and as much as he disagreed with the Bear, he respected what he wanted.

By the time he made it back, the Kharavian soldiers had bound the rest of the councilmen and were escorting them from the keep. Alexander stood at the window, looking out. Soren could hear cheering down below, in what could only be the calls of triumph in winning back the North. *Good*, it would soften his message.

"Unfortunate news," Soren said as he stepped back through the doorway. "Or you could look at it optimistically—you have one less councilman to hang."

But as Alexander turned, Soren's eyes locked on him and on the stream of blood pouring down the front of the Bear's armor.

Soren stopped in his step.

It was too much blood.

Alexander swayed, and Soren lunged forward to catch him.

"What happened?" he demanded.

Alexander scoffed. "Before or after I caught a blade to the stomach?"

"Damn you, man, this isn't a joke." He pulled the Bear's arm over his shoulder to support him. "We need to get you to the healer."

Alexander shook his head. "No, Destroyer," he said, breathing heavily. "This is my end."

The Bear's words knifed him. "If you say that again, I'll end you myself." Soren pulled him toward the stair.

Alexander grunted in pain. "I always thought you'd be the one to do it."

"There's still time," Soren cut back. "Hold yourself together." Where was Salara? He set his eyes on a nearby soldier. "Get Salara!" The soldier darted away.

Soren started forward again, but Alexander pulled him back.

"Soren," he gasped. "Stop."

There was a finality to his tone. The way he said his name—*no, no, no.* Soren shook his head. "You can't die now, Bear. Not now."

Alexander grew heavier as he weakened. "Let me down," he said.

Soren sank slowly to his knees, lowering the justice to the floor. He shifted behind him, holding him upright. "You have to hold on," Soren said. If he could just hold on...

The justice shook his head faintly.

"You have to hold on."

The Bear's body grew even heavier.

"You can't die," Soren told him. "They'll memorialize you, you bastard. Kids will be cursed with your name. And it's a fucking terrible name."

Alexander chuckled weakly.

"Of course you'd love that." Soren's lip trembled.

Alexander's breathing became labored. His face was pale now. Ghostly pale. Soren ripped off his armor to the blood-soaked shirt underneath. Alexander coughed, and more blood seeped from the wound in his stomach, tiding over his sides and puddling underneath them. It was dark blood. Life blood.

Soren bared his teeth, holding back the emotion. Death didn't deserve the Bear—the only worthy opponent he'd ever had. Soren had hated him for so long. He loved hating him. He wanted to keep hating him, to keep fighting him. He needed him.

"Don't even think about leaving yet," he said between his teeth. "You know she's coming."

"How do I look?" Alexander joked.

Soren grimaced. "Like a gutted pig."

He motioned to a soldier nearby. "Your cloak," he commanded. The soldier pulled it off quickly and covered the justice.

Soren nodded. "Now a little less gutted."

The justice's breaths came shallower. "Don't you pine after me when I'm gone."

Soren turned his head away, fighting the tears that stung his eyes. He had always planned to kill the Bear, but this...

"Soren." Alexander clutched him. "Norah, Adrian—watch over them." He squeezed Soren's arm, gasping for another breath. "I beg you. Brother."

Soren nodded, unable to speak.

Alexander's breath grew fainter, and the blink of his eyes slowed.

"Not yet." Soren shook him. "Not yet—Salara's coming." He looked around. Where was she? Shouts rang outside, with a shuffling below. "Salara!" he bellowed. He gripped the justice tightly. "She's coming. Norah's coming!"

Alexander drew in a breath, and Soren knew it was the last one. The last breath. The last of life.

The Bear stilled in his arms.

Soren slumped forward over the justice. He'd done everything in his power to kill this man all these years, and now he'd give anything to save him.

Salara's voice rang out below. "Alexander!"

Soren clung to him, unable to respond.

Footfalls hit the stairs. "Alexander!" she called again.

Soren leaned back, still holding the Bear up, and waited. He could do nothing more—he couldn't call to her; he couldn't even breathe.

She reached the top of the stair and stopped, horror flooding her face. "No!" she screamed, running to them and dropping to the floor. "Alexander!" she cried. She clutched his face and pulled it toward her. "Alexander!"

Soren watched her, his vision blurry. "He's gone," he said hoarsely.

"No!" she screamed. "No!" She clutched on to the Bear's shirt, shaking him. "Alexander! I'm here, come back. I'm here!"

Soren reached out a bloodied hand and grabbed her arm, pulling her still. She stopped, looking up at him, and he shook his head.

"Please," she begged him, like he had the power, like he could give the Bear back to her. But he didn't, and he couldn't. And it killed him.

A wail broke from her lips, a raw anguish that shook him to his soul. All the battles he'd fought, all the death he'd seen, but her cry—a long, keening wail—broke him. He'd never forget the sound.

Slowly, he eased out from behind the justice and laid him down gently.

She let out another sob and collapsed over him.

Soren waved out the remaining few soldiers. He stood and stretched his arm to the wall, leaning against it. He couldn't draw in a breath. The ache of loss in his chest was suffocating. He moved to the edge of the stair, looking back at his weeping queen.

He didn't know how he made it out. His legs felt like they might not hold him, but once outside the castle, he staggered through the carnage of the North. The weight of the air crushed him, but he turned his mind away from himself to someone more important. Soldiers called out to him, but he ignored them as he scanned the masses. He had to find him—where was he? A warrior trotted up to him, but Soren pushed him back, not hearing his words.

Where was he?

Then he saw him.

Although bloodstained and weary, Adrian's face held a wide grin. "Victory!" the young bear bellowed. He looked across the soldiers as they cheered around him.

Soren lingered, letting him reap the joy, if only for a moment.

Adrian spotted him and lifted his sword in triumph.

Soren moved toward him, slowly. Then he stopped, and Adrian's grin faded slightly. He pulled down the wrap from his face. Their stares locked.

The young bear stilled. "Where's Alec?" he called.

Soren hesitated.

Adrian's brows drew together. "Where's Alec?" he asked again.

Faintly, Soren shook his head.

His face twisted. "Where's Alec?" he asked more urgently. "Where is he?" Soren stepped toward him, but Adrian drew up his sword to halt him. "No. No! Where is he?" he demanded.

"Adrian." His voice cracked. "He's gone."

Adrian bared his teeth as he shook his head. "No." He shook his head again. "You're lying. Where is he?" he raged in desperation.

Soren let out a ragged breath. "He's gone."

Adrian shook his head again, refusing his answer. "Alec!" he cried out as he staggered back. He turned and stumbled in a circle, looking around for his brother. His eyes desperately combed the soldiers around him. "Alec!"

But there would be no answer.

Adrian dropped his sword from his hand and wavered as he stopped. "Alec!"

Soren caught him and pulled him close. Adrian was a large man now, not easily embraced, but Soren held him.

"Alec!" Adrian screamed into him.

Soren held him until his screams gave way to sobs, and then he held him longer. His own tears fell as he hugged him tightly. It wasn't right. The Bear should be the one alive—here. He had family, people who loved him, people who needed him. In that moment, Soren would have given anything to take his place. He held him tighter.

Adrian's body shook as he sobbed in the courtyard of death.

A slight breeze rippled over the carnage of the North, carrying the smell of blood and victory. Mikael stared down at the fallen mercenary commander of the Holy Knights.

Pity—they truly were a magnificent army. He surveyed the city. So many good soldiers lost, and the loss of good soldiers saddened him, even when they weren't his own. The mainway ran red with blood—blood of mercenaries, Northmen, and Kharavian warriors. But they'd taken back the North, and that was worth the cost.

He'd never stepped inside the kingdom of Mercia. Many times he'd imagined it, imagined the death-littered streets of the North that he'd hated for so long. But never like this. Never had he thought he'd fight to reclaim the throne for its queen—the woman he loved.

A mercenary stirred to his right and pushed himself to sit. He sputtered a broken cough, spitting blood down his chin, but he didn't seem fatally wounded.

Mikael stepped toward him. The soldier would be taken with the other survivors, made slaves—a tragic end for such men.

The soldier looked up at him, no fear in his eyes. "Shadow King," he panted with a hateful breath. "Come closer, that I might fight you with what little strength I have left."

Mikael snorted. Resilient bastards, he'd give them that. "Are you not afraid to die?"

The man took a raspy inhale. "What is death? I'll bask in the glory of the gods and be rewarded for my courage against evil."

"Evil," Mikael repeated. He stooped down beside the man. "Is that what you think I am?"

"What do you think you are?"

Mikael frowned. No one had ever asked him that. "A man." A salar. A husband.

The soldier chuckled before coughing and sputtering more blood down his chin. "If you're a man, have mercy as a man. Send me to my gods."

"Not all men have mercy."

"Honorable men do."

Mikael clasped the side of the soldier's neck, locking him with his gaze. "I'm not an honorable man." He pulled the soldier closer. "But you did fight with courage. Go to your gods." And he plunged his dagger into the soldier's chest, giving him a quick journey. For this man, he'd give mercy.

He laid the expired soldier back against the ground and wiped the blood from his dagger before sheathing it again at his waist.

"Salar!" Soren's voice came urgently from behind him.

Mikael turned.

The commander stopped, silent, as if words wouldn't come. It was the first time Mikael had seen him on the battlefield without his wrap. Anguish covered him. "The Bear," was all he said.

Mikael cast his eyes toward the castle. "What about the Bear?" Was he coming?

"He's dead."

A weight struck him. *No.* He couldn't have heard correctly. "What?"

"The Bear's dead."

Mikael shook his head. "No. That's not possible." He couldn't be dead. The Bear would be the one to bring his end. Mikael had seen it with his own eyes. This wasn't possible.

"You need to come. Now."

Mikael followed Soren through the field of the dead, to the castle, up the stairs, and down the marble halls darkening with the fading sun. Soren led him to the private mortium, where he stopped.

In the center of the room stood a stone slab table, where the body of the lord justice lay.

Salara sat beside him, leaning forward with her forehead against his shoulder as she wept. Mikael stepped into the room, and she looked up. Her eyes were swollen and red, her cheeks wet with tears. Blood stained her hands and arms, the blood of the Bear, no doubt.

The crimson saturating the front of his battle clothes told the story of his death—a weakness in the ornate Northern armor, where the breastplate met the waist piece.

And now the justice was dead.

The Bear was *dead*.

But this wasn't possible.

Mikael drew closer, looking down at him. He wasn't convinced this was real. This couldn't be real. He moved even closer to the side of the table. Slowly, he reached out, then stopped. To touch the Bear...

It was a violation of some kind.

The Bear had always been beyond his reach. This man, who had haunted him for so long. The only man he'd ever feared. Hated. Cursed. Resented.

Yet a man he now respected.

He dropped his hand to his side. The Bear would stay beyond his touch.

The head of the Northern Bear, its white fur splattered red, had been removed from the justice's shoulder and laid on the ground under the slab table. Perhaps it was best that it die too, for no one else was worthy of it.

His gaze shifted to Salara, who only watched Mikael as he stood there. Her eyes were the bluest they'd ever been, against her red-rimmed eyelids overflowing with sorrow. The initial anguish had passed, and now she sat in the quiet shock of grief, watching. Was she looking for something within him? Pleasure? Victory? Relief, even?

She would find none of it. He felt none of those things.

Her lip trembled. It was the slightest of movements, but it called him. Quickly he stepped around the table to her side, pulling her up and wrapping his arms around her. She let out a sob and clung to him. He said nothing. There were no words. He only held her. Tightly.

They stood for a long time, until the dark of night came and he felt her weight heavy against him. Keepers stepped into the mortium—those responsible for preparing the bodies of the dead to pass their souls to the next life. They lit candles throughout the room to chase back the night, then stood quietly, waiting to care for the body of the justice.

"Let me take you to your chamber," Mikael said softly. "You need to rest."

"I can't." Her voice was barely a bird's breath. "I can't leave him."

"The keepers are here. They'll take care of him."

Her head snapped up, and her eyes found them. She hadn't realized they'd come in. "No, they can't have him." Her eyes pleaded as she shook her head. "They can't take him."

Mikael gripped her shoulders, making her look at him. "They won't take him. I won't allow it." Then he softened his voice. "But don't let him lie like this, in his own blood. Let them clean him. And we'll stay."

She looked at the justice on the table and wiped her face with her hand. Her breaths still filled the silence of the room. Finally, she nodded.

Mikael led her to a bench against the wall and sat, gently guiding her down beside him and putting his arm around her. He nodded to the three men in gray robes, who silently stepped forward. They pulled off the rest of the justice's armor and cut away his clothing. A breathy cry escaped Salara as they stripped off the red-stained linen, revealing the deep wound to his stomach. Mikael pulled her closer to him. Two of the men brought a basin and started sponging the body clean, and one of the keepers prepared a needle and set to stitching the wound closed.

They worked with the care and reverence befitting a hero; that's what the Bear was to the North. And now Salara would have to find a way to fill his void. Mikael would have to find a way to help her.

When the keepers finished, they draped a white cloth over his body and bowed to Salara before leaving in silence.

He looked down at Salara but didn't dare suggest she leave again. "Has Adrian come?" he asked softly.

She nodded weakly. "Earlier, with my grandmother," she whispered. "He's not of right mind. Soren had to take him away."

The brother of the Bear would be devastated, as he knew Salara was. "Do you want to stay longer?"

Her red-rimmed eyes met his, and she nodded again.

He pulled her closer and kissed the top of her head. "I'll give you some space. Take all the time you need."

Mikael stood, squeezing her arm tenderly before leaving her the privacy to grieve.

CHAPTER ELEVEN

Norah sat beside the stone slab table that held Alexander. She didn't know how much time had passed. She could only stare at him. With his pallid skin and blue-tinged lips, she couldn't pretend he was only sleeping. His skin was cold to the touch.

How could this have happened?

She shouldn't have come. She'd been safe in Kharav. She'd had Mikael and Soren. She'd had Alexander. Even if she'd have never seen him again, he'd still be alive.

But she'd wanted her throne back. She'd wanted vengeance.

And this was what it cost her.

The tears came again, and she lay her head on his cold shoulder. Cold like the room. Like tomorrow, and every day after now. She'd brought this. She'd done this to him. To herself. To Adrian—*oh gods, Adrian.* And Catherine. How could she even face them again? She wanted their anger, their wrath. She needed it. She deserved no kindness, even in the bitter depths of her grief and loss.

There was a tremor in her mind, and she brought her fingers to her temples. She was exhausted, but she knew sleep wouldn't come. Not that it mattered—she didn't deserve sleep either.

A stirring rippled through the room, and Norah felt eyes on her. Her skin prickled. She lifted her head to see a man standing at the other end of the mortium, between two pillars in the shadows.

Just standing.

Watching.

She narrowed her eyes to focus better. And her breath left her as her chest seized.

Alexander.

She shook as she glanced down at his lifeless body under her hands, then looked back up at him on the other side of the room. Alexander was dead, right in front of her.

Yet his exact likeness stood at the edge of the room, as in life.

How?

"Alexander?" she breathed.

He was different—his hair was clipped shorter, and he was dressed in dark breeches with a gray tunic. His eyes were fierce, his face full of anger as he looked upon his body.

"Alexander?" she called again.

His attention jerked, his stare moving up from the body on the table slab to find her, as if just noticing her for the first time, and he took a step back.

"Is it really you?" she asked him.

His brow relaxed from its hold of anger, but his eyes gave way to alarm. No recognition came from him, no warmth. He backed farther into the shadows, and she feared she'd lose him.

"Wait!" she cried. "Don't go! Please."

He paused as she staggered up and drew around the table, closer to him.

"How is this possible?" she whispered. "How are you here?" She swallowed back a cry.

He shifted, leaning back on his heel, still on the verge of flight.

"Do you not know me?" Is this what death did to a man's spirit?

Alexander neither moved nor spoke, but he watched her apprehensively as she came closer—close enough to touch him.

She brought her hand up hesitantly to his face, but he pulled back. His eyes didn't know her. "It's me," she whispered, crying softly. "It's me, Norah."

He didn't respond, but his stance eased ever so slightly.

Markings on his neck caught her eye. Ink markings—different from the markings Mikael and Soren wore, yet they seemed familiar. When he noticed her gaze on them, he reached up to cover them and pulled back, his alarm returning. He retreated farther into the shadows.

"Wait!" she called to him. "Alexander!"

But he stepped backward, into the darkness, and disappeared.

"Wait! Don't go!" She ran past the columns and into the shadowed hall, looking desperately for him. "Alexander!"

The darkness swirled around her, and she woke abruptly, sitting up at the table beside Alexander's body once again. She jerked her head to her right, and then her left, scanning the room. She was alone. A cold sweat beaded on her brow, and her heart thundered in her chest. She forced herself to take deep breaths, willing back the calm.

She'd been dreaming.

But it had felt so real.

She wiped her face. Mikael's cloak lay around her. He must have come back to check on her. How long had she been there? It was still night.

"Norah."

She jumped at the voice behind her and turned. "Adrian," she said breathlessly.

His face was pale and hollowed from grieving, his eyes without the light they normally held. Her heart broke for him. She rose from the bench beside Alexander, ignoring the stiff ache in her muscles from sitting all night.

His eyes traveled over Alexander's body, then back to her, and his nostrils flared. The ache in her heart grew to a pain as her pulse quickened. She tried to form some kind of apology—where could she even start? But as her mouth struggled to shape the words that didn't exist, his face twisted in a silent grief, and he swept forward and pulled her close, embracing her tightly. Her body shook, or maybe it was his. She didn't know.

They stood, holding each other in their loss. She didn't know for how long. She didn't care. That he would embrace her at all brought another wave of emotion—she hadn't lost him too.

When their tears ran dry, they both sat on the bench by the table, clasping each other's hands. Silence filled the room. She was glad the keepers had cleaned Alexander—glad that Adrian didn't have to see him again in that state. But she'd never be able to clean the memory from her mind.

Adrian finally spoke. "You can't let them take him," he whispered.

She looked at him, but his eyes were fixed on Alexander. "What?"

"You can't let them take him to the pyre. You can't send him to the gods. He needs to stay here—he belongs in Mercia."

"Adrian," she said softly. "You would chain his spirit here?"

"He would want to stay, to watch over Mercia. To watch over you." His lip trembled slightly. "And he wouldn't leave me." He clutched her hands. "Don't send him," he begged as he turned to her. His eyes welled again. "Don't send him."

Norah didn't want to send Alexander to the gods, but she couldn't make that decision right now. She only clutched Adrian's hand tighter, and they both surrendered to the silence.

Adrian left just as the faint light of morning peeked over the horizon. Norah knew she needed to go clean up; she still had Alexander's blood on her skin.

She could only stare at him lying on the table. What would she do now? She'd never imagined her life without him. A life apart from him, yes, but never a life without him. Adrian's ask came back to her. Would she send him to the gods? Would Alexander want to go?

"What do you want me to do?" she whispered.

He'd always been a man of faith.

"Surely you want to join the gods. You deserve to join them, to bask in glory."

But Alexander had never been a man for glory. He was a man of duty, of sacrifice. He wouldn't want to leave Mercia, but could she really keep him from the gods? And what would she do otherwise? Mercia didn't bury their dead. She couldn't put him in the Hall of Souls—the tomb of Mercia's kings and queens.

How could she decide? That she needed to decide at all made anger flash through her.

"Damn you," she whispered. "I'll never forgive you for this."

Tears threatened again, and she laid her head forward onto his shoulder. This couldn't be real. He couldn't be gone. The bewilderment of grief was overwhelming, and exhaustion still pervaded her. All of it was too much, and she couldn't be there anymore.

Norah walked out of the mortium and into the rising sun, her legs numb. She kept her head down, shielding her eyes from the brightness. Bhastian and Kiran were at her side in a moment, but she waved them back.

"Please," she said softly. Space. She needed space and quiet and stillness. And darkness. It was too bright outside.

She didn't remember the walk to her chamber, only that when she reached it, it was empty. No one would have expected her there.

Norah stood. It was the first time she'd been back in her chamber since she'd returned to Mercia. When she'd been there last, it was before she'd fled. When she'd been there last, Alexander had been alive. She pressed her eyes closed—she couldn't think about that right now. She needed to hold herself together.

Norah glanced around the chamber and the adjoining bathroom. She desperately needed a bath, but the energy escaped her. The bed was too inviting, and she let herself fall back onto it. Just for a moment. She closed her eyes and gave in to her sorrow again.

A whisper stirred in her spirit, and she opened her eyes. She blinked, focusing. She lay in her bed in the middle of a tree-lined path. Slowly, she sat up. It was summer. Norah loved the summer. Was it summer already? She couldn't remember.

She dropped her legs over the edge of the bed and stood. Her mind was in a haze. Was she dreaming? Where was she? Flowers of all colors surrounded her. She closed her eyes and breathed in, but she couldn't smell their fragrance. Almost, but not quite. Puzzled, she opened her eyes again, and she saw him.

He stood at the end of the path between the rows of trees.

Alexander. She smiled.

She hadn't seen him since she'd left Mercia. No, that wasn't right... The haze in her mind cleared.

Alexander.

Her breath seized in her chest. Alexander was dead. *Dead.* And she was in Mercia. But where? And where was the mortium? Where was his body? Was this his body, alive again somehow? She swept her eyes around her. The bed she'd risen from was gone. Only the tree-lined path remained, and Alexander stood at the end of it. Another dream?

It didn't feel like a dream.

She started slowly toward him, not daring to take her eyes from him for fear that he would disappear again. This time, he waited for her. As she came close, he shifted uncomfortably, but he didn't step away.

"Please," she said softly. She feared her emotion might choke her. "Please don't leave."

He let her step closer. He looked... not like in the dream before, but more like himself now. He was dressed in his Mercian battle armor, everything but the head of the Northern bear, and his hair wasn't clipped quite so short. The markings on his skin were gone.

She searched his face for the affection he'd held in life, but she found none. Tears threatened. "Am I a stranger to you now?" she whispered.

He watched her curiously but didn't answer.

"Say something. How are you here?"

His silence crushed her.

"Say something," she begged him.

But there was only emptiness. Norah stepped closer. He wasn't really there, she told herself. She reached out. He leaned back but didn't completely avoid her, letting her touch find him.

She sucked in a breath as her fingers met the hardness of his body. How was this possible? How could she feel him? She spread her hand wide against his chest. But his eyes still held no knowing, no recognition.

Alexander reached up and caught her wrist. His message was clear: *Enough.* He brought her hand down but didn't release her as he pulled something from his pocket.

A vial of a red tonic.

No, not tonic. *Blood.*

He removed the top of the vial, then spread her hand wide and smeared a drop across her palm. His eyes burned a brilliant blue as he closed her hand in his. Her breath came faster, and he leaned closer, then closer still. He reached up and brushed his fingers over her eyes, bidding her to close them. And she did.

Her mind shuddered.

Norah woke with a start, and again found herself on her bed inside her chamber. Her breaths came fast, her lungs struggling for air. Had she been dreaming? She opened her hand and glanced at her palm, but there was no blood smear. No tree-lined path. No summer. No life in Alexander's body.

But she'd *felt* him. No, that was the madness coming through, the lack of sleep. She clutched her hands to her chest. Her grief was playing tricks on her. She took a deep inhale to focus herself.

She heard footfalls, and she sat up, but she didn't need to look to know who it was. Mikael. She knew his sound and welcomed the comfort that came with it. He'd help calm her mind. She pushed herself to stand.

He stepped from around the hanging panels to the bed and met her before she could find the strength to move to him. The warmth of his arms came around her, pulling her close. She reached up and held on to him. Gods, she needed him.

"Salara," he said softly. "You should eat something. Bathe. Rest."

There would be no rest. "I can't."

"You have to take care of yourself."

But there were so many other things she had to do first. "I have to figure out what I'm going to do with Alexander."

"Caspian is looking after him. You have time."

Caspian. She hadn't seen him since she'd left him wounded by the library. If he was tending Alexander, then he was doing better. And she could trust him, until she could think. Until she could figure out what to do.

"You need to eat."

"I'm not hungry."

He held her tightly. "Let's at least get you in the bath."

Finally, she nodded.

The door opened again, and Serene stepped inside. Her Mercian maid greeted her with tears in her eyes before moving quickly to prepare a bath. It was the first time she'd seen Serene since returning, and while she was happy to see her, she couldn't muster the energy of joy. Serene said something, but Norah wasn't sure what, and she couldn't bring herself to answer.

Norah stood numbly as Mikael pulled the tie from her hair and gently worked out the braid. Then he loosened the back of her gown and helped her step out of it.

Serene returned, but Mikael said, "I'll tend her." Then he led Norah to the bath.

She sank into the tub and tinged the water rust and brown. She couldn't move, she couldn't speak. She could only sit as Mikael washed her hair and scrubbed the last traces of blood and battle from her skin. Then she let him pull her out and dress her for sleep.

The overwhelming ache of loss left Norah exhausted, and she sank heavily onto the bed. She let her eyes close, but she knew sleep wouldn't come. There were no distractions from her grief in the darkness. Mikael crawled into bed beside her and held her as she wept long into the night. And when she thought she had no more tears, she wept some more.

CHAPTER TWELVE

Norah's legs felt like they might not hold her as she walked to the courtyard. The sun had risen, and it shined its warmth down through the crisp fall morning, but it wasn't enough warmth to stop the shaking inside her. She knew what was to come. She'd been here before—had seen it before—and she wasn't sure she could face it. But she had to.

The Kharavian warriors parted for her. She was glad they were here. It was easier to accept the darkness when it supported her. And despite the sun, this morning would be dark. Mikael walked behind her, giving her the lead to show a re-risen queen, but stayed close and occasionally brushed her back to remind her he was there.

She paused when she saw the gallows in the center of the courtyard. They'd been temporarily erected, but they seemed so sturdy. So permanent. She pushed out a breath—she'd have them broken down as soon as they were finished.

Three ropes hung from the beam above. There would have been five, but James and Alastair were already dead. She breathed a prayer of thanks that she didn't have to watch James hang. Despite his betrayal, she knew how much he'd meant to Alexander.

Norah took her place. Mikael once again brushed her back, and she slipped her hand behind her to lace her fingers into his. She skimmed the growing crowd. Not far to her left, she spotted Evangeline, who gave a small curtsy when their gazes caught. Norah nodded back. She didn't fault her for the circumstance, or anything that had happened. The girl had been a pawn of the council, as Norah had once been. Norah had welcomed her to stay at the castle, but with the death of her father, Lord Allan, during the battle to take back the kingdom, Evangeline had asked to return to her home city of Damask to live with her aunt. It was an understandable request, and one that Norah was happy to grant, and she also ensured Evangeline was provided everything fitting of a royal. It was the right thing to do. Evangeline would stay in the line of succession, should Norah have no heir.

So Evangeline would be queen one day.

The soldiers parted on the opposite side of the courtyard, both Kharavian and Mercian soldiers, and Soren pushed three men forward. Three councilmen. One man cowered behind the other two—Edward, unsurprisingly. Soren prodded them forward with the eye spear on his battle-axe, and they staggered to the gallows.

Edward's panicked eyes found Norah. Her fingers clutched Mikael's hand tighter, but she didn't waver. These men deserved death. And they'd receive it.

"The gods strike you all!" Edward screamed. "Be damned! You'll be damned by Hammel himself, in the darkest depths of the hells!"

The corners of Soren's eyes turned up. He was smiling underneath his wrap. "Good," he replied. "Then I'll see you there, where I can kill you again—but the way that I truly want to."

Edward gasped.

Soren pushed them under each rope, looping the noose and tightening it around each of their necks. The other two councilmen stood silently, but the eyes of all three were wide with terror.

Soren didn't look at her as he worked. After the battle, she had expected she'd have to restrain him from slaying the councilmen on sight, but he'd taken the laws of Mercia seriously, not just allowing a trial but requiring it—albeit a short trial. He brought the councilmen before her in the throne room, and he judged them in the name of Alexander—judged them as guilty and sentenced them to death.

He stood now, all preparations made, and finally looked to Norah. Her heart pounded in her chest. Faster. Then faster still. He turned and nodded to a man on the side of the gallows.

The floor fell out from underneath the feet of the councilmen, and even though she knew what was coming, she flinched. Mikael leaned into her back, ever so slightly, giving her the power of his body behind her. Two of the councilmen hung limply, their necks immediately broken, but Edward squirmed at the end of his rope. A sickening groan escaped his lips. Death was necessary, yes, but it was supposed to be quick. She needed it to be quick.

"Soren," she gasped.

He pulled a dagger and ran Edward through with the blade. The councilman stilled, then swung from his rope with the hilt of the dagger from his ribs. Soren turned back to her, his dark eyes burning.

Norah swallowed the bile building in her throat, and he dropped his head with a hint of apology. She leaned against Mikael, and let his warmth calm her.

It was over, and she could breathe.

Salara only stared at her breakfast as Mikael watched her. She put nothing in her mouth. She just stared at it. But he knew she wasn't looking at the food, wasn't seeing it.

The councilmen had been executed the day before, but no doubt it was still fresh in her mind, as it was in his. It had been too quick a death, too kind, but neither he nor Soren intervened to change it. Salara had needed it to be over, and he'd given her that.

He wished he could give her more. He wished he could give her the Bear. It was a strange feeling, watching one's wife grieve so deeply over another man, but he couldn't muster any jealousy, not anymore. He'd come to accept that the Bear held a piece of her heart. Mikael had the assurance she loved him—he knew she was faithful to him, and she chose him over and over again. And maybe he'd also come to accept that the Bear deserved her love. Maybe it was a combination of those things that let him be at peace with it.

Mikael had foregone his seat at the opposite end of the table in order to sit next to her. He knew she needed him near.

Her eyes closed, and it was a long moment before she opened them again. She swallowed cautiously, as if her own tongue might choke her. Mikael reached across the corner of the table and took her hand. He didn't try to make her eat. He didn't ask her questions or prompt her to speak. He just sat in the silence, letting her know he was there by his touch.

The grandmother sat stoically to Salara's left, across the table from him. Her face was pale, and her lined eyes were trenched in grief. She'd spent the early morning in the mortium with the Bear. This woman had seen a lot of death over her years, had lost many she'd cared about. But Mikael knew she loved the Bear as her own blood and the loss cut her deeply. It was a wound he wasn't sure her heart would ever fully recover from.

Catherine's voice came barely above a whisper, but it broke the quiet of the hall. "When are we sending him to the gods?" she asked.

Salara swallowed again, and her eyes drifted slowly up from her plate to her grandmother. It had been three days since the Bear's death. Mikael hadn't pressed her, but she'd have to make a decision soon.

For a moment, he wasn't sure she'd answer.

Then she said, "Adrian thinks he would have wanted to remain here, to watch over Mercia."

Catherine drew in an even breath as she stared at her granddaughter. "Are you thinking of not sending him?"

Salara didn't answer. Mikael knew she didn't want to talk about this right now. But she would have to, eventually.

"You would keep him from his glory? Give him no rest?" Her grandmother looked at Mikael, but he offered no reaction, no support. This wasn't his decision. The old woman shook her head. "Norah, you cannot."

Mikael didn't necessarily agree with that.

"I haven't decided," Salara replied.

"What is there to decide?" her grandmother pressed her. "You have to send him to the life beyond."

Yes, that was how things were done in the North, but as someone who didn't believe in a life beyond, Mikael deemed a body all the more sacred—it was all that was left of a person. And for a person so loved...

He'd laid his father into the earth, and his sister. To have burned what was left—he wondered if he could've done that. It was hard to imagine.

"I'm just not sure that's what he would want," Salara said.

"Not what he would want?" the old woman asked sharply. "Or not what *you* want?"

Salara fell quiet. Anger coiled inside him. He didn't think this was about what Salara wanted—she didn't want any of this—and he didn't like that assumption placed on her.

"And where would you put him?" her grandmother asked. "Are you going to keep him in the mortium?"

Salara leaned forward with her elbow on the table and rubbed her temple. "I don't know. In the Hall of Souls, maybe."

"You can't put him in the Hall of Souls. There's no place for him!"

"I've been in there, I've seen it. There are lots of places." She was close to breaking; he could hear it in her voice.

"For future kings and queens, as they are bound to watch over Mercia. But you must relieve Alexander of his duty."

"He wouldn't want to be relieved!" Salara cried, her grief rising to the surface again and spilling down her cheeks.

The room quieted.

Still, Mikael said nothing.

Salara rested her forehead against her palm. She wasn't in a state to decide this now.

"Norah," her grandmother said, softly now. "You have to let him go."

She cut the old woman a fierce gaze. "How can you say that so easily? You love him too!"

"I say this *because* I love him. He should go to the gods. There's no place for him here."

Salara shook her head. "How can there not be a place for him?" she cried. "He is my lord justice! He gave his life for Mercia!"

"He can have my place," Mikael said, silencing them both.

Catherine and Norah both stopped and gaped at him in surprise.

"What?" the grandmother said breathlessly.

"Am I not king of Mercia?" he asked.

Her grandmother gave a faint nod. "Yes."

"Do I have a place?" It was likely not a place planned for him, but he'd claim it all the same.

The old woman pressed out a breath. "Well... I... I suppose, but..."

He took Salara's hand and his eyes locked with hers. "When I die, I'll return to Kharav, to the earth from which I came. You can give him my place."

Her lower lip trembled, and she brought his hand up and kissed it.

He looked at the untouched plate in front of her. "Are you finished?"

She nodded.

He stood and pulled her up. "Lady Catherine," he said with a polite nod to her grandmother, and led Salara from the dining hall.

She clung to him as they walked.

"Are you all right?" he asked.

She nodded and wiped her face. "I shouldn't have been so harsh with her. She does love Alexander. And she truly believes I'm keeping him from his glory."

"I know," he said.

She stopped them. "What do you think?"

He'd been hesitant to weigh in on this matter. He cast his gaze around and let out a long exhale. He hoped he didn't come to regret this, but...

"The Bear doesn't care about glory. He would have wanted whatever you wanted."

"I love you, Mikael. This isn't… This doesn't mean—"

"I know," he said, quieting her.

Her breath came easier. "And you?" she asked. "Is it really what you want—to return to the earth of Kharav when you die?"

He gave a frown. "It's what I've always expected. But… I also want whatever you want."

She threaded her fingers between his. "I want us to never be parted."

He tilted his head to one side and then the other. "Well, we may have to share an eternal bed then, as I've just given mine away."

A laugh escaped through her tears. "I'd love to share an eternal bed with you."

He smiled, and they picked their walk back up again. "Does this mean I have to deal with the Bear in the afterlife as well?"

"You don't even believe in the afterlife."

"Thank the North gods. But if I'm wrong and there *is* a life beyond, I'd want to make sure I was with you."

She held his arm tighter, but she was smiling.

The ceremony had been short and private. Only those closest to Alexander were there to see him placed in the tomb of the king in the Hall of Souls. Soren and Mikael had helped seal it. Adrian had stood silently beside Norah, still mourning his brother. Catherine had given no more objections to Alexander taking a place in the Hall of Souls. Surely she, too, couldn't bring herself to let him go.

After, Norah sat in the gardens. Had she made the right decision? There was comfort in knowing Alexander was still with her, that his spirit was still watching over. Was he watching her now? If she spoke to him, would he hear her?

"Queen Norah," Caspian's voice came from behind. It held an urgency that made her stiffen. "You need to come," he said. "A letter has arrived from Kharav."

Who would have sent a letter? "Has something happened?"

"Katya writes of Rael amassing forces at the border. She thinks they're preparing to attack."

"Where is my husband now?"

"In the judisaept, with most of the others."

The others—those who had become her de facto council—Soren, Adrian, Caspian, and three of several nobles who had been loyal to Norah through the coup: Lord Bosley, Lord Branton, and Lord Semaine.

Norah hurried toward the judisaept. Catherine joined her in the hall and hurried along beside her.

"Have you heard?" Norah said breathlessly.

"Just now."

Mikael was waiting when they arrived. He held a letter in his hand and gave it to Norah as she neared him.

"I have to return," he said. "Their numbers near the eastern pass double each day. I brought the entire Kharavian army to take back the North. Now there's no one to protect Kharav other than the border forces and the Uru. The Canyonlands provide natural protection, but even if a small army gets through, they could take the kingdom."

"And what about you?" she countered. "If they move to confront you on your journey back—alone against Japheth and Rael, you can't take them both."

"I'll march the army back through the Tribelands and through the western pass, then move north so the eastern Canyonlands will be between us. It will take longer to get the army through, but we should be able to clear it before anyone knows."

Her stomach turned at the thought of him leaving her. "I'm going with you."

He shook his head. "No. You just got your kingdom back. You'll stay here."

"We have to leave today," Soren said.

Mikael drew in a long breath, and his eyes met his commander's. "Brother," he said softly. "I don't want to deny you a good fight should it come to that with Rael, but you know what's most important to me."

Soren glanced at Norah and then back at Mikael. He gave a stiff nod.

No, he needed Soren. "You need a commander," Norah insisted.

The corner of his mouth gave the hint of a smile. "I've told you this before, but I'm beginning to think you don't believe me—I *can* command an army."

Norah took his hand. "Of course you can, but I don't like the thought of you going alone."

"I won't be alone. I have the entire Kharavian army. And I'll take Adrian."

Adrian gave a nod.

Mikael reached up and brushed Norah's cheek, giving her a soft kiss on her forehead, then he led Adrian out to prepare the forces for departure.

Soren followed after with Caspian and the lords, leaving Norah and Catherine.

Norah glanced at Catherine, but the woman said nothing. She narrowed her eyes. "No objections to him taking Adrian?"

Her grandmother frowned. "Why would I?"

Why *wouldn't* she?

"You've brought Mercia a strong king, Norah," Catherine said. "A fiendish king, with his... fiendlings... but a protector of the North. We should make an effort to keep him."

An emotional smile worked its way along her mouth. "You'd like Kharav, you know."

Catherine scowled. "Don't push it."

CHAPTER THIRTEEN

The fog of her breath lingered as Norah stood in the courtyard in the cold of morning. Winter was almost upon them. Mikael and his warriors readied to depart. The Kharavian army waited on the mainland outside the castle isle. It would take them two weeks to reach the Canyonlands and pass through its maze on the western side as Japheth and Rael amassed their forces in the east.

The Canyonlands posed fatal threats to those who didn't know them. Most who tried to pass got lost, then died of hunger or dehydration. Deep trenches funneled large armies into smaller groups, who could be picked off by arrows from the top. The smaller Kharavian army could defend against one three times its size, or more. But if they didn't reach the Canyonlands, they'd be overwhelmed and defeated with Rael's numbers.

It was a significant risk, but Mikael had left Kharav undefended in order to retake Mercia, and he had no choice—he had to return, and he had to return now.

The Kharavian army was feared by many, but these men were not the monsters of stories told. Regardless of how skilled they were, they were only men. Norah worried for them, and for her Shadow King husband. They needed to reach the safety of the Canyonlands, and Kharav beyond.

Soren stood beside her, no worry in his eyes. How was he so calm? As if they were marching to dinner.

Adrian checked the saddle on his horse, then turned to Norah. He gave her a respectful bow of his head, but she reached out and pulled him into a hug.

"Stay safe," she told him. "The gods watch over you."

"And Alec," he said.

"And Alec," she whispered back.

He mounted his horse.

Soren stepped up, waving him close, and Adrian leaned down. Soren clutched him by the breastplate and pulled him even closer. "This is what you've trained for, Little Bear. Protect your king."

Norah smiled at Soren's nickname for him. She'd heard it a few times now. *Little Bear.* Adrian was anything but little. He was larger than Alexander, larger than most Northmen, almost as large as Mikael. But to Soren he was the little Bear.

Adrian nodded.

"Keep your shield up. You get markings for kills, not wounds. Salta Tau will see them all." Soren released him and gave an affectionate beat on his breastplate with his fist. "Keep well, brother."

When they were ready to depart, Mikael stepped to her. His face was long, and shadows hung from his brow.

"Why do you look worried?" she asked him. "I'm the one who should be worried."

"Don't worry for me. I'll be safe as soon as I reach the Canyonlands."

"I know you won't listen, but I still think you should take a Northern legion as well."

He shook his head. "No. If things go poorly, I want the entire Northern army here with you. We still don't know Aleon's intentions."

"Well, Phillip's not going to attack Mercia with Japheth and Rael still threatening."

He clasped the side of her neck warmly. "I take no chances when it comes to you." He dropped his head and kissed her. "I love you."

"I love you," she whispered.

He looked to the castle at the top of the stair, where her grandmother stood, and gave the woman a nod before mounting his destrier.

Norah watched as they rode out of the courtyard and across the bridge to the mainland and beyond. She stood there, her cloak pulled tight around her, until long after they were gone. And as Mikael disappeared from her sight, she couldn't shake the sweeping feeling of loss, that she was all alone now. *No.* She wasn't alone, she reminded herself, and looked at Soren, who stood beside her.

"I want to start dining together again in the evenings," she told him. "Like we did in Kharav."

"Is your grandmother all right with that?"

"She told me to tell you to come."

His brow raised in surprise. "Did she?"

Damn. She pulled her lip between her teeth. "No. But she probably would."

"Would she?"

Damn. "No." She swallowed. "I just want you there."

"Then I'll be there."

She gave him a relieved smile. "Thank you," she whispered, and turned toward the castle.

Mercia was beautiful in the beams of the morning sun. Even in the cold. It was easy to pretend that everything was the way it had always been, that nothing had changed—no battle, no blood, no loss. Alexander could still be in his study, as he usually was in the mornings.

Alexander.

She could pretend, if only for a moment, Alexander was still there.

But he wasn't.

Norah paused on the stair and gripped the railing. She thought she'd battled the worst of the grief, but it swelled inside her again and threatened to cripple her.

"Salara," Bhastian called from behind. "Are you all right?"

She nodded. "I just want to go to my chamber."

"Do you need help?"

"No, I'm fine," she said quickly. She just needed to get to her chamber and catch her breath. Norah waved him off and forced herself up the rest of the stairs and into the castle. She took the halls as quickly as she could, trying to bite back her emotion. As she reached her own hall and turned the corner, the free fall of her mind momentarily stopped. She spotted a familiar face standing guard outside her door.

"Titus!"

The large guard bowed his head, respectfully formal, but Norah didn't care about formalities. She crossed the distance between them, leapt up, and threw her arms around his shoulders.

"I'm so glad you're here, and well!"

She hadn't seen the Northman since she'd fled Mercia. Or had she? Perhaps he'd been near, she just hadn't noticed him in the chaos of her return. A pang of guilt needled her that he hadn't crossed her mind in the days she'd been back, that she hadn't sought him out.

He patted the back of her shoulder but refrained from hugging her back. Still, she let herself hold on to him a little longer before releasing him. She couldn't handle any more loss, and seeing Titus walked her back from the sorrow's edge that had threatened her composure just moments before.

He cleared his throat, and she finally pulled back.

"Queen Norah, it's very important to me that you know I would have given my life to stop the council. But I wasn't on guard, and I didn't know what had happened until after you'd fled."

"I know." She clutched his arm in reassurance. "Titus, I never doubted you. Not for a moment. I only worried that those I cared about had suffered or been harmed in some way, including you. I'm so relieved to see you well, and back in my service."

A slight smile touched his lips. "I'm glad to be back in your service. And to see you back on your throne."

"How's your wife?"

He nodded. "She's well. As is my daughter."

"A daughter!" Norah grinned. "Titus, congratulations!"

The guardsman smiled. "Thank you, Regal High."

She squeezed his arm again. "I really needed some good news. Thank *you*." She smiled again, and he bowed his head as she stepped into her chamber and closed the door behind her.

Serene was straightening the room when she entered. Norah hadn't said much to her since she'd been back. She hadn't had the chance, or the mental wherewithal. But now, alone in the quiet... she was so happy to see her. She stared at her maid for a moment.

"Are you all right, Regal High?"

Norah nodded. "I've really missed you, Serene."

The maid's eyes glistened, and she smiled. "I've missed you too."

They both gave an emotional laugh as they embraced and held each other. Things would never feel right again, but they were starting to feel better.

"What happened to Vitalia?" Norah asked softly. Her maid had died when she fled Mercia during the coup. "What did they do with her?"

Serene held her hands. "The lord justice sent her body to the sea, as is the custom where she was from."

The sea. Vitalia was sent to the next life in the way she would have wanted. Norah nodded as tears came; she was so grateful that Alexander had known what to do and had seen it done. And here she was, still uncovering his mercies even after he was gone.

"I'm so sorry," Serene whispered. "I know you loved him. We all did."

Yes, Alexander was loved by many. She could only nod.

Norah looked around her chamber, trying to avoid the next wave of emotion that would come at any moment. On the vanity, a small box wrapped with a ribbon caught her attention.

"What's that?" she asked Serene.

"Oh, I don't know. But it was sitting on the balcony."

Odd. Who would have sent her something? Norah stepped to the vanity and picked up the box. She pulled the ribbon free and opened the lid. Inside sat a small glass vial.

A vial of blood...

The same vial of blood from her dream of Alexander.

Chapter Fourteen

Red.

Back and forth. Rolling like an ocean wave. A blood ocean.

Norah sat alone at her vanity, tilting the vial back and forth between her thumb and forefinger, rolling the blood within. The vial was small, no larger than her smallest finger, and tapered to its base. Where had it come from? *Who* had it come from? This was the same vial Alexander had held in her dream. Had he sent it to her?

That would be impossible.

Alexander was gone. She'd only dreamed of him.

Hadn't she?

She set it down on the polished wood and sat back in the chair, wishing for Mikael. She wished she could show him, talk to him. Grief made it hard to think. He'd calm the wildness of her mind and help her make sense of everything. But Mikael was gone, tending concerns far greater than dream trickeries. She'd need to figure this out on her own.

Norah poked at the vial, moving it from one side of the vanity to the other. What was she supposed to do with it? In the dream, Alexander had brushed a drop onto her skin. Across the palm of her hand. Seemingly, that was the appropriate action, but what would happen?

She could ask Soren what he thought.

No. He would make her throw it out. And there was a purpose here.

Alexander had given it to her in the dream. And blood... Seers used blood. Or rather, traveler seers did. Her hand curled around the vial. They had to be related somehow. Her mind spun through her memories—through everything she knew.

When they'd gone to the Wild, both Wild women had thought Alexander was a seer. They'd been sure of it. And he did have some kind of power—a power strong enough to keep the women from entering his mind. What if he'd been a seer and didn't know? Or maybe he'd been something entirely different. If he had power that let him bridge the void between the living and the dead...

Before she could talk herself out of it, she pulled the stopper from the top and touched it to her finger, turning it. Then she brushed a stroke of blood across her palm and curled her fingers closed.

And she waited.

Her heart raced in her chest.

She glanced around the room, still waiting. This was what she was supposed to do. This was what Alexander had shown her. Hadn't he? Or had she imagined it all?

Either way, she wasn't imagining the vial in her hands right now. It was very real, and very... full of blood. The vial and the dream had to be connected.

But all was quiet.

"Well, that's... strangely disappointing," she whispered to herself. Heat flushed her cheeks from the embarrassment that she'd expected anything at all from merely dabbing blood onto her skin. At least she was alone in her embarrassment—thank the gods she hadn't involved Soren. He would have thought she'd lost her mind completely.

Norah opened her palm and stared down at the blood smeared across her skin. Whose blood was this anyway? A small flutter whispered in her mind, like a bird's breath. When she looked back at her reflection in the vanity mirror, she jumped out of her chair, knocking it back and overturning it.

Just behind her stood Alexander.

She whirled to face him.

But the room was empty. He wasn't there.

No one was.

Shakily, she turned back to the mirror and sucked in a breath as he stood looking back at her again.

"How is this possible?" she whispered. She spun back to where he should have been standing behind her, but again, no one was there.

Norah turned back to the mirror. His image crushed her heart. "How are you here?" she whispered. Everything came all at once: sadness, happiness, relief, confusion. It was overwhelming. She forced herself to breathe. "Is it really you?"

He didn't speak. Could he not? Or did he just not want to?

She finally found words. "Does the blood bring you?"

He gave no answer.

Of course it did. She glanced down at the vial of blood. This didn't make sense. It was as if he were a traveler. But not.

"How? I didn't consume it, I only..." She looked down at her palm again. "Is this how you came to me in the mortium? Your blood on my skin?"

He still said nothing, but the slight tightening under his eyes told her she was right. He'd come while his blood had been on her skin. Like his blood was on her skin now.

"I wasn't really dreaming then. And I'm not dreaming now. Are you in my mind?"

The corners of his lips turned up slightly. Then he relaxed his face and closed his eyes. And waited.

Slowly, she followed suit and closed her eyes. And in the depths of her mind, he stood in front of her.

"How are you here?" she whispered as she stepped closer to him. "Is it really you?"

But he still didn't answer.

"Can you not speak?"

Again, no answer.

She knew he was just a vision in her mind. She couldn't touch him, couldn't feel him. And yet she couldn't help herself—she reached out her hand. But where she expected nothing, her fingers met the firmness of his body.

Norah let out a ragged breath. She *could* feel him. This wasn't just a vision.

And then she remembered, she'd felt him in her dream as well.

"How is this possible?" But she didn't care how it was possible, she only cared that he was there. He wasn't gone—not completely.

She pulled back and looked up at him. He was different, somehow. He seemed to recognize her... but not *know* her.

"Is this what happens when you leave life?"

His expression changed, but she couldn't read it. The wall of her chamber fell away to reveal the tree-lined walk that had been in her dream. He gave a slight motion toward it with his hand.

A walk? So... strange, yet not. So seemingly familiar, yet not. Like him. Slowly, she started forward, and they made their way down the path.

"Please, talk to me."

He glanced down at her for a moment, then looked ahead again. How she wished he would speak.

"I miss you, Alexander." The sudden sorrow returned, and she had to stop. Stupid emotion. She hated it. It crippled her. She clutched her chest. "It hurts," she breathed.

But the hurt turned to anger. It wasn't anger at him, or maybe it was. Maybe it was anger at herself, at the gods, at the world. He'd been taken from her.

"I need you." She needed her lord justice. He knew her, knew her heart. He'd always been someone who knew what to do, someone she trusted, someone who listened. She needed someone to listen now.

He took her hand. She stared at it a moment before looking up at him. His eyes moved back and forth between hers, their blue so settling. He was listening.

"I feel so lost. And scared." Just talking to him made her feel better. "Mikael went back to Kharav. And, of course, he's made Soren stay with me. He's all alone."

Alexander stilled. It was as if words were trapped inside his lips. He didn't speak.

"I'm worried for him. If Japheth and Rael attack before he makes it through the Canyonlands, it could be disastrous. He'll try to make it through the western pass. If he does, he'll be safe. But until then..."

Until then, she'd be sick with worry. Should she have done something different? Should she have sent a legion of Northmen? She still could. They'd be only a few days behind the Kharavian army.

"Should I send a legion?"

But he didn't seem to be listening anymore. The garden path around them flickered.

She caught his arm. "Alexander." He stiffened and leaned back, pulling away. A darkness crept around them, and once again they were back in her chamber. Their walk was over.

"Alexander," she said softly, but he stepped back farther. Why was he so distant, so cold? "I don't understand. Have you only returned to take silent walks with me? Why have you come?"

He stepped back, farther into the shadows.

"Are you leaving?"

His eyes held a stone gaze.

"Wait. Will you come back?"

And he disappeared into the darkness.

Norah paced the floor of her chamber. Her hands were sweaty, but chills prickled her skin. She clasped the vial tightly. She still didn't understand it.

A rough knock sounded at the door, and then it swung open. Soren stepped inside. "What's wrong?" he said as he swept the door closed behind him. "Bhastian said it was urgent."

"It is." She swallowed and clenched her hands around the vial. It had taken her two days to gather the nerve to tell him, but *now* it was urgent. "I need to tell you something, and it's going to sound completely mad."

His eyes narrowed.

"Sit down."

He shook his head. "I don't think so."

No matter. Either way he'd think she'd lost her mind. Might as well get it out. "Alexander's still here," she said. "Somehow. His spirit."

Soren frowned. "Did you expect something different? Did you not trap him here?"

"No—" She stopped. Is that why he had come to her? Had she trapped him by not sending him to the gods? No... She shook her head. It had to be something more. "He came to me. I've seen him."

Soren only stood, staring at her. Yes, she knew it sounded mad.

"It first happened in the mortium," she continued. "I had Alexander's blood on me, and he came to me, as the seer did in Odepeth. I mean, not exactly like the seer. With Bhasim, I had to drink the blood—"

Soren's eyes narrowed.

Speed it along, she told herself. "Anyway, I thought it was a dream, but he came back, again, here in my chamber after I left the mortium. Which makes sense because I still had his blood on me. Then, in the dream, or the vision, or whatever it was, he showed me a vial of blood and smeared a drop on my hand."

The lines at the corners of his eyes deepened, but still he said nothing.

"And two days ago, I received this." Her hands shook as she showed him the vial.

Soren stepped closer.

"Just like the one Alexander gave me in the dream."

His breath came with a deep vibration. "Whatever you think that dream is telling you to do, it's a lie. Don't do it."

Norah swallowed. "That's... the thing I wanted to talk to you about. I thought about it, and I was thinking..." Her words came all over the place. "I thought—"

"Don't do it. That's not the Bear's blood."

"But it was Alexander's blood in the mortium—"

"Salara, don't do it."

"I kind of already have," she blurted.

Soren's eyes blazed.

"He came back!"

"Salara," he said through his teeth. "Why would you do such a stupid thing?"

"Because he's trying to talk to me!"

"And what did he say?" he demanded.

Nothing. Her breath left her. "Nothing. I don't think... he can speak. It's like a... a vision, where you see but can't hear."

"That is *not* Alexander," he said angrily. "It's a trick, and a cruel trick at that."

"No." She shook her head. "Soren, I saw him. It's Alexander. I felt him!"

"It's not Alexander." He grabbed the vial from her hand and flung it into the fireplace.

"No!" she cried as it shattered into pieces.

He grabbed her arm and pulled her to look at him. "That is not Alexander," he said firmly, his eyes burning into her. "Don't let someone use your grief to trick you."

Her lip trembled. "Soren," she pleaded.

147

He softened, and his grip on her arm relaxed. But he didn't release her. He only pulled her closer. "Salara," he said softly. "He's gone. And whatever you think you see, it's not real. Do you understand?"

No. It *was* real. It was very real.

He caught her chin and forced her to look at him. "It's not the Bear."

She yielded, nodding. He squeezed her arm, as much of a consolation she would get from the Destroyer, and he left her to the quiet of the afternoon.

Norah sank to the stone floor beside the fireplace and wiped the tears from her face. No fire burned inside, but the small shards of glass lay in the ash at the bottom.

If this was a trick, who would do such a thing? Who could? They'd have to possess the power of a traveler, or something like it.

But...

Alexander *did* have power. Nothing she could define, or explain; Alexander hadn't understood it himself. But he had *something*. The Wild hadn't been able to see him. The Wild sisters hadn't been able to enter his mind. He was strong, Naavi had told Norah—strong enough that his shield had covered them all while they escaped.

Was he strong enough to deny death?

She needed to see him again. She needed to ask him. But what remained of the blood had soaked into the logs and ash.

All but one drop, which had splattered on the metal andirons.

Her breath came faster, and her hand shook as she ran her forefinger up the iron and scooped the last of the blood. Then she curled it in her palm, closed her eyes, and waited, praying it was enough.

She imagined herself sitting on the bench in the garden in the light of the sun and waited for him to return.

And he did.

She didn't turn when she felt his presence. She didn't look; she didn't want to drive him away again. But she knew he was there.

Alexander.

He sat down beside her.

"Is it your power that allows you to come to me?" she asked, finally looking at him. "The same power that kept the Wild from entering your mind, kept them from seeing you?"

His eyes flashed with surprise, yet he still didn't speak. But he could hear her. And understand her.

"How do you come through the blood? Are you a traveler?"

The corners of his mouth twitched slightly. Was it the hint of a smile? Was she right?

"How did you get the vial to me?"

He leaned back against the bench. She wasn't sure whether he didn't want to give her an answer or just didn't have one for her. Was she pressing him too much?

"Soren tells me this is a trick." But her eyes ran over every detail of his face, his body. Everything about him was just as she knew him to be. Exactly. An impossible trick, surely.

His hands lay still in his lap. Her eye snagged on his wrist and a small bracelet of tiny shells. She sucked in a breath. It was the bracelet she'd woven for him so long ago. No one else would have known about it—*except Alexander.*

This couldn't be a trick, but how was he here? And why?

"Are you here because I haven't sent you to the gods?" she whispered. "Do you want to go?"

His lips formed, as if to speak, but he remained silent. Then he gave a slow, faint shake of his head.

Her heart leapt. An answer from him. Finally. It was the bare minimum of communication, but she'd take it. She forced her breath calm. "I... I didn't know what you would have wanted. I feared I'd trapped you." She stopped. Her eyes welled. Why was this making her so emotional? "But this is the last time I can bring you back. I don't have any more blood."

His brows drew together, and the garden fell into nothingness around them. She felt unsteady as he pulled forward her memories in front of them and reeled through to the one of Soren throwing the vial into the fireplace. His ability to pull it so easily surprised her. How much freedom did he have of her mind? What else was he able to do?

Anger lined his face.

"Don't be angry with him," she said. "He cares for me. And worries."

His brow creased in confusion.

"He took your death hard. He won't admit it, but I see it in him. Adrian did too. He was devastated. Still is." She sucked in a breath. "Are you able to go to others—"

He stood. She *was* pressing him too hard.

"All right," she said quickly, and she stood too. "I just thought, at least Adrian."

Adrian's name brought no reaction from him, no semblance of recognition.

"Do you not remember your brother?" she asked him.

He stilled, and his eyes widened.

"He misses you. Terribly."

His expression was still one of surprise, but his eyes shifted down as sadness moved over him. How cruel fate was. All Alexander had known was loss—loss of family, of love. Of life.

And she owned a piece of that. What she wouldn't do to go back and give him a different life...

She reached out and placed her hand on his arm. He didn't balk. "I'm sorry," she whispered. "For everything. For any pain I've ever caused you, I'm sorry." Tears sprung from her eyes. "You deserved so much more, so much better than me, and so much better than what fate gave you."

His eyes softened as they met hers, and his lips parted slightly. He covered her hand with his.

"Alexander," she breathed.

Suddenly his expression changed, hardened, and he pulled back.

"Alexander," she said again, and she stepped forward, following him as the darkness closed around her. "Alexander!"

But he was gone.

Norah opened her eyes and found herself again on the floor of her chamber, near the fireplace. She crossed her arms and hugged herself to ease her shaking.

This was no madness of the mind.

Alexander wasn't dead.

CHAPTER FIFTEEN

The young bear rode ahead of him. Soren had charged him with protecting his king, and Mikael knew it was a charge Adrian took as seriously as life. In such a short time, he'd grown from a boy to man, from simple soldier to warrior. Mikael had noted a change in Soren toward him too—a shift from enemy to friend. To brother.

It was good. Soren needed more brothers.

They traveled with only the sound of their horses' hoofbeats. Adrian's eyes swept the horizon diligently—assessing every ridge, every rock, every detail—as they made their way through the flats of the Tribelands. They stayed wary through their grueling pace, with good reason. They had to reach the Canyonlands to protect Kharav, and to protect themselves. Only with the canyons could they defend against the combined armies of Japheth and Rael. Although, even with the canyons...

Mikael pushed the thought from his mind. Kharav had never been conquered. He wouldn't allow it now.

Adrian glanced over his shoulder, and their gazes met. Each day he looked more like his brother—more serious, more determined, more purposeful.

Fearless and loyal.

The Bear brothers were nothing if not fearless and loyal. Caution to the man who fought against them, and fortune to the man with one by his side. Mikael reached up and brushed the scar on his face that the Bear had given him so long ago. It was faint now, barely noticeable, but a reminder, as if he'd ever forget. He'd been fortunate that day to keep his life, and in looking at the young bear now, he considered himself fortunate still.

Adrian's armor bore the winterhawk crest of the North, but the dark color of Kharav, the only armor of its kind. Adrian had it made after Soren had mentioned him taking up his brother's armor, the armor that had once belonged to their father. Adrian had flatly refused. Mikael could understand. There were two ways to honor fallen blood: wear the armor or display it.

The Bear's armor now hung in the judisaept of the North, where his shield hung as well. Although it was a chamber frequently used by Salara and the council for matters of rule, the judisaept was a sacred place. Mikael had known it the moment he'd set foot in it. Along the high walls hung shields of bravery past. He had recognized the shield of the North King, Aamon. The Bear's now hung beside it, the only shield not a king's, just like his body was the only body not a royal's to lay in the Hall of Souls. But he was worthy.

Mikael turned his thoughts home. When he'd left Kharav, he couldn't shake the feeling he wouldn't return. He'd been so sure that the battle to win back the North would be the battle that sealed his fate. Yet he hadn't feared it. Mikael had never been one to fear death, but he did fear failure. He had feared not winning back the North for Salara. Now he feared not protecting Kharav from Japheth and Rael. If he didn't make it to the canyons, that's exactly what would happen, and the stakes were higher now. The North needed Kharav. Salara needed Kharav, especially without the Bear.

Mikael still couldn't believe he was gone. He hadn't wanted to leave Salara so soon after his death, with her still so raw and broken, but time was against him and there was nothing he could do. It would be a grief she would always carry, as would Adrian. The young bear's signature smile hadn't shown itself since the justice's death. All his youth seemed gone. That's what grief did—it stole one's youth.

And Mikael carried a grief of his own—not just the loss of a great man, but also the loss of knowing his fate. He'd always thought it was a curse knowing he'd die, and how. But now with that knowing gone, he realized it had given him confidence and security. To be at a distance from the Bear—at a distance from his fate—had made him feel invincible. To know what his end was going to be meant that he'd known what wasn't. It made him all the bolder. But now... his new fate could come at any moment. It could come now, with Rael and Japheth.

When he'd first left the North, he set his intention on visiting the seer as soon as he reached Kharav. But now, as the journey allowed his mind to think, he wasn't so sure he would. When a man knew his fate, it became an obsession. And Mikael had obsessed for so long.

Their urgency to reach the Canyonlands pushed them to travel both night and day, resting only a few hours at a time, to sleep, and leaving them all the weaker if they did face a battle.

They had traveled rapidly to the North, warred a battle that had tested the limits of their skill and determination, and now they traveled rapidly home. Weary. Worn. It wasn't a state the Kharavian army was accustomed to. Yes, they were warriors—the greatest of warriors—but their strength was the lowest it had ever been. Even the great warlord,

Jarik, nodded off as he rode. Still, they pressed on. They needed to make it to the Canyonlands.

On the tenth day, the army's spirit started to lift. Only two more days and they'd reach the pass. Mikael's hope grew with each hour, but he dared not call it a victory yet. It would take time to get the army through. The western pass was narrower than the eastern pass, and it was the less favored of the two. But it was closest.

The sun broke through the clouds. The day was beautiful. Absent the circumstance, Salara would have loved being out for a ride. Only ten days had passed since he'd left her, but it was ten days too long, and an eternity longer before he'd see her again.

A shout rang out.

Adrian pulled up his horse abruptly. Mikael broke from his thoughts and straightened, following his gaze east to see movement on the horizon.

A single rider galloped toward them. Dust plumed behind him.

It was a Kharavian rider, driving his mount faster than a horse should go.

"Rael!" he bellowed as he drew closer. "Rael!"

Adrian cast Mikael a quick glance and reigned his horse closer. Jarik urged his destrier to Mikael's other side.

The rider pulled up his mount, which was lathered with sweat and mud. Blood streaked the animal's legs.

"Rael is coming," the scout panted. His horse stumbled in exhaustion, and the warrior slid to the ground. His legs gave way underneath him, and he dropped to a knee, but he didn't let it keep him from delivering the news. "They come with numbers much greater than ours." He gasped for breath between words. "Twofold at least."

A warrior close by grabbed the scout and helped him stand.

"How far?" Mikael asked him.

"A day's ride at most."

Two days it would take to reach the Canyonlands. One day until Rael reached them. Mikael's army wouldn't make it.

"Water," the scout begged.

Another warrior stepped forward with a water skin, and the scout drank deeply, coughing between swallows.

"And Japheth is with them?" Adrian asked.

The scout shook his head. "Not that I saw. Only the banner of Rael."

Mikael and Adrian looked at each other in surprise. "That doesn't mean Cyrus comes alone," Mikael said.

"We should rest the army," Jarik said. "Prepare to meet him."

"Or we could still get as close as we can to the Canyonlands," Yassar, a field captain, said.

Jarik cut him a disapproving glance. "But that would leave our men without the strength for battle," he argued. "This is an army of freed slaves—many have never held a weapon in their lives. Even if their numbers are three times our size, we can prevail, so long as we're rested."

"Unless they have the blood sport fighters," Yassar countered. "Or if Japheth is with them. Then it won't matter how rested we are."

"Being closer to the Canyonlands only matters if you plan on retreating," Jarik quipped back.

"No one is planning on retreating," Yassar replied, his tone rising, "but if Japheth is with Rael, and it would be stupid if they weren't, we all know this is a battle we cannot win."

"Unless we split the army," Adrian said, finally speaking.

Everyone stopped and stared at him.

Adrian's eyes burned with a determination that reminded Mikael so much of the Bear.

"I can stay, with half our forces, and hold them long enough for you and Jarik to take the other half and reach the Canyonlands," Adrian told him. "Once there, you'll be able to defend the pass, and protect Kharav."

"Defend Kharav with half an army?" Yassar asked.

"It's better than no army," Adrian said. "And their numbers will be less, too, by the time they reach you. We'll launch a defensive here, and take as many as we can."

Jarik snorted. "You think I'm going to let a Northman hold off our enemy while I retreat?"

"Not retreating," Adrian countered. "Kharav needs you to defend her. I'm only buying you time to get there."

Mikael stared at Adrian, someone he knew so well and yet a man who never ceased to surprise him. This was a solid plan—a plan that could save Kharav. A plan by a Northman.

"All who stay will be lost," Mikael said.

Adrian gave a somber nod. "Yet if you reach the Canyonlands, all will be won."

Perhaps. It was a gamble. But what other choice did they have? Mikael sighed and looked to Jarik, who nodded his reluctant agreement.

"I still have to think on it," Mikael said. "Rest the men for now, and I'll let you know my answer."

The army slept under the last bit of warmth of the setting sun. It was a developed skill of a good warrior—to sleep anywhere, at any time.

Mikael's eyes found Adrian, who lay awake, fidgeting with something instead of sleeping—sometimes he was not a good warrior. As Mikael drew near, he saw there was a small parchment and pen in Adrian's hands.

"What are you writing?" Mikael asked.

Adrian looked up, then back at the parchment. He hesitated, pulling his dry lips between his teeth, then said, "Instructions."

Mikael dropped down to sit beside him. "For what?"

Adrian scribbled the last of his writing, then put down the pen and folded the piece of parchment before tucking it into a small pouch that hung around his neck under his armor. "For when I die. If my body is recovered, I don't want to be sent to the pyre."

The words struck him, and Mikael needed a moment. He looked out at the resting army, gathering his words. "You don't want to be sent to your gods?" he asked finally.

Adrian looked down. "I want to see my brother again."

Mikael could only sit in silence. The Kharavians would recover their dead, and honor Adrian's wishes. They'd put him into the earth. Mikael would do it himself, just as he himself had laid the Bear to rest.

Adrian reached into his pocket and pulled out a piece of polished wood. He handed it to Mikael. "Will you give this to my son?"

Mikael turned it over in his hand, and he immediately recognized the small metal plate set into the bottom with the image of a bear. A seal.

"It's my family seal. I don't know if Theisen will ever want to use it, but... I want him to have it."

Curse this Northman. Mikael had become quite fond of him. He pursed his lips as he clutched the seal in his fist, then he held it for Adrian to take back. "You'll give it to him yourself. You're going to Kharav with Jarik."

Adrian's brows dipped. "What?" He leaned back and away. "No. I'm staying. It's what the lord commander would expect."

"Your salar orders you to go."

"My queen would say different," Adrian argued.

"She would not have you die!"

"She'd have her husband live!"

Norah wouldn't let either of them stay. And Kharav would fall.

"I'm staying," Mikael said.

Adrian's face held firm. "Then I'm staying with you."

Mikael knew there was nothing he could say to convince him. This bear wouldn't listen to him. Just like his brother.

It was almost night as Mikael watched Jarik prepare to depart. The warlord would lead half the army under the cover of darkness, getting as far as they could toward the Canyonlands before the sun rose. With luck, Rael would keep their attention fixed on Mikael and not notice them.

Mikael selected his best to send. He needed the confidence that they'd be able to defend Kharav, and Salara, if the need arose. He walked the legions of men, ensuring everything was set. He stopped when he reached Jarik.

"The army is ready, Salar," the warlord said. "But you should be leading them. I should be the one staying."

Mikael shook his head. "Cyrus won't waste his time on a distraction. To hold him from Kharav, to buy you enough time, it must be me."

The lines around the warlord's eyes deepened. Reluctantly, Jarik nodded.

Mikael sighed. He wasn't one for goodbyes, but words needed to be said. "Jarik. We haven't always agreed, but I know you've always had Kharav's best interest at heart."

"After today," Jarik said, "I can't say you haven't." He paused. "I hope the North gods are with you, Salar."

Mikael nodded. He did too.

"I'll await word from the lord commander, and you have my promise—I'll follow his order and ensure the others do the same."

Mikael extended his arm, and Jarik grasped it.

"For Kharav," Jarik said.

"For Kharav."

Adrian stood beside Mikael. Jarik extended his hand, and Adrian clasped his arm in return.

"For Salar," Jarik said.

The line between Adrian's brow creased in confusion, and Jarik held him tighter. Adrian moved to pull back, but Jarik didn't let him go. Three other warriors quickly stepped behind the young bear—two grabbed his arms, and one locked a grip around his shoulders.

"What—" Adrian struggled, but they held him.

Jarik pulled out a cord.

Adrian fought, but with three seasoned warriors holding him, there wasn't anything he could do. Jarik bound his hands.

"What are you doing?" Adrian raged.

Mikael stepped in front of him. It didn't give him pleasure to see Adrian this way, but it was for his own good. For Salara. And Soren.

Adrian's face twisted in anger.

Mikael reached out and gripped his shoulder. "I'm sorry. You'll have to wait a little longer to see your brother. Salara needs you alive." He pulled the seal from his own pocket and pushed it into Adrian's. "So does your son."

Mikael nodded to Jarik and the warriors, and they pushed Adrian onto a horse and tied his hands to the saddle pommel.

"No, Salar—"

"Goodbye, Adrian," Mikael said somberly.

"Salar!"

Jarik mounted his destrier and the army started out.

"Salar!" Adrian bellowed.

They disappeared into the night.

"Mikael!" Adrian's voice carried back.

Mikael watched them leave. Then he turned to wait for his enemy.

CHAPTER SIXTEEN

Norah held out her hand for the most delicate of flakes to land. It melted the moment it touched her skin. It was the first snow of the season. It had been almost three weeks since Mikael had left, but it felt like months. She stood on a terrace in the southern tower. She came here often to watch the sky and wait impatiently for word. A bird should have come already to tell her he'd made it to the Canyonlands safely. Why hadn't it come? He would know she'd be waiting.

"Tell me about your daughter," she said over her shoulder to Titus, who stood with Bhastian by the doors leading inside, to the upper south halls. She needed something to occupy her mind between her worry for Mikael and her thoughts of Alexander—*gods,* she couldn't fall back into thinking of Alexander right now.

"She's three months old now," Titus said.

She could hear the smile in his voice and turned to face him.

"Sarah is her name."

Norah smiled. "That's beautiful."

His own smile grew. "She is too. She looks like her mother."

"Thank your gods," Bhastian said with a smirk.

They all laughed.

"I never thought of having a daughter, of wanting one," Titus said. "But she has my heart. We're still praying for a son, though. To carry the legacy."

"What do you mean?" Bhastian asked.

"My family's served the crown for generations. I want it to continue."

Bhastian frowned. "Why can't it?"

"What?" Titus asked.

"Your daughter. She carries your name, no?"

Titus looked at him in confusion. "She can't be a soldier, though. She's a woman."

Bhastian snorted. "Tell that to Katya. See if she doesn't make you a woman."

Norah laughed. If Titus were wise, he most certainly wouldn't say that to the Kharavian captain.

Just then, Bhastian's eyes darted to the sky. "Salara."

She followed his gaze to the horizon. And the bird it carried.

Her heart leapt to her throat. She raced back into the castle and down the stairs. Bhastian and Titus followed close behind. Damn the avian tower—it had to be all the way across the courtyard, above the library. It took an eternity to reach it. She pushed against the large oaken doors of the library, not waiting for them to fully open before sliding inside and bounding up the stairs of the tower to where Rector Tusten would have received the bird.

"Did he make it?" she asked breathlessly as she burst in.

The rector stood by the window, a bird in his hands. He turned abruptly at her entrance. "Regal High," he greeted in surprise, then he glanced down at the bird in his hands. He pulled the capsule tied around its leg and held it out for her.

Norah reached for it eagerly, breaking it open and fumbling with the tightly rolled parchment.

And she sucked in a breath.

Soren burst into the room, obviously seeking the same news. Her hands shook as she held it for him.

"What does he say?" he asked.

"Cyrus moved to attack before he was able to reach the western pass." Soren grabbed the small piece of parchment.

"But Aleon forces moved south and stopped Rael's advance," she said. "He made it. Mikael made it through the pass." Her eyes stung as she said the words. *He'd made it.*

The note was short. Word that traveled by bird was always short. More would follow by messenger, she knew. She would have to wait. But she couldn't.

Her heart raced at the thought of what could have happened had Aleon not moved to stop Rael. But why? She hadn't heard from King Phillip since her council had tried to kill her. "Why would Phillip help Mikael?" she asked.

But Soren seemed distracted.

"What's wrong?" she asked him.

"How did Cyrus know Salar would be headed for the western pass? The eastern pass is more favorable; the canyons are wider, allowing an army to move through more quickly. If I were him, I would have anticipated Salar returning through the eastern pass."

Norah shook her head. "You said it yourself. Mikael's moving an entire army. I'm sure they've been seen."

"Kharavian warriors aren't seen."

Norah sighed. "I know you have pride in your army, but we're talking tens of thousands of warriors. You don't move an army that size in complete secrecy."

The shadow darkened under his brow. "It's how we marched to Mercia. The Holy Knights didn't know we were coming, and they were some of the greatest mercenaries in the world."

"I'd like to think Alexander had a hand in that."

"That he did," Soren admitted. "But Cyrus knew Salar would go through the western pass. How?"

Norah shook her head. There was so much she didn't have answers for.

The dining hall was quiet, save the *tick tick tick* of their forks against their plates as they ate. Soren had started joining for dinner, as Norah had asked, with surprisingly little objection from her grandmother. Catherine absolutely refused him having a blood bowl, and Norah found herself speechless that Soren obliged her. He did, however, continue to take bites of food from his knife instead of his fork, for which Catherine cast him a constant judging eye.

A week had passed since the news had come of Mikael safely making it through the Canyonlands, but she still awaited a messenger with more detail. Couldn't he have just sent more birds? He'd taken several with him, couldn't he have sent them all?

Things seemed to be settling, yet Norah didn't feel settled. Cyrus had pulled back his forces at the sight of Aleon's army, which was still a mystery, as was the fact that Japheth hadn't joined the initial move on Kharav.

The doors to the dining hall opened, and a servant entered with a letter. "This just arrived for you, Salara," he said with a bow.

Finally. Thank the gods. A message from Mikael.

Norah took it eagerly, but as she flipped it over, she stopped. On the back wasn't the black seal of Kharav but the royal-blue seal of Aleon. She looked up at her grandmother, then Soren. "It's from King Phillip."

Catherine set down her fork, and they stared at each other for a moment.

Then Norah looked at Soren.

"Well, read it," he said impatiently.

Right. Read it. She broke the seal and unfolded the parchment to find the words. "Dearest Norah," she started. She swallowed. Why was reading so hard right now? "I've never celebrated another kingdom as I've celebrated your retaking of Mercia. It was a victory I personally felt."

"Interesting," Soren said sourly, "as he played no part in helping."

"Nor did he help the Mercian council," Catherine countered.

"Perhaps he's a coward all around," Soren quipped.

Catherine scoffed. "King Phillip is no coward."

Norah rolled her eyes and continued. "As you're aware, the situation with Japheth and Rael is escalating, and I have decided to expedite my marriage to the princess of Osan."

"What?" Catherine gasped. "He plans to marry the princess of Osan?"

Norah paused. The princess of Osan? She read the line again as she tried to wrap her mind around it herself. "Osan has a formidable naval fleet, and King Tagasi has agreed to join our cause."

"We have a fleet," Catherine said. "Mercian ships are world renowned."

"Unsinkable ships, yes," Soren cut in. "But Osan has warships with cannons. They would be an asset against Gregor and Cyrus, to stop the route along the channel between Japheth and Rael. To stop them from moving forces. That's excellent."

Catherine straightened. "Finally, something positive from you about Aleon."

Soren's brows dipped. "It's not about Aleon, it's about Osan."

Norah pursed her lips. She was already regretting reading aloud. "I extend a warm invitation that you might attend the wedding here in the capital city of Valour, for Mercia has always been the closest of friends with Aleon. It's important to me that you're here."

Soren snorted.

"What?" Catherine challenged him. "Mercia and Aleon have ruled side by side for generations. It's proper Phillip would have her attend."

"Salara does not come to his call."

"It's an invitation," her grandmother said, "not a demand."

"Given the growing threat against our kingdoms," Norah said, speaking over them, "I pray you'll forgive the short notice. The wedding will be held in the upcoming fourth septimana."

"That's hardly any time!" Catherine said. "Even if you leave tomorrow, you might not make it."

"You can't seriously be considering going," Soren pressed.

"I don't know what I'm considering!" Norah snapped. "Let me finish the gods-damned letter!"

Catherine and Soren quieted, and she drew her eyes back to the parchment.

"I understand if you hesitate, but I hope Mercia and Kharav recognize the recent actions of Aleon as that of a friend and have faith in future intentions. The northern kingdoms are united, as they've always been and always will be. Your support would honor my marriage, and I most look forward to seeing you again, Norah. Please come. I eagerly await your reply. Most sincerely, I am, Phillip."

Soren's eyes burned into her as she folded back the letter.

"Say what you're going to say," she told him.

"You don't find this highly suspicious? You hear nothing from him when you need his friendship most, when you're trying to take back your kingdom. But now that Salar has returned to Kharav, now that you're alone, he calls you to Aleon?"

"He does not *call* me. And I'm not alone. You're here."

Soren's lips thinned. "Well, how does the Osan princess get to Valour so quickly? It would have taken more than three weeks to travel from Osan to Aleon."

"He said *expedite* his marriage. She's probably already there."

His nostrils flared. "Don't be so quick to take him for an ally, or one to be trusted. Sharing a common foe doesn't make one a friend."

"The kingdoms of Aleon and Mercia have been allies and friends for generations," Catherine interjected.

Soren locked eyes with Norah. "Until you set the North on a different course with an alliance with Kharav."

She leaned back in her chair. "But I feel like not going to his marriage would be a slight."

"That's if he's really getting married," Soren countered.

Norah sighed. She didn't know what to believe. "I do think Phillip has shown himself to be a friend. He gave me forces to defend Mercia against the attacks on our villages—"

"In exchange for Bahoul," he countered, "which he'd already taken, by the way."

"He warned Mikael to close his ports, which saved Kharav from fever."

He tilted his head. "Yes, people are capable of doing nice things while still having an agenda."

"Then why would he defend Kharav against Rael?"

"If he's also facing war with Japheth and Rael, he has a joint interest in Kharav not falling."

She shook her head. "Soren, any one of these individually, I agree with you. But together, they're compelling. Phillip presents himself as a friend, and I believe him. I think I should attend the wedding. And I want to see him—meet him face-to-face. I'll determine if this is truly an alliance we can trust."

"That's the worst idea you've had yet," he insisted.

She shrugged. "Well, I'm still going."

His jaw tightened. "Then I'm going with you."

"I don't think—"

"Take him, Norah," Catherine said. "He might be a fiend, but he's a fiend that will see you safe. I don't doubt Phillip's intentions, but I do fear your journey, and would see you back to Mercia as quickly as possible."

Norah shifted her eyes between the both of them, then sighed. "Fine. We'll leave tomorrow."

CHAPTER SEVENTEEN

The late afternoon sun gleamed off the bright city of Valour, the capital of Aleon. It was breathtakingly beautiful. The architecture shone white, like Mercia, but rather than the tall spires and turrets of the Northern kingdom, Valour was topped with patinated copper domes. And unlike Mercia, green scapes and fountains layered the city, creating a garden paradise. Autumn hung in the air, but there was no sign of winter yet.

The journey had been uneventful. Norah supposed that was the best kind of journey, although she would have given anything to keep her roaming mind from the worries of Mikael and Rael. And from Alexander, whose being still haunted her. Her only relief—and it was a painful relief—had been the distraction of Soren's unending attempts to talk her out of going to Phillip's wedding. She didn't think it was possible, but he talked more than Calla along the way. Calla took Soren's side, only fueling him more. Norah almost wished she'd left the girl back with Cohen and Catherine. Her grandmother had already taken to the siblings, pecking them around the castle like her new adoptees.

But Norah wouldn't be talked out of this. She needed to go—this, she was certain, although it didn't settle the gnawing angst in her stomach.

She wished she remembered Phillip. Would it make this easier? Of course it would, she told herself. Did they have a friendship? His letter sounded like they did. How well did he know her? She wasn't sure if she'd tell him about the loss of her memories. Would he know something was different now? She'd have to determine all that when she arrived.

Bells chimed with their entry through the gates, and they rode down the mainway toward the center citadel. The Crest rode close to her in tight formation, but nothing seemed sinister—quite the opposite. People lined the street, throwing flower petals into the air.

"Quite the welcome," Calla said.

Norah raised a brow to Soren riding beside her. "Do they know who I am? Do you think they've confused me with the princess of Osan?"

"If they think the princess of Osan rides with the Destroyer under the flags of the North, you're lucky you didn't marry the Aleon king and have to rule these idiots."

She couldn't help a laugh.

"But really, I think they see a beautiful queen worthy of a rose-petal welcome," he added.

She looked over at him with a smile on her lips. "I think that's one of the nicest things you've ever said to me."

He rolled his eyes. "I'm already regretting it."

As they neared the citadel, an entourage emerged and made their way down the steps, led by a man that could be no other than Phillip, king of Aleon. He was a tall man, lean but well muscled, which was apparent even through a tunic and vest.

"The fuck," Soren breathed beside her, and she glanced to see his eyes on the king. He seemed shaken, but she didn't have time to try to understand as Phillip stepped toward her.

"Queen Norah." He greeted her with a smile. "Welcome to Aleon."

Norah slipped down from Sephir, and Phillip took her hand and brought it to his lips. He paused after planting a kiss against her skin, still holding her, as his eyes locked with hers. The painted portrait she remembered didn't do him justice. Of course, he looked even better having shaved the small animal off his top lip. She judged him to be the same age as Mikael and Soren, but unlike the darkness they carried, Phillip had an air of light. His blue eyes smiled with a boyish enchantment, and his tousled bronze locks fell over his brow. A glow of wild spirit hung around him. He was warm. Likable.

"It's been a long time," he said. "I'm so happy you've come. I honestly... didn't know if I would ever see you again. This is a fortunate day." He stared at her. She stood frozen, not expecting this warmth. He stepped even closer, almost like he might embrace her. Was he going to? His eyes were happy, but they held something else too—a sadness, something still unsaid.

She moved back slightly. "King Phillip." Her voice cracked as she spoke, and she hoped he hadn't noticed. His brow twitched.

He released her hand, and she took a breath—she hadn't realized she'd been holding it in. His eyes stayed locked on her, as if trying to figure her out. Perhaps he'd known her well in the past, perhaps well enough to know there was something off about her now.

But he only smiled politely. "Well, let me show you—"

His words cut off as his eyes moved past her and stopped. She turned to see they'd landed on Soren.

"You bring the Destroyer," he said.

Soren wasn't generally a welcomed presence, and she cursed herself that she hadn't even thought that bringing him might feel more of a threat than a friendly visit.

But Phillip gave a small smile. "A fortunate day indeed."

Norah raised a brow. Wait, what? Most people avoided Soren. At all costs.

"And how do you find Aleon, Destroyer?" Phillip asked Soren as the commander swung down from his destrier.

Soren didn't answer. He only stood with the look of war in his eye and the rigidity of restraint. She pursed her lips. He'd had this entire journey to resolve his feelings of coming to Aleon, of meeting King Phillip. Could he not at least pretend to be civil?

Phillip was a tall man. Not as tall as Soren, and certainly leaner, but he didn't shy from the mountain of a man in front of him. It was bold. Or stupid.

"The demon of war," the king said, not taking his eyes from him. "Or so they say."

Norah frowned. *Partly* true, perhaps.

Phillip stepped nearer to him.

That was close enough, really. She clamped her clammy hands together.

"But you don't look like a demon," he added.

Did he not? Soren could look very scary when he wanted to. Still, her commander didn't answer.

"I want to see his face," Phillip told her, seemingly unbothered with Soren's refusal to converse with him.

Norah's eyes locked with Soren's, and his silent warning scorched the air between them.

She forced a calm breath and a steady voice. "Kharav believes the markings of accomplishment show a man's true self, not his face."

Phillip cast his gaze over the markings covering Soren's bare arms and torso. "And if I require it?" he pressed.

"That's how you lose yourself an Aleon king," Soren snarled to Norah.

Phillip rocked back slightly on his heel. But then he gave a light chuckle, as if more amused than threatened.

"I'd rather you not try to require it," Norah told Phillip with her sweetest voice. And it would certainly be a *try* because there would be no requiring Soren to do anything. Not by the king of Aleon, and not on this matter.

Phillip shifted his gaze back to her. There was an intensity in his eye that made her stomach clench. There was no fear in him. Again, it was bold, or stupid. But then he shifted back, and a warm smile broke across his lips. "Then I'll refrain, as you wish."

She let out an appreciative breath. Excellent. Aleon might see its king live yet another day.

Phillip held his arm out for Norah. "Shall we?"

Here we go, she thought. She glanced back at Soren with a scowl before accepting and letting Phillip lead her into the castle.

"I have to admit, I was starting to worry you might not make it, with the wedding in two days' time," Phillip told her as he led them through the high-arched halls dripping in golden sunlight. "But I'm grateful you're here. The journey wasn't too uncomfortable, I hope."

"The journey was fine, thank you." It really had been, despite its boredom. It had given her a chance to think, to question herself, to convince herself she was still sane, and to question herself again. And now she was here, in Aleon. It all felt so strange.

"How long will you stay?" he asked.

"Oh, um... a few days past the wedding, I suppose." She glanced around them. "Is Princess Daiyona here?"

"She is, and I would love to introduce you."

So it appeared there *was* to be a wedding, and the princess was here. A relief.

"There is a pre-celebration dinner tomorrow evening," he said, "although I'll arrange something for us tonight."

"No, that's all right," she said quickly. "It's late, and I'm quite tired, actually. Tomorrow is perfect. It will give me some time to put myself back together and look somewhat presentable."

He chuckled. "Norah." His hand clasped warmly over hers on his arm. "It's hard to imagine you any more beautiful than you are now."

"Oh, he's a charmer," came Calla's voice behind her.

Norah cut the girl a daggered glance to hush her. Calla shrugged innocently. Norah looked back at Phillip, whose lips held a smile. She feigned one of her own.

But it wasn't lost on her that he called her by her name. And the way he held her hand. So casually. So freely. As if they were close.

Soren was up before the sun, unable to sleep, unable to quiet his mind. The Aleon king. *The Aleon king.* His skin burned with anger. He felt... betrayed, but no one had betrayed him. Deceived, but no one had deceived him. He didn't know what he was feeling, only that he needed to get ahold of himself, of his anger. He needed to get his senses back.

He left Titus and Kiran at Salara's door and headed out to have a look around, not bothering to take Caspian either. He didn't want conversation. He hadn't told the captain about Tahla and the child. And he wouldn't. Not yet. He needed Caspian sharp and focused.

The morning light peeked over the horizon as he stepped out onto the polished cobblestone mainway. Salara had been impressed by the sight of the city. It was beautiful, he'd give her that, with its celestial gardens and utopian aura. Absolutely beautiful. And it made him even more angry.

The morning air was cool, but not cool enough to pull the heat radiating from his body. Why had he come here? To this entitled kingdom with this entitled king. This man was the enemy, not to be trusted. And if this king expected anything other than a fight, he'd be sorely disappointed.

He walked the mainway, toward what was clearly the war office and army sector of the city. Men of arms stopped and gave respectful bows of their heads as he passed. *Bastards.* Niceties wouldn't win him over. He ignored them. Behind the war office, he found the sparring fields and training arena. Beautiful, like the city. Too beautiful. Too perfect. Not used enough, and empty now.

Soren ran his hand along the side of the weapons' hold. The polished wood was smooth to the touch. He pulled open a locker to find a row of swords hanging in a perfect line. Running his finger down a blade, he snorted. Mercian steel. Of course. Kings would kill for a sword of Mercian steel, and Aleon had practice arms of it.

He turned his attention to the perfectly parallel posts lining the field and their colorful archery target markings. Fancy. But no matter. Aleon's archers weren't as good as his Northmen, or even as good as his Kharavian warriors. He cursed himself for leaving Calla back at the castle. His farm girl would show the shit out of these pretentious pricks.

Soren pulled the small battle-axe from his side and flung it down the field, burying it into one of the closer pole targets. *Not bad.*

"Impressive," a voice called from behind him, and he whipped around to see a man approaching.

His pulse thrummed faster. It couldn't be. But it was.

The Aleon king. No guard—unprotected. A careless decision.

"How are you with a sword?" the king asked with a friendly smile.

But Soren didn't like friendly people. And he didn't like Aleon kings.

"Are you up for a spar? It would be an honor to try my hand with the great Destroyer."

Soren eyed the king. He wore only light armor. Pretty armor. Too pretty to have experienced the hardship of battle. And his invitation to test blades—*another* careless decision.

The king pulled his sword from its scabbard and swept his arms out with an amicable bow of his head. Soren could crucify him against the field rail like that. Perhaps he might. He pulled his own sword and looked around the field again. They were alone, and Soren stepped forward to the challenge.

They circled one another, each waiting for the other to strike. The Aleon king was calm, steady.

Interesting.

Soren launched the first attack with a lunge and a powerful swing. He could already tell the king had some skill just by his fluidity of movement. But not enough skill to save him. Soren chuckled silently to himself—he would flay this man.

The king was quick and met his sword with a firm counter before launching an attack of his own. Soren had to shift swiftly to keep from being driven back.

Very interesting.

They broke and circled again, but the Aleon king didn't give Soren much time before launching another attack. He arced a series of swings, and Soren had no choice but to take defense. As they broke, the king shot him a grin.

What was even happening? Anger coursed through him.

Soren shifted his mind. For blood. He leapt forward in a lethal sequence, each strike carrying with it the power of death. The Aleon king met each one with a skilled counter but slowly gave up ground. Soren refused to relent. He wielded his blade with more speed, more power, driving the king back farther, toward the rail. He would pin him to it, soak the wood in his blood. Soren was stronger, but the king was faster, and as they drew nearer to the rail, the king twisted in another counter and spun right, repositioning himself toward the field and out of the path of Soren's drive toward death.

The king gave another grin, seemingly unrattled. "I think you're even better than the stories," he said. He took another step back and paused, a call to end, and slid his sword back in its scabbard. Their spar was finished, and Soren silently cursed his missed opportunity. But he couldn't bring himself to sheath his own blade.

"You're impressive, Destroyer. But I'm not surprised. I know I don't match your skill. Or your power." He gave a sly smile. "And I do appreciate your restraint."

Restraint. Soren could still kill him. He wanted to kill him, more than anything. For what he'd done. For who he was—Soren hated him for who he was. But Salara wouldn't be pleased. The opposite, in fact. Yes, not killing him now required restraint.

The king drew nearer to him. "Do you ever show your face?" he asked. He stepped even closer, but Soren brought the tip of his blade to the king's chest, stopping him.

The act would have earned him a lashing in Kharav. Salar would have flayed any man who raised a sword to him, but this king wasn't Salar.

The Aleon king only looked down at the sword against his chest. Then he gave a light chuckle with a smiling frown. "I hope you'll entertain a conversation with me while you're here. I'd really like to know—and see—the great Destroyer." Then he gave a nod, turned, and headed back toward the castle.

Soren could only watch as the king disappeared back into the safety of the citadel. He let him go, and he cursed himself. What was he even doing? He cursed again. Then, he stalked back himself, his sword still in hand, unable to sheath it. Unable to sheath his anger.

His mind reeled. He'd tried to temper his reaction to this man, tried to act as though seeing him—meeting him—hadn't possessed him with an all-consuming fury. Soren tried to act like he didn't know who and what this man was.

But he did.

CHAPTER EIGHTEEN

The castle buzzed with activity. Norah stepped out into the hall from her chamber, feeling the excitement in the air, and headed toward the sound of celebration. It was the night before the wedding of King Phillip and Princess Daiyona of Osan.

Cascades of vining flowers draped the hall's arches and flowed down the pillars to the ground, and bright silk swags with colorful bouquets crested every door. White-clothed tables hosted assortments of sweet treats and wine, and she hadn't even reached the great hall yet.

Norah looked back at Titus behind her. "Fancy."

She stepped into the great hall, and a hush fell over the room as all heads turned toward her. Then the crowd brought their hands together and clapped. Heat sprang to her cheeks, and she resisted the urge to crawl under a table. She glanced back at Titus, who was also not one for attention and was doing his best to conceal a scowl. Kiran, beside him, raised his brow.

As she turned her focus back, Phillip appeared before her, taking her hand and lifting it to his lips.

"Queen Norah," he said with a smile.

"You certainly know how to make someone feel like a guest of honor."

"As you should. You were almost queen of Aleon."

She wasn't sure if it was a jest or a jab, or simply a genuine statement. She supposed they would talk about their failed alliance at some point, how she broke their betrothal. Preferably that point wouldn't be here. Or now.

Phillip pulled her hand around his arm assumingly and led her toward the center banquet table. As they approached, a petite woman stood. Her skin was dark, like the people of Kharav, and her hair was black as night. But her eyes slanted back like trails of teardrops. Elegant. Beautiful.

"Queen Norah, may I present my betrothed, Princess Daiyona."

The Osan princess curtsied respectfully with a warm smile and a bow of her head. "Queen Norah. It's an honor." She bowed again. "And I've not forgotten the kindness you showed my brother when he so foolishly crossed the border into the Shadowlands."

"Oh," Norah breathed. She *had* almost forgotten. Not long after she'd first arrived in Kharav, the Osan prince had crossed the border with several of his friends, and Norah had sent him home. Only he encountered Soren on the return, and barely made it back alive. His friends were not so fortunate.

She glanced around the room, looking for the lord commander. If Daiyona knew about Norah trying to send the trespassing prince home, she'd surely know about the lord commander so savagely killing the men accompanying him. It was a memory she had tried to forget, and hopefully it wasn't something that would come back to haunt her now. "Well, thank you," she managed to get out. "And I'm looking forward to us becoming fast friends."

Norah glanced around the hall again, hoping Soren had decided not to come, which was likely. He hated socials. She spotted Caspian, but he stood alone.

The princess smiled. "Absolutely, Your Majesty."

Past their easy pleasantries, Princess Daiyona was swept away with other guests, and Phillip took a place beside Norah.

"She's very beautiful," she said.

Phillip glanced out at the Osan princess and frowned. "Yes, I suppose she is."

Not the response she'd expected. *All right, then.*

"And where is your Destroyer?" he asked.

"My lord commander?" Not here, hopefully, but she wished she knew. "He had something to tend to."

He paused. "Lord commander. Is that what he wishes to be called?"

"It's his title, and what *I* would like him to be called."

He gave a smiling nod. "Very well then."

They stood together, looking out over the festivities. People gathered around tables of tiered food, and more filled the dance floor.

"Why didn't you marry me, Norah?"

Here it was. Did he really want to have this conversation now? *Fine.* "You know why. I wanted peace. Kharav was the only one who could offer that."

"But did you really get peace? You just finished waging a war to take back your own kingdom, and a war with Japheth and Rael waits for us still."

Norah glanced down at her hands clasped at her waist in front of her. Heat flushed her cheeks.

No. She wouldn't let him do this.

She straightened and met his gaze. "Are you trying to rub my naivety in my face? Should a queen not expect her council to support her sacrifice for peace and her kingdom's prosperity, and not try to overthrow her for their own subversive agenda?"

"Our marriage would have given us what we both wanted."

She shook her head. "I didn't want war. An alliance with Kharav brought the real *possibility* for peace, even if I didn't achieve it."

He was silent a moment. "Is that what you've reduced us to? Mere war partners?"

She wasn't sure how to answer that. "Is that not what we were?"

His brow creased, and he pulled his eyes from her and roved his gaze back across the great hall. His face held steady, but his throat moved with a hurt swallow. Then he gave her a polite nod. "Enjoy the evening, Queen Norah." And he stepped away, in the direction of his betrothed.

Her mind swirled around her as she tried to piece together this puzzle of the past. Why was he acting so strangely? What had been between them?

Norah stared into the mirror as Serene pulled tight the lacing on the back of her dress. In a few hours, Phillip would be wed to the Osan princess, and in a few days, Norah would be on her way back to Mercia. And she was very much looking forward to that. However, she couldn't shake the sinking feeling in her gut from her conversation with Phillip the evening before. Her refusal of marriage had more than hurt his pride. There was something else.

But what?

And why?

Her chamber door opened, and Soren stalked inside.

Her brows drew together. "I could have not been dressed yet, you know."

"Well, then you would've been late, and it would've been your own fault," he said shortly, not caring. "Everyone is assembling. It's time to go."

Norah pushed a stray lock of hair behind her ear and turned to him with a frown. "About that. I was thinking you could find something else to do while I go to the wedding."

His face wrinkled in disapproval. "Why?"

"You don't even want to go."

His eyes narrowed. "Maybe I do."

"No, you don't."

"Well, I don't want you to not want me to go."

She sighed. "It's not that I don't *want* you to go. Princess Daiyona remembers—and brought up—what happened to her brother when he foolishly crossed the border into Kharav. You know, when you killed his friends like a manic fiend? I just don't want to stir up ill feelings. We're guests, and it's her wedding day."

"Well, what am I supposed to do?"

She shrugged. "I don't know, whatever you did yesterday. Or take Calla to the sparring field because she *really* doesn't want to go to the wedding either."

"I don't," chimed Calla from the corner chair she sat in. She'd been so quiet Norah had almost forgotten she was there.

He grumbled. "I already saw the sparring field, and tested swords against the Aleon king."

"Wait... what?" Her heart quickened. "Did you hurt him?"

"He made it to the celebration last night, didn't he?" He pushed out an irritated breath. "He's... very good with a sword. Unfortunately."

Curse the gods. She just wanted to get through this wedding and back to Mercia with everyone alive. Specifically Phillip. Things hadn't started off as well as she would've liked, and she feared them going even more poorly.

"Just stay here, or at least out of sight," she said.

He scowled at her.

"Watch him," she told Calla.

The girl gave a smile, happy to be out of going to the wedding, and Norah stepped out of the chamber. Titus and Caspian picked up behind her, followed by the rest of the Crest.

After a series of awkward wrong turns, she made it to the great hall. Soren was right—everyone had assembled.

"I hope they don't do the clapping thing," Titus muttered.

No one clapped, thankfully, and Norah made her way to the front right of the hall as the guest of honor and took her seat. Titus, Caspian, and the rest of the Crest took their posts against the wall.

Phillip stood at the front of the room and gave her a small smile. Despite the awkward end to their conversation the night before, he seemed to hold no personal animosity now. Suddenly, everyone rose. Norah turned around to see Princess Daiyona entering through the double iron doors at the back of the hall.

The Osan princess walked the mainway, toward Phillip. This was what Norah's wedding would have been. This is what her future would have been—queen of an empire, living in a beautiful city in wealth and extravagance.

But all she could think about was how much she missed Mikael. As beautiful as Valour was, she'd give anything to slip back into the comfort of the shadows and find warmth in the arms of the man she loved. They were too far apart, and she needed to get back to him.

The wedding passed as weddings typically do—meaningful words spoken, people smiling... and waiting for the end. They exchanged rings, and the priest wrapped a ribbon around their joined hands and pronounced them married. Daiyona looked at Phillip with a broad smile on her face. She was happy about this wedding.

And Norah was happy for her.

The celebration followed in normal fare and fashion, with no expense spared. Norah stood contently at the side of the floor, watching the dancing as she shoved another shrimp into her mouth. The food was delicious.

"You seem to be enjoying yourself," Caspian said beside her.

She shrugged. "Why shouldn't I? It's not *my* wedding."

He chuckled.

Phillip approached, and Caspian gave her a small bow and left them to take a position against the far wall.

"Congratulations," she said warmly as Phillip stepped beside her.

He glanced sideways at her with a slight smile. "Thank you."

"You're a married man now."

"And everyone is finally happy," he added.

She looked at him, his face pleasant and kind as usual, yet a sadness seemed to linger. One that unsettled her.

"But you're not happy?" she asked.

Her words seemed to hit him strangely, but she couldn't decipher why.

His blue eyes caught hers. "I'm as happy as I'll ever be," he said finally. He gave a respectful bow. "Enjoy the evening, Queen Norah." Then he stepped away to other guests who came to offer their congratulations.

She watched him go.

What did *that* mean?

"I think Phillip is in love with me."

Soren snorted as they stood in her chamber. "Not everyone just falls in love with you."

Norah puffed a breath of annoyance. "This isn't my ego speaking. He's acting very strange. He still seems bothered I broke off our marriage."

"You did promise him an alliance that would help him get revenge against his brother, and then you ran off and married his brother's ally."

"I didn't *run off*," she cut back. "I was abducted. You know this, you were there."

Soren shrugged. "You still dumped him and married his brother's ally."

She shook her head. "No, there's something else there. It's like I've personally wounded him." Norah pushed open the doors of her balcony and breathed in the morning air as the sun warmed her face. "I think we were close. I feel like there was some kind of connection between us. I just can't remember."

She gazed across the city. Norah liked the buildings of Aleon: the tall arched windows that let the sun spill in, the airy colors that bounced the light. Everywhere around her seemed bright and beautiful.

As she looked down, a sight caught her eye. Princess Daiyona's army had assembled—Phillip's new bride was preparing to depart, the day after her wedding. How strange. Was something wrong? Why was she leaving?

"Soren," she called back to him.

He stepped out beside her.

"The queen's leaving." She leaned slightly over the railing, as if it would give her a better view. "Already."

"Are you sure?"

She waved to the scene below. "Well, what does it look like?"

He gave a yielding shrug. "Like she's leaving."

She stepped back into her chamber and pulled her cloak over her shoulders. "I have to go find Phillip. I have to find out what's happening. You stay here."

"All I've been doing is staying here," he protested.

"Except when you tried to kill Phillip on the sparring field."

He threw out his hands. "That was one time."

"Where's Calla?"

"I don't need to be watched."

She pursed her lips. "Stay here."

Norah walked quickly from her chamber, with Titus close behind, through the side hall and then down the curved stair. When she reached the bottom, she hurried down the main hall and through to the front.

Phillip walked in from the outside just as she reached the door. He smiled when he saw her, and everything seemed... perfectly normal. "Queen Norah," he greeted her. "Good morning."

"King Phillip," she greeted him back, trying to hide her breathlessness. "Is everything all right?"

"Why wouldn't it be?"

She gave a small shrug. "It's just... a little unusual for your new wife to depart the morning after her wedding, before even the guests."

The corner of his mouth twitched as he stood in silence for a moment. He paused, before saying, "I gave her the same choice I gave you."

Unhelpful. "And what choice would that be?"

His eyes narrowed. He glanced at Titus and then back to her. "Will you walk with me? Privately?"

She looked back at Titus, then nodded and waved him to stay. Phillip offered his arm. She hesitated, then took it and let him lead her outside and into the gardens. They watched the tail end of Daiyona's army leaving until the red-and-yellow banners disappeared through the gates.

"We had a plan, Norah." He stopped when they reached a fountain in the center of the scrolling topiary and turned to her. "Why do you act as though it meant nothing? Did your love mean nothing?"

She stood speechless for a moment. "Ummm... I don't know what you think you and I had, but—"

"We had an arrangement," he said, cutting her off. There was a sharpness in his voice now.

"Things change."

"Did your love change?" he asked.

Oh gods. "Phillip, I don't love you. I don't think I ever did."

His brow dipped as he took a step back. "Me? Of course you didn't."

Oh gods, oh gods... She didn't know what to say.

"Wait..." He raised a brow. "Did you think I'd fallen in love with you?"

Soren was going to enjoy hearing how this conversation went. Immensely. She swallowed and cursed in her mind again. "Ummm... I think I may have read this entire situation wrong."

189

His mouth moved to form words, but nothing came out.

There was no way to redirect the conversation. Norah sighed, taking his hand and pulling him toward a bench. "Come, sit down with me." She let him go and wiped her face with her hands as she drew in a deep breath. Where to begin?

First, sit. She sat. And he sat beside her.

"Phillip, this is going to sound a bit incredulous and strange, but I have to tell you something."

He only waited for her to speak.

"The reason I was missing for three years was because my father took me away to keep me safe from the Shadow King."

"Yes, I know. Although you've still not told me where you were."

"That's... a small detail... but, to truly keep me hidden, my memories were taken from me."

His brow dipped. "What?"

"Everything was taken from me to hide me, erasing everything I was before. And when I returned to Mercia, I remembered nothing." She watched as he seemed to absorb the information. "I quickly learned that I was betrothed to you, with the plan to go to war against Japheth and Kharav, save Mercia, help avenge the death of your younger brother, take the throne of the Shadow King, and banish his so-called evil from this world."

He still only watched her. Not speaking.

"And I know my decision to... marry the Shadow King instead did nothing for your cause," she continued. "But I found that Kharav was not the evil kingdom it was made out to be, and I saw a real opportunity for peace. So I took it. And Mikael..." She smiled. "He's a good man. I think you'd like him."

His brow twitched in surprise. "You love him?"

More than loved him. "I do," she said, but sometimes words just weren't enough. "I'm sorry, Phillip, for how things turned out for you. But I hope you can understand."

He crossed his arms and sat back against the bench, staring out at the fountain. Then he gave a chuckle. But it wasn't an amused chuckle. His face held a sadness.

"And you don't remember? Still?" he asked.

She shook her head. "No."

"Then you don't remember our friendship?"

So they did have a friendship. "No," she whispered.

"Or our circumstance?"

What was their *circumstance*? She shook her head again, slowly, and resisted the urge to ask. It was coming. She waited.

He stared into the fountain for a long time. When he finally spoke, his voice came soft. "You must have asked yourself, why the princess of Osan for my queen?"

Yes, that was true.

"Well, first and foremost, it's because Osan will make an effective ally. But equally important, to me anyway, it's because she doesn't want to be married. She wants freedom."

Norah scoffed. "And so you decided to marry her?" Well, that was cruel.

"We made the same arrangement as you and I once had—giving ourselves the freedom to love who we chose, while keeping our kingdoms relatively happy. You were to return to your love in Mercia, as Daiyona returned to hers in Osan this morning."

What? Her mouth fell open, but she couldn't speak. *That* was the arrangement he was talking about. She would have returned to Mercia after wedding Phillip. She would have returned to her love.

To Alexander.

Norah couldn't breathe. She swallowed back the choking sensation in her throat. Her mind swirled around her as she forced the words to come.

"How much did you know about..." She didn't want to say Alexander's name. "How much did you know?"

He gave a thoughtful frown. "Not who he was. Only that you loved another. As I did."

His words hit her like a physical strike, and she swayed slightly. If she had married Phillip, she could have stayed with Alexander. She struggled to pull her mind back. She couldn't let herself think about that. Not now.

"Do you remember him?" he asked. "The one you left?"

Tears threatened, but she blinked them back. "He's gone," she whispered. "He died in taking back Mercia."

He gave the moment silence. "I'm sorry."

She couldn't talk about Alexander. Not now. Maybe not ever, but especially not now. Norah swallowed, forcing herself to speak. "With Daiyona returning to Osan, at least you can finally be with your love."

He sat quietly, but then shook his head. "No. He died too. When I took Tarsus."

He. "Oh," she breathed. Her heart hurt for him. "Phillip, I'm so sorry."

He smiled sadly. "It was a good plan we had, though, wasn't it? A good effort?"

She nodded.

They sat in silence.

"Why did you take Tarsus?" she asked finally. Mikael and Soren had been so sure Phillip was driven to accomplish what his grandfather could not—taking the island trading nation and further building his empire. It fueled their suspicion he would do the same to Kharav.

"Because it was Gregor's primary source of trade revenues. When I heard rumors that he was pressing the Shadowlands for a change in trade terms and that the alliance was souring, I saw it as an opportunity for him to lose it all. It would have been a significant blow to him financially, and perhaps a fatal blow in my favor, as he employs mercenaries and must keep paying them to wage war against me. So I took Tarsus. But with heavy losses."

Norah started to piece everything together. Gregor had been pressing Mikael for new terms and had even ventured so far as to skip due trade. Gregor had been so confident with Tarsus to fall back on, but Phillip had taken that away from him. Gregor needed a new alliance, and he must have found that in the Raelean king.

"Taking Tarsus was necessary," he added. "But I still question if it was worth it. Had I known... what would happen to Jonah... I wouldn't have."

"His name was Jonah?"

Phillip nodded as he stared into the fountain. He let out a heavy sigh and turned his gaze back to her. Gently, he took her hand. "I'm not angry with you, Norah. I thought I'd brought the gods' disfavor with the shame of my sin in whom I loved."

Norah shook her head. "Don't say that. There is no sin in love."

His eyes glistened, and he gave an emotional smile. "I would feel favored once more to be considered a friend again, both to you and this Shadow King you speak so highly of."

She put her hand over his and smiled. "I would love that."

"And I'd like to invite your lord commander hunting with me tomorrow."

She wrinkled her nose. "I don't know if that's a good idea."

"He doesn't like hunting?"

Soren liked hunting. "He doesn't like people."

He chuckled. "Well, will you ask him?"

She pursed her lips into a polite smile and forced a nod.

CHAPTER NINETEEN

Soren's eyes blazed. "If I go hunting with that bastard, he'll end up gutted."

Norah shot him a disapproving look. "Soren, this is a diplomatic visit; can you try to be a little more... you know... diplomatic?"

"I'm not a diplomatic man."

"Then pretend," she snapped, her patience waning. "You insisted on coming. And perhaps no one's ever told you this before, but being a commander is more than war and hate and wanting to kill people."

"Alexander was the diplomat."

"Alexander's gone!" She sucked in a breath. "He's gone. And I need more from you."

Norah moved to the edge of the bed and sat down, struggling against the emotion that threatened. She waited for the calm to return.

"Phillip's not an enemy," she said as she gained back control. "He and I knew each other before I lost my memories. Surprisingly well, actually." She looked down at her hands. "I found out we had an agreement, a long time ago: to wed and let each other be free. I was going to return to Alexander, and Phillip would have been free to be with his own love."

Soren shifted. Quiet came, and they let it hang between them awhile. Then he sat on the edge of the bed beside her. "I'm sorry," he said softly.

"Me too," she whispered.

"Do you regret things now?" he asked. "Not marrying him?"

Her lip trembled. It was the question that she feared asking herself. One that she'd avoided asking, but one she couldn't keep avoiding. "What kind of person would I be if I said I wouldn't change my choice to wed Mikael?" She covered her face in her hands.

Soren sighed. "It doesn't mean you would have chosen the Bear's fate, or that you wanted it for him."

She sniffed and looked up at him. Sometimes Soren was a beautiful person.

"In fact," he added, "even if your arrangement would have played out, he still would have died. I would have killed him. More horribly."

And the beauty rapidly left. She shook her head and grimaced. "I know you're trying to make me feel better."

He nodded. "Yeah."

"Stop," she whispered.

"Okay."

It grew quiet between them again.

"Is the Aleon king with his love now?" he asked. "Is that why the princess of Osan departed?"

She pulled herself from her emotion and wiped her cheeks. "They made the same arrangement, yes. But Phillip's love is gone too. He died when taking Tarsus."

Soren's weight shifted back, as surprised at Phillip's news as she had been, she was sure.

Norah let out a breath. "But now he's making a valiant effort to bring together our three kingdoms in friendship, and I really want that. So, you'll go hunting tomorrow morning, and not bring back a dead king of Aleon."

He stared at her a moment, as if about to say something, then stopped.

"Will you go?" she asked. "Please?"

A protest rumbled from his chest.

"Please, Soren?"

Finally, he nodded. "Fine."

She gave a tired smile. "Thank you."

Soren sat on his destrier, struggling against the impatience twisting through him—he had thought *Salar* took too long departing places. Curse the North gods. They could have been well on the hunt by now, but this Aleon king took an eternity. And this man defined hunting as riding along with an army of men and a pack of noisy dogs. What was this madness?

"Are you ready?" the Aleon king asked him as he finally mounted his horse.

Was he serious? Soren cursed under his breath again. He should have made Caspian come. At least then he'd have someone else to witness this lunacy. And to complain to. Or Calla. He cursed himself again. He'd have loved to see his farm girl outshoot these cowards. But this was better, he supposed. If he wasn't with Salara, he wanted people he trusted with her.

They urged their mounts through the gates, toward the forested hills, surrounded by hound vocals that could surely be heard across the four kingdoms.

Soren let the Aleon king lead, silently judging him from behind.

The lands of Aleon were breathtaking, much like the capital city. Everything seemed perfect. They passed a grove of autumn-laden aspens that made Soren want to stop and stare, but he pushed himself on. Over dreams of rolling hills they rode, then through wheaten grass so tall it brushed the calves of his boots. When they reached the edge of the pine forest, the Aleon king grinned back at him. "Beautiful, isn't it?"

Of course it was beautiful—the curse of this place. It could draw a man in, make him not want to leave. But Soren wanted to leave.

The hounds let out a series of howling barks and raced deeper ahead, into the wood.

"They've got a scent!" Phillip called out, and they all kicked their mounts into a gallop to follow.

They chased the hounds to the base of a sprawling tree, where the dogs barked up at their catch. Soren shifted his eyes upward to find a large mountain lion in the far branches.

"Look at that beauty!" Phillip exclaimed excitedly. He dropped down from his mount and pulled his crossbow.

Wait, wait, wait. "You're going to kill it?" Soren asked.

"Of course I am."

Was this man serious? "Are you going to eat it?"

Phillip chuckled. "I'm going to stuff it."

"And for that, you'll kill this animal?" Soren reached down to settle his destrier, who moved under the rage of its master.

The Aleon king eyed him in surprise. "I thought you enjoyed hunting."

Soren did enjoy hunting, but... "This isn't hunting. There's no need. If you're going to waste a life, let it be your own."

Phillip's smile fell from his face. "I see."

Soren shifted his shoulder, readying to pull the sword from his back. Surely this would be the start of battle—where he would have to kill this king. He glanced around at the surrounding men. He definitely should have brought Calla with her bow. It would be hard getting out of this alone.

"What would you rather?" the king asked.

His question took Soren by surprise, and it made him pause. "What?"

"The morning's still early."

Soren snorted. *Barely.*

"What would you rather?" Phillip asked again. "Duck? Deer? What do you want to eat tonight?"

"Deer need to hang. You can't eat them the same day you hunt."

Phillip stepped closer to Soren's mount, looking up at him. "Do you not see my effort?" he asked so that only Soren could hear. "Can you not manage a little of your own?"

No. He couldn't. He didn't want to. But Soren did promise Salara he'd hunt. He sighed. "How's your grouse hunting?"

The corners of the king's mouth turned up. "Did you see the aspens to the south?"

Obviously. "That's why I ask."

"Back to the castle with the dogs," Phillip ordered out. "The lord commander and I will keep out."

They would go alone?

"Majesty," a fair-haired man beside the king said to him, a not-so-subtle warning—the only man of intelligence among them.

The king met Soren's stare and gave a smile. "Let Queen Norah know that the lord commander and I will be out awhile longer," he said to his men. "We'll return later this afternoon."

Soren clenched his jaw. If the Aleon bastard thought that reminding him about Salara would protect him... Damn the North gods, he might be right. *Might.*

The king's men reluctantly started back toward the castle, surrounded by the flurry of barking hounds. Phillip swung up onto his horse, and then they turned and urged their mounts south, toward the aspens.

Norah stood on the balcony of her chamber, watching the mainway toward the gates of the city. She hadn't been able to sit still since receiving the message that Soren and Phillip were hunting alone.

"Watching for them will only make them take longer," Calla said.

Norah groaned and stepped back inside to pace the room. She stretched out her fingers to stop wringing them.

Alone. Phillip would be alone... without his guard... with Soren... and with weapons. Which would be perfectly safe, she told herself.

"They're going to be fine," Norah said aloud. Yes, they'd been enemies for ten years, at war for ten years. And Phillip had given men to her father to help capture Bahoul from Kharav—the battle where Soren lost his family. But... "The war is behind us," she said, more to herself than to Calla. "And Soren knows the importance of a relationship with Aleon now." She bit her lip. "Surely he can put aside old animosities, now that the opportunity for peace and friendship is within our grasp."

Calla snorted. "Because the lord commander is so good at peace and friendship."

Norah cursed under her breath, and her stomach twisted. Calla was right. Why had she made him go? She should have known.

No. She had to think positively. Soren would be fine with Phillip. He loved hunting.

He would love...

Nine hells. He'd love to kill the king of Aleon.

She wrung her hands, her worry growing as the afternoon waned. Where were they?

Movement caught her eye, and she nearly tripped as she stumbled out to the balcony. As she squinted, she made out Soren walking toward the castle from the south. He hadn't come through the gates and down the mainway? Why not? "Where's Phillip?"

"Uh-oh," Calla said. "That doesn't seem good."

"You're not helping. Stay here." She turned and walked quickly from her chamber, down the hall, and to the stairs. If anything had happened... she'd kill him herself.

She reached the entry hall, just as Soren entered.

"Where have you been?" she demanded. "Where's Phillip? And—"

The sight of dried blood down his front stopped her in her steps.

"What have you done?" she asked breathlessly.

"He killed a charging boar that we startled while hunting," Phillip's voice called, and she whipped her head past Soren to see Phillip. She let out a sigh of relief.

"Were you worried, Salara?" Soren asked. His eyes smiled. He knew exactly what she'd been thinking.

She feigned a scowl. "Well, you look like you enjoyed yourself. So yes."

Phillip chuckled as he clapped Soren on the shoulder. "I venture to say he did, as did I."

Soren's eyes darkened at Phillip's touch, and Norah saw the warning. She stepped forward.

"I have to admit," Phillip added with a grin, "if one would have told me a few months ago I'd strike up a friendship with the Destroyer, I would have called them a liar."

Before Norah could react, Soren spun, snatching Phillip's wrist from his shoulder and clutching him by his leathers. "Do not mistake my tolerance for friendship," he snarled. "And touch me again only if you no longer value your life."

Norah's heart leapt into her throat as four door sentries pulled their swords. "Soren!" she cried. What was wrong with him? Behind her, Caspian and Titus pulled their own swords. She hadn't even realized they'd trailed her.

She held out her hand, desperate to settle everyone. "Soren," she said again.

Soren released his grip, and Phillip held out his own hand to stay his guards. Phillip's face was serious now as both men faced each other, poised with fight. Norah's heart pulsed in her ears. This would not end well. Soren had crossed the line of no return, so boldly threatening a king in his own kingdom, but she didn't know how to bring them back to the floor of reason.

They all stood frozen in the silence.

Then Phillip straightened as he dropped his hand, and the tension settled ever so slightly. "I know it takes time to heal from the damages of war," he said, "but I've been a patient man, Lord Commander, and a friend to both Mercia and the Shadowlands. You'll find my patience waning now."

Was Phillip giving him a warning? Was that all? She begged the gods that Soren would take it and keep his mouth shut, but she knew him better.

"I'm so sorry, Phillip," she interjected as she cut Soren a daggered eye. "You've given the lord commander a great deal to reflect on. Thank you for that."

Phillip looked to Norah. "I know you journey back to Mercia tomorrow. I invite you to dine with me this evening." He glanced back at Soren. "Both of you, if you can find the civility within you." Then he gave a short nod and left them in the quiet of the hall.

Soren didn't look at Norah before he turned toward his own chamber.

"Soren," she called after him, but he didn't stop. By the gods, she'd murder this man with her bare hands. "Soren," she called again. She picked up after him, needing almost the full length of the hall to catch up.

When they reached the end, she grabbed his arm. "Soren! Are you going to tell me what happened back there? What was that?"

"He takes too many freedoms," he said angrily.

"He is king!"

"Not over me! Not over you."

Norah hushed him as she pushed him inside his chamber and closed the door behind them. She grabbed him again and made him look at her. She was done with this nonsense.

"What's the matter with you?" she hissed. "Phillip's done nothing but extend the hand of friendship since we got here, and you spit on it."

"I don't want his friendship!" he thundered.

"It's not about what you want. Phillip is the king of Aleon, he—"

"It's *him*! The man in the vision, it's *him*." He pulled down his wrap and roughly wiped his face. "He's the one the seer showed me."

Norah stopped. They hadn't talked about Soren's vision for a long time—the vision of a man he didn't know. A lover.

A quiet came between them.

Slowly, he moved to the bed and sat down on the edge. He pulled the wrap from his head, as if he needed to escape it, as if he couldn't breathe. Then he just sat. Lost.

Norah sat down beside him. But she didn't know what to say.

His breaths were shallow. His voice wavered slightly. "I'd never seen the Aleon king before. But I recognized him from the vision the moment he greeted us."

"Why didn't you tell me?" she whispered.

He shook his head. "I don't know. I was upset. And... ashamed."

"But I already knew about the vision."

His eyes glistened with anger. "It wasn't just a vision," he said through his teeth. "Once it was in my mind, once he was in my mind, he stayed. And when something occupies your mind long enough, it becomes real, it feels real. And he's occupied my mind for a long time."

"But why are you so angry?"

"Because he's taken that from me! I know who he is now." He drew in a breath. "And I'm angry because I let myself..."

He had let himself dream. And he let himself feel for a dream. She had no place to judge him for that; she'd fallen in love with dreams. She sighed. "You haven't even tried to know him."

"I don't want to know him. He's the Aleon king."

"Uh, you're the one they call the Destroyer. Talk about *perceptions*."

He snorted, and it brought a small smile to her own lips.

"Soren, if you want to hate him, then hate him. But you have to control yourself. We need this alliance. And for gods' sakes, stop trying to kill him."

"I didn't try to kill him today."

"Then stop threatening to kill him. I know it's hard, what's happened in the past, and I know you don't trust him, but you have to at least pretend civility. Phillip is deeply offended, and you have to help me smooth things over."

He gave a reluctant nod.

"And, Soren, I don't want you to feel shame. Even now that you know who he is, if he... continues to occupy your mind, that's okay. And if you ever find yourself... wanting to get to know him, that's okay too. You deserve to be happy."

"No one deserves to be happy. We're all wretched creatures."

She put her hand on his arm, making him look at her. "Well, deserved or not, I want you to be happy. I love you, Soren."

His eyes glistened, and his nostrils flared. "Then you're the most wretched of us all."

She smiled as she leaned her head against his shoulder.

Evening had set over Aleon. Norah looked forward to the morning, for when they'd start the journey back to Mercia, but first, dinner with Phillip. She searched her mind for how to mend things after what had happened with Soren. Of course, she'd apologize, and she'd explain... What would she explain? She couldn't tell him about Soren's vision, or his struggles. She shook her head. She'd just have to rely on her own rapport with him and try to build their friendship further. It shouldn't be terribly hard, with just the two of them. She stepped into her silk slippers and opened the door to her chamber, then stopped abruptly.

Soren stood in the hall. Without his head wrap. She could only gape at him.

"What?" he said irritably.

She shook her head, raising her brows in surprise. "I almost didn't recognize you."

"You know what I look like." He missed her jest completely.

"I just didn't expect to see you like this. Or to see you at all."

He creased his brow. "I was invited."

"I know," she answered quickly. "I... I just didn't think you'd come."

He hesitated, glancing to the floor. Then he swallowed. "I wanted to come."

"Oh," she said. Then her breath caught. *Oh.*

"Stop grinning like a fat-fed hound."

Was she grinning? She pulled her lips between her teeth.

They started their walk toward the dining hall.

Norah glanced at him. "You look nice."

"It's not my intention to look nice," he replied, annoyed.

"Really?" He'd washed and trimmed his beard... and was actually wearing a tunic. *Really?*

"What?" he asked shortly.

She smiled. "Nothing."

His brow etched deeper, and a shadow hung over his eyes. "What?" he asked again.

She wouldn't say it. "Nothing," she said again, and kept toward the dining hall.

They reached the hall, where Phillip was waiting. He turned when they entered. "Queen Norah," he greeted her politely, but his eyes widened when he saw Soren. "Lord Commander," he said in surprise.

Soren didn't answer, but he gave an ever-so-slight, stiff bow of his head.

Phillip drew closer. Norah clenched her hands so tightly her nails dug into her palms. He was close enough. But Soren didn't balk. He stood silently, giving himself to be looked upon. Phillip stepped even closer. His eyes traveled over Soren's face—his pulled-back hair, his jaw, his lips—and back to lock their stare.

Norah pulled her gaze away. It felt... too intimate to watch.

"Thank you for coming," Phillip told him. He waved his hand toward the dining table, then said to both of them, "Please."

Norah stepped to the table and sat down. Soren seated himself to her right as Phillip took his chair at the opposite end.

"I am sure you're eager to get back to Mercia," Phillip started as the servants busied themselves filling their plates with food.

She smiled. "I've quite enjoyed the time here, but it'll be good to return."

"You're welcome back anytime." He turned his gaze to Soren. "As are you, Lord Commander."

She smiled at Soren and raised a brow, and he cut her back a daggered glance.

Time passed quickly, and conversation came easier. Norah couldn't help but notice Phillip's gaze roll back to Soren as he talked. His smile was natural and warm, and his laugh light and infectious. And she almost thought she saw the corners of Soren's mouth curve slightly upward once. Maybe.

Norah watched her friend with her heart full, and for his wounds of the past, she felt the beginnings of healing. For them both.

CHAPTER TWENTY

Morning came quickly. Norah was happy to be on her way back to Mercia but sad to be departing Aleon so soon. Dinner the evening before had set them on the course of friendship with Phillip, and leaving now seemed to cut it too short.

She had penned a letter to Mikael in the early hours, telling him of her decision to go to Aleon, of the wedding, of this new friendship, and of her safe journey home—well, by the time it reached him, she would be safely home. Soren had pressed her to write him before going to Aleon, but she knew that would have drawn Mikael in full force back to Mercia, no matter what threats lay before Kharav. She had no intention of keeping the visit from him, but she wanted to make sure she had a good-news message that wouldn't take his attention away from Kharav and drive him to return.

Looking back, it was a risky decision, but one she was right about and glad she had made. Mikael would still be angry, of course, but he would come around to understanding, she was sure.

Soren gave Sephir a pat on the neck as Norah mounted in the courtyard of the citadel. The mare tolerated him now—she seemed to like him even. Two kind stable hands and the commander were all she permitted to touch her. Norah smiled. Soren had a way of growing on a person, even on the spirit of the Wild.

Phillip stepped forward from where he had been waiting while the company readied in the mainway. He looked up at Norah with a warm smile. "Thank you for coming, Norah. And for trusting me. I can see why you wouldn't have, but I'm glad you did." His eyes moved to Soren and then back to her. "Let's not wait so long to see one another again."

"I'm glad I came too. And I'm thankful for your friendship and hospitality. You're welcome to visit Mercia anytime."

"I'd like that." He looked back to Soren, who had mounted his destrier. "Lord Commander. It was an honor to meet you, and I hope... I hope we meet again. And not on opposite sides of the battlefield."

Soren hesitated a moment, then gave a nod of his head.

Phillip's gaze met hers again. "Goodbye, Norah."

"Goodbye, Phillip." First names, because this time, they really did feel like friends.

She gave a final smile, and they urged their mounts down the mainway with the rest of their party behind them. Crowds had lined to see them off, waving them through.

"They're happy to see us leaving," she said to Soren in jest.

"They were happy when we came," he said. "I think they're just generally happy people."

"Did he really just say that?" Calla said.

Norah laughed. "Look at you, being all positive," she teased him.

"I didn't say I liked it," he cut back. When they reached the main gates, he cast a glance back at the castle.

She pulled Sephir closer, dropping her voice for more privacy. "Did you enjoy yesterday evening? Phillip seemed—"

"Stop."

"I'm just—"

"No," he said firmly, with his eyes forward and avoiding hers. "I want you to forget yesterday."

Wait, what? "Soren—"

"I don't want to talk about it," he said sharply.

He was obviously still battling the demons in his own mind. She puffed out a breath between her lips. He wore more armor on the inside than out.

An autumn blanket of red, orange, and yellow covered the hills as they rode through the morning. Norah tried to soak in as much of it as she could. In only a short time, they'd reach the snow of the North, and winter would be long. Longer without Mikael. How long would he have to be in Kharav? As long as Japheth and Rael posed a threat, she supposed. But now with Aleon and Osan joining them, there was hope in seeing him again soon.

"You were right about something, though," Soren said after a while, breaking the quiet.

She cast him a playful scowl. "You say that like I'm never right."

He shrugged, and she rolled her eyes.

"Well, what was I right about?"

"I'm not a diplomat. Nor can I be."

Where was this coming from? And where was it headed? "I think you managed all right."

He pulled the wrap down from his face, and her stomach dipped slightly. He was Serious Soren when he took down his wrap to speak—more serious than usual. He had a hard message.

"You need to name a new lord justice."

A knot formed at the base of her throat at the mention. She shook her head. "No."

"You have to."

"No, I don't," she argued. "I have you. I don't need another."

"Salara, I'm your agent of war. But for the North, for peace, you need another." He paused and looked back at Caspian trailing their unit. "And there is a ready and capable man. The Bear named him his second. Will you not trust that?"

Of course she trusted Alexander's endorsement, although it wasn't his decision. She trusted Caspian, but she wasn't ready to name another. And—she turned her mind back to what the visit to Aleon had almost distracted her from—Alexander wasn't gone.

Snow covered the ground. Norah wished she'd spent just a few more days in Aleon's autumnal beauty, but it was still good to be back in Mercia. Catherine had made her recount each detail of the wedding. Norah stuck *only* to the wedding, keeping her discovery of her and Phillip's arrangement, and other private matters, to herself. She found she remembered more about the food than the ceremony, drawing her grandmother's ire.

Late into the evening, Norah found herself in Alexander's study. Everything was just as he'd left it. No one entered this room. It wasn't a room she'd been in often, but it was one she imagined he'd spent quite a lot of time in. She trailed her fingers the length of his desk as she moved by it. How many hours had he sat here? Her eyes traveled over the shelves of books and ledgers. Caspian would know what to make of all this, and what needed to be done. Why did she hesitate to name him justice?

She sank into the oversize chair by the window. The cold leather prickled her skin through her gown. Had Alexander sat here, mulling hard decisions? She stared out the windowpanes and into the courtyard below.

No.

She stood and moved back to his desk, easing herself into the chair behind it. This was where he'd done his work. She brushed her hands across the top of the desk, over the parchments and maps strewn across the wood.

"Norah!" Catherine's voice came urgently as she burst in. "There you are. What are you even doing in here? I've been looking all over for you."

She silently cursed herself. Now what? "Why? What's wrong?"

"You have to come."

"Where?" What was so urgent? Her stomach knotted as her mind turned to Mikael. "Has something happened?"

"Samuel's had a vision." Catherine waved her up. "Quickly!"

The seer? "What is it?" she asked as she followed her grandmother out of Alexander's study, through the castle, into the courtyard, and around to the seer's gallery.

"You have to see."

Norah wanted to shake her. Why couldn't she just tell her?

They reached the gallery, and Catherine maneuvered through the narrow walkway and the stacks of paintings as if she'd done so a hundred times. Norah bumped a few trying to keep up as she followed her to the back room.

Samuel looked up as they entered, his face pale, his lips pressed in silent worry. He held a paintbrush in his hand—he hadn't even finished. What had been so urgent? As Norah stepped around it, her breath left her lungs.

In the center of the canvas stood Alexander.

In his hand, he held a horned helm, bloodied and separated from its wearer. Her stomach twisted. She thought she might be sick.

She knew the dark, armored body that lay at his feet—a body she knew as well as her own.

Alexander's eyes blazed in triumphant hatred, staring off the canvas at her. A deep shudder gripped her spine. She reached out and clutched Samuel's chair for balance.

No.

"This isn't possible," she whispered. Tears stung her eyes. How had this vision not perished with Alexander? Was Mikael still in danger? Had his fate not changed? "Maybe... maybe it's an old vision?"

Samuel shook his head. "The power that carries this vision is still very much alive. And with its detail... it's very strong. Stronger than it's ever been."

Norah couldn't stop her shaking. "Get the lord commander," she whispered.

Samuel stood frozen.

"Get him!" she cried.

He quickly shuffled from the room, still holding his brush.

Norah shook her head. "This can't be," she said. Even if Alexander still lived, he wouldn't do this. He wouldn't take Mikael from her. Would he? But if he wasn't himself...

And there was something strange about this vision. Alexander's hair was cut shorter than how he'd normally worn it. And he wasn't wearing his signature battle armor with the pauldron of the great Northern bear. Instead, he was armored in black and red. Her eyes narrowed. Markings on the skin of his neck just above his breastplate caught her attention, as did those on his wrists peeking out from under the armor along his forearm. She'd seen these markings before...

Catherine had moved to the next room and was sifting feverishly through all the new paintings Samuel had done.

Soren charged in with Samuel close behind. He knocked back stacks of paintings along the narrow path as he made his way through the gallery, but when he reached Norah and saw the image, he stopped.

She gave him a moment to comprehend what he was looking at before asking, "How is this possible?"

He shook his head. "It's not. The Bear's dead."

"But what if he's not?" she whispered, wary of Catherine in the room nearby. "I know I saw him. I know he came to me."

"Salara," he said, low. His lips moved to protest more, but he said nothing else. He didn't believe her; he didn't believe she called Alexander with the blood.

"Then explain this," she pressed. "How can you not believe it now?"

"I don't believe that's the Bear."

"Because, as you like to remind me, he's dead?" she snapped.

He clasped her shoulders and made her look at him. "No," he said. "Because I know him. I would trust the Bear with Salar's life, as I would my own. That is not him." He looked back to the painting. "But I will find out who it is."

The day seemed to have gotten colder as Norah walked toward her chamber. Her mind and her stomach twisted all at once. She needed Mikael back. She needed to see him, hold him, keep him from this cursed fate that refused to release him.

She reached her chamber and pulled off her cloak before even fully getting through the door.

And stopped.

On her vanity was a small package with a ribbon. She didn't have to open it to know what was inside.

A vial of blood.

Chapter Twenty-One

Norah clutched the vial in her hand, her thumb numb from pressing it against the decorative beveled point at its top. She lay on her back across the bed in her chamber as she stared up at the ceiling.

They were supposed to be past this, past the vision. Mikael was supposed to be safe.

The cool air sat stagnant around her. It was suffocating.

How could this be Mikael's fate still?

And Alexander. Soren was so certain there was someone else behind it all—someone tricking her. But the vision in the painting had been clear, as had the one in her mind. It was Alexander.

Norah sat up and looked at the vial in her hand. She tilted it to one side, then the other. She knew Alexander, more than anyone else. She would know if it was him, or if it wasn't. Wouldn't she?

She would.

Then why was she doubting?

She needed to see him again. She would know. She would know if it was him. Norah clutched the vial tighter. She would know, she told herself again.

Before she could talk herself out of it, she dabbed a smear of blood across her palm and closed her eyes.

Her skin prickled with nervousness. This was a stupid idea. Soren would rage through the floorboards if he found out.

No, it wasn't stupid. She had to see Alexander. She needed to know how he came to her, and if he truly posed a threat to Mikael.

She waited, but all was quiet.

This was a stupid idea.

Her pulse quickened. It wasn't too late. She could wipe off the blood. But she didn't.

And then she felt him.

He entered her mind like a gentle breeze, not as invasive as the traveler seers Nemus and Bhasim. He entered softly, gracefully, as if it were natural. As if he'd done it a thousand times.

He stood in front of her, in normal attire—dark brown breeches with a white, long-sleeved tunic. He looked every bit the Alexander she knew.

Norah eyed him warily, then rose from where she had been sitting on the bed. She studied him—every part of him, every detail.

He seemed to know this was a different calling, a different visit. He didn't speak, but he waited patiently.

Norah stepped silently to him. Her eyes moved over his face, his hair, his eyes, his mouth. To his chest and down his front and back up. Around him, she walked, moving slowly. Every line, every detail—it was everything she knew. And yet something she didn't... Something wasn't quite right. She moved closer as she came back around in front of him.

Still, he waited.

Norah reached out and took his hand. She expected him to pull away, but he didn't. Unlike the previous visits, he was... amenable. She pushed up the sleeve of his tunic and searched his arm, looking for the markings she'd seen in the painting. There were none. Her eyes moved to his neck, and she reached and pulled down his collar. No markings were on his skin.

He stood, unmoving.

She released him. The Alexander in front of her was not the Alexander in the painting. His eyes didn't hold the same hatred, the same rage.

"How are you here?" she asked him.

A question he wouldn't answer.

Yes or no questions, she told herself. "Can you come whenever you want?"

He eyed her for a moment, then gave a single shake of his head. *No.*

Her pulse quickened. "You need the blood."

Only a single nod in reply. *Yes.*

He was talking to her. Two answers now. This was further than she'd gotten with him before. He was *talking*. Her heart beat faster. "But how did you send it to me? How can you... engage?"

No answer.

She sighed, frustrated. "Is it *your* blood?"

He pulled back slightly. His mouth opened, then closed. Then he stilled. He wasn't going to answer.

Of course he wouldn't. Because it wasn't his blood.

She brought her hand to her forehead, clutching her temples. She should have listened to Soren.

But his touch on her arm made her pause. He pulled her hand down for her to look at him.

Then he gave a nod.

Her eyes narrowed. Was he answering her? "Yes, it's your blood?"

He nodded again.

"That's not possible."

He only watched her.

"No," she insisted.

But the blues of his eyes looking back at her—they weren't lying. He nodded again.

She gritted her teeth. "Gods, why do I believe you?" she whispered. She stared at him. "But your body... How? How is that possible? I saw you sealed in the Hall of Souls. Your body is... there should be no blood to send. And even if there were..." She rubbed her hand over her face. This didn't make any sense. Alexander's dead body was sealed in a sarcophagus, in a hall under guard. How could he reach her?

Unless it wasn't Alexander. Soren was so sure. But as she looked at him, he couldn't be anyone else. There were details that lived only in her memories, things only she and Alexander would have known—the shell bracelet. Yet... there was something...

"Do you deceive me?"

His eyes—she couldn't read them now. They almost seemed... sad.

Just as she was about to ask him again, he reached behind him and pulled out a box. A navy velvet box. Her heart beat even faster.

She knew this box.

Gently, he placed it in her hands.

Norah couldn't breathe. Her fingers trembled as she stepped to the vanity and set it down. She could only stare at it.

Norah glanced back at him in disbelief, and the corners of his mouth turned up ever so slightly. He gave a small nod.

She turned back to the box, finally summoning the courage to open it, and blinked back her tears.

Her mother's crown.

"Where did you find this?" she whispered.

No. He couldn't have found it. This was a vision. It wasn't real. When she left this dream, she'd leave the crown too. But to hold it in her hands, see it, touch it—this was truly a gift, and only people who loved her would know how much it meant to her.

She stood and turned to him, and without even thinking, pulled him into an embrace. "Thank you," she whispered.

He wrapped his arms around her and embraced her back—an embrace Alexander would give, because somehow this was Alexander.

The table was quiet as dinner was served. Her grandmother hadn't said much since seeing the painting. Neither had Soren. But she knew what was on their minds, what was on all their minds.

"I'll head out in the morning," Soren said, breaking the silence.

Norah's head jerked up. "What? Why?"

"To get to the bottom of this. I'll take the pair." *The pair*—what he called Calla and Cohen, who had become somewhat of his little sidekicks. As if she hadn't noticed.

"And what are you expecting to find?" she asked.

"Who's behind this. Who's in your head."

Catherine looked at Norah with a bent brow. "What do you mean?"

Norah cut Soren a daggered glance. She hadn't told her grandmother about Alexander coming to her. She hadn't planned to. But Soren's chastising gaze told her he wouldn't let her keep it to herself.

"Norah," Catherine pressed.

How to explain this as sanely as possible... "I've been having visions."

Her grandmother's eyes widened. "You've seen what is to come? The future?"

"No, not like the seers." She shot Soren a frustrated scowl as she searched for words. Then turning back to her grandmother, she said, "They're not exactly visions, but more like... visits."

"Visits?" Catherine frowned. "From whom?"

"That's what I mean to get to the bottom of," Soren said.

Norah pursed her lips. "I know who it is."

Soren shifted back in his chair. "Salara."

He didn't believe her, but it didn't matter. "It's Alexander." Her heart pulsed in her throat as Catherine gaped at her.

Her grandmother looked at Soren, then back at her.

Norah could feel Soren's eyes on her, but she couldn't meet them.

"It's a trick," he said.

"It's Alexander," she argued, now looking at Catherine. Someone needed to believe her. "He's come to me, as only I would know. It sounds like madness, yes, but it's him." A desperation washed over her. She needed her grandmother to believe her. "He gave me back my mother's crown."

Catherine drew in a breath. "You have it?"

"No, I mean..." This was certainly sounding like madness. "He gave it back to me in a vision."

"You saw him again?" Soren asked angrily.

Curse the gods. This was getting worse. She finally faced him. "How could I not after Samuel's vision? I'm trying to get to the bottom of this too."

His nostrils flared, and the muscle along his jaw tightened.

"Don't you see?" she begged him. "He knows what would have been important to me—something only those close to me would know."

"Everyone knows that crown is important to you," he snapped back. "I've lit up half this cursed world searching for it."

Norah quieted. She'd forgotten about that, and a wave of guilt washed over her. Still, it changed nothing of how she felt. Soren hadn't been there—he hadn't seen Alexander like she had.

Catherine's face was hard to read. Did she believe her? Norah searched her eyes... and her heart sank. Oh gods, she didn't. Worse than that, her eyes were the eyes of pity. At least Soren believed she saw *someone*, even if he believed it wasn't Alexander.

She desperately missed Mikael. He would have believed her.

A servant entered the dining hall. "Regal High, this arrived for you," he said as he held out a crimson, fabric-wrapped box for her.

Norah glanced at Catherine and Soren. Who would have sent her something? Soren's eyes narrowed, annoyed. At least it was a distraction to break the tension. She took the box and set it on the table in front of her before pulling the thick satin ribbon from around it.

But on lifting the lid, she rose with a start.

Soren stood abruptly. "What is it?" he asked.

But Norah couldn't speak. She could only stare at the box in front of her. Inside of it was a smaller box—a navy velvet box.

But she didn't open it. She couldn't. If the crown was inside, Alexander wouldn't have just given it to her in the vision, but in life as well. How? How had he found it? And how had he sent it to her?

Soren moved to her side. Norah stepped back as he reached in and pulled out the velvet box. Catherine rose.

He opened it. And pulled out her mother's crown.

Catherine gasped, and Norah's own breath shook.

"The bastard's had it this entire time," he said.

Norah shook her head. "No, Alexander would have given it to me sooner if he'd had it. He must have found it."

He clenched the crown in his hand. "I'm telling you it wasn't to be found. It wasn't lost. He had it."

Just because Soren couldn't find the crown didn't mean Alexander couldn't.

He bared his teeth, his anger growing. "Salara, this didn't come from the Bear."

"You don't know that!"

"I watched him die!" he thundered. "I saw him gutted, the blood run out of him, and I watched him die! And I sealed him in that sarcophagus myself. Even if by some miracle he wasn't dead when I put him in, he's certainly dead and rotting now." His words and his tone were like knives—angry, searing knives.

Her lip trembled. "Get out," she whispered.

He let out a long breath as his shoulders dropped. His face sobered, and he shook his head apologetically. "Salara," he said softly.

"Get out!" she cried.

He hesitated a moment, then gave a small nod. Leaving the crown on the table beside the box, he stepped from the dining room.

Norah's eyes found Catherine's.

Her grandmother opened her mouth.

"Don't," Norah warned. She was in no mood to argue about this any longer. She would find out what was happening herself.

Soren beat on the thick oaken door. There was no answer, and he beat again. He knew she was in there. He wouldn't let her avoid him, even if *he* wanted to avoid *her*.

Finally, the door swung open, and the grandmother stood with a scathing scowl.

"By the gods, fiend, what's the matter with you?" she snapped at him. "Must you beat down the door?"

Irritation rumbled in his chest. "You weren't answering."

"I was walking to answer!"

"Too slowly."

She pursed her lips with a glare that would freeze the wind.

"Take me to him," he told her.

Loathing shadowed her eyes. "To whom?"

"The Bear. Your guards don't allow me to pass. Don't make me kill them."

She puffed a breath. "I'll have you know there are more civilized ways."

Soren gritted his teeth. "This is me being civilized. Now take me to him."

"Absolutely not—"

"Woman!" He was losing his patience. He culled his irritation. That would get him nowhere with her. He drew in a long breath and let it out slowly. "Please. Take me to him. Salara's not safe, and I have to find out what's going on."

She stared at him a moment. "Fine," she said finally. Then she stepped into the hall, and he followed.

He knew where the tombs were, where he had helped seal in the Bear, but he let the old woman lead him through a series of halls. When they reached the Hall of Souls, she waved the guards to step aside. They looked at Soren warily but did as they were bid and let them pass.

Bastards.

She led him down the wide, winding stair to the bottom. The glass of the high ceiling spilled light down to the floor. It had been night when he was here before, but now in the day, he realized how beautiful this place of death was.

Tombs lined the walls, generations of Northern rulers, each within a carved alcove of stone. The Northmen believed them to be watching over Mercia. Were they watching now? He almost smiled. Were their bones twisting in their beds of stone at a Shadowman among them?

He followed the woman to a side dais with a sarcophagus draped in silver-embroidered linen. It was just as he remembered. She put her hand on top.

Soren reached and pulled off the silver cloth.

"What are you doing?" she demanded.

"Hold this," he said, pushing the cloth into her arms.

"You have no right—"

He clasped the top of the sarcophagus.

"No, don't!" she cried—not the cry of anger, but one of pain. A plea. "You can't."

He stopped, then turned to her. With the greatest effort of compassion, he said, "Alexander would want me to find out what's happening. And see Salara safe."

"By wreaking havoc on his place of rest? Destroying it? Disturbing his body?"

"I'm not destroying it. And you burn bodies, by the way. Moving his around a bit won't make a difference."

Her face still held the look of horror. He probably could have handled that a little softer.

"And when did he ever care about rest?" he added, trying to change his approach. "Nothing as it relates to Salara could ever disturb him. He would be doing this himself if he could."

"This is the madness of grief," she argued. "Her thinking that he comes back to her even in death! She's not accepting that he's gone."

"She's not mad," he cut back. "She *does* see something. Someone is toying with her. And I'm going to find out who it is." He clutched the cover of the sarcophagus again.

"You won't be able to open it. It took four men to put it on."

Soren gritted his teeth again. Yes, he knew—he'd been one of them. He strained against the heavy stone and pushed the lid sideways. The stench of death filled the room, and the woman gasped. He looked into the sarcophagus, and there lay the body of the Bear, adorned in the colors of the North. His face was unrecognizable, but Soren knew the golden locks.

This was the Bear. A very dead Bear.

Relief filled him. Not that he actually believed him to be alive again, or to have cheated death. But Salara was a smart woman, and it would be very difficult to fool her, especially using the image of a man she knew so well—a man she loved. He'd been so sure it wasn't the Bear, but for her to believe so strongly, it had begun to eat away at his confidence. And she said she'd touched him, felt him. He ran his eyes over the remains—not this body, she hadn't.

"Sorry, brother," he said quietly. Then he pushed the top of the sarcophagus back into place.

Soren looked and found Salara's grandmother off to the side. She had lowered herself to sit on a bench along the wall. His opening of the tomb had shaken her. To breathe in the death of one lost, that would stay with her. And he pitied her.

Her lips were pursed, but he knew it was to control her emotion. Slowly, he approached and sat beside her.

They sat in silence for a long time.

"I raised him, you know," she said finally. "After his mother went mad. His father... Well, the work of a justice is unending, and so I saw to the boys. I raised Alexander to be a proper lord. He was a sweet child. Kind, loyal. He was easy to love, and I did so like he was my own. Both of them." A tear escaped down her cheek, and she wiped it back.

"You raised good men," he told her. He looked back at the sarcophagus. "The Bear was the only adversary I've ever grieved. And in the end, one of the few men who ever truly knew me." He stopped. Curse the North gods, he was starting to feel emotional himself.

The woman leaned back slightly. "You are surprisingly gracious for one so fiendish in nature."

Soren snorted. From her, he'd take that as a compliment.

She looked across the room. "And you care for Norah, I can tell."

He did. And it was annoying.

"What are you going to do now?" she asked.

"I'm going to take her back to Kharav."

The woman stood abruptly. "Have you lost your mind? Closer to Rael and Japheth? Closer to war? Is that not why you brought her to Mercia in the first place?"

He stood too. "She's in danger here."

"This is her home! This is where she's protected!"

"Yet this trickster of the mind is reaching her here. Do you know how she sees him? He can't just come to her. He needs his blood to touch her skin, and she finds the vials in her chamber. He's getting *into her chamber* somehow."

Catherine's eyes widened, and her breath quickened. "Then we'll increase the guard."

"I already have." Was she really going to try to tell him how to protect Salara?

She shook her head. "And you think her being in Mercia is more dangerous than the Shadowlands? I think not!"

"Circumstances have changed, now that we've confirmed our alliance with Aleon and Osan. And I can protect her better in Kharav."

"Like you protected her from the assassins?"

He grew quiet. "That was a failure I take very personally." He softened toward the woman. He understood her hesitance. "Salara's not safe here. And yes, there are dangers in Kharav, but these are dangers I know, dangers I can fight and defend against. I don't know what's happening here." He sighed. "And I think it will be better for her mind to get away from the things that constantly remind her of him, to get back to the one person who can help her heal."

She stood quietly, uncertainty still on her face.

He needed the grandmother's help in convincing Salara to appoint a justice; she couldn't leave Mercia without one. He clenched his jaw. The woman needed more convincing herself, but what else did he have?

"Lady grandmother," he said as respectfully as he could. "She needs to set up the North so she can return to Kharav. She needs to name another lord justice. I'm sworn to her. I wouldn't press this if I didn't believe it was best. And I know you don't trust my king, but you would be sending her back to the man who loves her above all else."

Her lip twitched slightly as she looked around the hall again. Finally, she nodded. "I'll talk to Norah about a justice," she said. "There are a few lords—"

"Caspian. The Bear trusted Caspian. As do I."

She hesitated, but then nodded. "All right."

Uncurse the North gods. *Finally.*

"And about your king," she added. "I don't like him. But he's a good king, and I do trust him."

Soren gave a faint smile under his wrap. "Perhaps one day you'll feel the same about me."

"No, Destroyer," she said. "I actually like you."

He looked at her from the corner of his eye with a hidden smirk. He might actually like her too.

CHAPTER TWENTY-TWO

It smelled like shit—not of the animals as he passed the stables, but of the chaos that fouled the air around them all. Soren knew he'd spoken harshly to Salara, and undeservedly so. She truly thought she'd seen the Bear. Clever bastard—whoever was behind the elaborate scheme. He'd find them. And gut them.

He carried the crimson box that had held Salara's crown as he strode toward the sparring field where he knew he'd find the pair of raven-haired siblings. He'd come to rely on them. Often. Soren trusted very few—select members of the Crest, the young bear, Caspian, and the pair.

Cohen saw him first as he approached, but both came immediately to meet him.

Soren pulled down his wrap from his face. "I've a task for you," he told them as they neared, and he held out the box. "Salara received a gift yesterday. It came in this. I want to know if anyone saw anything."

"What was in it?" Calla asked.

He eyed her in annoyance. Always so many questions. At least they weren't stupid questions. "Her crown."

The girl's mouth popped open. "Her mother's crown? The one you lost when you first took her and haven't been able to find?"

Well, most of her questions weren't stupid questions. "I didn't lose—" He looked at the boy in disbelief. Cohen shrugged.

Curse the North gods. Soren didn't have time for this. "I want to know who sent it."

Where was it delivered? Cohen asked.

Soren liked the boy's silent language. He wished the girl would use it more. He wished everyone would use it more.

"The servant who brought it in said it had been left in the entry of the main doors," he told them. "Someone had to have seen something."

Cohen frowned. *Do you think the sender means harm to Salara?*

"I do."

Calla took the box. "Do you think it's a Northman?"

He let out a long breath. "I want to say no. But I don't know how an outsider's getting through to her here."

She nodded, with her normal determination coming to her eyes—that determination that Soren needed. "We'll see what we can find."

Norah stared at the crown in front of her as she sat at her vanity under the light of morning. She clenched the blood vial in her hand and thumbed the top as she mulled.

How had Alexander found her crown? Where had it been? And how had he gotten it to her? Here. Now. Perhaps it was the same way as he'd gotten her the vials.

When he'd given her the crown in the vision, she'd thought it was a symbol—something he knew would be important to her to show her he was real. But it wasn't a symbol. He had truly given it to her, and now even more questions flooded her mind.

She wanted to call him back, but how many answers would he give her? And how long could she keep calling him? Perhaps indefinitely, so long as she had the blood. But where was the blood coming from?

The door to her chamber opened, and she jumped, quickly shoving the vial into the pocket of her gown and turning.

Her grandmother swept in, with Serene carrying a plate of fruit and cheese behind her. "I thought we could take breakfast in here together this morning," Catherine said as she pushed the draperies wider, letting in more light.

Norah forced a smile. *Great*—a private conversation. No doubt to question her sanity after learning of her visions of Alexander. She rose from the vanity with a sigh and joined Catherine at the small table by the window. Serene poured a hot cup of tea for both of them. Her grandmother flicked her hand, and Serene added a chalice of wine. Then the maid saw herself out, closing the door behind her.

Norah sat. Where would they start? Would she be made to recount everything she'd seen in the visions? Likely. All the while being told it was a product of her grief, a lapse in her sanity.

"It's time, Norah," Catherine said directly. "Mercia needs a justice."

Norah stiffened. That wasn't what she'd expected. She would have rather talked about her sanity. Her grandmother let the silence sit between them, waiting for her to respond. And she'd have to respond. Eventually. She took Catherine's chalice and swallowed a large swig of wine.

"I don't need a lord justice, I have the lord commander," she said finally.

"Yes, well, as pleasant as he is, he's a beast of the Shadowlands. That's where he belongs."

"I'm not sending him back—"

"You'll need him by your side when *you* go back."

Norah jerked her head up. "What?"

"With Aleon and Osan now, you don't need to hide away in Mercia. And I'll not play ignorant, I know your heart is in the Shadowlands."

Her pulse raced. She could go back to Kharav? Back to Mikael?

"However, Mercia needs a proper justice, and a proper council."

But Mercia didn't deserve anything less than Alexander. "I'm sure you've already prepared a recommendation?" Most likely one of the elder lords—

"Caspian."

Norah sat back. That, too, was unexpected.

Catherine took a drink from their now-shared wine chalice. "You and I both know he was Alexander's choice, not that it was or is his choice to make. But I trust it's the right decision."

Caspian. Soren had felt the same. If she didn't know him and her grandmother better, she would have thought them to be colluding. She drew in a long breath. Caspian had been Alexander's choice. If she were to name *anyone*, it should be him.

"Of course, then you'll have to name a new captain," Catherine added.

Or let Soren do it. Or Caspian. That sounded like a justice's task anyway.

"Norah, you can continue to mourn for as long as you need, but see Mercia well. Don't forget your duty, or your people. They look to you."

The thought of seeing Mikael again, and so soon, filled her with a rush of emotion. She needed him. She needed to be home again. He could help make things right, if ever things could truly be right again.

Norah turned her mind to Mercia—she did need to move her kingdom forward, both with a justice and a council. Especially if she would be returning to Kharav. And she most certainly would be returning to Kharav. She nodded. "All right."

Catherine gave a sad smile, then reached across the table and clasped her hand. "I love you, my darling. I don't say those words enough."

Norah clutched her hand through her tears. They were exactly the words she needed to hear.

Soren sat at the large desk in the Bear's study. He'd been using it as his own quite a bit lately. At first it seemed sacrilegious, but thoughts came easier here—in the place where the Bear had planned and strategized. Maybe his spirit lingered, watching over and helping him, like Norah and the Northmen believed. More likely the Bear was annoyed by Soren's complete disregard for how everything had been meticulously situated. Soren had moved the larger chair from the window to the desk—it was more comfortable—and he'd pushed the desk forward to create more room from the shelves behind. Yes, that was more likely—he was sitting in the Bear's irritation. Soren gave a small chuckle. *Good*. "That's what you get for dying, you bastard."

He looked up from his thoughts to see the pair as they stepped inside from the hall. "What have you found?" he asked.

"No one has seen outsiders that seem suspicious," Calla said. "But there was a man who saw this box." The siblings looked at each other hesitantly.

"And?" Soren prompted them.

"He said a dog was carrying it."

"A dog?"

"Large dog, big jowls, short hair, black. No ears and no tail."

Soren frowned. "A dog with no ears and no tail?"

Calla's face twisted. "He said it looked like they'd been removed."

Men were disgusting animals. "He said this dog was carrying the box?"

She nodded.

"You believe him?"

No one has lied to us, Cohen said.

Cohen's read on people was absolute. Soren nodded. It was a dog then. But how had the blood vial been delivered to Salara's chamber? A dog wouldn't have been able to do that. So much remained unanswered. But they had a start.

"Find that dog," he told him. "And we'll find its master."

"Caspian Frey. Come forward."

Norah stood in the throne room filled with the nobles of Mercia. Her grandmother and the members of her newly formed council stood in front, watching the appointment of their new lord justice. It had been six weeks since she'd retaken her kingdom.

Six weeks since Alexander had died.

It felt even longer that she'd been without Mikael. She needed to get back to him. And this was the first step.

But all morning, she'd felt in a daze, like this reality wasn't real. Like she was there, but she wasn't. Why was it so hard? This was the right thing to do. It was the obvious thing to do. It's what would get her back to Mikael. And it was Caspian—a man she trusted with her life and her kingdom.

Caspian stepped forward, coming in front of her.

"Kneel," she told him.

He dropped to his knees and held out his hands, palms up, as Alexander had once knelt in front of her.

"Caspian Frey." Her voice broke as she spoke. "I appoint you..."

A knot formed in her throat. This shouldn't be this hard. It was the right decision. She had no doubt. She tried to start again. "I appoint you..."

Why couldn't she speak? Why couldn't she breathe?

"Norah," Caspian whispered as she stood frozen.

But she couldn't answer. She couldn't move.

"Norah," he whispered again, and she looked down and locked eyes with his. "I'm not here to replace him," he said softly. "I'm here to join him by your side." He nodded his reassurance, and she found herself nodding in return. The gods bless this man—the only man who could get her through this.

"I appoint you," she continued, "lord justice of Mercia"—those words were the hardest—"high commander, proxy of the queen, and protector of the North and her people."

The priest held a bowl of oil beside her, and she dipped her fingers into it. Slowly, she drew her fingertips along his palms, as she had done with Alexander. "May your hands be my hands."

As she ran her thumb across his lips, her hands shook. "May your words be my words."

She reached and scribed a line on his breastplate with her fingers, just above the winterhawk. The same winterhawk that had marked Alexander's breastplate. But she couldn't say the words.

Caspian reached up and covered her hand with his against his chest. "Take your time," he said quietly. "There's no hurry. Although"—he grimaced—"it would be unfortunate, at this point, if you were having second thoughts and would rather choose someone different."

She didn't know why she laughed. But she did. It helped curb the threatening tears. She shook her head. "No. No one different."

He let out a breath. "Good," he said, nodding. "I don't consider myself a prideful man, but having come this far, it would be slightly embarrassing."

She laughed again. This was the justice she needed. She squeezed his hand and pulled hers free, then finished her mark across his breastplate. "May your heart be my heart."

And it was done.

Norah smiled down at him, her eyes blurry. "Thank you, Caspian," she whispered, then, louder, "Rise, Lord Justice."

CHAPTER TWENTY-THREE

Snow fell heavily on the northern castle isle, but nothing could frost her spirits. Her heart beat happily at the thought of returning to Kharav. It would be a cold journey, but it didn't matter. She missed Mikael terribly.

As she swept her eyes around her, she stopped on Bhastian. He stood to the side of the rest of the Crest, in a slightly different stance.

She narrowed her eyes as she stepped in front of him. "There's something different about you."

The slight creases at the corners of his eyes gave away the hidden smile underneath his wrap. "Yes, Salara."

"He's been promoted to Captain of the Crest," Caspian said, coming up beside her.

She popped her mouth open with a big grin. "Bhastian!" She laughed and swept him into an embrace. "Congratulations!"

He bent stiffly to receive it, but he didn't embrace her back. He just gave an awkward bow of his head as she squeezed him. "Thank you, Salara."

She pulled back. Bhastian would be the perfect captain. She wrinkled her nose as she cut him another grin and turned and mounted Sephir.

"Are you ready?" Soren asked her after she'd settled in the saddle.

"I've been ready."

His eyes smiled. He was happy to be heading back too.

Catherine stood at the top of the stair. They'd said their emotional goodbyes inside. As regent again, her grandmother would look after Mercia in Norah's absence, with the support of the newly formed council. Norah gave her a final wave before they urged their mounts out of the gates and across the bridge.

They traveled lightly, with the Crest and the siblings. Caspian also joined them. He'd see Norah back to Kharav, then return to Mercia to help manage things with her grandmother. It was the first time he was returning to Kharav since the council's coup, and he seemed in good spirits. Serene came as well. Norah was surprised the maid had decided to return with her, but was thankful to have her company again, although she still painfully missed Vitalia.

When they reached the outskirts of the city, Norah urged Sephir into a gallop. She stretched forward, giving the mare her head to run. The icy wind brought tears to her eyes and froze them across her temples. She smiled. This was the feeling of freedom, the feeling of going home.

They rode until the sun dipped below the horizon, and just as Norah thought she might turn to ice, they stopped and made camp. Serene laid out bedrolls for them in their tent, and Soren laid out one for himself. When Mikael wasn't with her, Soren slept inside, not trusting her safety with anyone else while they traveled, especially considering the situation with Alexander.

"It's going to be a cold night," Serene said. "I hope it doesn't storm. I'll get more furs for us." She darted back out of the tent.

"I remember the last time we were caught in a storm while traveling," Soren said as he pulled off his weapons strap and sank down onto his bedroll. A deep chuckle rumbled from him. "The look of horror on your face when you woke."

She rolled her eyes, remembering as well—losing consciousness in the cold and waking in the ruins of Aviron not long after she'd first been captured by Mikael. "You were completely naked after being quite mean to me, let me remind you, and I was a proper lady. Of course I was mortified. How did you expect me to feel?"

His chuckle grew to a hearty laugh. "That was exactly how I expected you'd feel—or hoped, anyway."

"You were absolutely terrible."

He laughed again. She hadn't heard him laugh in a long time, and it was nice. It prompted her own smile.

"And I don't know what's funnier," he added, "remembering that look, or you thinking you were a proper lady."

Norah pursed her lips. "Yeah, well, looking back, if I'd been smarter, I would have pretended to enjoy it. That would have scatted you away."

"Well, you weren't smarter."

She scowled at him.

Serene returned with more furs. Soren shook one out over him and held up the corner. "Come on," he said to Norah, nodding to the space beside him. "Get in here. Even the Crest are tented and sleeping back-to-back."

It wasn't an unwelcome invitation, and she sidled up against the heat of his body as he pulled the furs over them. The warmth was nice. Quite nice. She might actually be able to get some sleep.

"If you start snoring..." he warned.

"I don't snore." *The nerve.* But she would get more comfortable. She accidentally kneed him while slipping off her boots, and he grunted—served him right. Then she stuck her freezing toes under the warmth of his calves, eliciting a growl.

"What about Serene?" she asked as she got settled. Serene would be cold, too, although she doubted her Mercian maid would be keen on cozying up to the Destroyer.

His lips thinned in irritation "Fine," he hissed. "Come on." Surprisingly, Serene sidled in on his opposite side, shimmying close. "Curse the North gods!" he spat. "Are all women's feet made of ice?"

Serene gave a giggle, and Norah smiled as she tucked her frigid fingers in the fold of his arm, drawing another snarl.

Despite the cold, sleep came quickly.

They rode for two weeks, stopping late into the night to make camp and rest. It warmed as they traveled south, and Caspian was grateful. The first few nights he thought he might freeze to death, but thoughts of seeing Tahla again warmed him. He wondered how she was and if she missed him. Surely, she knew what had happened, what had kept him away. He prayed she knew he'd find a way to return to her.

Evening came again. They set up camp in the low of the rocky hills. Caspian laid out his bedroll bedside Bhastian's. They were far enough south that the air wasn't freezing, but it was still cold, and while they didn't use the tents anymore, the warriors still slept back-to-back for warmth. He checked on the men taking watch, then took off his sword to settle in, but he paused when he saw the lord commander walking toward him. Bhastian moved to give them some space to speak privately.

The commander swept his eyes around the camp as he drew near, and when he reached Caspian, he stepped close—uncomfortably close. "We'll reach the Uru tomorrow," the commander said quietly. "But circumstances have changed since you last saw Tahla."

Caspian's pulse quickened. What did that mean? "Changed how?"

The lord commander let out a long sigh and pulled down his wrap. "This isn't my news to tell, but I don't want you caught unaware, and I need you to remember your duty." He clasped Caspian's shoulder. "You have a child, Caspian."

Caspian sucked in a breath. His mind swirled around him, and he swayed. A child. *A child.*

The commander's hand gripped his shoulder tighter. "I wanted to tell you sooner, but I needed your mind clear in the North."

His mind clear. Yes, this would have certainly muddied it. As it did now. *A child.* "Does Norah know?" he asked finally, his voice barely a whisper.

"She knows of the babe, but not that it's yours. No one knows. Tahla hasn't shared who the father is, but she was heavy with child when we last passed through."

He couldn't imagine Tahla with child. "And you're sure it's mine?"

The commander's eyes blazed with anger. "Who else's would it be, you dumb fuck?"

"No, that's not..." He didn't mean it like that. "I want it to be my child." It would crush him if it weren't his. "I want it to be mine."

The commander settled and finally nodded. "Well, I'm telling you because you need to remember your duty. You're lord justice now. Salara needs you more than ever. Take tonight before we get there. Steep your mind in it, figure out a way to manage yourself."

Caspian nodded.

The commander cuffed him on the shoulder and left him alone in the dark.

The night passed without bringing sleep. Caspian didn't know if he was warm or cold, happy or sad. Did Tahla want a child? Surely this made her life harder now. It would make things between them harder. Would she deny him still?

Caspian rose well before the sun, while the rest of the warriors slept. He joined Kiran, who stood watch.

"Can't sleep?" the warrior asked.

Caspian smiled weakly. "Just a lot on my mind." He nodded back toward the camp. "Go get some rest before we leave. I'll take over."

Kiran nodded his thanks and headed to where the other men slept.

Caspian breathed in the sharp air. In a day's time, he would see Tahla. What would he say when he saw her? What would she say to him? The possibilities swirled around him—ones that made him smile, ones that gutted him. But deep inside, fear sprouted, and that fear gnawed at his soul.

Footfalls behind him made him turn. The lord commander approached. Caspian shifted his gaze back over the hills. He hadn't realized the sun had started to peek over the horizon.

"Did you sleep?" the commander asked.

He shook his head. "No."

"Is your mind right?"

What was *right*? Claiming the child? Loving it? Pretending it didn't exist for the sake of his duty? But he nodded.

The commander gripped the top of Caspian's breastplate and pulled him close. The dark pools of his eyes searched Caspian's. Weakness—he was looking for weakness. "Is your mind right?" he asked again.

Caspian would have to figure it out. And quickly. He nodded again. "Yes."

"Get something to eat," the commander said, releasing him. "We're leaving."

Before the sun had fully risen, they were on their way. Norah seemed in high spirits as she rode; no doubt excitement was coursing through her in returning home. Caspian was happy for her. She deserved it, especially after everything she'd been through.

After the endless day, the sun set too soon, and they reached the Uru. Caspian's heart pulsed in his chest. They dismounted, and he followed closely behind Norah into the village.

As they neared the center house, he almost stumbled as he caught sight of Tahla approaching. Behind her, an Urun woman followed holding a small bundle in her arms.

"Tahla!" Norah exclaimed.

The daughter of the chief smiled. "Salara."

Norah hurried forward in excitement. "Let me see!"

Tahla laughed as she turned to the woman who held the infant. She took the child from the woman's arms and held it to Norah. "His name is Katakah."

Caspian's chest tightened. Tahla had borne a son. He had a son. *Katakah.*

Norah smiled as she took the boy into her arms. "Hello, Katakah Otay," she cooed. Then she glanced up at Tahla. "He's got your eyes."

Tahla smiled. "Yes, he does. Come, let's get something for you to eat."

The words between the women blurred together. All Caspian could think about was the child. His child. He stepped forward but a hand gripped his arm, stopping him.

The lord commander. "You'll wait," the commander told him.

Caspian watched the women, his head spinning. Suddenly, Tahla's eyes locked with his. And she smiled. Then she turned and walked toward the center house with Norah.

He stood in a daze. He couldn't move, he couldn't breathe. The lord commander said something to him, but he didn't understand.

"Caspian," the lord commander's voice came more sternly.

Caspian looked at him.

"Settle the men and go to your accommodations."

He nodded.

"Are you well, Lord Justice?" Bhastian asked as Caspian walked back toward the men.

Lord Justice. Caspian had almost forgotten. He felt so unworthy of the name. So unworthy of the title Alexander had once held. Unworthy of the title of father. He nodded, but he wasn't well.

He never imagined himself a father. Of course, he had dreamed, but it was never a life he'd dared to expect. Most soldiers married. Lord justices married. But there was only one woman he wanted, and she was beyond his reach. Now he had a son. And while joy sprang from every fiber of his being, so did an overwhelming sadness. Would he be able to be a father to the boy? Would the child even know him?

He worked numbly through his duties. He found himself in the house the Uru had provided without remembering the activity. Had he done everything? Food had been left on the table, but he couldn't eat. He paced the room. Would Tahla come to him? Would she bring the boy? He had to see him.

Night came, and Tahla didn't. He finally sat on the edge of the bed. But he knew he wouldn't sleep.

A knock on the door made him jump to his feet, and he swung it open. Only it wasn't Tahla. His heart fell. It was the lord commander.

"Come with me," the commander said.

Caspian, his pulse racing, followed Soren through the darkness to a large house off the mainway. The commander opened the door, but he didn't enter. He only waited for Caspian to step inside, then closed it behind him, leaving Caspian alone in the house.

"Northman," Tahla's voice came, and he whirled to see her step from behind a hanging panel that separated the adjoining room.

She was more beautiful than the day he'd met her, if that was even possible. Her skin glowed in the candlelight like sparkling sands under the sun. Her dark hair hung long and wavy from its loosened braids.

Caspian couldn't speak. He could only step closer. He reached up and brushed her cheek with his fingertips, and she smiled as she brought her hand over his.

"Tahla," he whispered.

"After Salara fled the North, I feared I wouldn't see you again," she told him. "I thought something had happened to you. But Soren told me you lived, and I knew you'd come again." She held his hand and looked down at their entwined fingers. "I've missed you, Northman. And I'm glad you're here." She stepped closer. "We have so much to talk about. With the child."

With the child. She had to be considering their lives together now. Surely.

She gave a warm smile. "Do you want to see him?"

His heart stopped. Of course he wanted to see him. But he couldn't speak. All he could do was nod. She pulled his hand and led him behind the panel to the adjoining room. Inside sat a small crib with the sleeping child. His breath shook as he drew closer to look at him—he was the most beautiful thing he'd ever seen.

"Can I hold him?" he whispered.

"Of course."

Tahla reached into the crib and gently lifted the child without waking him. Ever so carefully, she placed him in Caspian's arms.

Caspian moved and sat down on the edge of the bed. He couldn't take his eyes from the boy. He drew the infant's small hand between his fingers—the skin was so soft and warm. He moved his fingertips to the roundness of his plump cheeks, grazing them lovingly. The child opened his eyes and let out a large yawn.

Caspian chuckled as tears came to his eyes. This was his child. His son.

"Katakah," Tahla said. "His name means golden light."

He chuckled again, looking at the boy's dark hair and brown eyes now staring back up at him. "I don't think there's any gold about him."

"He's filled with it. From his father."

Caspian looked up at her. This woman in front him, his child in his arms—never had his heart felt so full. He stood and stepped to her, holding the child between them. "Tahla," he said softly as he reached his hand and pulled them together. "Marry me. I know I'm not worthy, but I would be a good husband, a good father."

But sadness filled her eyes. "Caspian." The way his name sat on her lips crushed him. "No one is more worthy," she said. "But it's not about being worthy."

She took the child back and gently laid him in his crib, and Katakah promptly closed his eyes and fell back asleep.

"I can't," she said.

It was as he feared. "Why?" His voice broke to match his heart.

Tahla sat on the edge of the bed and pulled him down beside her. She smiled, but there were tears in her eyes.

"Are you betrothed to another?" he asked.

She shook her head. "No, of course not."

"Then why?"

"You know why. I will be chieftess. I belong to the Uru, and so must Katakah. And you belong to Salara and the North. We can't pull each other from our duties."

"I would never pull you away from the Uru, nor will I abandon Salara. I only want to know you as my wife, and for my son to know his father."

"Katakah will be chief one day. I can't have him torn between the North and the Uru."

What did that mean? "So you would keep him from his father altogether?"

"There will be strong men in his life. My father. Salar. Soren." She looked at him. "And you—lord justice of the North, a role model for any man. But I want him to know he is Urun, and only Urun, and his duty is to the Urun people."

Caspian's heart shattered. He watched the sleeping child—he already loved him. He would give his own life for him, betray everything for him, and for Tahla, which meant she was right. Blood ties weakened the pull of duty. They already weakened his own, and he didn't want that for his son. He didn't want that for Tahla. "I respect your wishes," he said finally. "But I want to be a part of his life as much as I can."

"I want you to as well. But as Caspian, lord justice. Not Caspian, his father."

It wasn't enough. But it would have to be.

She curved her hand around the back of his neck and pulled him close. "Will you stay with me tonight, Northman?" She ran her fingers up the back of his head and threaded them into his hair. "I've missed you."

"Is this how we're to be, then? Together but forever apart?"

"Or just together, as fate allows." Her eyes drew him in and held him. "Kiss me, Northman."

He couldn't deny her his love, and he lowered his mouth to hers.

CHAPTER TWENTY-FOUR

The Canyonlands—a dark and twisted labyrinth of rock and trench that swallowed men caught unaware—marked the entry to Kharav. Many had died in these folds of earth, lost and abandoned or picked off from the top ridges by those who called Kharav home. Norah followed Soren through. It would take many more times before she knew the way, but she floated through the arms of darkness with a joy building in her heart. On the other side, Mikael would be waiting.

They emerged from the Canyonlands and made their way up the ridge to where the breathtaking scape of rice terraces rolled as far as the eye could see. In a month or two, they'd be steeped in snow, creating a whole new magical world. Winter was almost to Kharav, bringing frosted mornings and light afternoon snows that melted as they touched the ground. Norah hated winter, but in Kharav, it didn't matter. She loved all seasons here. Gods, she missed this place.

They reached the capital city of Ashan the following day. She hadn't slept at all the night before, and her stomach tumbled as they rode through the gates. The city bustled with a familiarity that she'd missed. The wind brought smells of home, and when she saw the castle, her heart leapt. This was where she belonged.

"You'll tell him?" Soren said, pushing his destrier up beside hers as they rode.

It was the one thing she wasn't looking forward to. She nodded. "Yes, I'll tell him what we saw in the painting."

"And about the blood. And the visions."

Right. "Of course." That would be equally as difficult.

When they reached the courtyard, Mikael was waiting. Before she even fully came to a stop, he was beside her, reaching up and bringing his hands to her sides to ease her down from the mare. He kissed her, deeply.

When he pulled back, he still held her tightly. "I only received your letter a few days ago that you were returning. I almost came to meet you partway. You should have stayed in the North." He glanced at Soren, clearly displeased at him for bringing her back. Then he looked down to her. "It's safer for you there."

"Don't look at him like that," she chided. "I wanted to come home. I'll be apart from you only in dire circumstances, and now with Aleon and Osan, things are no longer dire."

"We don't hold a formal alliance with Aleon. There's still risk."

"Not enough to keep me from you. Say what you want. I've never been so happy to be home, and I'm *not* leaving."

He held her cheek in his palm. "I don't want you to leave," he said softly.

Her smile widened. "Then take me inside, husband."

Mikael swept her up in his arms and carried her into the castle. The feel of his body drew a new wave of longing through her, and she spread her hand against the hardness of his chest. Too long it had been, and she needed him. But there was so much she needed to tell him first.

"Salar," a voice called from behind them, and she looked over Mikael's shoulder to see a messenger approaching.

"No," Mikael called out to the messenger, not turning, not slowing his step.

Wait... "What if it's important?" she pressed, as much as she hated to. She had her own important things to tell him.

"It's not," he said firmly, and continued to their chamber.

"How do you know?"

He carried her inside and kicked the door closed behind them. Setting her down, he still held her close. "Nothing else is important right now."

She raised a brow. "What if Rael is marching against us again?"

From around her waist, his hands ran up her back and then down again, curving around her buttocks through her riding gown as he walked her backward toward the bed. "It will take them some time to get here."

Gods, she missed this man. Perhaps her own important things could wait just a little longer. "They could be at our gates," she warned playfully.

He didn't stop his movement toward the bed. "Did you see them when you came through?"

She bit her bottom lip and shook her head.

"Then we have some time yet." His voice came lower now. "Kiss me before I go to battle."

Hunger radiated off him, and the muscle tightened under his skin, but before they reached the bed, she put a hand on his chest to still him. "I need to clean up." And calm things down to tell him about the visions of Alexander.

He slowed but didn't stop. "I'm not waiting."

"Mikael, I'm so dirty."

"Then we'll both be dirty." They reached the bed, and he pushed her back onto it with his frame, but his arms supported her, and he lowered her gently to the furs.

"I smell like... I've been on a horse for weeks—"

"I like horses." He lowered himself over her.

Norah couldn't help a laugh. He moved his hips between her thighs.

"I need to talk to you," she said.

"After."

The air changed, and she quieted. The dark pools of his eyes traced her face, moving from her eyes to her hair, then back down to her lips.

He was quiet.

And then he wasn't.

An urgency came to him, and he reached underneath her skirts. Need trembled through him. She shifted her weight, helping him free her of the riding breeches and undergarments. Mikael stripped them both of everything that kept their skin from touching, everything that kept them apart. Grasping, pulling, tearing. He moved with a feral need, violent but not hurtful, and they became one as he sank inside her.

A calm returned, and he stilled. He buried his face into her neck, and the heat of his breath licked her skin. As they lay quietly, he trailed kisses along her jaw.

Her eyes narrowed. "You'd better not be finished."

He chuckled. "No," he said softly. His flesh pulsed inside her, hard and thick, offering proof. He lifted himself to look at her again, and his eyes shone bright, but there was a seriousness to them. "I just needed to be close to you right now."

She tightened her thighs around him. "Is this close enough?"

But he shook his head slowly. "Nothing with you is ever enough."

Norah reached up and softly scored her fingertips through the short cut of his beard. "I've missed you," she whispered. She had missed everything about him—his touch, his voice, his love, the way he needed her.

"I've missed you too." And he lowered himself back to her waiting lips.

Morning brought the sun, and Norah walked to the dining hall. Mikael had left early to see what unimportant news the messenger from the day before had delivered. It gave her a moment to get her thoughts in order. She reached her hand inside the pocket of her gown and clutched the small vial. She'd show it to Mikael today. Or maybe she shouldn't. Maybe she should just tell him about it, and not show him. What if he told her to call Alexander? What if he wanted to see for himself? Would it work this far from Mercia? It had been a month since she'd received the vial and had last seen Alexander. Would it work at all? Or would its power fade with time? It wasn't like normal blood—it didn't clot or separate. Perhaps something had been mixed with it. Or perhaps it wasn't normal blood. She mocked herself. Obviously it wasn't normal blood.

Soren fell into step beside her, and she jerked her hand from her pocket.

"Did you tell him?" he asked.

About the visions. She glanced at him out of the corner of her eye as she kept walking. "Not yet."

His eyes burned into her, but she avoided them. "Why not?" he demanded.

She pursed her lips. "It wasn't the right time."

"What do you mean 'it wasn't the right time'?"

"Not while we're getting reacquainted."

"You had all night."

She didn't have the energy for this. "I said not while we're getting reacquainted."

He grimaced. "You rutted all night?"

"Soren!" She stopped abruptly and smacked his arm. "Do you have to be so foul? And that's none of your business."

The corners of his lips turned up slightly. "Are you going to tell me you're a proper lady again?"

She scowled at him. "I hate you."

"I don't believe that."

Gods help her.

They reached the dining hall, and Soren stopped at the door. She'd almost forgotten. In Kharav, he respected the mornings as Salara-Mae's time and didn't eat breakfast with them. With Catherine's tolerance in Mercia, Norah had grown used to sharing nearly every meal with him over the past several months. Being without him now seemed... amiss. She'd have to talk to Salara-Mae, but one thing at a time.

"You have to tell him," he pressed.

"I will. Today."

He gave a short nod, doubt still filling his eyes, and then left her at the door. She stepped inside and moved to the table where Salara-Mae sat sipping her morning tea.

Norah took her place at the end.

Mikael's mother set down her cup and smiled at her. It was the most warmth she had ever shown. "It's good to have you back."

Norah smiled back at her. "It's good to be home." The woman seemed in high spirits. Maybe now *was* a good time to talk about Soren. "Salara-Mae, there's something I'd like to talk to you about."

The woman gave an agreeable lift to her brow.

Mikael entered and stopped by her chair. He gently clasped under her jaw and pulled her lips up as he leaned down to kiss her. His kiss was hungry and left her completely forgetting her train of thought. She blushed as they broke, all too aware of his mother's nearness. But Salara-Mae said nothing. She took another drink of her tea as if she hadn't even noticed. Norah smiled at him with chastising eyes, and he moved to take his seat at the opposite end.

What had she been thinking about? *Oh right*—Soren at breakfast, but she didn't want to have that conversation in front of Mikael.

"Maybe we could resume our walks after breakfast again, this morning even, if you'd like," she said, picking back up her conversation with Mikael's mother.

Salara-Mae nodded. "I would like that, although I can't this morning, I have new gown fittings." She took another sip of her tea. "You should come; you need more gowns yourself."

Absolutely not. "Oh... uh, no, I can't, I—"

"You were just going to go for a walk."

Damn. She wasn't getting out of this one.

Norah glanced at Mikael, and he smiled at her. She sighed. Well, she wasn't making any progress on either of her tasks at the moment: talking to Mikael or getting Soren back to the table. Time spent in dress fittings wouldn't get her any further, and time with Salara-Mae meant time away from Mikael. Later, she promised herself.

"What news came yesterday?" she asked Mikael, remembering the messenger.

He swallowed his bite of food and took a drink. "There are rumors that the alliance between Gregor and Cyrus is weakening."

"What?" That was great news. "Are you sure?"

"One is never sure of gossip. But it appears Rael is focused on Kharav, and Japheth on Aleon."

"It would explain why Gregor didn't join Cyrus when Rael moved against you." She frowned. "But they're bickering over who to go to war with? Surely now they know Aleon, Mercia, and Kharav stand together, so what would it matter? And, if anything, the threat should strengthen their alliance."

He nodded. "As I said, one can never be sure of gossip." He took another drink from his cup. "I would like you to come with me to Salta Tau. Tonight."

Salta Tau was the ink mastera who marked the stories on his skin. "Oh," she breathed. His comment caught her by surprise.

"For the story of taking the North," he said.

Taking the North. The idea knifed her and left her breathless—it hurt. Why? Of course he'd want to get the markings of victory for taking Mercia, and why shouldn't he?

Because it wasn't an accomplishment. It wasn't something to celebrate. Having to march against her own kingdom was a great tragedy, and with everything she'd lost in the process... for him to want it proudly displayed on his skin felt like a slap in the face.

She couldn't speak. She only found herself nodding, but why? Why was she nodding? She didn't want to see the markings. She didn't want them on his skin. Forever. But after everything he'd done for her, she couldn't bring herself to tell him not to.

He rose from the table and stopped beside her, leaning down to kiss her as he had done when he arrived. "I'll see you this evening."

"This evening," she echoed blankly.

Salara-Mae stood as well. "Be at my chamber within the hour. I'll have the seamstresses ready a fitting space for you." Then she whisked out of the room, leaving Norah to herself.

Norah sat at the table in silence. She tried to shake off the misgiving growing in her stomach. Don't be ridiculous, she scolded herself. Why shouldn't Mikael be proud? It was a significant feat to take back Mercia from the council, which had been defended by some of the most renowned mercenaries in the world, and it was to put her back on the throne. But no matter how logical she made it sound to herself, she still couldn't shake the emotion against it.

She pushed a breath out. She still needed to tell him of the visions—that his fate still remained—and how Alexander had come to her. In Mercia, she'd been desperate to tell him, to have him help her make sense of it all, but now it seemed an impossible task. Why was it so hard?

Because she'd loved Alexander.

A dress fitting was the opposite of what she wanted to be doing right now. She leaned forward against the table and rested her cheek against her palm. There was really no avoiding it. She stood and headed to Salara-Mae's chamber.

As she walked down the hall, she spotted Katya outside through the glass. A woman stood beside her, holding a small child. Norah's heart beat with happiness. Of course Katya would have had her baby by now. She made her way quickly to the doors at the end and out to catch them.

"Katya!" she called as she approached.

"Salara," Katya bowed her head in greeting.

"Is this your little one?"

Katya nodded. "Yes. I'm sorry, Salara. My mother only brought him by to say hello."

"Don't be sorry! I'm so happy to see you." She stepped closer to the child.

Katya smiled as she presented him. "My son, Araseth. And my mother, Delina."

"Lovely to meet you," Norah told the older woman, who smiled with a bow of her head. Then she turned her attention to the boy. He was a plump child with a full head of black hair. But his eyes were a deep cerulean blue. A Northman's eyes, no doubt. "Katya. He's beautiful."

The captain's smile grew. "That he is." She looked to the ground, her smile fading and her pain showing through. "His father fell taking back Mercia."

Norah reached out and clasped her arm. "Oh, Katya, I'm so sorry." Norah knew loss, yes, but to lose the father of a child, she couldn't imagine. To raise a child alone... Then she remembered: "Katya, Mercia grants provisions for children of fallen heroes. If you only record the child—"

"No," Katya said quickly. "I know that Kharav and the North view intimacy and marriage differently. And a child out of wedlock... I won't dishonor his father's legacy."

Norah stared at her, speechless. Then she shook her head. "You know what, it's perfectly fine. You don't even need to record the child. I'll make sure—"

"No, Salara. Really. I want for nothing here. I have everything I need."

Norah's heart broke. She wanted to do more, to offer more, but Katya would refuse, she knew. She nodded. "All right. Well, if there's ever anything..."

"I'll let you know."

Norah nodded again. "Well, bring Araseth to the castle anytime. It would be wonderful to have a child around."

Katya's smile returned. "You're too kind, Salara."

Norah meant every word.

Chapter Twenty-Five

It was late afternoon before Norah could escape to her chamber. She sat at her vanity, staring at her own image, yet her mind wasn't on herself. Her stomach twisted. She still hadn't told Mikael his fate remained. Or that Alexander had come to her with the blood. She needed to. It was important. But their brief time alone together had been spent in each other's arms—poor timing to share this news.

And now the evening ahead would be special for Mikael; she couldn't tell him tonight. *Tomorrow.* It would have to be tomorrow.

Soren would be furious.

Her mind turned to the evening ahead—something else that turned her stomach—when Mikael would get his markings for taking Mercia.

For her, taking back Mercia was the correction of a great wrong, but still the stain remained, and the loss suffered in doing so made her question if it was even worth it. But for Mikael, it was an accomplishment. He'd always wanted to take Mercia, and while it had been in a different form and under very different circumstances, he'd finally done it. It was now a significant part of his story—his story that she would have to look at every day, and be reminded of...

No, she didn't have to look at it. She wouldn't look at it.

What if it was on his neck? Or on his face? She groaned to herself. Did Kharavian warriors mark their faces? Master archers bore fletching-patterned marks on their bow-side eye. Other than that, she hadn't seen any others—which was a small relief, but one that brought little comfort. This would be Mikael's greatest accomplishment, and surely it would be bold and prominent across his body.

Norah moved her gaze over her reflection. She wore a gown the color of night, the color of Kharav. And right now, it was the color of her heart.

"Are you all right?" Mikael asked, coming up behind her.

She gave a small start; she hadn't realized he'd come in. Her eyes met his in the mirror, and she nodded. Why did she nod? Of course she wasn't all right. She should just say something. But she couldn't. It was only a marking. She should let him have it—for all he had done for her, and all he had done for Mercia.

"Are you ready?" he asked.

No. She nodded again and rose.

Mikael took her hand, and they walked through the castle, into the courtyard, and across the gardens to the temple of Salta Tau.

It was just as she remembered from the last time she'd been there, when Mikael had gotten the marking of her crown.

The crown that she'd lost.

The crown that was now hidden in its velvet box in her vanity drawer.

They walked a series of halls back to a large open chamber. Salara-Mae and Soren were already there, just as they had been before. They stood on opposite sides of the chamber from each other, as they had before.

Salta Tau stood in the room's center, wearing a cream linen gown and her hair pulled back in a braid. She bowed as they drew near. "Salar. Salara."

"Salta Tau," Mikael replied, and both he and Norah bowed their heads in return.

The old woman spoke in the Kharavian tongue, which Norah understood now. "What do you seek to record?" Her voice was gravelly from age, but there was a smoothness to it still.

Norah cursed herself silently. She should have said something, told him how she felt about the marking. Now it was too late.

"I come for the story of taking the North," Mikael said.

Norah hated those words—*taking the North*.

Salta Tau took Mikael's hands before closing her eyes and speaking her spell into the air. She swayed in her chant, her voice drifting in and out, echoing through the chamber. Then she stopped. The old woman opened her eyes and stood for a moment, silent, looking forward but at nothing in particular.

What did she see?

Salta Tau's words made Norah freeze. "The story of the North, it brings you sorrow," she said to Mikael in the Kharavian tongue.

Sorrow? Not pride? Not accomplishment? But sorrow?

Mikael nodded.

The old woman frowned. "And you still want this story on your skin?"

He looked at Norah, then back to Salta Tau. "I do."

Norah's eyes welled. He wasn't celebrating Mercia. He felt her loss with her. Even in his triumph, even in the happiness of having believed he'd changed his fate, he felt sorrow.

Salta Tau motioned for him to lie down on the mat.

No. No, *no*. He couldn't do this. "Wait!" she cried.

Mikael's brows drew together as he shifted his weight back. "What?"

"You wouldn't feel sorrow if you knew the truth." Her words came before they could stop them. "Alexander's not gone, and your fate's still unchanged. I saw it."

Salara-Mae covered her mouth with her hand.

A line spread deep across his brow. "What do you mean? My fate? You saw it?"

"Samuel painted it again. It hasn't changed." She shook her head. "Mikael, I'm sorry. I've been trying to tell you, but…"

"The Bear is dead."

Norah winced. "Yes. And no."

"What do you mean *no*?" Then his stare shifted from confusion to anger. "You saw this in the North? Why didn't you send word?"

"Because… I needed to tell you in person."

"But you didn't."

Norah cursed herself for it not being the first words off her lips when she saw him. She looked at Soren, and he gave a small nod of encouragement for her to tell him the rest.

Mikael twisted his head toward him. "You knew about this?"

"Don't blame Soren," she said quickly. "I told him I would tell you. I should have already, but I was waiting for the right time."

"Now would be the right time." His words simmered in anger.

The right time would have been sooner. This was a very wrong time, but she had no choice. She drew in a breath. "He's shown himself to me. Even after death. Visions, or his spirit, I don't know how to explain it, but he comes to me."

"The Bear is dead," he said again.

"I know, which is why I said I can't explain it."

His nostrils flared, and light caught the white of his teeth between his partially parted lips. "Who else has seen him?"

"He's come only to me."

The darks of his eyes were the darkest they'd ever been.

"Tell him how," said Soren.

She tried to swallow the growing lump in her throat. Her hand shook as she reached into her pocket and pulled out the blood vial. She felt Soren's searing gaze, but she didn't look at him. He hadn't known she had more. "I receive these," she told Mikael as she held it out for him. "When the blood touches my skin, he comes to me."

Mikael took the vial from her hand, looking at it closely. He was calm now. Too calm—the calm that came when he shifted to battle. "And you invite him?" he asked. "You call him to you?"

The perception was damning. "I'm trying to find out what's going on."

"And have you?"

She glanced at the floor. Of course she hadn't.

"What does he tell you?"

"He can't speak in the vision. But he finds other ways to show me he's real." She swallowed again and paused. "When he came to me in my mind, he gave me a gift. My mother's crown." She glanced at Soren. "The next day, it arrived at the castle."

The corners of Mikael's eyes creased, and he glanced down at its image on his chest. Then he looked back at Norah.

"He found it," she said.

"Or had it all along," Soren added.

"Alexander wouldn't have done that," she argued. "He wouldn't have kept it from me."

"It's not Alexander," Soren countered.

Norah reached out and clasped Mikael's hand. He had to believe her.

"Mikael, it *is* Alexander I see. Everything about him, every detail of things only he would know." *The shell bracelet.* "Things only *I* would know."

"You should have made them things I know," he said. He was angry, and he had every right to be. Still, his cold gaze crushed her. He pulled his hand from hers, then turned and strode from the room.

Norah stood in silence as Salara-Mae followed her son. She couldn't bring herself to look at Soren, who stood for a moment, then left as well.

Only Salta Tau remained. She stared at Norah, but not with eyes of judgment.

Norah glanced around the empty chamber, trying to keep herself together. Then to Salta Tau, she said, "I think I'm just going to sit here awhile," she whispered. "If that's okay."

The old woman bowed and left her to the cold of the empty room.

It was morning. Norah sat on the edge of the bed. Mikael hadn't returned to their chamber through the night. She didn't fault him. He'd been hit with two blows: The first was the false relief his fate had changed. To be struck with its truth again would surely be defeating. Second, Mikael thought himself free of Alexander. He would see him as a threat again, both to his crown and her heart. And she had willingly called Alexander back to her. Even with her pure intentions, she couldn't deny it looked damning.

The creak of the door opening made her look up, and Mikael stepped inside. She hadn't expected him to come, not so soon, not now, but she was glad he had. They could talk it out now, she could try to explain. She rose, her heart pounding in her ears.

He stepped toward her.

"Mikael, I—"

"Don't." He stood in front of her, the pools of his eyes dark and drowning.

Norah pulled her bottom lip between her teeth. She was desperate to set things right between them.

He pulled off his tunic, and she stepped back slightly. What was he doing? Her breath left her as she saw a wrap around his torso just under his chest—the kind of wrap one gets after visiting Salta Tau. Slowly, he removed the side pins and rolled back the linen strip that held the pads of healing mixture over the marking.

And she saw it.

It wasn't as she had imagined Salta Tau's marking would be. *Taking the North*, Mikael had called it. She'd expected a broken banner, perhaps a falling winterhawk or a castle in ruin. Not the glorious bird with wings spread wide against the sun. Mikael's sun. The same as the one on his shoulder. It was beautiful, so bold against his skin.

"You got it anyway?" she whispered.

"Nothing you've said makes me feel differently." He stepped closer to her and brought his hand to her face. "I don't know what's happening right now, or what you're seeing, but I know I sealed in the sarcophagus the body of the Bear—a great warrior, a man the North needs and lost. I saw a great kingdom taken from her queen, and that brings me sadness. All of it. Sadness for the North." He tipped her chin up. "Sadness for you. But we've set things right, you and I. And now we're the strongest we've ever been. Together. So yes, I got the marking."

He reached into his pocket and pulled out the vial he'd taken from her.

Her heart stopped.

It was empty.

Why was it empty?

"What have you done?" she breathed.

He held it out for her. "He didn't come."

Her eyes dropped in a long blink as she curled her hand around the vial. He had used it. But Alexander hadn't come. Relief washed over her. Then that relief turned to anger, and her eyes blazed back open.

"It wasn't meant for you," she snapped.

The shadow under his brow grew. "You're angry at *me*?"

Was he serious? "To have taken the liberty, yes! To give no thought of what this means to me."

"What this means to you?" His own voice was laced with anger now.

"You *know* what Alexander means to me!"

"So you wanted for me to just accept this?"

"I don't know!" she cried. "I wanted you not to have used it! So readily, without even speaking to me about it, and on top of that, to have no regard for yourself!"

"What am I to fear for myself?"

Gods, this man was an idiot sometimes. "I don't know what his power is. I don't know what he's capable of."

"Yet you call him to you?" he challenged.

"Because he's not here to harm me."

"You don't know that."

"No!" She pushed him back from her. "*You* don't know!" A tear escaped down her cheek, and her voice dropped to a whisper. "You don't understand." He wasn't even trying to understand.

Norah shouldered past him, out of the room, taking the empty vial with her.

CHAPTER TWENTY-SIX

Norah finished scanning the letter Soren had given her—a letter from Aleon. Communications flowed freely now between the two kingdoms. Phillip wrote to Soren directly even, sending him scout updates and military reports. In return, Soren sent information their own armies had collected on Japheth and Rael.

Mikael remained wary of the empire, as she expected, but he also realized the value of friendship between the kingdoms. He hadn't been happy about her attending Phillip's wedding, feeling it had been too great a risk, but it had been a risk she'd had to take. These Shadowmen might know war, but they didn't know the art of diplomacy, the power of politics.

She held the letter out for Mikael. A tension still hung between them. He'd apologized after their argument, and so had she, but the weight, the heaviness, of the circumstance lingered.

Norah watched him as he read the letter, and he nodded.

"It's not a surprise," he said.

Rael's forces were heavy in number and just inside Japheth's border, no doubt preparing to launch a joint attack. Following the rumors, if there *had* been a rift between the two kingdoms, clearly it wasn't enough to dissolve their pact.

"You don't find the numbers surprising?" she asked.

"We know slaves have been flocking to the army of Rael for months, from all kingdoms. Their numbers will continue to grow." He turned to Soren. "You'll go to Aleon, devise our joint strategy."

Soren shifted uneasily. "You need me in Kharav."

"No." Mikael shook his head. "I need you to figure out how to win this war when it comes." He handed the letter back to Norah and leaned to kiss her on the cheek. His eyes were somber. "I'll see you tonight."

She nodded. Then he left them to the quiet of the room.

"Did you put him up to this?" Soren asked after he'd gone, pulling her attention.

"Up to what?"

"Sending me to Aleon?"

"No, of course not." She didn't entirely trust that Soren wouldn't still try to kill Phillip. While it did seem like something she would do—creating opportunity for a budding relationship—there was no budding relationship. Soren learning that Phillip was the man in his vision had severely affected him, hurt him even, and he was still angry. She knew he felt like Phillip had taken something from him. Now she worried he might take something from Phillip. Like his life.

"You have to talk to him," he pressed. "I can't leave Kharav. I have matters to tend here. I have things to look after."

"You mean me?"

He stilled.

"Soren, you've done a fine job looking after me ever since... well, ever since I met you, but you're lord commander. You have to get back to...

lord commanding. War is coming. I don't want you to have to go to Aleon—I know what it means for you. But Mikael's right, we need you to go. I'll send word for Caspian to meet you there, and after you confer with him and Phillip, you'll decide our collective approach."

The muscle along his temple tightened. "You assume the Aleon king will follow my plan."

"I assume he'll appreciate the counsel of a renowned commander and will want a unified effort." As they all did.

"I can determine that from here."

"I also want you to determine how to better fortify Aleon. That you can't do from here."

"That's the responsibility of his own commander," he argued.

"Soren. You know your value. This is a completely appropriate duty."

He sighed. "Fine. I'll go. Just don't do anything stupid while I'm gone."

She narrowed her eyes. "When have I ever done anything stupid?"

Aleon was as Soren remembered—glorious, beautiful, welcoming.

Complete shit.

He wrestled with his mind the whole journey from Kharav. Memories of what the seer had shown him haunted his thoughts. Shame still hung around him, for the nameless face he'd thought about so often. But it was nameless no more, and he had to see things for what they were. This king had become an informal ally of the North and Kharav, that was true.

But he was not a friend.

In the Great War, the Aleon king had given the North King the forces to take Bahoul—the battle in which Kharav had lost its mountain stronghold and Soren had lost his family. And even if this king hadn't wielded the sword himself, he was still complicit, still to blame. He would continue to grow his empire, remaining an ally only so long as his and Salara's interests aligned. He couldn't be trusted, even if he *had* recently come to Mikael's aid when Rael moved against him.

Soren had made good time in traveling alone to Aleon's capital city of Valour, arriving even before the Northmen. He wanted to finish and return to Kharav as soon as possible. Return to... *looking after* Salara. That was what she had called it, but he wasn't only looking after her. Rael would move against Kharav soon, and he was needed at home. The faster he could finish with this Aleon king, the faster he could get back. It wasn't necessary to have traveled all this way. He knew what needed to be done; Norah could have sent a letter, giving the Aleon king instruction. He only needed to do as he was told. Soren ran his eyes over the brilliance of the mainway, its opulent splendor. This kingdom was built on pride. He hoped that pride wouldn't stand in his way.

People lined the street with his arrival, as they had done when he had come before with Salara. Only this time, they threw no flowers. Should he be offended? He almost chuckled. But they welcomed him with smiling faces. Like they knew him. Now that was *truly* offensive.

As he reached the citadel, the Aleon king was waiting, as he had been before. Was there nothing else for him to do? Did he just stare out his window waiting for visitors to arrive?

He was as Soren remembered him—bronze hair, messy, but in a perfect kind of way. He wore a stupid smile that made Soren want to gut him. But Soren was prepared this time. At least, he had thought he was prepared, but seeing Phillip struck something within, and a flash of anger swept through him. He pushed it down—he was here with a purpose, and he wouldn't let himself be distracted.

"Lord Commander," the king greeted as Soren slid down from his destrier. "I trust you journeyed well."

Journeyed unnecessarily. Diplomacy, Soren reminded himself. "Aleon King," he replied.

The king's smile widened, flashing a row of perfect teeth. "You're welcome to call me by my name. Phillip."

Soren would *not* be calling him by his name, and if this king was looking for reciprocation, he wouldn't get it. "Have the Northmen arrived?" Of course they hadn't.

"Not yet. But I received a message yesterday. They're yet another day or two out."

What was taking so long? Was Caspian fucking *walking*?

"I'll show you inside," the king said.

"I've seen inside." Soren knew what he meant, but he didn't want an escort.

"Then you'll act surprised."

Oh. Some wit, then. Soren narrowed his eyes.

Phillip's face still held a smile, was still friendly, only a little more serious now. Firm. The king turned and strode up the stairs to the castle.

Who did this man think he was? Did he think Soren would just follow? Like he could be commanded? Soren stood for a moment in his surprise. Curse this Aleon king. Then he pushed a snarl between his teeth and followed him inside.

The king looked over his shoulder as they entered. "I trust the chamber you stayed in before was suitable. I've had it prepared again."

It had been more than suitable—it had been excessive. It was the equivalent to the royal guest chambers in Kharav. "It's unnecessary." As were most things in Aleon. "Soldiers' quarters are suitable enough."

"I want your comfort."

Soren almost laughed. *Comfort*. This wasn't about comfort. It was a display of wealth and power.

They moved down a side hall to the guest chamber, where the king stopped in front of the door. "I'll send someone to make sure you have everything you need."

"I don't need anything." And he certainly didn't need someone else bothering him.

The king's expression changed, although not of annoyance, or frustration. His brow softened, and his lips parted slightly. "I am honored to host you again, Lord Commander."

His words felt... genuine, and the fight inside Soren ebbed slightly. But only for a moment.

"Please, settle in and make yourself comfortable." Then the king gave a friendly nod, left, and headed toward the main hall. Soren watched him go, his irritation returning. This man was infuriatingly pleasant.

Soren found his chamber to be as over-the-top as it had been before. An assortment of food sat on the table by the balcony door. Large windows let in the sight of the capital and all its beauty. He let himself fall back onto the bed. This was the bed he'd slept in during his last visit. It was ridiculous and overindulgent, so plush that he couldn't feel the frame underneath.

And he could easily sleep for a week.

Back in Kharav, he had thought about how he might recreate it, but he pushed it from his mind and forced himself up. That would have to wait. He wasn't here for his enjoyment. He looked around the room. *Settle*, Phillip had told him. There was nothing to settle. And he struck back out to explore things once again on his own.

Even with winter creeping in, the gardens of Kharav were beautiful. Their year-round green contrasted sharply against the light dusting of snow that now covered the earth. Norah sat on a bench between two topiaries, soaking in the false promise of warmth from the sun. She was grateful to not be in the North—she'd be bundled in layers and pausing by each fireplace in the castle every moment she got the chance.

And she was glad to be away from everything that reminded her of what she'd lost. Had it not been enough for fate to take her childhood, her memories, her parents? Everything she'd ever loved? Then to take Alexander from her too—a second time—was just cruel.

But just as much as she wanted to distance herself from the pain, she wanted to hang on—to not let go of any scrap of what she'd fought so hard to gain back. She wanted to cling to every piece of her shredded heart.

But Mikael didn't understand. He didn't know the pain of loss like this. He didn't know the fight to endure. He'd have her put Alexander behind her. But she couldn't. She wouldn't.

If there was something still remaining of him, she'd track it to the ends of the earth. If he was trying to speak to her, she'd listen.

She breathed in the cold winter air, then froze.

Her pulse quickened.

She hadn't even noticed the small white box on the end of the bench that was blending with the light layer of snow. Her hands shook as she placed it in her lap and opened the lid to what she knew she'd find inside—a vial of blood.

His legs burned. There were so many cursed stairs in this city. Soren grumbled as he cleared the last run of them to the top of a hill where there stood a temple larger than any he had ever seen. But he wasn't here for the temple—he'd come for the view. He ran his eyes over the city to the horizon. He would have given anything for this sight years ago in the height of the Great War. It was a sight he'd never dreamed he'd see. At least not in friendship. Still not in friendship, he reminded himself.

"And how are you finding Valour?" a voice called to his right. *The Aleon king.*

Did this man not relent? Could he not just leave him in peace until Caspian arrived? What did he want? Soren's honest opinion? *Doubtful.* He turned to look at him, and the king smiled.

"Well?" Phillip pressed, not even out of breath from walking up all the cursed stairs.

Fine. "Had I known there were no obstacles to your capital, I would have taken Aleon in the Great War."

The king chuckled. "You think you could have?"

Soren tightened his fist. The heat of challenge rose in his chest as he turned to him. "I know I could have."

Phillip raised a brow. "Gregor has tried with fervor and failed."

"Gregor's an idiot. He confronted your forces openly. Few armies can match your numbers."

The king stepped closer to him with an amused smile—a disarming smile, and Soren hated it.

"And what would you have done differently?" Phillip asked him.

"I would come in the night. Slaughter everyone in their sleep." He didn't use past tense. It wasn't a threat that had passed.

The king's smile fell. "Where's the honor in that?"

"There is no honor in war." Soren looked out across the city. "Rolling forestland surrounding the city, no walls, no barriers. So many places for an attacking army to hide, so many opportunities to create distraction—this is the perfect city to take by surprise. If only I had known. I could have brought your empire to the ground."

"You're quite confident."

Soren snorted. "I didn't name *myself* the Destroyer." He could tell his words troubled the king.

"Then why didn't you try to take Aleon?"

A great regret, now that he knew. "I expected more from an empire. A mistake on my part—Mercia was the goal, and I thought the path to victory was a direct one." Soren shook his head. "If only I had known. You were the North's weakness—they needed you. I could have just taken Aleon. Cut off the sword arm, cut off the ability to fight."

"They would have still been on the isle, behind their impenetrable walls, with their archers. What would you have done then?"

Soren shrugged. "Nothing. The starvation of winter would have finished them for me."

The king eyed him. "Why are you telling me this?"

"Because I've been tasked with a collective strategy, which means I must also look for the protection of Aleon."

"And you share with me the weakness of Mercia?"

"If you were a smart king, you would have already known this. In any regard, it's no longer true. The North's weakness is no longer Aleon. The North has Kharav. Salara has me."

A smile returned to the king's lips. "I would very much like to know... how does one *get* you, Lord Commander?"

The question caught Soren by surprise, but the answer was simple. Especially for this man. "One doesn't."

The king looked at him a moment, still smiling. "Well, as I've arranged with Norah and your king, you'll help determine our collective approach, so I look forward to your counsel."

Counsel. Soren snorted again. No, he would not simply give counsel. He would tell this king what he would do. And he would do it. There was so much to be done.

"Are you hungry?" Phillip asked.

He was practically starved. Soren hadn't eaten anything since the day before, but he had food in his chamber, where he'd rather be. Alone. "No."

"I am. We'll eat. Come." The king turned and headed down the steps toward the central castle.

Come? Soren watched him descend the stairs of the temple in disbelief. Had he just told him to *come*? Like a dog? So casual Phillip was, so smug in his confidence. Well, curse him. Curse the North gods. He hated this king. He hated this place. Perhaps he'd take Aleon after all. But he hadn't brought an army. Where were Caspian and his Northmen?

Curse everything. He stood as he stewed, his fists clenched. Then he sucked in a breath through his teeth and blew it out slowly.

There was nothing he could do.

Except follow after Phillip.

The dining hall was as he remembered—too big with too much... stuff. He wanted to break away, return to his chamber, but he was committed now. He had followed the king this far. He had followed *the Aleon king.* He clenched his teeth so tightly they ached. He should have left him to walk back on his own. Eat on his own. Fuck off on his own. Now it was too late.

Now he was here, expected to eat. Expected to show his face. He had shown his face to the Aleon king before. Why had he done that? He had felt... What had he felt? An obligation to Salara to smooth the tension, yes, but something more...

He had wanted to show his face.

It had been a mistake.

"What would you like?" the king asked as they neared the table being prepared by servants.

Blood.

"Anything you want," Phillip added, "I'll have it made for you."

Enough. He couldn't bear it any longer. "Do you expect me to be impressed? Bow at your feet in thanks?"

The king whirled around, stopping them both abruptly. He didn't match Soren in size, but he certainly met his challenge. "I do want you to be impressed. *Destroyer.*" His eyes locked with Soren's boldly, unafraid. More than unafraid. Angry. "I'm the king of Aleon. I've defeated those undefeated. When I kill the man that I'm ashamed to call my brother, I'll have the largest empire in the world, riches unmeasurable. But you're not impressed, are you? And I know you're the last man who will bow to me."

Soren bristled at the king's sudden anger. "But that's what you want, isn't it?" he snarled back. "And you'll carry on with your riches, pursuing your glory, as you continue to take, continue to conquer and build your empire, as will the next Aleon king after."

Phillip's shoulders fell, and a calm returned. His anger seemed to dissipate as quickly as it came. "No," he said softly. He walked to the chair at the table's end and leaned against it, as if he suddenly didn't have the strength to stand. "No," he said again. "I'll have no heir."

What? Soren could only stare at him.

The king sat down and motioned for Soren to take the chair at the other end. "Please."

Still Soren stood.

Phillip sighed. He waved to the servants waiting near the door, and they disappeared into an adjoining room. Then he said, "When I take my final rest, I'll give the empire to the people."

What?

"I've been planning it, setting in place the laws that will govern and those who will enforce them and carry out the will of the people through elected officials."

Soren didn't understand, or if he did, he didn't believe it. "Aleon will no longer have a king?"

Phillip motioned again to the chair at the end of the table. "Please."

Finally, Soren moved to it and sat.

"Men are not meant to be ruled." Phillip let out a long breath. "And power... power corrupts everything it touches. It's taken everything and everyone I love."

Soren didn't agree. Men needed the strength of a ruler. And not everyone with power was corrupt. Not Salara. Not Salar. But he didn't offer an argument. "What do you want, then?" he asked instead.

Phillip frowned, ever so slightly leaning back in his chair. "To structure Aleon for the future. And to kill Gregor." He paused. "After that, I don't know. Perhaps then I'll feel complete." He raised his eyes to Soren's. "Do you feel complete, Lord Commander?"

Of course he was complete. He had everything he could ever ask for. He had Salara, and Salar. But why did the question hit him so heavily?

Mercifully, the servants reappeared with trays of assorted meats and vegetables, redirecting their attention and rescuing him from answering. A large platter was laid to Soren's right, and his stomach growled at the heavenly smell of herbs and spices.

"I don't go after Gregor with the lust of power," Phillip said. "I go to avenge my younger brother."

Soren knew the history. As Phillips's father lay on his deathbed, he split the empire between his three sons. Gregor, the oldest, was furious, and killed his youngest brother, joining the kingdom of Hetahl with his own kingdom of Japheth. He had tried to take Aleon and the lesser kingdoms from Phillip, but Salara's father stood as his ally, and that had been the beginning of the Great War.

"Aston was fourteen," Phillip said, staring at his chalice, but Soren knew he was staring into his memories. "Fourteen when Gregor slit his throat. He was just a boy."

Soren had always hated Gregor. Crowns in general were not kind to those who wore them, especially the young. But he didn't feel pity. "My brother was twelve when he died," he said. "My sister, nine." He had never spoken about them. Not since it happened. Only Mikael knew, and Salara. The words on his lips brought back the rage long buried.

Phillip's face grimaced slightly, and he nodded. "So, you understand. You understand the need."

Soren's fingers tightened around the knife beside his plate. "I understand."

The king nodded again and picked up his chalice of wine. "Did you lose them in the war?"

Everything within Soren tightened and coiled to strike. "I lost them when you gave the North King an army to take Bahoul."

Phillip paused, then set his chalice down. His face paled. They locked in their stare, frozen. Then his eyes moved to Soren's grip on his knife.

"Is this why you're truly here?" Phillip challenged.

Soren didn't want to think about why he was truly here. He didn't want to think about his obligations, his duty. "Have you nothing to say for yourself?" he hissed.

The king sat, unmoving, and then shook his head. "I didn't know about your family, but that's not an excuse. The truth is I would've done whatever Aamon asked of me."

Aamon. The North King. Soren clutched the knife tighter.

"I'm sorry for your family. I am. But if you'd have me recant my course, I won't."

"You continue this charade of loyalty to the North." This fakery.

Phillip's brow dipped. "Charade?" He straightened. "My father didn't prepare me for the crown. I was never meant to wear it. He saw what Gregor was becoming, the evil inside him, and decided to split the empire in his final days. He thought he'd given me enough to stand on my own, with Aleon and the smaller kingdoms. But I had no idea how to be king." He swallowed as he looked down at his plate, then back to Soren. "Aston... Well, Gregor went for him first. He didn't even make it to his coronation. I would have fallen, too, if not for King Aamon."

Phillip paused, and a quiet fell over the room. "Aamon spent a lot of time in Aleon," he continued. "And I in Mercia. He looked after me, became like a second father. He taught me things I should've learned early on, but never did. I thought I was a man at the time, but I was just a boy. He stood by my side against Gregor. Aamon taught me how to survive, how to lead a kingdom. I know you've seen devastation at his hand, but he was a good king, and he made me the man—the king—I am today. And I'm loyal to him still."

Soren didn't want to believe him. "Then why didn't you help Salara when the council took her throne?"

Phillip clasped his hands in front of him and rested them on the table. "It's a great regret, one I'll always live with. I would have harbored her, protected her, kept her safe, but she fled to the Shadowlands before I'd even learned what had happened. And then I was torn. I couldn't march against Mercia. It felt so wrong."

"So you did nothing."

"And I regret that now." He drew in a long breath and let it out. "If I could go back, change the past, I would." He finally took a drink of his chalice. "The council wrote to me. They wanted to reestablish the alliance. They offered me her cousin's hand."

Of course they had. Soren would forever be grateful he'd been able to see them hang. "What did you say to them?"

"Nothing. I didn't respond. Evangeline's a child, for gods' sakes, and she wasn't Mercia's true queen. Of course I wouldn't have agreed to that. But I said nothing. It's the only time in my life I felt like a coward. And then Norah's letter came. She didn't even ask me for help, she only asked if I knew how the people she cared about fared." Phillip's eyes welled. "But I said nothing." His face twisted in self-loathing. "To this day, I'm ashamed. I'm grateful to your king for stepping up in my failing. Grateful to you."

The room grew quiet again, and Phillip straightened. His eyes met Soren's. "And I'm grateful you're here now, Lord Commander."

Soren shifted back in his chair. He knew lies when he saw them, but this king carried no lies. This was perhaps the realest anyone had ever been with him, other than Salara and Salar. And not under threat of death or pain. This king laid himself open, willingly, and Soren didn't know what to do with him.

Slowly, he reached up and pulled down the wrap from his face. Then he stabbed a chunk of meat with his knife and pulled it to his plate and took a bite.

Curse the North gods. The food was delicious.

CHAPTER TWENTY-SEVEN

Mikael stripped off his tunic. Yes, it was winter, but Salara had a fire lit in every room of the castle. For a North queen, she certainly liked the warmth. He stared at their bed for a moment, with its heaping mounds of quilts and furs. When he'd been alone, he'd only used a sheet. This woman would sweat him out of his own castle. It was a small price, though.

The truth was, he'd give anything to make her happy, would pay any price. He'd burn his castle to the ground for her.

Yet he was losing her.

He could feel it—this distance between them, her grief and her pain; she was spiraling further away from him. Even in death, the Bear had the power to take her from him, regardless of whether this ghost was real or not. And the more Mikael fought against it, the more he pushed her away.

She was the furthest from him she'd ever been, even when she was right beside him. Mikael had used the blood, and it had upset her. He'd tried to call the ghost to him, to see what Salara had seen. She had seen *something*.

The blood only needed to touch Salara's skin for her to call the Bear, Soren had said. Mikael had poured it into his hand and waited. But no one came. He felt nothing, saw nothing. He went so far as to smear it up his arms and across his chest. All of it.

"Show yourself!" he'd snarled.

But nothing came of it.

Except Salara's unraveling.

He hadn't meant to upset her; he hadn't meant to hurt her. She was right—he hadn't thought of what it would mean to her. In his anger, he hadn't thought at all. Perhaps he was too desperate to know what it meant for himself. If the Bear still remained, so did his fate.

Or perhaps he was jealous that she still clung to another man. She'd always protected the Bear from Mikael. She'd loved the Bear, and still did. And Mikael wasn't a fool. If this was the Bear, he knew he wouldn't be able to keep her from him.

But nor would he try to.

No. It was neither of those things.

He was angry, yes, but not because he feared his fate or sharing her love. He feared this vision was a trickster that meant to do Salara harm. He feared not being able to keep her safe, and it was an ever-increasing fear.

They still had no heir. They didn't talk about it anymore—he'd told her they'd manage without—but it was no less a concern. It still haunted the shadows of his mind.

After his death, Salara would have to fight to keep Kharav. This had always been known, but things had been different before. She'd had Soren, and the Bear, and a formal offer of alliance from Aleon to fall back on. She'd been safely behind the impenetrable walls of the North. Now the Bear was gone, and the Aleon king had wed. She was deep within a kingdom surrounded by a growing enemy, and the political powers within would not be ruled by an outsider. She still had Soren and had gained the loyalty of a few other Kharavian nobles, but it wasn't enough. She wouldn't be able to keep the crown. Not without a child.

But there would be no child.

That left her with only one other option—one Mikael wasn't sure he could convince her of.

CHAPTER TWENTY-EIGHT

The Northmen arrived with the sun, and Soren was waiting. The Aleon king stood beside him at the top of the citadel stairs. Bells had chimed in the castle, alerting the arrival through the main gates, and they'd gone out to meet them.

"I love this," Phillip said.

Soren wrinkled his brow and looked at the smiling king—such a peculiar man. Was he always this happy? But it wasn't entirely annoying.

Phillip tilted his head back in question. "Don't you enjoy people arriving?"

Soren grimaced. "No."

The king chuckled.

Why was that funny? Soren shifted his gaze back to the approaching Northmen, and they both took the stairs to the bottom.

Caspian brought his horse to a halt and slid down. "Lord Commander," he said with a small bow of his head.

"What took you so long?" Soren rumbled.

Caspian's brows drew together. "I came immediately once I got the message."

"Lord Justice," the king greeted.

Caspian shifted his attention to the Aleon king and bowed his head. "King Phillip."

"Welcome back to Aleon, and congratulations on your position."

"Thank you. I appreciate that. And it's good to be back."

"How is the queen regent?"

"Well," Caspian said. "Very much herself."

Phillip chuckled.

Soren held back the impatience growing in his chest. There was work to be done, and they were standing here chatting.

The king motioned for a servant. "Prato will show you to your chamber," he told Caspian. "Freshen up. Get something to eat, then meet us in my study. He'll show you the way."

"Thank you," Caspian said. He gave another nod to Soren and then followed the servant to his chambers.

Phillip turned to Soren. "Shall we?"

Finally. "Lead the way," he replied irritably.

Soren followed the king down a series of halls. They reached a back study, and his eyes widened as he caught sight of a large table map of Aleon and the lands beyond. He stepped slowly to the table and ran his hands along the smooth edging of polished wood. Now this—this was a work of art. Kharav was exhaustive in planning, and Soren considered his own maps to be some of the best in the world, but this in front of him... he could only admire. The line topography was meticulous. Moveable figures in polished iron marked the placement of forces, both those of Aleon and of Mercia, as well as those of Japheth and Rael. And this Aleon king was well informed.

"Does it meet your expectations?" Phillip asked him.

Soren glanced at him, and the king smiled. Distractingly so. Soren forced his eyes back to the table. "It isn't disappointing."

He set his mind on the task at hand, staring at the figures of enemy forces along the inside border of Japheth. Rael would likely make the first move, and there were two options. Cyrus could advance north against Eilor, the southernmost kingdom of the Aleon Empire. This was the least-favored option to Soren, as Kharavian forces would have to give up the advantage of the Canyonlands to join the battle. But Soren had a hunch: Gregor wanted Aleon, and Cyrus wanted Kharav—they would attack Kharav. Rael was the more powerful force, Gregor the weaker in both strength and courage. Cyrus would get what he wanted. And Soren planned to make it a more appealing option as well.

Phillip stepped to the table map beside Soren. "What do you think, Lord Commander?"

Soren tapped on Aleon's southern kingdom of Eilor. "Put your forces on your southern border and show Aleon as a less desirable option. Push Rael and Japheth toward Kharav, and when they take the pass, you'll move south and keep pressure on them to stay along the canyons."

"And then?"

Soren drew his finger along the map and stopped at the central Canyonlands—the land he knew like his own flesh. "Once they reach here, you'll push them back into the canyons, where my men will finish them."

Phillip leaned across the table and clasped two of Aleon's battalion figurines. Soren's eyes caught on the lines of his lean-muscled arm, but he quickly pulled his gaze away. Phillip moved them on the map just north of the Canyonlands. "Two or three?"

Forcing his attention on the map, Soren said, "All of your forces."

Phillip looked at Soren in surprise. "All?"

"You have to come with enough power that they won't consider moving north."

He stared at Soren a moment. "All?"

"All."

"Even my forces in Bahoul?"

Especially his forces in Bahoul. "My Northmen will keep the stronghold."

Phillip chuckled. "And how do I know this isn't your strategy to get me out of there?"

Perhaps it was. The stronghold belonged to Kharav and the North, not to Aleon. "Even so, it's still the right move. I need your cavalry and swordsmen at the southern border of Eilor."

"You *need*?" Phillip's eyes were a piercing blue, challenging. "Are you commandeering my army, Lord Commander?"

"Is that not why I'm here?" Soren said shortly. Diplomacy, he reminded himself. He drew in a breath. "Forgive my overreach. It's not my intention to take command."

The corner of Phillip's mouth curved up ever so slightly. "Perhaps I want you to."

Their stares locked, and Soren froze. Was the king giving him the Aleon army? His pulse quickened. Was there another meaning to his words? *No.* He swallowed and tore his eyes away, looking back to the map. The army—the king meant the army. But when he raised his gaze again, he caught Phillip's smile, and the glint in his eye—

The doors to the study opened, and Caspian stepped in. *Thank the North gods.*

"Lord Justice," Phillip said, motioning to the map. "We were just talking about positioning."

Soren shifted.

Caspian stepped to the table and eyed the setup. "Impressive," he said.

Phillip smiled proudly as he looked back down at it. A bronze lock fell over his brow, and he brushed it back. He glanced up at Soren, his blue eyes shining. Soren hated blue eyes. But these blue eyes...

"The lord commander believes the best course is for me to move the entirety of my forces south to Eilor," Phillip said. "Push Japheth and Rael back into the Canyonlands."

Caspian nodded. "It makes sense, but it's a great risk. Your advantage before was your overwhelming numbers, but that's not in our favor now, not with Rael. It's essentially a bluff, and if they break through, you've no defenses to stop them from moving up through Aleon."

Phillip nodded, mulling. "I'd rather position my forces farther north, in Songs."

Caspian's brow creased. "You'd give up Eilor?"

"Temporarily, yes. For more advantageous ground. If I put all my forces south in Eilor and am overwhelmed, I would have to trust the Shadowlands to come to my defense."

"Do you not?" Soren quipped.

Phillip's eyes met Soren's again, locking them into a stare once more. "I want to."

The king's reply stole whatever smart response sat on his tongue.

Phillip looked back down at the table, pausing. "I've never shied from a risk, if the reward is worth it." Then he brought his gaze back to Soren's. "This is a dangerous path for me." He gave a faint smile. "But I'm willing."

That smile wasn't about the battle. Soren shook his head—of course he was talking about the battle. What else would he be talking about? Soren's pulse thrummed faster, and he clenched the edges of the table.

Phillip stepped around to where Soren stood, reaching across and taking Aleon's figurine from Bahoul. Their shoulders brushed. Soren tensed as a jolt of electricity ran through him. Their eyes locked again as Phillip moved the figurine to the border of Eilor.

"Together, or spread along the border?" Phillip asked.

Soren swallowed the fire that was building in his throat. He tried to push it down. "Together," he said. "Moving together as Rael progresses." A strange grip held him. He needed to get away from this man.

Phillip moved the rest of the Aleon figurines to Eilor. Their shoulders still touched as they both leaned on the table over the map.

Never had someone stood so casually close to him before. Never had someone dared to touch him. Still, Soren couldn't bring himself to move away.

"I'm choosing to trust you," Phillip said. He turned and his eyes found Soren's again.

Fire rippled across Soren's skin. Phillip was talking about the battle. Nothing else. But the way he looked at him...

"Let's think on it," Caspian said. "For now, I want to see if my men have settled in the barracks."

"Go," Phillip said, "we'll think more on it and reconvene."

Caspian gave a small nod and departed.

Soren moved to leave, but Phillip caught him.

"You own the next move, Lord Commander." The corners of his mouth turned upward, and he left out the door and disappeared down the hall.

The battle. He was talking about the battle. Soren pulled down his wrap and wiped his face. He pushed out a long breath. He needed to get his mind back.

The afternoon passed too slowly, and too quickly. Soren found himself back at the map with Phillip. They'd already met with Caspian again and confirmed the plan from before. Phillip would move the entirety of his forces south, putting pressure on Japheth and Rael to keep them along the Canyonlands and giving the advantage to Kharav. If they were lucky, they'd contain the war there, and finish it.

Caspian left to write orders for the legions.

It was a bold plan, and a risky one for Phillip, Soren knew. The Aleon king would be placing his trust in an enemy he had warred against for ten years, an enemy who had dreamed of his death many times over, who still dreamed of it. Although Soren had to admit, he dreamed of it a little less now. This king puzzled him, both in mind and... He didn't know how to describe it. Phillip was different from what he'd thought. It cooled Soren's anger toward him.

And the way Phillip looked at him...

Soren sucked in a breath. It was all in his head. He needed to get out of this kingdom. It was messing with his mind. He turned his thoughts to something he could think about more rationally—war. War was coming. He felt solid with this plan he'd devised with Phillip and Caspian.

That reminded him... "Where's your commander?" he asked Phillip as they stood at the table.

Phillip shifted back, hesitating before he answered. "I lost him when I took Tarsus. But I have my generals."

Wait... "You have the largest empire in the world, and you have no commander?"

"*I* am commander."

Soren could only stare at him in surprise. Was this man mad? "Who devises your strategies?"

Phillip frowned with a shrug. "I devise my own strategies."

"Who executes them?"

"As I said, I have my generals."

Even with generals, being both king and commander was too much for one person. "Do you not have a trusted man?"

Phillip sighed. "I'm working to dissolve the absolute power of an empire. As you can imagine, for those who reap the benefits of status, it's an unpopular plan." He looked back to the table. "I trust my enemies more than I trust my own heads of state." He raised his eyes to Soren's again. "Am I making a mistake by trusting *you*, Lord Commander?"

Absolutely. Soren would just as soon run him through than... he cursed himself silently. He hated the North gods more than he ever had. Because he wouldn't harm this man. "Maybe," he said simply.

Phillip nodded. "Yet I find myself doing just that." His voice dropped. "Perhaps because I see you, Soren."

Soren shifted back on his heel. For the king to so boldly call him by his name...

And the way he'd said it—all play gone, stripped and open, completely genuine. Soren's breath seized in his chest. He searched his mind for something—anything—to redirect the conversation. "You need a commander. You can't do this on your own."

A hint of a smile returned to Phillip's lips. "You sound… concerned for me."

"If you fail, we all fail."

Phillip nodded as he stepped closer. "Is that all?"

Was that all? What kind of question was that? What answer did he want? Soren shifted. It wasn't all. His heart hammered faster at the answer he didn't dare give.

The king gave a small chuckle. Did he notice? "Have I improved my standing with you, Lord Commander? Or do you still think of killing me?" Phillip stepped even closer. "I know you've thought about it. Killing me, that is. I've seen it in your eyes."

Soren swallowed. He wouldn't deny it, although it wasn't exactly true now—but *that* he would deny.

"Strange it doesn't make me wary of you." The king was so close now, close enough to touch. Too close. "Perhaps that's foolish of me," he added.

It was.

Phillip reached up and brought his hand to Soren's wrap. Soren didn't move to stop him. Perhaps it was the shock of it. Or perhaps he didn't want to. Ever so carefully, Phillip pulled the cloth down to reveal his face. No one had ever been so bold before.

"Am I foolish, Soren?"

Only a foolish man would touch him. "Very." But perhaps Soren was foolish for letting him.

Phillip leaned forward, lifting his face. His lips parted slightly. He was a beautiful man—a beautiful and powerful man. And something told Soren he was a very dangerous man…

Soren leaned forward, an invisible force drawing him closer. Then closer still. He couldn't breathe as the air conspired against him.

But suddenly his will broke through and something splintered within, freeing him. He jerked back.

The king drew back with a start as well.

Soren shook his head, but more at himself than Phillip. Had he lost his mind completely? The heat of embarrassment flushed across his skin, then a rush of anger. What was he doing? His hand wrapped around the dagger at his waist. His focus should be on the war at hand. Not... whatever this was.

It was nothing.

But it wasn't nothing.

And where did this leave them now?

"I'm sorry," said Phillip. "I shouldn't have done that." His eyes caught Soren's again, but it wasn't a reciprocation of shame Soren saw. The king's eyes gleamed with a hint of mischief. "I did say it was your move."

The shock still gripped him. Soren couldn't speak. He couldn't move.

The king turned to leave, but paused and looked back at him. His smile grew. "And, Lord Commander, when we become better friends, I'll tell you about a vision I've seen." Then he left Soren standing alone in the study.

Soren's heart pounded in his ears.

Phillip knew.

CHAPTER TWENTY-NINE

Adrian's nostrils flared. "The Aleon king needs a trusted man, and he can't pick one from the hundred thousand he already has?" He shook his head. "I can't go to Aleon."

Norah sighed. She didn't blame him. He didn't want to serve Aleon. He wanted to serve Kharav. He wanted to serve Mercia. She reached out and clasped his arm. "Phillip has given the lord commander control of his army. Think of it as Soren needing a trusted man, and he trusts you."

"What about Katya?" he argued. "She'd do far better than I would."

"The lord commander is a purposeful man, and he's called for *you*," Norah said. "He has a reason. And Katya's just had a child."

"You'll go," Mikael told him.

Adrian cut Mikael a sharp glance, one that would have normally garnered a swift and harsh punishment. Something had happened between them—she wasn't sure what. Whatever it was, it fueled Adrian with an anger rarely seen, and drew from Mikael a tolerance rarely given. Norah told herself to pry later.

"I belong here," Adrian said to Norah. "The Aleon king doesn't even know me."

"Adrian—"

"Norah, you need me here—"

Mikael's eyes blazed, and he grabbed Adrian's breastplate. "Your salar commands you. Your salara commands you. But that aside, if the lord commander has called you, you'll go. Do you understand?"

Adrian stilled, but he didn't respond.

"You leave tomorrow," Mikael said.

Adrian glanced back at Norah and, finally, gave a reluctant bow of his head. Then he left to prepare without further protest.

"Don't be angry with him," she said after Adrian was gone. "He's still young, unsure of himself."

"He knows exactly what he's capable of." He reached down and took her hand. "He just wants to stay with his queen. He worries for you here."

"He doesn't need to worry." She squeezed his hand. "I have you."

He lifted her chin to him. "I'm worried too, Salara. I want you to think about returning to the North."

She pulled back. "What?"

"It's safer for you there."

She shook her head. "No, I'm not leaving you. I've only been back a few weeks. And it's perfectly safe here, safer than traveling."

"You're only thinking about today. You need to think about tomorrow."

She paused, and her eyes narrowed. "What's that supposed to mean?"

"It means you have to think of the future, and about your strategy."

She only stared at him. Where was he going with this?

"You have to fortify yourself in the North," he said, "and continue to grow your friendship with Aleon and Osan." Then he paused and swallowed. "And you have to marry Soren after I'm gone."

Her mouth dropped open. "Have you lost your mind?" she hissed.

"He has claim to the throne. The nobles will support him."

She shook her head. "No. We've been through this. I won't bed him, and I certainly won't marry him."

"You'd have the same relationship you have now. He'll give you freedom. He'll protect you."

"He protects me now."

"You know what I mean!" His voice came thick with frustration. "I'm not talking about his strength or his fortitude. When I'm gone, you'll need his name."

His frustration fueled her own. "Because you don't think I'm strong enough without you?"

"That's not what I said."

"But it's what you meant. You think I'm weak. Because I'm a woman? Because I love? Because I grieve?" She stepped closer, seething. "I'm queen of Mercia and salara of Kharav, with or without a husband. If someone wants my crown, they'll have to pry it from my dead fingers, if they still have a head to wear it."

A deep horn sounded through the air, and Norah looked through the window from where she sat at her vanity.

"The lord commander must be returning," her maid Amara said as she finished pinning back a lock in Norah's hair.

Norah knew what the horn meant. She'd been waiting for it. "Send for him," she said. "Tell him I need to speak to him immediately."

Amara nodded and left to do as she was bid.

No doubt Mikael would be eager to speak to Soren too. But Norah couldn't wait. She hoped Soren would seek her out first.

Not long after, two knocks on the door gave her answer, and it swung open before she could even rise.

"What?" Soren said as he stepped inside. He looked like he'd been riding for weeks. And he smelled like he'd been riding for weeks. But Norah didn't care about his look or his smell, she was just grateful he was there.

"Is there still a king of Aleon?" she asked him. While she trusted Soren implicitly, she also knew he was confined to few boundaries, and wanted to make sure their new ally still had his head.

"He lives."

That was a miracle in itself. She nodded appreciatively. "I was surprised you called Adrian to go." And she was surprised Soren had left him there. Not that she worried for Adrian in Aleon, he was just still so young, and to be serving on his own in another kingdom...

Soren shifted slightly. "You wanted me to have asked you first?"

She shook her head. "No, you're making decisions for all our armies now, and I trust those decisions. I'm just saying I'm surprised, that's all."

He seemed to mull over her words, then he said, "The Aleon king has no commander."

Her brows drew together. Was that an explanation? "Adrian isn't a commander." Gods, he wasn't even a captain. He had no status, other than a Crest sword entitlement.

"Not yet. But he doesn't need to be. The Aleon king is a smart man, but he needs someone to challenge his thinking, someone who doesn't have his own agenda. And yes, surprisingly, this Aleon king is accepting of Kharav, but some of those around him are still wary."

She understood. "You couldn't send a Kharavian."

"So I sent him a Kharavian Northman." His eyes smiled.

She couldn't help a smile of her own. No doubt Adrian's being the brother of Mercia's former lord justice also helped. And he was right, Adrian was extremely clever and knew Kharavian battle standards and strategies, and he wouldn't shy away from challenging one's thinking—even a king's.

Soren gave a quick nod and then turned for the door. "Salar wants to see me."

"There is one more thing," she said, stopping him. He paused and looked at her, a wariness immediately coming to him. She didn't say anything else; she only turned her eyes to the small vial that sat on top of her vanity, waiting for him to react.

And he did. "You received that here? Just now?"

She shook her head. "No, while you were in Aleon."

"What did Salar say?"

Damn it. She rocked forward as she searched for the words.

"You *did* tell Salar. Didn't you?"

"I wanted to, but—"

"How could you not?" His voice was thick with anger.

Norah stood. "I panicked! Mikael used the last vial, and we're lucky nothing happened. We don't know what power we're dealing with. I didn't know how he'd react, or how Alexander would react. And when I didn't tell him the first day, the second day was even harder. Then the third, then the fourth." She looked down at her hands. "I can't tell him now. Now he'll think I'm hiding something."

"Well, you are," he snapped.

"You know what I mean," she cut back. Her stomach twisted, and she moved and sat on the edge of the bed. "Soren," she breathed. "Please. I don't know what to do."

He lingered by the vanity before picking up the vial. She couldn't look at him. She only waited for the lecture she knew would come.

But it didn't.

The bed sank under his weight as he sat beside her, and they let the quiet lay between them for a while.

"You truly believe this is the Bear?" he asked.

She didn't know what to believe anymore. "I don't know." Her lip trembled as her eyes welled. "I want it to be."

"And that's why you didn't tell Salar."

"He doesn't understand. He doesn't *try* to understand. But it's not what it appears, it's not like that—"

"I know." He stared at the vial in his hand. "Let's say it is Alexander." He looked at her. "There is a time where we all say goodbye."

The breath left her lungs. She knew this. But still...

"We have to move forward," he continued.

"It's easy for you to say," she whispered. "You hated him."

He sighed. Then he stood and slowly unclipped his cloak from his shoulders and pulled it off.

She gasped as she stood. Covering the broad stretch of skin across the center of his back was the image of a shield. But it wasn't just any shield—it was Alexander's shield.

She reached out and brushed her fingertips over the patterns that together formed a greater picture.

"I asked Salta Tau for the marking," he said, "for the loss of my greatest adversary. And she gave me his shield upon my back." He turned, and his eyes found hers again. "I carry him with me now. And so will you. But you have to say goodbye."

Say goodbye? She couldn't do that. "I'm still figuring things out."

He shook his head. "You're not figuring things out. There's no information he gives you. He doesn't speak. There's no purpose to seeing him, other than comfort. But that comfort will keep you from moving forward. You have to let him go." His brows drew together. "And he's supposed to be watching over the North, not visiting you in visions. Tell him to do his job, or I'll pull his worthless body from the Hall of Souls and send him to your gods."

His jest broke the tension, and she gave a small laugh through the tears that were threatening.

He held the vial for her, and she took it back, but he didn't release it immediately. A seriousness returned to him. "Say goodbye. Then that will be the end of this."

He let it go, and with a final nod, left her to the quiet of the room.

Norah watched him leave before looking back at the vial in her hands. *Say goodbye.* How simple, yet not. How could she say goodbye? But Soren was right. She needed to put an end to this and move forward. For herself, for Mikael, and for Alexander.

She inhaled deeply as she opened the vial and drew a line of blood across her palm. Then she closed her eyes and waited.

All was quiet.

Then he came.

Alexander stood in front of her in the depths of her mind and gave a small smile. Gods, she missed that smile. She had last called him when she had been in Mercia, and to see him now, again... A wave of emotion hit her.

His brows dipped, and he stepped closer.

"I wasn't sure you'd come, after Mikael..." She paused. "I'm sorry about that. I didn't know he'd use the blood. I'm sure that was a surprise."

His face showed no reaction.

"I... I thought about it a lot, him calling you. At first I thought it would have helped him understand if he'd seen you." She paused again, looking down at her hands. "But now"—she shook her head—"I think it would have made it worse, knowing you really are here. So thank you, for not engaging." And not doing anything else that this strange power allowed him to do.

She stared at him, chained by the blue eyes staring back at her. Gods, this was hard. "But Soren says it's time for me to say goodbye." She pulled her bottom lip between her teeth. "And he's right." She gave a sad smile and let out a laughing breath through her tears. "He said you need to start doing your job looking over Mercia and stop haunting me."

But Alexander's smile was gone, his face dark. He obviously didn't appreciate the humor as much as she had.

She cleared her throat and became serious again. "I know you're not yourself, at least not exactly, but I think it's what the old you would have wanted—for me to be able to move forward."

His face grew sharper and more shadowed. He stepped closer, shaking his head. Her words were upsetting him.

"I want you to know that I'm all right. That I'm cared for and looked after."

He shook his head again as he reached up and clasped her cheek. It broke her. She hadn't expected him to object. She thought this would bring closure.

"I'm all right, Alexander," she tried to encourage him again. And then she hugged him. Tightly. She gave herself only a moment.

Then she had to go. With tears in her eyes, she stepped up on her toes and brought her lips to his cheek.

"Goodbye," she whispered.

Norah opened her eyes to her empty chamber. She drew in a tear-laden breath and wiped off her hand, then looked down at the vial, at the blood still within. She sank to the floor of the fireplace and sat. She just sat.

The hours passed in a blur.

The day faded into evening.

Finally, she picked herself up off the floor and dropped the vial into the letter box on the vanity before leaving the chamber.

The sun had already set as she walked across the courtyard, but its colors still painted the sky. Through a window, she spotted Soren inside speaking to one of the nobles, but when he saw her, he excused himself and stepped outside. Norah picked up her walk along the castle toward the gardens, and he fell in step beside her.

"He didn't understand," she said, not looking at him as she spoke. "He didn't want to say goodbye."

"You did the right thing."

She shook her head. "What if he had a purpose, and I just cut him off?"

"It's not a pure purpose, I assure you."

Norah stopped abruptly by the wall of the tower. "You still don't think it's Alexander?"

He sighed.

"So all those heartfelt words of saying goodbye were a cart full of rubbish?"

"If it were Alexander, every word I said holds true. You can't keep him, Salara."

"I'm not trying to keep him!" she cried.

"Then what are you trying to do?"

The question left her speechless.

A noise in the distance caught her attention, and she turned toward it. She squinted and saw a large flock of birds flying toward the castle. Their multitudes created a giant swarm, twisting and floating through the painted sky.

"What's that?" she asked.

"Looks like a massive flock of starlings."

There were hundreds, maybe thousands of them. "It's amazing," she whispered, temporarily forgetting everything else in the moment.

The birds drew closer, and the collective sound of their wings grew louder. She stood mesmerized. The swarm moved as one, weaving in and out in a meticulously coordinated dance, like chaos through the halls of air but with beautiful purpose.

"Have you ever seen anything like it?"

Soren shook his head. "Farther south, but not this large."

Suddenly, the flock swarmed downward, and Norah let out a sharp cry as they plummeted into the side walls of the tower above her and then fell to the ground from overhead. Carcasses poured down like rain. She dropped to her knees with her hands over her head, and Soren covered her. He held her tightly, protecting her from the falling creatures. The Crest swept around them, their shields up. The sickening blows of death rang out as the birds dropped down over top of them. Norah covered her ears to muffle the sound.

When the last bird had fallen, a haunting silence came. The Crest drew back, and Soren rose slowly, pulling Norah up with him. The guard stood in a circle around her, their swords out, but equally as confused as to what had just happened. She covered her mouth in horror as she looked at the dead birds blanketing the earth around them.

"Get inside," Soren said to her as the Crest quickly made a path through the dead birds back to the entry hall.

Norah stumbled back to the castle in a daze. Inside, she let out a ragged breath, trying to keep herself calm. Caspian appeared beside her. Where had he come from? He was supposed to be in Mercia. But she couldn't think straight right now.

"I saw what happened," he said. "Are you all right?"

"No, I'm not all right!" she cried. She looked at Soren, who had followed her. "It's him, I know it's him."

Soren's brows drew together. "The Bear?"

She nodded, clutching her arms around her. "He's angry."

"Alexander?" Caspian asked, his face etched in confusion.

"Salara." Soren reached out and clasped her arms, making her look at him. "Angry or no, the Bear would never do this. You know him. He had respect for life and all things. I don't know what happened here, but whoever comes to you in these visions, if he is linked to this, it's not the Bear. I need to tell Salar."

She grabbed his hand. "No! Soren, no! Please!"

"You have to tell him what's going on!"

"He'll send me back to Mercia."

"Queen Norah," Caspian said, stepping forward. "You *have* to come back to Mercia. It's why I'm here."

She stopped and stared at him. "What? Why?"

He hesitated a moment, then said, "It's your grandmother. She's sick. Very sick."

She forgot about the birds. "How sick?"

"She's dying, Norah."

The cold had settled in her core, but she didn't have the energy to pull more blankets over her. Norah lay in her bed, staring blankly out the window, unseeing. Mikael had stayed with her for a time as the news about her grandmother sank in, then he had gone to prepare for the journey back to Mercia. As she had expected, the birds sparked a fury in him, as did the news about Alexander and the vial of blood, and he insisted on returning with her. It was nonsensical that both he and Soren would accompany her back, but he wouldn't hear of anything else. She tried to talk him out of it, but only half-heartedly. The truth was she was glad he'd stay with her. She needed him.

Her mind raced and stumbled all at once. The news of Catherine took the air from her lungs. She was all Norah had left. And despite her callousness at times, she was the matriarch that had held Mercia together, had made Norah strong, and Norah loved her. What would life be like without her? What would she even do with Mercia? Catherine took care of everything—Norah didn't even have to think about it. How was she going to run a kingdom on her own? Catherine couldn't leave her.

Like Alexander had.

Alexander.

Alexander had left her. More than left her—he was supposed to be watching over her, watching over Mercia, helping her, helping

Catherine. Her face twisted as the emotion washed over her. She ripped back the furs and stumbled to the vanity, clawing off the lid and finding the vial. She poured the blood out across her palm.

She demanded him to come. "Alexander!"

But there was no answer.

She tried to calm herself as she closed her eyes. "Where are you?" She heard the anger in her own voice. Anger at him. At her grandmother. At fate.

"Alexander!"

But she stood alone in the darkness of her mind. Would he not come? Was this what had become of them? She sank into the chair of the vanity. Even in her mind she didn't have the strength to stand.

"Alexander," she whispered.

Then... the faintest of stirring.

"I know you're there."

He stepped forward from the darkness, but she didn't stand.

"Did you send the birds?" she asked. Her voice cracked. "Did you do that?"

He drew closer, his eyes apologetic, sad.

She shook her head as emotion built in her throat. "Why?"

He stepped even closer, his mouth opening as if about to speak, but he stopped.

"Why would you do that to me?" she whispered. "How could you do that?"

In front of her, slowly, he sank to his knees. Asking forgiveness. A deep sorrow hung across his brow. Her anger dissipated.

"What happened to you?" she whispered. She leaned forward slightly and brought her hand to his cheek. "Is there anything left of the Alexander I knew?"

His eyes shifted down. Ever so slowly, he shook his head.

A cry rose in her throat, and she swallowed it down as she pulled back. "Then you're not Alexander. If you were, you aren't anymore. Not truly."

His chest rose and fell, and a pain etched his face. Again, he shook his head, but he took her hand and pulled it back to his cheek.

Her lip trembled. The tears came freely now. She needed him—not just the Alexander she once loved, not just her lord justice, but the man who had shared a bond with Catherine, the man who would have mourned her grandmother as his own, so that Norah wouldn't mourn her alone.

"Grandmother's dying." Her voice broke as she said it.

His brow dipped, and he clutched her hands tightly.

"Without her, I don't know what to do." She shook her head. "And without you too." Her voice dropped to a whisper. "I'm trying not to hate you for leaving me, but I do. I do sometimes."

Norah pulled her hands from his and wiped her face. "I'm leaving for Mercia tomorrow. I won't call you back again."

He shook his head, and it knifed her heart. She brought her hands back to his face, tracing the lines she knew so well. His eyes pleaded to her.

"Goodbye, Alexander," she whispered, and opened her eyes to the living.

The room was quiet.

Norah sat for a time, staring at her lap where Alexander had knelt in front of her in her mind. She pulled a small handkerchief from the vanity and wiped the blood from her hand, then rose unsteadily.

Move forward. That was what she needed to do.

She threw the vial into the fireplace.

CHAPTER THIRTY

Most of the Kharavian army stayed in Kharav, with only one legion accompanying Norah and the king back to Mercia. Caspian rode near the back as they traveled north. He was happy to be headed back to the Uru, where he'd been the week prior in coming to Kharav, but too soon he'd be leaving Tahla and his son again, and he didn't know when he'd see them next.

Caspian accepted this life, welcomed it even. He'd never imagined himself finding love or having a son. Now he had both, and he was grateful. Men wasted their joy on seeking perfection in it, but he'd relish every moment. He had to. He had to find joy where he could.

Alexander's death had hit him harder than he could have ever imagined. He missed the man he'd known his entire life, the man that was like a brother to him. Caspian had always expected himself to be the first between them to leave this world. To him, Alexander had been... invincible, his death impossible. Caspian would have given his life for him, and it's what he always thought he would do. When Alexander died, it had shaken everything within him, rocked his very foundation. And now he found himself in a role he wasn't worthy of, praying that he could fill it half as well as his friend had.

He'd worried for Adrian, but the young man had surprised him. Adrian had shown himself to be every part Alexander's brother, every part the son of the great Beurnat the Bear. He'd grieved deeply, but then he'd risen.

The lord commander had a hand in it, no doubt. And the king. They treated Adrian as if he were their own man—they had faith in him, and expectations of him—and he rose to those expectations. Now under the lord commander's watch, Adrian served beside King Phillip—a seemingly impossible circumstance. Yet here they were in seemingly impossible times—Mercia and Kharav united with Aleon, with Caspian as lord justice. Although months had passed, it still hadn't taken hold in his heart, but he'd give his everything to it.

His pulse raced as they neared the Canyonlands. It had only been a week, but he couldn't wait to hold his son in his arms again, to hold Tahla.

When they reached the tribe, he worked quickly to settle the legion outside. Then he made his way inside, to the village's center fire, where Norah and the others had settled among the Urun people, visiting. Norah sat on a large rock by the warmth of the fire, laughing and holding Katakah in her lap.

Caspian took a seat close by. He couldn't take his eyes from the infant. The child sat contently, bundled in furs, looking like a bedroll. He had to hold back his chuckle. He glanced up to see Norah looking back at him.

"Sorry," he murmured as he shifted his gaze to the fire.

The center of her brows twitched. "Why?"

He only shook his head. "I don't know. I didn't mean to stare."

She grinned. "How can you not?" She looked back down at the infant in her lap and scrunched her nose at him. "He's the most adorable thing."

Caspian couldn't help a smile as he looked at the child. "That he is."

"Do you want to hold him?"

Yes. Yes, he did. "No," he said quickly. "No." It would be awkward for the Mercian lord justice to hold an Urun baby. Norah never thought about what was awkward, only about sharing things that brought joy. This baby certainly brought joy, but Caspian had to decline. Still, he watched as she adjusted Katakah's cover more snugly over his head and around his cheeks to keep him warm. But there was no covering the plump rounds on the babe's face, and a chuckle escaped Caspian as Norah's attempts only squished the fat and puffed out the child's lips more.

Norah laughed too. "Did you see Katya's son?" she asked.

He nodded with a smile. "I did."

She laughed again. "These chub babies just melt my heart." She looked over at him. "Fatherhood would look good on you too, Caspian."

His smile died, and he had to force himself to keep it.

She must have noticed, as she stammered, "I-I mean... you should just know if it's what you wanted... I'd want it for you, that's all."

It was what he wanted. More than anything.

"Not that it's my business," she added. "I just, I, uh"—she smiled as she shook her head—"or maybe it is my business because Titus asked me. But I don't think you'd ask, so you should just know that you'd have my blessing if it was what you wanted."

He swallowed the lump forming in his throat. "Thank you."

While his heart leapt at her words, they didn't matter. He couldn't let them matter. This was Tahla's decision, and he respected it, regardless of how much it hurt. And it was the right decision. Whether Caspian had an heir was of no consequence—there was nothing to pass down, nothing to inherit. There was nothing at stake. But Tahla had a duty to her people. Katakah would be chief one day, and the Uru depended on that identity, that loyalty. He knew Tahla loved him, but he also knew duty. And for duty, they'd sacrifice.

Tahla appeared and stepped around the fire, and both Norah and Caspian shifted their attention to her. She paused when she saw him and gave a warm smile. "Lord Justice," she said.

He loved the sound of her voice, no matter what she said. He gave a respectful nod, as anyone would, grateful he didn't have to speak, because he didn't think he could.

"I think he's ready for bed," Norah said as she passed the child back to Tahla. "His eyes are sleepy."

"He most certainly is." Tahla scooped the baby into her arms, looking down at him. "I have to feed him and put him down. I'll see you off in the morning, Salara."

Norah clasped her arm with a smile. "I'll see you in the morning."

Tahla left with the child, and Caspian had to force himself not to watch her go. He waited until he had finished his soup and until Norah left for her own bed. Then he could wait no more.

He trailed the shadows of the village streets, moving quietly, back to where he knew Tahla resided with the child. He wasn't sure how she'd feel about him coming on his own. She'd always come to his dwelling, or invited him to her. But he couldn't wait for that. He didn't know when he'd see her or Katakah again, and he wanted every moment.

When he reached the house, he was surprised to find the door ajar. He paused, swaying to eye the candlelit room inside through the crack, but it seemed empty. Slowly, he pushed the door open and stepped inside.

"Back here," came Tahla's voice from the room behind a hanging panel.

Caspian closed the door behind him and moved toward the back room. Stepping around the panel, he drew in a breath as his eyes caught Tahla sitting in the center of the bed, cross-legged, with Katakah at her breast. Never had he seen her more beautiful.

She smiled at him. "I was hoping you wouldn't make me come get you."

He smiled back. "If I'm welcome, I'll come directly from now on."

She held out a hand for him. He closed the gap between them and took it, letting her pull him onto the bed beside her.

"You're always welcome," she said.

Caspian clasped her cheek and leaned in to kiss her. Her lips were warm and sweet. When he pulled back, he looked down at the child. "He's growing," he said softly.

"He is."

"He looks like you." He cupped the top of the child's head. The boy's dark hair was thick but soft, and there was a lot of it. Caspian could already see he'd have his mother's mane.

She smiled as she grazed the child's cheeks with her fingertips. "I still see you when I look at him." Her face turned serious. "I'm sorry, Caspian. For tonight. I know it's hard, and I know this isn't what you want."

He shook his head. "You don't have to apologize. You're making the right decision for Katakah and your people. I only want to share this life with you as much as I can. I love you, Tahla."

Her smile returned. "I love you," she whispered.

"There is something, though." He sat for a moment, swallowing the lump rising in his throat. Then he pulled the ring off his smallest finger and placed it in her hand.

"What's this?" she asked.

"It's customary in Mercia for a man to give a woman a ring when they're wed, to remind her of his love for her."

"Caspian," she breathed.

"I know," he said quickly as he shifted closer to her, being careful not to bump Katakah. "And I won't speak of it again after this. I won't ask you anymore. I only want you to know there will be no other in my heart but you. I make you this vow. I love you, Tahla. I love our child. And I want you to remember that every day." He paused and swallowed again. "And if you should ever find in your heart that you think of me as your husband, just wear this ring, and it will be so."

"Caspian, I—"

"Don't answer," he stopped her. "Don't answer. I say this only for you to know."

Her eyes glistened as she curled her fingers around the ring, and he brought his lips to hers.

CHAPTER THIRTY-ONE

The open markets smelled of cooking meat, and Norah's stomach grumbled. She followed the scent of smoke and spice through the streets of Redding, one of the Free Cities just beyond the outer reaches of Mercia. Mikael and Soren weren't keen on stopping in the Free Cities when traveling between Mercia and Kharav—they weren't keen on any city not in Kharav—but Mikael had surprised her with the idea, and Norah had quickly accepted. She needed a break, something to distract her mind.

She walked freely. The city was so used to travelers and merchants passing through that no one took notice of her, no one recognized her. She loved it. Only a few of the Crest moved through the crowds around her, at a distance, not close enough to draw attention to her, as she had asked of them. However, there was no convincing Mikael and Soren, who paid no mind to blending in and followed ridiculously close.

She finally found the source of the wonderful smell and stopped at the stall of the culprit.

"What'll ya 'ave?" asked a pot-bellied man without looking up. He stood over a grate along a pit fire, turning meats as they cooked.

"One of those sausages," she said, pointing to a steaming plate on the side.

"Two sum."

Norah puffed a breath through her lips. She had forgotten they dealt in a separate currency here. She pulled a gold coin from her pouch. "I think this will suffice?"

The man grinned and held out his hand, and she dropped it into his palm. Then he offered her the plate to take her pick. Norah pulled her dagger and speared the one on the end, and then smiled as she turned to continue walking. But she stopped when she saw Mikael and Soren staring at her in surprise.

"Did you just pay a gold coin for a sausage?" Soren asked with a snaked brow.

She looked at Mikael, then back at Soren. "No."

"I saw you."

She pursed her lips. "I was hungry."

"You could have at least gotten more than one then."

She eyed him directly as she took a bite of the sausage.

Mikael brushed her arm. "Do you want to stay longer?"

She shook her head and swallowed. "No, we should get going. It was nice to stop for a little while, though."

"We'll still reach the Fork by nightfall, so no time lost."

He was trying to keep pressure off her, and she appreciated that. "I'm good," she assured him, and looped her arm in his. She took another bite of her sausage as they headed out of the city and back to where the rest of the men waited.

"Do you want a bite?" she asked, holding the daggered meat up toward his lips.

Mikael leaned forward and bit the sausage, but instead of taking a piece, he polished off the rest.

She gasped. "I said a bite! Not my whole sausage!"

He chuckled and then swallowed the meat. Norah put on her best attempt at a mad face, but she couldn't keep it. It had been a while since she'd heard him laugh or seen him smile, and she'd missed it. She gazed up at him, and the air lightened. She'd missed that too. He grazed her cheek with his hand—she knew he missed the closeness between them as well.

He pulled her into a kiss. "I'll get you another," he said, and turned back to the market stall not far behind them.

She pursed her lips at Soren, who stood with a scowl. "Go get yourself one; I know you want to. I'll wait."

He mumbled what could only be curses under his wrap, but he followed after Mikael. She knew it—who could resist a sausage?

She caught sight of Bhastian across the way to her right, keeping his eye on her, and he shook his head in amusement.

Norah couldn't help a smile. Despite the heaviness of the circumstances, her heart was lighter than it had been in a while. Maybe it was this place. Freedom hung all around from her insignificance in the hustle and bustle of the city, and she simply stood and closed her eyes in its noisy peacefulness. A slight breeze danced around her, cold but refreshing, and the weight of everything fell away. The coming war, Japheth and Rael, Alexander, her grandmother—she dropped them from her mind, just for a moment. She didn't allow herself to enjoy these fleeting moments often. This one, she would. And soon she'd have another delicious sausage, so it would be even better.

Norah opened her eyes again and glanced back at Mikael, who was paying the merchant for the whole plate of sausages, and she laughed.

A faint wind swept through again, but colder this time.

It carried with it the feeling of being watched.

Her laugh quieted on her lips, and she stilled. Prickles rose across her skin underneath her cloak.

Norah turned and cast her gaze around the market: the cobbled mainway with its centered merchant stalls, the side shops and their open doors.

But all around her the market bustled; sellers continued on with their wares.

"Salara," Kiran called out from her left. "Are you all right?"

Was she all right?

Mikael appeared beside her. "Another sausage?" her offered, breaking her thought. He looked at her a moment, and then his brows stitched together. "Is something wrong?"

She glanced around one last time. There was nothing, and no one. "Um, no." She shook her head and gave a smile. "Of course not. Just waiting on my sausage."

He daggered one and held it out for her, and she gladly accepted. "Anything else you want to get here?" he asked.

She noticed Soren eyeing the plate of meat, but he wouldn't eat in the market. He wouldn't uncover his face until they were away from public view.

"No, we can go," she said. "This was a nice break, but I'm ready."

Mikael nodded, and they headed back to their horses outside the gates to rejoin the army and continue on their way.

Norah lay awake in the darkness. They'd stopped in Hanset for the night, the last of the Free Cities just before the Mercian border. The Fork was shortly beyond, where they'd planned to make camp, but the temperature had dipped low. The army continued on to make camp there, but Mikael suggested Norah stay at the town castle that had been converted into a merchant house and inn. She didn't need much convincing. She hadn't had a proper bath since she'd left Kharav, and she allowed herself a long soak in the tub—with a glass or two or three of wine—before collapsing onto the feather bed. It was more comfortable than she'd expected from an inn. Much more comfortable.

But despite the comfort and her weariness, and the effects of the wine, sleep wouldn't come. Her thoughts turned to her grandmother. Catherine was sick. She was dying. Norah had tried to deny it, push it from her mind, as if not accepting it would make it not true. But it *was* true, and she'd have to face that truth in only a few days. At least she had Mikael with her. She didn't know how long he'd be able to stay in Mercia. Perhaps with Katya remaining with the army in Kharav and overseeing things, he wouldn't have to go back immediately. Unlikely, she told herself. But she still hoped for it.

Norah sat up and took the chalice from the table beside the bed and polished off the last of the wine. She thought she could chase away the swirling thoughts from her mind, but instead she brought on a swirling room as well. She wiped her face with her hands, her cheeks flush, and she let herself sink back against the pillows.

Soren had gone to check the horses, and Mikael to bring back a hot meal. Mikael wasn't keen on her eating in the tavern on the far side of the castle. She didn't blame him. Even from a little distance, its rowdiness carried through the air. She also wasn't going to complain about being served a warm meal in a plush feather bed or being able to enjoy eating in the comforts of a nightgown instead of a stiff-fitted riding dress.

Muffled voices sounded in the hall—Bhastian and Kiran at their posts outside the door. Although Bhastian was captain now, he still took shifts accompanying her guard, and the men seemed to respect him even more for it. She hoped they'd get some rest; they had to be tired as well. Her eyelids grew heavy, and she let them fall. Time passed slowly. Maybe it was the wine. Everything always seemed longer with wine.

Cold air swept over her skin, and she opened her eyes. The side window was cracked open to the icy air outside.

Strange. It hadn't been open before. Had it?

She sat up slowly and blinked, pushing back the grogginess. Had she fallen asleep? *No.* The sounds of the tavern still lingered in the air, and the candle that had been burning was still tall. But its flame had been snuffed—recently—its fresh smoky coils still rising in the moonlight.

From the corner of her eye, a shadow moved in the darkness.

"Mikael?" she called softly.

All was quiet.

But she wasn't alone.

And it wasn't Mikael.

Her mind roiled through the effects of the alcohol, struggling for clarity. Where was her knife? She had peeled off her dress in the far corner, where it still lay in a pile, before changing into her nightgown. But where had she put her calf sheath and blade?

The air stirred again.

"I know you're there," she said into the darkness.

A shadow stepped forward and loomed into the moonlight beaming through the window. Her pulse quickened, but she wasn't afraid. Not of one man. She wasn't the weak woman she once was. Knife or no, she was salara. This man would do well to take care.

Norah remembered now—her calf strapping and blade lay on the tufted bench at the end of the bed. She rose to her knees and moved to the edge. Slowly, she stepped down onto the floor, putting the bed between her and this stranger. The hooded figure waited, unmoving.

"What do you want?" she demanded. She moved carefully around the far edge of the bed, to the end, until her thigh touched the bench. *Just a little more.* She took another step. The flow of her nightgown concealed her reach, and she exhaled a thankful breath as she found her knife and curled her hand around the hilt.

He didn't answer her. His silhouette held no weapon—a mistake.

She moved closer, her knife now in hand and hidden in the hanging folds of her nightgown. "Why are you here?"

Still, he didn't answer.

Norah cocked her head to the side. "I should tell you about the last time I woke to a strange man in my room." She tightened her grip on her blade. "I hate to spoil a good story, but it didn't end well for him. For any of them."

She drew closer—she was right in front of him now, but still he made no move. Was he not here to harm her? That didn't mean she wouldn't harm him. Foolish man.

She whipped the dagger to his throat. "Final words?" she hissed.

He held his hands up, showing her they were empty in the pale light of the moon. Then, ever so slowly, he reached up and pulled back his hood.

Norah sucked in a breath. The knife in her hand clambered to the floor as she lost her grip on it.

Alexander stood, looking back at her.

The moonlight showed only half of his face, but there was no mistaking him—the high of his cheekbones, the line of his jaw.

She stumbled back. "What magic is this?" she whispered. No blood. No calling him. No going to the depths of her mind to see him. He was here. In front of her.

No. She had to be dreaming.

He didn't answer, the same as before. But he stood, waiting patiently.

She stepped forward again, reaching out. Her hands shook as she tested her fingertips against his chest, and they met the hardness of muscle through his tunic. She spread her hand flat against him. Warmth seeped into her—the warmth of life. In the visions she could touch him, but she couldn't feel warmth. Not like this.

She couldn't be dreaming. He was really here.

"How is this possible?" she whispered.

Norah ran her gaze from her hand on his chest to his face. Tears sprang to her eyes as the emotion flooded back—the pain, the loss.

"How are you here?" All she could do was ask him the same question over and over again. But its answer still escaped her.

Still, he said nothing.

He raised a hand to her cheek, and she closed her eyes against his warmth. Life—it was life she felt in him now. He had a beating heart, blood coursing through his veins. This was more than a spirit.

And before she could stop herself, she threw her arms around him and pulled him tightly against her. He was really here. And just to embrace him—truly—she couldn't do anything but simply hold on to him. She'd never gotten to tell him goodbye in life, not the way she wanted. But he was here now. He was here, and she clung to him.

Alexander hugged her back, his arms warm around her. There was a strength to him, and it permeated to her core. She needed this strength, and she soaked it in.

They finally broke, and she stepped back, but still held on to his hands. There were so many things she wanted to say, but no words would come.

He brought his hand to her cheek again and brushed her skin softly with the back of his fingers. She tilted her head into his touch.

Then he stepped forward and caught her mouth with his. Surprise jolted through her, and her eyes flashed open. His lips were firm—not harsh, but they weren't tender.

He used his body to push her up against the bed, and she stumbled, but he caught her and laid her back on the feather mattress. She tried to blink back the still-swirling fog of her mind as he moved over her and brought his lips to hers again.

He smelled like smoky pear, deliciously sweet, but not like Alexander. And Alexander wouldn't kiss her like this; he wouldn't be here like this. Alexander knew her heart.

She spread her palms against his chest and pushed him to stop. "Alexander," she breathed as she broke from him. "No."

The shadow of his brows drew together, confused. Did he really not remember? He paused a moment, then dropped his head to hers again.

"No," she said more firmly, pushing him back farther. "This isn't who you are, or who I am. This isn't what we were."

He stopped, seeming to study her. Was he still confused?

"My heart belongs to another," she said. "You can't be here. Not like this."

He only stared at her.

"Alexander," she whispered.

Even in the darkness, his face grew more shadowed, and he pulled himself from her and stood. How was he even here? Her mind swirled around her. The wine didn't help.

She wiped her face, drawing in a breath, but when she pushed herself up and rose from the bed, she was alone in the night.

He was gone.

Her breath started to shake. Had that really just happened? She couldn't have imagined it all. Perhaps it was the wine. But... *No.* She brought her fingertips to her lips where she still felt him, tasted him. She knew it had all been real.

The chamber door opened, and she jumped.

"Salara," Mikael's voice came. In his hand he held a covered plate of food. When he saw her, he set it down on the small side table.

She let out a breath as emotion flooded her.

"Are you all right?" he asked, glancing around the room.

But she couldn't speak. She couldn't tell him what had happened. She couldn't explain it without sounding like she'd lost her mind. And what had just happened... how he would react...

The wind swept through the open window, pulling his attention, and he moved to close it. But when he turned back, he stopped. He stared at her in her nightgown in the moonlight, then he looked around the room again, as if recognizing something. He moved toward her slowly, his breaths coming heavier now.

"Salara," he said, his voice low. "Was the Bear here?"

How did he know? Had he seen him too? Her heart raced in her chest. Slowly, she nodded.

His eyes combed the room again, and he moved quickly back to the window and threw it open, leaning to look out from their second-story room.

Finding nothing, he turned back to her. Then his eyes found the knife on the floor. He picked it up. "Did he hurt you?"

She shook her head.

"Did he—" He stopped, and his breaths came faster. His voice came lower. "Did he take you?"

She shook her head again. "No," she said quickly, "but he..." She drew her fingers back up to her lips.

He clutched the knife in his hand, and his teeth flashed. "I've seen this moment before."

Oh gods, the vision from the seer. He'd told her he'd seen Alexander come to her bed, that he'd seen her take him. This had to be the moment.

She shook her head again. "Mikael, I promise you nothing happened. He kissed me, and I stopped him. I told him that's not how we were. I promise you."

His face hardened. "Did you call him to you?"

Her heart pulsed quicker. "Of course not."

But his eyes betrayed his doubt.

She stepped forward and grasped his arm, squeezing it tightly. "No. I promise you. Mikael."

His stance didn't soften.

"Mikael," she said again. "I didn't call him. Please. You have to believe this."

But she wasn't sure he did.

Salara was asleep. Her breaths came deep and rhythmic as Mikael held her in his arms in the bed at the inn. But anger coursed through him. He shouldn't have brought her here. The plan had been to make camp at the Fork, that's where the army was now. Yes, it was cold, but they could have made do with a tent.

He cursed himself again. He'd been lax with her safety, knowing the happiness it would bring her to walk through the markets of the Free Cities, and how she'd enjoy a bath and bed as a break from the travel. He'd wanted to take her mind from the pressures that weighted her spirit.

But they were so close to the North; they could have waited. She hadn't even asked him to stop in the Free Cities. He'd done it simply for her enjoyment. As much as it killed him to admit it, he shouldn't have stopped here.

He couldn't shake the doubt that lingered. She'd said she hadn't called the Bear. Everything in him wanted to believe that, was desperate to believe it... Why couldn't he?

She'd had no blood on her, no vial. So why couldn't he believe?

Because the Bear could take her from him. She'd lied for the Bear before, had kept things from Mikael. Given a worthy enough cause, Mikael knew, she'd do it again. He didn't doubt her heart; he knew she loved him. But they both had drastically different ideas on the best way to handle things.

If the Bear was in her mind, he would have needed the blood—she had to have called him.

Suddenly, Mikael stiffened. *If* the Bear was in her mind. *If.*

If he wasn't in her mind, it meant he had come in person. And she wouldn't have called his person...

Carefully, he slipped his arm out from underneath Salara and rose. He pulled on his boots and jacket and quietly opened the door to Bhastian, who stood right outside. Mikael waved the Crest captain in. He wouldn't risk leaving her alone again while he went to find Soren.

Bhastian took his post just inside the door, and Mikael closed it behind him as he stepped into the hall.

His anger built—for Salara, not at her. He'd long since accepted the Bear's place in her heart, understood it even, but continuing to see him wasn't allowing her the space to heal. With her grandmother now dying, could she handle both?

Mikael tried not to think about what the Bear's continued presence meant for his own fate, although the thought haunted him still. The Bear would bring his end. From the dead, apparently.

No—this man wasn't the Bear. He couldn't be. And if this wasn't a ghost in her mind, someone was toying with her, and doing it by getting dangerously close to her.

Mikael strode outside, toward a few of the Crest standing together with Soren. They hadn't captured anyone, as he'd hoped. Perhaps no one had truly been there.

Mikael had thought the worst case would be her calling the Bear back to her mind. That would have hurt the most. But even so, he found himself wishing it were what had happened. For if she didn't call him, this man now had the power to visit her without the blood, which was alarming. Worse yet, if he came in person, he had the ability to hurt her. Mikael prayed to gods he didn't believe in that she'd called him.

"We even swept the tavern," Soren said as he approached.

"So, he's in her mind."

"I thought the same," Soren replied. "But come here." He led Mikael to the wall of the castle, under the window of the room in which Salara slept on the second story. Soren crouched down, holding out the lantern in his hand. "What do you make of these?" he asked as he motioned to the ground in front of him, and Mikael shifted his eyes to boot prints in the dirt.

CHAPTER THIRTY-TWO

Mercia stood exactly as it had the day she'd left it, but it seemed a little darker now. The white of the castle seemed more gray, and even the stained glass windows didn't hold the same shine. Maybe it was the winter skies, or maybe it was the darkness hanging over her heart.

She tried not to think about the journey, or Alexander, but the memory of the night before kept creeping back into her mind. Why had he come to her? How had he come?

And just when she thought things were settling with Mikael, this brought back the distance between them. She'd seen it—the doubt in his eyes when she'd told him she hadn't called Alexander. She couldn't be angry with him; she hadn't been entirely honest with him in the past when it had come to Alexander. But his doubt still hurt.

When they crossed the bridge to the castle isle and reached the courtyard, Catherine was waiting for them. She sat in a wheeled chair with a fur draped over her lap. Her cheekbones seemed a little higher on her face, or perhaps the recesses of her eyes had dipped farther, making them look that way. She was so thin.

Norah stopped, then slowly slid down from Sephir.

Catherine stood shakily, but steadied and reached out her hand.

Norah wavered. Caspian had told her Catherine had a terminal sickness, but that she was still active and somewhat herself. Norah hadn't known it was this bad yet. Her eyes welled as she took Catherine's hand.

"Took you long enough to get here," her grandmother said, hiding her own emotion in jest.

Norah looked over her frail body and glanced at the wheeled chair. Hold it together, she told herself. But her lip trembled.

"Oh, my dear," Catherine said softly, and she pulled Norah closer. "Come here."

Norah stepped forward and hugged her grandmother. Tightly. She smelled of oranges, her grandmother's favorite fruit from her home kingdom of Eilor, and Norah breathed it in.

"I'm glad you came," Catherine said into her ear.

"Of course I came." Norah pulled back and looked at her. "Although if you wanted me to come back, you could have just asked." She sniffed. "You didn't need to be so dramatic and start dying."

Catherine gave a weak laugh, and her eyes glistened. "Come inside, child. There's so much to talk about."

Norah nodded.

Shakily, her grandmother sat back down in her wheeled chair, and the guard turned it and started her toward the castle.

Norah turned to Mikael, looking to take his arm, but his attention was fixed on the sky. She followed his gaze to the Mercian banner on one of the turrets. His eyes found hers again in surprise.

She couldn't help a smile. It had been over a month since she'd sent the changes of her sigil back to Mercia, and it was the first time she'd seen it on something other than a parchment drawing. She let herself take it in, in all its glory against the sky. It was the same image that was marked on

Mikael's skin. A winterhawk rising with the sun, as she had risen with him. The original symbol had never truly felt like her own. Now it did, because it had a piece of him in it.

He gave a smile of his own. And that made her happy.

Mercia almost felt like home with Mikael there. He seemed more and more like he belonged, and Soren seemed... less Destroyer-like, especially when he pushed her grandmother around in her wheeled chair.

And, of course, Catherine loved it.

As evening fell, they entered the dining hall. Soren pushed Catherine to her place at the table and then took his own seat as Norah and Mikael took theirs. Mikael raised a brow at Soren's joining, then looked at Catherine. But her grandmother only took another large swig from her wineglass as if nothing was amiss. Because it wasn't.

Norah looked at Mikael and smiled at him. She'd forgotten to fill him in that Soren had a place at the table with Catherine for all meals. Her grandmother had even stopped scowling at the commander for eating with his knife.

It was nice—their being together. She wondered how long Mikael would stay. Katya had sent a quarter of the Kharavian army to Bahoul and held the rest along the Canyonlands, ready, and Phillip had his forces in Eilor, all according to plan. But Mikael couldn't be away from Kharav for long, especially if things escalated with Japheth and Rael. He shouldn't have come at all, but he'd have things no other way. And she loved him for it.

Catherine took another deep drink of wine. "We must discuss the regency," she said, rather abruptly.

Norah stopped and stared at her. "What... what about it?"

"We need to discuss who's to be named regent."

Why was she raising this now? That wasn't—no, they didn't need to talk about this now. Catherine still had plenty of time. They could talk about this later. They had time. *She* had time.

"Norah?"

She glanced back up to find her grandmother looking back at her. But she just shook her head. "No, we should talk about this with the council. Later."

Catherine frowned. "I want us to talk about it now, before there's pressure to make a decision quickly."

"We still have plenty of time," Norah argued. And she wasn't ready.

"There isn't as much time as you think."

Norah clenched her fork in her hand to force down the rise of emotion. "I said I don't want to talk about it right now." She couldn't. She needed her mind calm to talk about this, and right now... it wasn't. And this conversation was so sudden. Too sudden.

"Norah, I know it's a difficult—"

"No!"

"We don't have to talk about it now," Mikael said, interrupting and quieting the room.

Norah inhaled and pushed her breath out slowly. Under the table, she relaxed her fist, where her fingernails were digging into her palm. When she raised her gaze, Mikael was watching her. She couldn't read his expression.

They finished dinner quietly, and after, Mikael walked her back to their chamber.

"Thank you," she said softly as they stepped inside.

Mikael waved out Serene and closed the door behind her.

She pushed out another breath. "I just... I can't even think about the regency right now."

He pulled her close and gently smoothed her hair back over her shoulder. Hesitation sat on his lips. "Salara," he said softly, "I don't think the North needs a regent."

It was true the collective council could look after Mercia. She could take her time to make a decision. That made her feel a little better.

"Not if her queen is here," he added.

She stopped. "What?" What was that supposed to mean?

He clasped her hands in his and held them to his chest. "Salara. Your place is here now."

She shook her head. Was he serious? "No, it's not. My place is in Kharav."

"You're the North Queen."

"I'm salara!" She pulled her hands from his. "I'm going back to Kharav with you."

Pain etched across his brow. His lips parted, but he paused before saying, "I'm not going back to Kharav again."

The finality of his words shook her. She couldn't speak.

His eyes were heavy with his own emotion. "You and I both know my fate. You must be prepared... to rule alone. And you should be here. Whatever is left of the Kharavian army, if Kharav still stands at the end of all this—"

"Stop." She shook her head.

"Listen to me—"

"No."

"Salara," he pressed.

"No!"

He clutched her firmly by the arms. "Listen!"

Tears streamed down her cheeks as she quieted.

Mikael brought his hand up to her face and held her to look at him. "When I fall, it's likely Kharav will as well. Even if it doesn't, it won't be safe for you there."

"I'm not marrying Soren—"

"I'm not asking you to again."

He dropped his head for a moment and then looked back at her. "Soren will stay in the North. With you. What's left of the army will follow him and add to your defenses. With Soren and Adrian and Caspian, and this king of Aleon, you'll have most of what you need."

But that wasn't what she needed.

"But you have to stay in the North," he said. "Do you understand?"

No.

"I know you're a strong queen, the strongest there's ever been. And you'll stay strong. Here." He clutched her tighter. "Promise me."

She wouldn't.

"Promise me!" he demanded.

Another tear escaped down her cheek. She shook her head.

"Norah," he said softly. It broke her. "Promise me," he said again.

She let out a trembling breath through her tears. "I promise."

He gave a sad smile as he brushed her face with his fingertips. Then he pulled her close and wrapped his arms around her. She breathed him in—his scent, his nearness, his being. No, she told herself. If he thought he was just going to traipse off to war and kill himself, he was wrong. They'd find a way to get through this, and they'd go back to Kharav together.

She couldn't lose him. She wouldn't.

He nuzzled the top of her head. "Can I make love to you, wife?" he whispered.

She looked up at him and ran her hand around the back of his neck and pulled him down to kiss her. Then he picked her up and carried her to the bed.

Two days passed, but tears threatened every time she thought about the conversation between her and Mikael, every time she thought about his fate and about the possibility of never returning to Kharav again.

Then she resolved herself. She'd find a way to stop it. How, she didn't know. All she knew is that she'd keep Mikael. Or join him in death in the pursuit of trying. Either way, Mercia would need someone, and it gave her the strength to talk about the regency.

Norah knocked on Catherine's door. She'd take her grandmother for a walk outside for some fresh air, then talk about options. She was sure Catherine had already put together some recommendations.

"Come back later," came Catherine's voice.

Norah almost smiled and opened the door.

"Oh, it's you," her grandmother said as she stepped inside.

"You sound disappointed."

"No, no. You can get my robe."

This time Norah did smile. "Glad I can be of help."

"Well, I sent the maid away because I actually wanted to rest awhile longer, but then I couldn't."

"That explains why you're not dressed yet." Catherine was always put together, no matter the circumstance. It probably bothered her that she wasn't right now.

Norah walked into the side chamber and pulled out a dress. "Here, I'll help you."

"I don't like that one," her grandmother said as Norah stepped back to the bed and held it up.

Norah pushed a breath between her lips and pulled another. As she stepped back to the bed, Catherine moved to rise, then lost her balance.

"Grandmother!" Norah dropped the dress and caught her in her fall. They landed awkwardly but were otherwise fine.

Catherine gripped her arm tightly, then resigned to sit. She waved her back. "I don't think I'm going to go."

"It's all right. It was just a misstep. Here, let's get you dressed."

"I said no."

Norah stopped. She sighed and moved to pick up the dropped dress from the floor. "All right. We can go later."

"No, Norah. I don't think I'm going out again."

Wait... *again*? "Why not again?"

"I just don't have the energy anymore."

Norah stared at her.

"Plus, being outside is overrated. I hate the cold." Catherine shifted back. "Just help me get situated back in bed, and I'd like that book over there on the cabinet."

Norah looked over and stared at the book. Not go out again? How could she say it so casually? She got the book and slowly handed it to her grandmother.

Settled back in her bed with her book, Catherine asked, "Did you want to stay for a while, my dear?"

Norah only stared at her. Catherine talked like everything was so normal... so... fine. But it wasn't fine. She was dying. And she was perfectly accepting of it—planning a new regent, reading her book, deciding she just wouldn't go outside anymore.

Just like Mikael was so accepting of his fate.

Why were they so accepting?

She couldn't breathe.

"Norah? Are you going to stay?"

"Um..." She couldn't. She needed to breathe, to think, just for a moment. "Maybe I'll come back in a little bit? I was just going to tend to some things."

"Very well." Catherine opened her book. To read. Dying.

Norah walked numbly down the hall. It wouldn't be long now. Catherine had been right—she didn't have as much time as Norah had thought. Her world was caving in around her, and what could she do? She stepped outside but didn't feel the cold.

She did need to see to one thing, though. She found Soren with Caspian on the bridge, discussing more fortifications and defensive efforts.

"We'll keep the ships moving through the channel," Caspian was saying. "It's cold enough for ice to form, and we'll keep it clear."

"Let it form in the areas where it won't support weight. If someone is stupid enough to attack the North, let them venture out onto it. We'll let winter help us."

Not a pleasant thought—men being swallowed by the icy waters—but effective, she supposed. The benefits of having a man of war plan war strategies.

Soren stopped when he saw her. "What do you want?" he asked in his normal gruff voice, but she knew it wasn't a gruff question. He genuinely wanted to know what she wanted, and he'd make sure she got it. He wouldn't like this request, though...

"I need Adrian to come home."

He shifted his weight back. He definitely didn't like the request.

"There's not much time now, and..." She closed her eyes and shook her head as she gathered herself again. "And he needs to be able to say goodbye. If even for a short time."

Catherine had raised Adrian, loved him, and he loved her. He hadn't gotten the chance to say goodbye to Alexander, but she could bring him home for Catherine. Of course, Soren would be against the idea. Adrian was in service to Phillip in Aleon, where he was helping prepare for war—an important task. But this was important too.

"All right," he said.

She snapped her gaze up in surprise. Not even an argument?

"I'll send a message and tell him to come with urgency," he added.

She stood, still frozen in her surprise. "O-Okay, thank you." The thought of Adrian coming home made her heart suddenly feel not quite so heavy.

CHAPTER THIRTY-THREE

Soren hammered the last nail into the iron shoe around his destrier's hoof before clipping and smoothing the outer edges. When it came to the care of the animal he depended so much on, he trusted only himself, as with Salar's destrier as well. Salara's mare, the horse of the Wild, didn't need shoes or maintaining, but he checked on her regularly regardless.

He released the animal's leg and patted the stallion on the shoulder—a horse he'd trained himself, the best he'd had yet. It was a strong beast, black as night, smart and fearless; he earned every bit of his noble name, Khalel al'Dakar V. Of course, he followed Khalel IV—the horse Soren had been forced to fell at the base of Bahoul to prevent Salara from escaping those years ago. It had been a great loss.

The original Khalel had been the famed destrier of his father—well, the father that had raised Soren—captain of the Crest, Tyrhar Nazim. And Khalel al'Dakar became the name of every destrier Soren trusted to carry him into battle.

When he'd fled with Salara back to Kharav after the council had tried to kill her, he'd left the animal behind. He didn't think he'd find him again in returning to the North, but when he did, he nearly wept. Soren didn't have many things. Besides his father's sword, this horse was the most important thing to him.

Soren's eye caught on the small braid in the animal's mane, and he scowled.

Salara.

Kal, she called him. Kal sounded like a packhorse name, but the animal came to it nonetheless, much to Soren's dismay. She was always giving him sugar and fruit, spoiling him, as she had the dogs. He missed the dogs. Brave beasts. If there were gods, and if anyone or anything deserved to be among them, it was the selfless animals that had given their all.

Soren pulled off his leather farrier's apron and draped it over the rail, then unclipped the animal's halter from the wall. "Come on, Kal," he said as he led the great destrier back to his stall.

The light of morning brought little warmth as he stepped into the frigid air, but Soren was in high spirits, and that was enough to warm him. Adrian would be arriving soon, something he was looking forward to. He'd never been a proud man, but he was proud now. Adrian had grown into a warrior, a leader, and a man respected by three of the greatest kingdoms in the world, and Soren loved him like his own blood. But it was under sad circumstances he was returning. Death would come soon for the grandmother. This was the woman who had raised Salara, and the Bear, and Adrian. She was a woman greatly respected, and she'd be a woman greatly mourned.

It shouldn't take Adrian too long to reach the castle. Last Soren had received word from him, he'd been on his way to Praetoria, the westernmost kingdom of the Aleon Empire.

Aleon.

Soren tried not to think about Aleon. He'd left the king with an awkwardness between them. Phillip had told him it was his move. And he'd simply left.

The bells rang out, and Soren's lips curved into a smile under his wrap. Adrian had arrived. He pulled his cloak around him, clipped it in place, and started toward the castle. The stables sat on the lower west bank, and it was a long walk for such a small isle. He reached the west doors and wove through the halls, but when he stepped into the great hall, it was empty. Unusual.

"Where's the arrival?" he called to a servant.

"Queen Norah is in the throne room, my lord."

The throne room? That was a bit much to receive Adrian, but this was the North, and they were strange here. He picked up toward the throne room and entered from a side hall to see Salara and Salar both on their thrones. Mikael didn't like the Northern throne; he didn't like to sit on it. Strange that he would take it now. Perhaps this place was turning him strange too.

Adrian stood with a small cluster of Aleon soldiers, his helm under his arm. A smile broke across his face when he saw Soren. "Lord Commander," he greeted.

Soren crossed the space between them and clasped Adrian's shoulder in warm welcome. "Little Bear."

"Soren!" Salara exclaimed as she stood. "Where were you? I've been looking all over for you." There was urgency in her voice, and Soren jerked his head toward her in surprise. Why would—

The doors of the throne room opened, quieting the hall, and another group of Aleon soldiers entered.

And leading them—*the Aleon king.*

Soren froze. The king swept forward with a graceful strength, his movement sure and fluid. His long strides covered the length of the throne room faster than Soren could wrap his mind around his arrival.

The king stopped a short distance from him, his eyes on Salar and Salara.

"King Phillip," Salara said, "welcome to Mercia."

He'd come to the North. *Why?*

"Queen Norah," Phillip greeted in return. "I know I come on little notice, but when I heard about Lady Catherine, and given your invitation when last in Aleon, I couldn't not."

"I'm glad you did," she said. "My grandmother will be very happy to see you." Salara stood and held out her hand.

Phillip stepped forward and took it, bringing it to his lips with a slight dip of his head. As he released Salara's hand, he locked stares with Salar. They stood in silence, taking each other in.

Mikael stood as well. His face remained fixed, showing nothing, but this was the first time he'd met the Aleon king face-to-face. Surely this surprise visit wouldn't come easily.

Salara reached back and looped her hand under Mikael's arm. "Let me present my husband, Mikael Ratha Shal, salar of Kharav and king of Mercia."

"Salar Mikael," Phillip greeted, dipping his head respectfully.

Mikael stood for a moment, then did the same. "King Phillip," he said, and the air lightened. But only ever so slightly.

The Aleon king turned his head, and his eyes found Soren's. Their stares caught, perhaps a little too long. Soren knew the other eyes in the room were on them, but he couldn't pull his gaze from the king. "Lord Commander," Phillip greeted finally.

But Soren was lost for words. He said nothing.

Salara stepped to Phillip's side with an uneasy smile. "I'm sure you'd like to freshen up. I know it's been a long journey. Let me show you to your chamber, and then we can catch up on everything at dinner."

"That would be wonderful," he said. He gave a nod to Mikael and glanced once more at Soren before letting Salara lead him away.

Soren numbly stepped beside Mikael, and they both watched the Aleon king leave. When Phillip was out of sight, he could finally breathe, and he turned to Mikael. "Did you know about this?"

"We received word earlier this morning. Salara had given him an open invitation when she was in Aleon, but I didn't think he'd actually come."

"And now that he has?"

Mikael turned to him. "You'll not harm him. Let him stay. And let him leave."

But Soren's mind wasn't on harming the Aleon king.

Norah smoothed the front of her gown and drew in a deep breath before she dared to step into the great hall. It had taken Adrian a little less than a week to arrive in Mercia after receiving the message. She was surprised he'd come so quickly. And with Phillip. And although a week seemed no time at all, it did give her some space to wrap her mind around the circumstance and come to terms with the things she *had* to accept—rationally, at least. Catherine would be with her for only a short while longer. There was nothing she could do to stop it, and this she'd come to accept.

But Mikael... Mikael—*no*. Nothing would make her accept that. Nothing would make her accept his fate. They'd find a way through. *She'd* find a way through. But for now, she'd focus on tonight.

Music carried from inside the great hall and out through the castle—merry music—but she wasn't in the spirit for merrymaking. She and Phillip had spent the afternoon with Catherine, who was certainly thrilled about the visit of a king in her name, and in seeing Adrian. Her grandmother properly enjoyed every bit of attention she could manage. Even though Catherine was confined to her bed, it was good to see her enjoying herself. She was so frail now, so weak, a shell of what she once was. But with Phillip's charm and Adrian's smile, Catherine had color in her cheeks and even managed a few laughs.

Now with her grandmother tended to and resting for the night, Norah turned her attention to the evening. While it was proper to host a dinner for Phillip, and despite being happy to see him again, she wasn't exactly looking forward to the social. Tonight would be about brokering relations between Aleon and Kharav, between Phillip and Mikael: enemies-forced-allies now together for the first time. It was complicated by Soren, who no doubt would be facing struggles of his own. She wasn't entirely sure where the lord commander now sat on the spectrum of complete hatred and cautious interest. She'd thought she'd seen a glimmer of something when they'd had dinner with Phillip in Aleon. And Soren had since traveled to Aleon, and not only did Phillip still live but Soren had sent Adrian to his service. Did Phillip hold an importance to Soren beyond pure duty now?

Norah pushed out a breath. It was none of her business, she scolded herself. But curse the gods, who was she kidding? The wonder was killing her.

With another deep breath, she stepped inside. The hall was alive with conversation and laughter. A few nobles from Aleon were in attendance, and they stood among the Mercian nobles as old friends. She spotted Mikael at the front, with Caspian and two Mercian councilmen beside him. Conversation passed easily between them, and she paused. It was a sight she thought she'd never see, and it brought a smile to her face.

Mikael caught sight of her and smiled as she approached. His thick, dark hair was tied back as it usually was, and his beard was cut short, almost to the skin. But unlike his normal attire, he wore an embellished black doublet over a long-sleeved black tunic, covering his markings. The Kharavians took care for modesty in Mercia, and the effort wasn't lost on her. He held his hand out for her, and she took it. "You look beautiful," he said.

Caspian and the councilmen gave a small bow and left them some space.

"You're quite handsome yourself," she said, squeezing his hand. "People might actually start believing you're king of Mercia now."

He chuckled. But then he quieted as his eyes drifted across the room, and his smile fell.

"What's wrong?" She followed his gaze to see Soren at the end of the hall, and beside him stood Phillip. Her pulse quickened, and her smile widened. Perhaps she'd get an answer to her wonderings sooner than she'd thought.

Phillip spoke with a genuine smile, clearly engaged with whatever he was saying. Soren didn't appear like he was on the brink of murder—which was always a good sign. Was he actually enjoying himself?

"What are they doing?" Mikael asked.

His voice brought her back; she'd almost forgotten he was standing there. "It looks like they're talking." *Miraculously.*

"I'm going over there."

She tightened her hand around his. "Soren's perfectly capable of taking care of himself."

"I didn't say he wasn't." He started again toward his commander, but she pulled him back.

"If you interrupt them, I'll properly cut you," she warned.

He gaped at her in surprise. "What?"

"You heard me. Leave them alone." She threaded her fingers in his for a better hold on him and set her eyes back on Soren. "Just stand here and spy on them with me," she whispered.

"Why are you spying on them?"

"Hush, I'm trying to hear." She strained her ears. "Is Soren smiling?" *Damn the wrap.* She wasn't close enough to see his eyes to tell.

"Why would he be smiling?"

Well, she didn't know if the lord commander *was* actually smiling. She squinted, trying to focus on the telltale creases of his eyes. She hated not being able to see his face right now.

"Why would he be smiling?" Mikael asked again. His voice was different now, and Norah glanced up to see his expression had changed.

She held on to his hand. Mikael knew who Soren was. Now the question would be if he could support Soren in his happiness. She watched him closely as the realization came to him. His nostrils flared, and his breath came slightly uneven.

"Don't get weird," she said.

His lips tightened. "I'm not getting weird," he quipped back, as he stood, getting weird.

She kept her hold on him and leaned into him softly. "He deserves this."

He glanced down at her. "This?" he said angrily.

"Yes, whatever you call the happiness of being with another. Soren deserves it."

"But not with..." He stifled a snarl as he looked back out at Soren and Phillip.

"Not with a man?"

"That's not what I was going to say." The hard line of his lips turned into a slight frown. "Not with that one." His frown deepened. "A better one."

"Better than the ruler of an empire?"

"When has that mattered?"

The corner of her mouth tugged down. *True.* But Phillip was more. "Phillip's beautiful and smart, and makes you feel happy, and he's good with a sword. And you know that sword part has always mattered to Soren."

He grimaced and looked down at her. "You think the Aleon king is beautiful?"

"Are we not looking at the same man?"

He puffed a breath between his teeth as he looked back across the floor. "Soren can do better."

Was he serious? "Fine. Name your match."

His brows drew together. "I'm not going to mate-match my lord commander."

"Ha!" She grinned triumphantly. "Because you don't have a match." He crossed his arms. She wedged her hand between them and tugged at him to open up. "Phillip's shown himself to be a good king and friend. If

Soren sees your disapproval, he won't allow himself that happiness. But he deserves to. Would you keep him from that?"

He was quiet for a time, then said finally, "I want him to be happy."

"Then you should let him know. But take care. I never told him you knew about him." And she pulled him down and kissed his cheek.

Soren drew in a deep breath of winter air out on the terrace. The music and laughing carried from the inside out into the night. He needed a moment of quiet, but he supposed this would do. He typically skipped socials; he didn't know what had made him come to this one.

That was a lie—yes, he did. He cursed the Aleon king under his breath.

Back in Aleon, Phillip had made his interest quite clear. Of course, Soren's interest had been in killing the man who wore the face of a dream he'd carried for some time. Of all the people, why did it have to be the Aleon king? He had hated Phillip for ruining it.

And then something changed. Soren started to like the ruin. The man in his dream hadn't smiled, but Phillip smiled. Often. And he laughed—something Soren despised. Until he found himself not despising it anymore.

Something felt different now, and he wasn't sure if it frightened him or excited him. He wasn't sure of anything anymore with this man. Only that he wanted more.

But that wasn't possible. He couldn't face Mikael with this ask. Mikael wouldn't understand. No one would, except for Salara.

A presence came beside him. He didn't need to look to know who it was.

"Salara is dancing with the Aleon king," Mikael said, breaking the quiet.

"I'm sure she's being polite," Soren assured him.

"Oh, she's quite enjoying herself. She says he's a beautiful man."

Soren chuckled. That he was. "You know she means nothing by it."

"No, I know. And I don't mind. Especially as she's trying to convince me that he's good enough for you."

Soren's heart stopped, and he struggled to force his breath calm and silent. He looked across the torchlit city. Had he heard him correctly?

"She says he's beautiful and smart and makes people happy, and he's good with a sword." Mikael turned and looked at him. "But you don't even like happy."

Soren turned, and their eyes locked. He knew. *Mikael knew.* Soren searched his face for judgment, disapproval—disgust, even. He found none of those things. Emotion breached the walls he fought so desperately to hold in place, and he broke away to blink it back. He looked back out at the city, gripping the balcony railing. "Maybe I'm starting to," he said hoarsely.

Mikael turned and leaned his back against the rail. Their eyes locked again. His gaze was penetrating, and Soren could barely hold it. Just as he was about to break, Mikael said, "He better make you pretty damned happy, then." He cuffed the top of Soren's shoulder and left to return inside.

Soren gripped the rail so tight his knuckles whitened. He couldn't breathe. He reached up and ripped the wrap from his face and sucked in the icy air. Mikael knew. He knew about Phillip.

More—he knew about Soren; he knew who he was.

Soren cursed under panting breaths. He had to pull himself together. He wiped his face with his hands.

"Are you going to stand out here all night?" Salara said, coming up behind him.

He straightened and sucked in another breath of winter. Wiping his face again, he quickly composed himself and pulled up his wrap. "Aren't you supposed to be dancing?" he asked as coolly as he could manage.

"Phillip's free now if you'd like a twirl about."

He snorted.

She clasped the railing beside him and rocked against it. "I saw Mikael out here."

Of course she had. "You told him about me."

She shook her head. "He's always known."

His pulse picked back up, and their stares locked. "How much?" he asked.

She didn't answer.

Soren grabbed her arm, pulling her still. "How much does he know?"

Her eyes darted back and forth between his, and ever so slightly, she winced. But he saw it. "Everything," she whispered.

He could barely speak. "How I felt before?"

Silently, she nodded.

All this time?

He released her and leaned heavily against the rail, returning his gaze across the city. Mikael knew. He had known all along.

"But he loves you," she said. "And he wants you to be happy. Like I do."

He couldn't reply. They only stood. Salara leaned against him—whether to steal some of his warmth or to comfort him, he didn't care. He was glad she was there.

They stayed on the terrace awhile, until Salara squeezed his arm and then left him for the warmth inside. He stayed long after the activities died down inside, and after most had retired for the evening.

He only stood, breathing in the night. Mikael's judgment, his disappointment, his rejection as his friend and now brother—these things had been Soren's greatest fears—to lose Mikael's love. But that hadn't happened. And now something felt new. For the first time, he felt... free.

There was something he needed to do.

He turned and strode back through the empty halls, his heart thrumming. The surge of the hunt raced through his veins. He reached the royal guest chamber and pushed open the door without knocking.

Phillip stood in the center of the room, his back to the door, reading a letter in his hands. He turned as Soren latched the lock behind him. Their stares locked, and Phillip's lips parted, yet he didn't speak.

His scent was faint—an autumn breeze—but one that Soren knew. One that he'd dreamed about.

Soren crossed the room, ripping his wrap down from his face as he closed the space between them. He caught Phillip just under his jaw and pushed him to the wall, covering his mouth with his own. To taste him was even better than he'd imagined, and it threatened his control—his very small scrap of control.

Soren was a larger man than the king, and he held him to the wall with a force. But Phillip wasn't a man to be forced. He yielded willingly. Still,

Soren felt the power of his body, and he slid his hand down and tightened it around Phillip's neck. That power—held in his grip.

They broke from their kiss, and their eyes locked. Phillip reached his hand to Soren's chest, spreading it wide across his skin, then ran it up toward his face. But Soren caught it. It was too intimate, too close. Too much.

"Do you not want me to touch you?" Phillip asked.

This man didn't know him to touch him this way.

Phillip's eyes moved back and forth between his. "Take what you want, then."

Soren's breath faltered. He would just give himself?

Phillip reached up and clasped the weapons strap across Soren's chest and pulled Soren to him, bringing their mouths back together.

Then Soren's control was gone. He spun Phillip to face the wall and stripped his vest and shirt from him. Linen tore, and buttons fell to the floor. Not that Soren cared. He pushed him hard against the stone. The muscle across Phillip's back bulged. Soren let his eyes take in the beauty. Unlike his own back, marred by scars of battle and scars of the whip, Phillip's skin was smooth. Perfection. Soren raked the pads of his fingertips down it, and red marks sprang to the surface. Phillip writhed under his bruising hold, and Soren gripped him harder.

"Do you want my pain?" Phillip panted.

Soren paused. *Pain.*

"Is that what you like?"

He frowned. There were times Soren liked pain—liked inflicting it, sometimes even receiving it. But he didn't want Phillip's pain. He loosened his grip. "No." His voice came softer than what he'd expected. "I don't want to hurt you."

Phillip turned to face him, and the corners of his mouth turned up. "I'm glad to hear it, although..." His lips parted slightly. "You don't have to be gentle." And the Aleon king sank to the floor in front of him.

Soren's breaths came faster. Phillip unlaced Soren's breeches and pulled them down, releasing his flesh and wrapping his hand around him. Soren let his head fall back. It felt... so good. Too good. And when Phillip's mouth found him, he worried he might not be able to keep standing. He panted as he reached out and caught himself against the wall.

Never had he let someone be so free with him, so free in touching him. And never had someone made him want to relinquish control. He forced himself to keep it. "Get on the bed," he rasped.

Phillip looked up at him, his lips still around his head. He took Soren all the way into his throat before pulling his mouth away, leaving a string of saliva between them. It was almost Soren's undoing.

It took all his control to wait for Phillip to move to the bed before he came behind him. He gripped the nape of his neck and pushed the king forward onto his stomach. Slower, he told himself. He slid his length down Phillip's center and positioned himself, but Phillip was tight against him. Too tight. Phillip had had a male lover before, but it was clear to Soren now with the king beneath him, he wasn't a man accustomed to being taken. Soren was still wet from Phillip's mouth, but not enough. He glanced around the room. On the small table near the bed was a tray of bread and cheese, with a side bowl of olive oil. Soren pulled back and took it. Then he dropped a trail of the oil between them and spread it with his fingers.

Soren repositioned. Lowering himself over the king again, he brought his mouth to Phillip's ear and breathed, "Let me inside you." Phillip's body eased. Soren pushed against him, testing, and Phillip gave. Soren pushed harder, and they both gasped as he sank fully inside him. Then he stilled, giving them both a moment.

Soren had been with women before, but he'd never had the strength of a man. He'd dreamed about it, craved it—the hard steel of a masculine body, a body that could handle his own strength. With the softness of a woman, it took effort for pleasure to come. But here, with Phillip—pure power underneath him—it took effort to not lose himself completely.

He moved slowly to start, then faster. Harder. Phillip didn't quail underneath him. Instead, he pushed back against him, asking for more. And Soren gave it to him.

Phillip's body called to him—called him to own it, to relish it, to touch it. So he did. He curled his arm around Phillip's hips and pulled him back hard, driving himself deeper. Phillip arched against him, reaching back and gripping Soren to pull him even deeper.

The king's arousal fueled his own. He took Phillip's flesh in his hand and stroked his length as he drove harder. They were both close now, their breaths shorter and faster. The heat built between them until he feared they would both catch fire. And then Phillip's body tightened under him. Liquid warmth pulsed into Soren's hand and onto the bed underneath them. It was too much to keep control, and he let out a growl as he shattered in his own release. He pushed himself deeper, then deeper still. He pushed until he was completely spent and empty, completely enraptured by this man.

They collapsed, still joined, both panting. The air smelled of male and sex and power, and Soren breathed it in. Everything about this king was intoxicating.

Phillip chuckled under Soren's weight. "I'll call for new bedding."

Soren bared his teeth against his neck. "You say that like I'm finished with you."

Phillip chuckled again.

The hours passed quickly. Soren took him two more times, not able to get enough, not able to pull himself away from Phillip's body. Then finally, exhausted, they both lay in the quiet of the candlelight, facing each other.

Phillip's eyes burned blue, blue like the brightest gems. He stretched his hand wide against Soren's skin, just under his shoulder. Their stares remained locked as he drew his fingers softly down the dell of his chest. Soren's mind told him to pull back, but he didn't. He kept his eyes on the Aleon king and let himself stay, let the king touch him. He wanted his touch.

Phillip's mouth moved to speak, but he hesitated. Soren waited. Almost fearing it. He knew what he'd ask. It was what everyone who he'd ever taken to bed asked—about the future. And his answer would be offensive. It wasn't meant to be offensive. He wanted this man. But want wasn't enough. And Phillip wouldn't understand. No one did.

The Aleon king gave a small smile. He grazed his fingers across Soren's skin again. "I know you don't belong to me," he said softly. "Your loyalty, your devotion to Norah and your king—I would never ask you to betray that. And when you let me touch you, when you let me have you, I see it for exactly what it is. A gift." He drew Soren's hand up to his lips and kissed his palm. "Thank you for this gift."

Soren's breath shook. This man understood him. He saw him.

And that was a dangerous thing.

CHAPTER THIRTY-FOUR

Soren lay in the quiet of the rising sun. He watched the Aleon king sleep—inhaling deeply and then releasing—the rise of his chest, the glow of his skin under the morning rays.

Phillip was a beautiful man, sculpted of strength and light. His nose sat straight between the thick, dark lashes of his eyelids. The square of his jaw tapered gently to his chin, just underneath the perfection of his lips. Hints of copper in his bronze locks begged the touch of fingers, and Soren couldn't help himself.

It hurt. Phillip had said he would never pull him from his duty, but any pull at all was a pull away from duty. Soren couldn't allow it. He clenched his jaw until it ached to match the ache in his chest as he drew his fingers through Phillip's hair.

The king's eyes opened slowly, and he smiled. He looked like an Aleon god. Soren loved how he smiled. He hated that he loved it. It made it all the harder. He cursed himself—he shouldn't have come.

"I have to go," Soren said.

"Will you come later, then—"

"No. I can't come back to you."

Phillip stilled, and his brows drew together. "I don't understand."

Soren didn't expect him to. "This can't happen again. I shouldn't have come."

Phillip pushed himself up and reached for him. "Soren, I—"

He pulled back and moved to stand, but Phillip caught him. "Soren, wait."

Soren pulled against his hold, but Phillip tightened his grasp. Soren wanted to wait, wanted to stay, but he couldn't. "Let me go," he warned.

"I said wait."

"Let me go," he said again.

"No."

The longer Soren waited, the more he might stay. But he couldn't stay. So he couldn't wait. Soren twisted against Phillip's hold, but Phillip was a powerful man, and fast, and he jerked Soren forward. Soren's balance gave way, and he fell back onto the bed. Phillip sprung over him, pinning him down.

"Stop!" Phillip demanded. "You'll stop. And talk to me."

Soren could have fought back, overpowered him. But there was a heartbroken ferocity in Phillip's eyes that stole his strength. So he stopped.

Phillip's voice came softer now. "Why? I told you I would never ask you to betray your duty. Why can't you return? Can we not simply enjoy each other?"

It was such a simple question, yet such a difficult answer. It was more than simply enjoying each other now, more than just sating the needs of the flesh. "Because you're a distraction," Soren said. *A dangerous distraction.*

"A distraction?" Phillip nodded, but it wasn't a nod of agreement. "You see me as a weakness?"

"Love makes one weak."

"Is that so?" Phillip's grip softened, but he didn't release him. His eyes dipped in sorrow. No, not sorrow—pity, as if Soren didn't understand. What didn't he understand?

"Did you not become lord commander because the king loves you?" Phillip asked.

What was his point?

"And Norah, she has a lord justice, but you control Mercia's army because she loves you and trusts you above all others. And now..." Phillip leaned closer. "Now, you control the king of Aleon, who will submit to your every ask. You think that love makes you weak, but has it not made you the most powerful man in the world?"

Soren blinked back his emotion. How did this man affect him like this? He couldn't let him, no matter how convincing his words. "I'm not a man who can love." He shoved Phillip back and off him. "I'm not a man who can be loved."

Then Soren left before he lost the power to do so.

He kept his eyes on the map stretched out on the table. His wrap was suffocating. Soren had never felt that way about it in all the years he'd worn it, but over the past few days, he'd felt it often. Mikael stood beside him, with Caspian across from him, next to Phillip. They'd just run through the battle strategy for a sixth time, making sure they missed nothing, forgot nothing. It was a solid plan. Yet Soren felt anything but solid.

After he'd left Phillip's chamber, the king let him be, as if Soren were in control. Except standing here now, with only a table between them, Soren was certainly not in control.

Phillip pulled the battalion figurines back to their original position. Soren's eyes followed his hands. Strong hands. He knew those hands—they were hands that had touched him. So softly, and not so softly. He closed his eyes and sucked in a breath. *Control.*

"It's a great risk," Mikael said, helping break through the fog in Soren's head.

Soren focused his mind back on the battle. This plan *was* a great risk for Phillip. It was one that turned his own stomach.

"As I've told the lord commander, I'm willing," Phillip said. His eyes were on him. Soren took care not to look, not to get caught in their snare, but he felt them—the eyes that knew him so intimately.

"And I understand the risk," Phillip added, "but this alliance promises me something greater, and I'm willing to take it."

Soren's inhale stuttered in his chest. Was he still talking about the battle?

"This is unconventional, this alliance," Mikael said.

Phillip gave a soft chuckle, and Soren could almost feel the puffs of breath on his skin, where he'd felt Phillip's chuckle the night before. On his hip, on his thighs—

He sucked in another breath.

"I'm an unconventional man," Phillip said. "And I'm sure you agree that convention holds us back. This is about knowing the opportunity and taking it. Doing the most with what we have and what we're given."

Soren lifted his gaze. Phillip's eyes were fixed on him, as he knew they had been, and he was caught. But his mind was on Phillip's words. This was no longer a conversation about battle. Or maybe it was, just not the battle against Rael.

"I agree," Mikael said.

"And if we respect one another, we can hold true to our values," Phillip said. "Hold what's important to each of us."

"I think that's possible," Mikael answered.

But it wasn't possible. Soren remained pinned under Phillip's gaze—the gaze that laid him open and bare and vulnerable, that tested his heart against his duty. He couldn't shoulder them separately. It wasn't possible. His heart *was* his duty. Salar and Salara were his heart. Salar and Salara were his duty. Phillip was...

Phillip was...

It wasn't possible. Just like it wasn't possible for Soren to stay in this room any longer. Without air. He ripped himself free of those eyes and pushed off the table. But as he headed to the door, Mikael caught his arm.

Mikael's brow dipped. "Where are you going?"

Soren had nothing in answer. To think? He couldn't think. He'd forgotten how. He needed to... He didn't know what he needed to do, other than get away. "Let me go," he said quietly, so that only Mikael could hear. "Please." He was practically begging.

Mikael's eyes moved back and forth between his. He didn't press. He knew something was wrong. Soren prayed he wouldn't keep him longer. And Mikael didn't. He only nodded and let him go.

He stood in the day's fading light, his back against the wall in the room's quiet. Soren wasn't sure what had come over him earlier that afternoon. He'd lost himself, lost his mind, and he'd had to walk nearly the entire city before he could get it back.

Now, he could breathe again, think again.

Even so, a tempest still raged.

This man. *Phillip.* Just the thought of him stirred Soren's arousal. The smoothness of his skin, the hardness of his muscle. His touch, his scent, his taste. Soren pulled off his wrap and wiped his face. Fire rippled through him, but he forced it down. This wasn't about desire. It was about what pulled him from deep within—that was the danger.

But Soren knew his duty, and nothing could pull him from it.

So now he waited in Phillip's chamber, his dagger in hand.

The door to the chamber opened, then closed.

Soren stilled, silent, hidden in the small recess of the wall. Then he moved quickly. He had his blade to Phillip's throat before Phillip even knew he was there. The king stopped. His mouth moved to speak, but when his eyes met Soren's, he quieted. Soren pressed the blade more firmly against his skin.

Phillip didn't react. He said nothing. He simply dropped his head back slightly, offering more of his neck. Was that submission? Or a challenge?

It didn't matter. Soren's voice came low, thick with his purpose. "If you move against Salara, against Salar, I won't hesitate to kill you."

Phillip's face stayed fixed, but his eyes smiled. "From anyone else, that's a threat. From you, Destroyer... Well, this feels strangely like courtship."

"I need to make sure you understand."

Faster than Soren thought possible, Phillip slammed against his forearm with a stinging force that made him drop the blade. Phillip snatched it and turned it back on him. He dug the tip into Soren's throat. And smiled. That smile—beautiful and disarming. It had the power to make Soren forget how strong this king actually was. How deadly. Like he'd forgotten just now.

Phillip's voice came in a whisper, but it held the weight of a roar. "There may come a day that we find ourselves on opposite sides of the battlefield. And I welcome you to try to kill me. If you can."

Soren's body flamed. This king was skilled *and* bold. His breeches grew tight against him. He felt the trickle of blood down his neck from where Phillip broke the skin with his own blade, and it made him even harder.

"But I told you," Phillip said, "I'll never ask you to betray your duty. I don't ask for your loyalty. Your heart, maybe, in time. But never your loyalty."

Those eyes pierced him more than any blade could. Soren couldn't hold his gaze, yet he couldn't look away. "What do you ask for now, then?"

"You. Your body. Your pleasure." Phillip pressed the blade harder against him. A tremor ran up Soren's spine, but not from fear. Phillip's eyes danced. "And just to make sure *you* understand," he added, "I'm not asking."

Soren snorted. "You should know me well enough to know I don't respond to demands."

"Take off your clothes."

Soren didn't *think* he responded to demands, but his body said otherwise. He shifted—he was painfully hard now. His hands betrayed him and unbuckled his strappings and unlaced his breeches. He kicked them off with his boots before he realized what he was doing. The tip of the dagger cut deeper into his skin with his movements, but there was something thrilling about the pain, something exquisite. And there was something exquisite about the gleam in Phillip's eye as he watched him. Without his clothing, there was no hiding his arousal, no hiding his want. Naked, Soren waited for the next demand.

Phillip still held the dagger. Soren didn't try to take it back. He knew he couldn't. While he was larger than Phillip, and stronger, he wasn't faster. His mind flashed back to sparring on the practice field with the king in Aleon. Phillip had matched him in skill with a sword; he should have guessed he'd be keen with a dagger as well. Soren couldn't take it back. And he didn't want to.

So close they stood.

A small trickle of blood ran down Soren's chest, and Phillip leaned forward and caught it with his tongue. Soren quivered under what was surely the most erotic and arousing thing he'd ever experienced. This man was... He didn't know what this man was. And he didn't know how to react. So, he stood, unmoving. Slowly, Phillip followed the trickle, his tongue lapping tormenting caresses upward. Soren's body threatened to burst from the confines of his skin.

When Phillip reached his neck, he pulled the blade away and covered the cut he'd made with his mouth. He sucked gently, bringing back memories of what his mouth had done to other parts of Soren's body. Soren clung to control. By a thread.

Pulling back, Phillip met Soren's eyes again, blood on his bottom lip. He flicked out his tongue across it and smiled.

Soren lost himself. He surged forward and caught Phillip's lips with his. He tasted his blood—blood mixed with desire—and he chased it with his tongue. Phillip opened his mouth to him, and Soren drank him in. This man knew what Soren wanted, what he needed, what he didn't even know he needed. Phillip knew where there were limits, but right now, there were no limits.

He ripped Phillip's clothing from him as the king pushed him backward toward the bed. Phillip flung the dagger and lodged it into the headboard. He grinned. "In case I need it later."

Soren couldn't help a smile of his own.

Then Phillip's hands were on him—roaming, feeling, gripping, driving him mad with want. Soren slid his hand down between Phillip's muscled thighs to feel if he wanted this as much as Soren.

Phillip groaned—he did.

The backs of Soren's legs brushed against the bed, and he shifted to move behind the king. But Phillip caught him.

"No."

Soren paused.

"I want to see you," Phillip said. He moved onto the bed, and slowly lay back on the pillows. Soren edged over him, leading but following, prowling but caught. He wasn't sure whether he was predator or prey.

He didn't care. He seized Phillip's mouth again with his. Soren had never liked kissing. Kissing was too intimate, too much. But with this man, he couldn't get enough.

He needed more.

Soren stopped and glanced around the room. His eyes found a small bowl of oil on the table by the bed, and he stopped. *Convenient.*

Phillip gave a wry smile. "I knew you'd come back."

"You say that like you know me." Soren had meant his words to be playful, but they didn't come out that way.

Phillip's face grew serious, and Soren searched his mind for how to bring them back.

"I want to know you," Phillip said softly. He reached his hand around the nape of Soren's neck. "Will you let me know you?"

Soren studied his face. He'd let this man do almost anything. "Do I make it difficult?"

Phillip chuckled. "Where's that dagger?" He pulled Soren down, and their mouths found each other again. He tasted of sweet and citrus, like something to be devoured, and Soren wanted to devour him.

Soren broke away to coat himself with oil, then moved between Phillip's thighs, positioning them both. Skin against skin, hard muscle brushing either side of his hips, male power underneath him—he had to work to keep control. Phillip blinked slowly, his breaths long and heavy. Soren gripped Phillip's thigh and watched him as he pushed inside. Phillip surrendered to him, panting a breath that made Soren almost lose himself. Soren pushed deeper and stilled. He needed to be inside him—to claim him, to be close. To be part of him.

He forced himself to be slow, trying to deny the fever of urgency. But Phillip's body rocked against him and drove him faster. It drove him harder. He clasped Phillip's hands and pushed them above his head and dipped his head to drink from his mouth again. The want was so intense it hurt. The storm grew between them—building, roiling—threatening to consume them both.

Then Phillip's body pulsed underneath him, tightening, and warmth spurted up between their stomachs. He groaned into Soren's mouth, and Soren unraveled. He drove himself deeper, erupting within and seeding his claim.

This man was his.

They both stilled, panting. Soren let himself collapse. Phillip was a large enough man that he could hold his weight. It was bliss to simply lay.

Soft fingers trailed through Soren's hair, raising prickles across his skin. "Stay," Phillip whispered.

Soren lifted his head to the piercing blue eyes staring back at him. He'd given himself permission to love this man, and permission to kill him.

He had no intention of going anywhere.

The soft silk of Norah's shoes fell silently through the hall as she made her way to the dining room for dinner. She was late, having lost track of time. She didn't even have a reason—she'd been sitting in the side chair of her chamber, wrapped in her thoughts: of Soren and whatever was happening between him and Phillip, of the impending war, and of Catherine, who drifted further and further from her with each day.

Mikael would wait for her, but she didn't want him to, and she picked up her pace even more. As she swept past the drawing room, she paused. Soren stood by the window, looking across the isle. Why wasn't he in the dining room?

"Are you coming to eat?" she asked him, and he turned with a start. "I didn't mean to startle you," she added.

"You didn't startle me," he replied quickly.

The corners of her mouth turned up. "Okay." But Soren wasn't in a light mood, and her smile fell. "What's wrong?"

He was silent for a moment, then he said, "A message arrived this morning. The full Aleon army has amassed in Eilor. They're prepared for when Japheth and Rael march."

She nodded slowly. That *was* the plan... "Sounds like a good thing."

"The Aleon king has decided to join his army."

While typically kings—and queens—remained safely back from the front lines of war, it also wasn't unusual for them to be with their army. And although this was something she had expected Soren to praise, it clearly wasn't a decision he was pleased with.

"He wanted to position his army in the mountains of Songs," he told her. "He'd give up Eilor temporarily but hold more favorable ground in the mountains. I told him I needed his forces in Eilor to push Rael into the Canyonlands."

"Was it the wrong decision? For him to move his forces to Eilor?"

He shook his head. "No. Not for the overall strategy. But it's dangerous for Aleon. Our plan assumes Rael will be more inclined to drive the war to Kharav. If they strike Aleon up through Eilor, Phillip's army isn't at an advantage, and they could be broken."

And then she realized. "You worry for him." It wasn't a question.

They stood quietly.

"It's different," he said after a while.

She looked up at him. "What is?"

"With Salar, I felt like... together we could conquer the world. And simply standing beside him, being loved by him was enough. Enough to be content. Happy." He glanced down at his hands. "But Phillip—Phillip is different. There's... a wanting. A hunger that can't be sated, a thirst that can't be quenched, like nothing will ever be enough.

I don't want..." He drew in a deep breath and let it out slowly. "I don't want him to go."

"Phillip is a very competent king," she assured him, "with one of the largest armies in the world surrounding him. And you yourself have tested his skills. He can certainly take care of himself."

"It's not enough."

She understood that feeling—she felt it with Mikael. So, she offered him the choice she had wanted: "Do you want to go with him? Do you want to go to Eilor?" With Phillip and the guarantee of blood and battle, she was certain he would take her up the suggestion.

But his brows drew together. "My place is here. With you."

"Just because you're sworn to me doesn't mean you have to stay in Mercia."

He shook his head. "I promised to watch over you."

"Mikael understands that Eilor—"

"Not Salar. I promised the Bear. If Eilor falls and Rael advances north, you'll need me. My place is here."

"Soren—"

"Stop," he said sharply, and she quieted. He sighed. "This is where my family is—you and Salar. Where my duty is. I don't want to go. I won't."

"Okay," she said, softer now. "But we can't let Aleon fall. If Phillip needs you, you'll have to go. I'd want you to go."

Finally, he nodded. "If he needs me."

"Now come on, we're late for dinner. Phillip will be by himself with Mikael, and while things have been going well so far, I'd like to not push it."

Soren snorted, and they headed toward the dining room.

Despite the army of men in the courtyard preparing to take the Aleon king to Eilor, the halls of the castle were eerily silent. Soren reached Phillip's chamber and raised his fist to the door, but paused. He cursed himself. He'd told Salara he didn't want to go, but he did. It had been a long time since he'd quenched his thirst for battle, but that wasn't what called him. Eilor would be dangerous, even for a king like Phillip. Soren would send Adrian back to Phillip after the grandmother passed, sooner if Rael attacked. But even with Adrian by his side, Phillip wouldn't be safe enough. He pulled down his wrap and drew in a breath.

Suddenly the door opened, and he jerked up to find the king looking back at him.

Phillip took a step back in surprise. Then he smiled—that smile. "Lord Commander." He stepped back farther, opening the door, and Soren swept inside.

"The army's ready," Soren told him. "Are you?"

Phillip nodded. "I was just headed down."

They stood, staring at each other.

Phillip stepped closer to him. "I wish I didn't have to go."

"Then don't."

"Would you not? If you were me?"

Soren couldn't answer that, because his answer would be different from what he wanted the king to do.

Phillip moved even closer. His voice came softly, almost a whisper. "These past couple days have been... I didn't think it was possible. To feel this way again. But..." Then he smiled that smile again.

Soren grabbed the king at the top of his breastplate and pressed him against the wall, catching him in a kiss. Phillip tasted of honey and sunlight and summer, and everything he never knew he needed. But now he knew.

They broke, but Soren still clutched Phillip's breastplate firmly. "Do *not* fucking die. Do you understand me?"

Phillip smiled. "Very clearly."

"I'll send Adrian to you soon. Listen to him and take no risks. If Rael attacks and your forces are failing, ride for Mercia."

"I can't abandon Aleon."

Spoken like a noble king. Soren hated it. "Then fall back to the mountains of Songs. I'll come to you."

Phillip smiled again, but not the smile of sunlight. It was the smile of sorrow, of not believing. "If you don't, I understand."

He clutched Phillip tighter. "I *will* come for you," he promised.

CHAPTER THIRTY-FIVE

Norah sat at the dining table, barely breathing, staring at the letter in her hand. Phillip had departed for Eilor the day before, and she already found herself wanting to call him back. Not that he'd provide anything Mikael or Soren couldn't, but they were all one team now—friends, allies—and a collective thought around the morning's situation would certainly help.

She hadn't recognized the letter's seal—red with a short sword sigil—until the messenger had announced his master.

From King Cyrus of Rael and Serra, he had said. Caspian stood beside him, having escorted him in.

She sent the messenger away to read the letter privately, or as privately as she could in front of Mikael, Soren, and her justice. Why would Cyrus write to *her*?

Norah stared at the words and read them for a third time.

Queen Norah,

Is this not an unexpected world in which we find ourselves? Gregor's cause is not my own. Yet we've advanced directly to the commitment of war, without even a conversation between us.

I wish to remedy that.

Are we not rational people? As I've come to learn more about you, I wonder if we're not as different as I once thought. I would like us to meet, on neutral terms, if only even to grant each other the respect of acknowledgment.

I await your reply,

Cyrus

She passed the note down to Mikael and didn't take her eyes from his face as he read it. Strangely, he seemed unbothered. When he was finished, he passed it to Soren.

"He only wants to meet Salara?" Soren asked.

"It's a trick," Mikael said.

Soren shrugged. "Or he thinks Salara's the only one who won't knife him." Mikael looked at Soren and they both chuckled.

"What's so funny?" Norah asked. "I'm the most peaceful person here."

"You've literally stabbed everyone in this room," Soren said.

Norah's mouth dropped open, and she scoffed. "First, Caspian was an accident." She cast him a glance. "Sorry again."

Her justice smiled. "It's all right."

"And Mikael"—she eyed her husband accusatively—"in fairness, you were kidnapping me." She looked back at Soren. "As were you."

Soren's deep, rumbling chuckle came again.

Norah narrowed her eyes at him. "Keep it up and I might give you another scar to reminisce about."

The smile still didn't leave his face.

"What if his intentions are true?" she asked, shifting them back to the matter at hand. "What if he wants to talk about a possible treaty?" Didn't they see? This was an opportunity to change the course of war—perhaps a very small opportunity, but an opportunity nonetheless.

"His intentions aren't true, Salara," Mikael said.

"You don't know that."

"I know," he said firmly.

She could only stare at him with her mouth slightly agape. "I'm just to tell him no?"

"You'll tell him nothing."

"So... I'm to send his messenger back with *nothing*? That's the same thing as telling him no."

"You won't send his messenger back."

"I'll take care of him," Soren said.

She dropped her napkin down beside her plate. "Absolutely not. I won't respond to a letter of peace with blood." That certainly wouldn't help prevent war.

"I can do it without blood," Soren said.

She scowled at him. "I said no." She needed to buy more time to talk to Mikael, to get him to see reason and to convince him of the value of diplomacy. "Put him somewhere until we can decide what to do with him. Not the cells. Somewhere comfortable."

The center of Mikael's brow creased. "You would put our enemy's messenger somewhere comfortable?"

Soren snorted. "Is that a rhetorical question?" he asked, drawing a sharp glance from Mikael.

Caspian shifted his gaze from Norah to Mikael, then back to Norah again. "I will put him in a guest chamber."

Norah kept her eyes on her husband. He had an objection—she could see it. But he only took a drink from his chalice, yielding. It was a start.

Norah pulled her fingers from between Mikael's and balled her fist against his palm to get more of his warmth. They walked the long hall of the castle, toward the study, and she was cold. She was always cold, it seemed. Castles were cold. He chuckled and pulled her hand over his arm and covered it with his own. Gods, she loved his warmth. She shuffled closer to him.

"Any word from Soren's Aleon king?" he asked.

"They're almost to Songs. Making good progress." The corners of her mouth turned up. *Soren's Aleon king.* She hadn't been sure that Mikael would accept Phillip, and in many ways he hadn't. As a no-choice ally, yes, but not as someone he trusted, and certainly not as a friend. But he accepted him as Soren's, and so accepted him as a man that needed to remain alive and well. Soren loved Phillip, and Mikael loved Soren. Perhaps that protected Phillip more than any alliance.

As they neared the end of the hall, Caspian and Soren came around the corner, their strides full of purpose.

"A letter," Soren said as they reached them. "Another one. From Cyrus." Caspian held it for Norah.

She broke the seal and found the words. Her heart beat faster.

Queen Norah,

My letter goes unanswered, but as my messenger has been treated kindly, I don't believe this to be a complete refusal. Perhaps it's not a refusal at all; perhaps it's only hesitation, which I understand. To show my intent, I'll come meet you in the outer reaches of Mercia, on your terms. Let's meet and speak, for I'm sure we'll find common ground.

Cyrus.

She gave it to Mikael. His face hardened as he read it. "Bold that he assumes we don't have intention to answer when only two days have passed since his first letter," he said, and he passed the letter to Soren.

"Well, he's not wrong," Norah pointed out.

Soren's eyes scanned the parchment. "And how does he know his messenger's been treated kindly?"

"I don't know," Norah answered, "but we have two of them now. For a second message to come this quickly, he has to be close. What if he's already in Mercia?"

"He wouldn't be so foolish," Mikael said. "It has to be a trick."

"We should hear what he has to say," she urged. Cyrus wanted to talk, and talking brought the real opportunity for peace. "Mikael, this is an invitation to potentially avoid war. If I can just speak to him—"

"You're not going alone to meet this man," he said firmly.

"Soren will go with me." She wasn't sure if she was closer or further from convincing him, and it made her all the more desperate. "And you and Caspian can be ready with the army close by," she added. "It's a big risk for Cyrus to meet in Mercia. If he comes alone, we could take him. But Mikael, if we can reach an agreement, gain an ally, we could bring an end to this threat. We could end it all."

"Only blood can end it all."

She shook her head. "I don't believe that," she said. "You know his army is at Japheth's border, too far to be an immediate threat, and we could make sure he comes alone. It's but a small risk."

His lips thinned.

She took his hand. "Mikael, we have to try. *Please.* I have to try."

He glanced at Soren, who returned a skeptical stare of his own. Then Soren shrugged. Mikael sighed. "Fine. We'll meet him in the valley in the outer reaches."

Her heart leapt. This was it—this was their chance. And she knew the valley he spoke about. It dipped low and was surrounded by the ridges of the highlands. It was a perfect place to meet; it was out in the open and they'd be able to see everything around them.

"I'll bring the Northern army to the ridge," he said. "Should Cyrus try anything, anything at all, then you must be prepared it will start this war."

To that, she could agree. "And I'll know I'll have done everything I could to prevent it."

The same day they released the messengers back to Cyrus, they received another message—to meet in two days.

Two days.

She didn't know how word could have reached him so quickly—no bird could have carried it that fast. Nor did she know how he was prepared to meet her so soon. It would be difficult even for her to make it to the valley with the army in two days' time.

But they'd go. They had to. They had to stop this war.

CHAPTER THIRTY-SIX

The Raelean king, or who she assumed was the Raelean king, waited atop his horse on the far ridge. He sat tall, confident. Behind him was another group of riders, not large enough to be an army. Norah glanced over her shoulder at the ridge where Mikael waited with Caspian, the Crest, and half of the Mercian army. Adrian stayed with Calla and Cohen and the remaining half of the army closer to the capital, at the risk the meeting might be a distraction.

Norah looked at Soren beside her. Hopefully seeing Cyrus with no army settled him and Mikael slightly, but it didn't necessarily settle her. This day would be the start of peace or the start of war. Her stomach turned at not knowing which.

Cyrus advanced his horse down the ridge toward them with only one rider beside him, and Norah and Soren did the same. As they drew closer to each other, Norah could make out more of his appearance. He wore black-plated armor with accents of earthy red, like blood. Black and blood. A sharp helm covered his face, with a daggered crown fused on top. Across his back he wore a sword with a large red stone set in the tip of the hilt that reflected the light.

The rider beside him wasn't a soldier, but a woman. Her dark, curly hair hung long down the breast of her winter riding dress, but her face was hidden by the hood of her cloak.

They stopped a few lengths from each other. Soren gripped the hilt of his sword, but no one moved. All was quiet.

Norah couldn't see Cyrus's face, but she was certain he was smiling behind his helm. He sat like he was smiling. Cold needled down her spine, and suddenly, she felt like Mikael might have been right. Was this a trick? She forced herself calm.

"King Cyrus," she greeted him.

He didn't reply. And no one moved. Her heart beat faster. She glanced at Soren, who was tense and coiled, waiting for a reason to spring for blood. She turned her eyes back to the king.

Slowly, Cyrus reached up and pulled his helm from his head.

Norah gasped. The face that looked back at her nearly broke her.

The blond hair.

The square jaw.

The blue eyes.

"Alexander?" she breathed. Her mind had to be fooling her. She glanced at Soren for validation that he saw the same, and his dark stare told her he did. Her eyes darted back to Alexander. She could only sit with her mouth agape, unable to speak, unable to breathe.

How was this possible? It wasn't. As she looked closer, she saw this wasn't Alexander. He had the same face, the same hair, the same eyes, but he was different. An imposter—Cyrus was an imposter.

Suddenly the air shook. Cyrus jerked up his shield as two bolts from Soren's crossbow buried themselves into the black metal.

Soren was attacking.

"No!" she cried.

But it was too late. His horse charged.

The woman beside Cyrus raised her arms and whispered foreign words into the air. A stinging wind swept through. Soren's destrier reared and lashed out with its front hooves, as if fighting an invisible enemy, but it didn't continue its charge.

Sephir tossed her head and reared. Norah clutched the mare to keep from falling off and dropped a hand to the animal's neck to calm her.

Soren twisted atop his mount, his hand straining for the small battle-axe at his side, but he couldn't grab it, and Norah realized he was being held by an unseen force. A growl of pain ripped from his lips.

"Stop!" she screamed as she reached for him, but she wasn't close enough to touch him. And there was nothing she could do to help. Soren bellowed again.

"Stop!" She shot a glance at the ridge where Mikael was waiting. Was he seeing this? Why wasn't he coming? She needed him.

"The Shadow King cannot see." Cyrus said calmly, answering. "Nothing looks amiss for him." The voice was Alexander's, but this couldn't be Alexander.

Norah glanced at the woman beside him, who continued to mouth silent words into the air. She turned her eyes back to the ridge, where Mikael still waited. He had no idea what was really happening. She was on her own.

Soren groaned again, and Norah looked back to Cyrus. "Please," she said, forcing her voice steady. "Stop. You're hurting him."

The corners of his mouth turned up ever so slightly, then he cut a look to the woman beside him.

Soren's body sagged in relief, but he still sat unnaturally, held by the unseen force.

Norah stared back at the Raelean king. She knew this wasn't Alexander, but she couldn't take her eyes from all his familiar features. Her lip trembled. "Who are you?"

"Perhaps the name Lucien may be more familiar to you," he said.

Lucien? "Alexander's brother?" she asked. Alexander had a brother who'd died as a child. Only, this man was very much alive.

His eyes gave a cruel smirk as he watched the realization hit her.

"You're his exact likeness," she whispered.

"As many twins are."

Twins. She hadn't known they were twins. Apparently, there was a lot she hadn't known. Norah shook her head in disbelief. "You're supposed to be dead."

Lucien gave a slight tilt of his head. "Yes, I am. At least that was the intent of my mother."

"But now you're king of Rael?"

"Now I'm king of Rael and Serra."

She knew now—this was the man she'd been seeing. Not Alexander. The loss flooded back. The realization ripped her chest open again. She'd taken comfort that he was still with her somehow. But now she knew.

Alexander was gone.

Norah wavered, then caught herself. She couldn't let grief take her, not now. Her kingdoms were depending on her. Mikael was depending on her. She drew in a breath and released it slowly.

He was an imposter, a pretender, but he still held the crown. Regardless of her emotions, this man was king, she was queen, and together they had the ability to stop this war. She forced her mind to focus on her purpose. No one was dying today.

She kept her voice steady and her eyes on Lucien. "I did *not* come here for blood."

Lucien looked at Soren. "He seems to have other intentions."

"He doesn't respond well to deception," she said coldly. "Neither do I." She could hear the sharpness of her own voice, and she exhaled another breath to soften her stance. "But I have come to talk."

Lucien's eyes moved to the ridge where Mikael waited. "With an army?" Then his gaze found Soren again. "And the Destroyer."

"Well, you didn't come alone either, with your..." She looked at the woman and paused.

"Witch?" the woman said as a cruel smile touched her lips. "You can say it."

But Norah didn't want to say it. She hadn't even thought witches were real.

Soren strained again, but the witch's power held. This wasn't going well, and Norah desperately needed it to go well. If she could just speak to Lucien alone...

"Can we take a walk?" she asked him. "Just you and me?"

"Salara," Soren hissed, but she ignored him.

"I would love a walk," Lucien said.

Norah looked back at the ridge. "Will he see?" No doubt a walk alone beside the Raelean king would bring Mikael in full force.

Lucien shook his head. "No."

Norah slid down from Sephir, and Lucien did the same.

Soren snarled and wrenched against his hold again. She hated this for him, but he was a liability.

"You won't hurt him?" she asked.

"Not too much," the witch said with a wry smile.

"She won't hurt him," Lucien assured her. Norah believed him.

"Salara," Soren growled, thrashing again. But she ignored him. She was the only one who could manage a civil conversation right now.

She let her gaze travel over Lucien. He held up his hands, showing them empty, but she wasn't a fool. She knew who he was and that he had power beyond weapons. Still, there was something that told her she could trust him, at least for today. She stepped toward him, and he motioned for them to continue together away from Soren and the witch. Away from listening ears.

A calm settled between them as they walked.

"It was you," she said finally. "It was you who came to me."

He didn't answer.

"All this time. The visions, the dreams, it was all you."

He still didn't answer, but she knew she was right.

"You're a seer? No, not just a seer, a traveler."

A small smile came to his lips. "You continue to surprise me, Norah."

A faint memory flickered. Had he told her that before?

Norah spotted something on his neck and stopped. He stopped too. She stepped closer, not that she trusted him, but she had to see... She eyed the ink that marked his skin, just above his armor. Her pulse quickened. She knew these markings. He'd had them when she'd first seen him in the mortium.

As she studied him, all the pieces fell into place. When he'd returned to her, he must have modified his image, like the traveler Nemus had been able to do in Mercia. He'd made himself as Alexander.

Lucien stood quietly, giving himself to her questioning eyes and roving mind.

"It was your blood," she said. And it was his blood that allowed him into her mind.

Then another thought came to her. Her chest tightened as her heart pounded in her ears. "But in the Free Cities, in the inn, that wasn't a vision," she said. "You really were there." Her pulse was racing now.

He didn't deny it.

"You came to my bed," she whispered. Her heart ached as she looked into the same eyes as Alexander's. "I let you close," she said. "An enemy of Mercia and Kharav, you could have killed me then. Why didn't you?"

He held the same expressions as Alexander did, the same mannerisms. Her question bothered him. Or perhaps he didn't favor his answer. Why didn't he say something?

Anger flashed through her. "Is this all you wanted?" she snapped. "We came all this way to meet only so that I could see your face?"

"No," he said finally. "I came to give you this, in person this time." He pulled out a small vial and held it for her. *Blood.*

She stared at him. "What's that?"

"You know what it is. Invite me back, and I'll tell you everything."

The audacity. "You've told me nothing!"

"I will," he promised. "I need more time, time we don't have here. Let me come to you."

She shook her head. "Absolutely not."

"Did you really think we'd settle things so quickly? With your army on the ridge and a few fleeting moments?"

Norah swallowed. She didn't know what she'd thought. But reality hit her that it wouldn't be that simple.

He held the vial for her. "Take it," he said. "And then decide."

Norah glanced back at Soren, who was still held by the witch's magic. He continued to fight with everything he had, to no avail. There was no way he and Mikael would let her take the blood again.

Lucien closed his empty hand into a fist, and when he opened it again, a small necklace lay across his palm. He reached out and put the vial and necklace into her hand.

"What's this for?" she asked of the necklace.

His eyes moved back to Soren. "A small gift. To use."

What did *that* mean?

The corners of his mouth curved up, and he turned back toward his own horse, leaving her standing alone.

Norah could only watch him as he walked back and mounted his destrier before departing with his witch. When they reached the base of the ridge and started up, Soren's body jolted as the hold released him. Freed, he thundered to the ground and started toward her as she made her own way back.

"What did he say?" he snarled with a raging brow. "What did he give you?"

She hesitated.

His eyes burned into her. "How can you walk with him and be so trusting?" he seethed. "Now that you know what he's done! How he's deceived you!"

Her own anger simmered at his tone. She wasn't an idiot.

"What did he give you?" he demanded.

She ignored his question. "I came here to talk, and that's what I did."

"You walk with him like he's a friend. He's not the Bear!"

"I know he's not!" she snapped back.

"That makes it even worse."

His words were like knives; they stung. His eyes still blazed. "What did he give you?" he demanded again. But he was in no mind for her to show him the vial yet. Not with the want for battle radiating from his skin and Lucien still so close.

To use, Lucien had said. She pulled the necklace from her pocket and shoved it into his hand. "A customary greeting gift," she said shortly. Then she pushed past him to Sephir.

The short ride back up the ridge to Mikael and the waiting Mercian army with Soren beside her took an eternity. Soren boiled in a pool of anger as he rode. Well, he could be angry at himself. He was the one who chose violence at a meeting meant for peace. She'd come to talk to Cyrus—Lucien—and they'd talked.

They reached the top of the ridge, and Mikael and Caspian urged their mounts to meet them.

"What happened?" Mikael asked when they reached them. "What did he say? It didn't even look like you were talking."

She hesitated as she glanced at Soren.

"Oh, they were talking, and walking, and having a great conversation," Soren said angrily.

Mikael's forehead creased. "What?"

"He put some trickery in place to keep you from seeing, and bound me so I couldn't move."

This wasn't helping. "It's Lucien," she said.

Caspian shifted back on his horse, and his mouth opened in surprise. He knew who Lucien was and was obviously just as shocked at the news he still lived.

"Who's Lucien?" Mikael asked.

She swallowed. "Alexander's brother."

Mikael glanced at Soren, then back to Norah. "Then where's Cyrus?"

"No." She shook her head. "There is no Cyrus. I mean, there is, but he's one and the same. Lucien *is* Cyrus."

Mikael only stared at her as it sank in. Then he looked out over the valley from which Lucien had long since left.

She looked at Caspian. Her voice dropped to almost a whisper. "He's Alexander's exact likeness."

Caspian let out a long exhale. "As he was when they were children."

Mikael's eyes jerked back to her, and the shadow under his brow darkened. "It was him coming to you all this time? Cyrus? Lucien?"

She nodded reluctantly. "He's a seer."

"A powerful one," Soren added. "And he's got a fucking witch, on top of everything else."

A quiet came, and they all sat, letting the realization settle. Where did they go from here?

"Are you going to tell Adrian?" Caspian asked her after a time.

She hesitated. "I want to, but..." She shook her head. "Not yet. I just have to... I don't know, I just need to think. It's all so much."

Mikael's expression changed, but she wasn't sure to what. He dropped down from his horse and stepped to the ridge, away from them. Something was wrong. Or rather, something was *more* wrong...

Norah slipped off Sephir and followed. She waited for more of his anger.

But it didn't come.

Instead, he turned and held out his hand. She took it, and he pulled her close and drew her chin up to look at him. "He looks just like the Bear?"

She nodded.

His voice dropped to just above a whisper. "I know that must be hard for you. I'm sorry."

Gods, she loved this man, and she hugged him tightly. "Thank you. For us coming. For just being here."

"Always." And he held her closer.

As she pulled back, her eye caught something, and she froze. In a tree not far away sat a small bird—a small, brown bird, with a blood mark on its head. She clutched Mikael's arm.

"Are you all right?" he asked.

"The bird," she whispered.

Both Mikael and Soren, who was dropping down from his own mount, looked to where she stared.

"It's his," she said, realizing. "The birds are his." It all fell into place. Her pulse beat faster as her mind swirled. "That means he's the one who sent the assassins."

She flinched as Soren grabbed his crossbow from the back of his saddle and loosed an arrow, dropping the bird to the ground.

Mikael pulled her back to look at him, his face gravely serious. "Salara, you understand there can be no peace with this man."

She jerked back. "Wait, what?"

"He tried to take your life."

"That was quite a while ago. Circumstances can change. People can change."

His eyes grew darker. "You defend him?"

"No, I just don't want to throw away the possibility for peace based on something he did before he even knew me!"

"He doesn't know you!" he said, louder now. "And you don't know him. He's violated your mind and deceived you, and you can't trust him."

She wouldn't deny that, but she couldn't skip so quickly to war for actions of the past. She needed to let her mind calm and talk it through when the tension faded.

"Can we just go home?" she asked. "And talk about this then?"

He quieted and sighed. "Of course."

They mounted their horses and started back north.

CHAPTER THIRTY-SEVEN

Calm.

Calm, she told herself.

But Norah was anything but calm. The journey back hadn't brought her to a rational place; it had only allowed her mind the space to rehash everything Lucien had done. And it made her angry.

Back at the castle in her chamber, she clutched the vial of blood in her hand as that anger grew. He'd lied to her. She clenched her teeth until they hurt—*so stupid*—she was so stupid. All this time she'd thought it could be Alexander somehow. Of course it wasn't Alexander. She should have known. He wore Alexander's face, but everything about him was wrong. She should have known. Even Soren knew it wasn't him. And Mikael. How could she not have known? How could she have been so blind?

She stood in front of the fireplace in her chamber.

Throw it in, her anger told her.

He had said he'd explain everything, if she'd only call him back. That he'd even have the audacity to ask her to invite his return...

Throw it into the fire.

He didn't deserve to explain. He'd used her pain to get close to her. He'd used her most private thoughts, her most private weaknesses. He had used *her*. He'd let her talk to him, tell him things.

Throw it in.

It was Lucien—not Alexander—who she had told that Mikael would be traveling through the western pass when he had first returned to Kharav, and Lucien had used it to advance his army and attack. Thank the gods Phillip had moved his army to stop them.

And she'd told Lucien she was traveling back to Mercia after Catherine had fallen ill. He came to her because he knew where she'd be, and because he could. But not to harm her. Why? It would have been so easy for him. What did he want?

Well, she wanted to tell him a thing or two...

She fumed with fury.

She needed answers.

Before she could talk herself out of it, she drew the blood across her palm and closed her fist over it. Then she closed her eyes and stood in her chamber in her mind.

Norah knew he was here. She could feel him.

The door of her chamber opened, but no one entered. Cautiously, she walked toward it. As she stepped into the hall, it was no longer a hall but a bright grassy knoll atop a large cliff, overlooking the sea.

And she saw him. Lucien.

He sat on a rock near the edge of the cliff, staring out over the water.

Norah walked slowly toward him. He was different now. His hair was cropped short, and he wore dark breeches and a loose-fitting gray shirt. Ink marked his skin, just above the neck of his tunic. He looked as he had the first time she saw him in the mortium.

"This is my favorite place," he said, not turning as she approached. His voice surprised her.

"You speak? Have you been able to speak this entire time?"

He didn't answer her.

Of course he wouldn't. "Why?" she demanded. "Why didn't you?"

"I didn't know his sound. Only his image."

What did that mean? "What?"

He pulled a long blade of grass from in front of him. "I didn't know his voice, his words. I couldn't speak as he did."

Then it occurred to her—the limitations of the gift of sight—he could only see the memories in her mind, not hear them. Alexander's speech was the only thing he couldn't copy. Her blood boiled. "So to keep up your charade, you said nothing?"

"I didn't intend to deceive you."

"Yes, you did," she snapped back. "Otherwise, you would have told me exactly who you were."

He stood, and the vision of the coast fell away. "You asked me if I was Alexander, and I told you no."

"You knew my context! I thought death changed you!"

"I never lied to you."

"That's all you've done! Deception is a lie, whether you spoke the words directly or not. And you"—she sucked in a breath—"you made yourself him. You showed yourself as Alexander." The worst lie of all.

He quieted. The earth changed below her feet, and they stood in a sun-filled forest. These visions were not from her memory. He was choosing the locations. He was creating the vision around them.

"I'm sorry," he said softly.

His apology surprised her, but it wasn't enough. "You're sorry you tried to kill me?"

He shifted his weight back.

"That's right, I know. I know it was you who sent the assassins. It was you who spoke through them."

He eyed her before answering. "I've done many terrible things I should probably be sorry for. Many I'm not, but"—he paused—"that has become one."

"Why did you do it?"

"Because you were the wife of the Shadow King. And Alexander's queen—I knew it would destroy him."

"You did it to hurt Alexander?"

"I did it to hurt them both," he snapped. His eyes blazed, and the forest around them darkened.

Yes—he'd come for vengeance. She remembered. "Why?"

He drew in a long breath, and the sun returned. But he didn't answer.

"You said you would explain everything." That was why she'd called him. "Explain."

He swept his eyes to the trees in hesitation, then back to her. "Where do you want me to start?"

Norah sat on a fallen tree. "From the beginning," she said as she crossed her arms. "What are you?" She had already guessed a traveler seer, but he hadn't actually acknowledged it.

He nodded slowly and sat on the opposite end of the tree. He took his time, wiping his hand over the bottom half of his face. "The Evil is what my mother called it. I didn't know how I was able to do it, get inside her mind, but I could. Not Alexander's, but I could hers."

Caspian had said their mother had gone mad. Was it madness? Or was it Lucien?

"I would have dreams," he continued. "Some were... terrible things. The worst was when I was scared. I just wanted to be near her, but she cast me out. I tried to show her."

Norah's chest tightened. To be a child...

He leaned forward with his forearms on his knees and his hands clasped. The landscape around them turned to winter. "I was so young, but I remember. I remember how she took me away. And left me in the forest." Snow blanketed the ground around them now. The trees stood like skeletons, stripped of their leaves. "I ran after her as she rode away. I ran until my legs wouldn't work and I couldn't feel my face for the cold." His voice was stoic, unemotional. "I fell, and I lay there, looking up at the tops of the trees, calling out for her. For my father. Calling out for Alexander. And that's how I was found."

Caspian said Lucien had died of a sickness. That must have been what his mother had told everyone. A pain seeped deeper into her heart.

"Who found you?" she asked, softer now.

He seemed to snap back to the present, and the corner of his mouth turned up. "By fate or by luck, the man who came upon me had a wife. They had for a long time tried to conceive a child but couldn't." Lucien smiled to himself. "And they raised me as their own."

Norah exhaled out a small breath of relief.

But then Lucien chuckled darkly and shook his head. "No. That's not what happened. It's what I imagined had happened many times over in my life. How... different... things would have been. But that's not what happened."

Norah's stomach twisted.

He stood, and the earth swirled under her feet again. Everything went dark. She staggered up but couldn't see.

When his voice came, it was all around her. "I was found by a demon in the night, and he took me to his hell."

Norah almost screamed as the darkness broke, and cages came down around her. Men filled the cages, stripped of their armor and most of their clothing, even though it was the dead of winter. Some were bloodied, as though they'd just seen war. Others were emaciated, as if they'd been in the cages for some time. She couldn't hear them, but terror still filled her. A man to her right retched his stomach contents through the bars of the cage onto the wheel of the wagon that carried them. Another man was hunched in a corner. His uncovered toes were black as death. Perhaps he *was* dead.

"This isn't real," she whispered to herself, trying to quell the panic. *It's just a vision.*

"Oh, it's real," he hissed. "It's very real."

The wagon stopped, and all the men around her were dragged from their cage. The vision shifted, and she was now among them. She gasped as she saw their captors. Their faces were wrapped in black like the night, and ink marked their skin. Shadowmen. Darkness loomed over her, and she jerked her head up. Her heart stopped. She knew this man, this horn-helmed giant. *Mikael.*

He spoke to a tall man with a shaved head beside him.

Norah was afraid to ask, but she forced herself to anyway. "Who's he talking to? What are they saying?"

"A Serran slaver. And he's deciding whether a small boy is worth any price at all, or if I should just be killed."

Oh gods. He was just a child.

Mikael gave a short nod and left the slaver to his cargo, but she didn't take her eyes from him. His movements were heavier, slower. And he was older. This wasn't Mikael. This was long ago, and she would have been a child herself. This wasn't Mikael—it was his father.

"Everyone I loved abandoned me," Lucien said, "including Alexander."

No. No, that wasn't true. "He didn't abandon you! Your brother loved you."

The cages and men in chains fell away, and Lucien and Norah stood again in the winter forest.

Lucien snorted, shaking his head. "No. If he loved me, he would have looked for me. He would have tried to find me."

"He was only a boy! He thought you were dead."

"He would have felt me!" he thundered. "The way I have felt him all these years."

"He didn't have your gift!"

"He did," he insisted. "He had a shield. I couldn't see him."

"No, it wasn't the same. It was... different."

He paused, and his face sobered. "How?"

How could she explain it? She couldn't, and she shook her head. "I... We don't know. He was only starting to uncover it when he died. But I swear to you, he didn't know you were alive. He would have gone to the ends of the world to find you."

He stared at her, not believing.

"I mean it," she said. "If he had any idea you were still alive, he would have come for you."

The anger on his skin cooled slightly.

"He would have come," she said again, "as soon as he was able."

His face softened, and his shoulders slumped forward. "I spent my entire life hating him. I followed the news of his rise, planning how I'd kill him too."

Too? Her pulse quickened. "What happened to your mother?"

His eyes locked with hers, dark blue like stormy seas. "I learned how to control my power. And use it."

Her heart raced. "Did you make her take her life?"

"I told you. I've done terrible things." He didn't look like Alexander anymore. She could see the differences now. The lines between his eyes were more pronounced. His face was... harsher.

She swallowed. This man was not Alexander. But she could see him—she could see the pain. And this wasn't wholly who he was.

She stepped closer to him. "Lucien, your brother loved you. Family was so important to him. And to Adrian—do you know what it would mean to him to learn that you're alive?"

For the first time, a sense of heart flickered across his face. His eyes glistened. "I never knew I had another brother. Not until you told me."

He hadn't known? Her heart hurt. "He's such a beautiful person."

"Is he... like... us? Alexander and me?" He rested his hand on his chest.

She shook her head. "No, there's nothing weird about him. He's perfectly normal." *Wait.* She bit her lip as she squirmed. "That didn't come out right."

He gave a small smile, a genuine one, and her heart leapt—the beginnings of goodness. This was what they needed. She knew if they could just connect and talk and work through things—

Suddenly, Norah was ripped from the vision. Her eyes flew open to being shaken abruptly.

"Salara!"

She gasped. Where was she? On the floor in her chamber. Mikael stared down at her as he clutched her shoulders. Soren knelt beside him. *Wait...*

No. No, no, no...

"Salara," Mikael called again, an urgency in his voice.

Soren gripped her hand, peeling open her fingers and wiping Lucien's blood away with a cloth.

"No," she cried as she tried to jerk it away. "No! I have to go back."

Mikael's eyes were dark and angry. And something else—scared. "What are you doing?" he raged. "You called him to you?"

"Mikael, please! He's there. I have to go back!"

The look in his eyes killed her—the look of betrayal.

"No. Mikael, he's talking to me. I'm getting through to him! His anger's built on perceptions that... that aren't true. And those he seeks vengeance against, they're all gone. It's not you he holds ill will for, it's your father. And he's learned about Adrian. I can see it—I'm getting through to him!"

"Salara," he said between his teeth as he shook his head.

She had to get him to understand. "Do you see what this means? What if I can convince him? Break his alliance with Gregor? Mikael, I could stop all of this. I could stop this war!"

He shook his head again.

"Please! I have to go back."

He clutched her tightly. "This man is deceiving you."

"Not anymore, he's not!"

He held up the vial. "Where did you get this?"

Damn it. She couldn't answer.

"Where did you get it?" he demanded again.

"He gave it to me," she confessed finally, "when I met him in the valley." She avoided Soren's burning glare.

Mikael stood. "You kept this from me?" he asked angrily.

"Because I knew you'd take it from me."

"So you lied?"

"I didn't lie. I just didn't tell you."

"That's lying!" he thundered.

She wanted to yell back, but—gods damn it... *Fair*.

He started toward the door, but he still had the blood.

"Wait!" she called, scrambling to her feet. "I need that!"

With a final look of insult, he stepped from the chamber.

"Mikael!" she called after him.

Her eyes found Soren staring back at her, but not with the anger she expected. Disappointment. That was worse.

"Soren—"

But he turned and followed Mikael from the room.

Gods damn it all. She sank into the chair at her vanity and covered her face with her hands. She breathed. In and out.

The calm returned. She couldn't be angry at Mikael. Of course he'd be upset. He didn't understand. He didn't see what she saw in Lucien. He thought she was being naive, and maybe she was before. But not now. She had to get him to understand.

Everything depended on it.

Dinner was quiet. Quieter than usual. Catherine ate in her chamber. She never left her room now.

At the end of the table in the dining hall, Mikael hardly touched his food. He was angry with her, Norah knew. As was Soren. She'd lied to him. He'd asked her what Lucien gave her, and she had only given him the necklace. Guilt ate at her, but she couldn't make herself regret it. If she had told either of them about the vial, she would have never been able to connect with Lucien at all.

After dinner, Mikael walked her back to their chamber. He still looped her arm through his, even in his anger. Her heart beat steadier. They were okay. He was still angry, but they were okay. When they reached the chamber, he pulled her to look at him, and brushed her cheek softly.

She needed to get him to understand. "Mikael. I need you to trust me."

He sighed. "I know. And I do."

She smiled up at him. *Finally.*

"But I know your weakness for his face," he said.

She rocked back on her heel in surprise. "I'm sorry, what?" Was he serious? "My *weakness for his face*?" Her voice came stronger with her own anger now. "I know you fear he's using my heart—"

"No," he said heatedly, responding to her anger with his own. "I fear he holds a piece of your heart, and he's not even the Bear."

Norah stopped. Did he really think that? Her anger dissipated. She shook her head. "No. That's not true." She reached up and brought a hand to his cheek. "That's not true. I need you to believe this if nothing else."

His anger evaporated, and he let out a long exhale. "I believe you," he said softly. "It was a fear in the moment, when you wanted the blood back."

She nodded. That she could understand. "Now you know." She leaned closer and ran her hand down to his chest, over his heart. He covered it with his own. "But I do need the blood back," she said. "I have to talk to him."

The muscle tightened under her hand. Heat grew across his body. "You won't. I know you're doing what you think is right—"

She pulled her hand away. "It *is* right! If it's a chance to prevent war, we have to try!"

"I said no."

"You won't tell me what I won't do." She was queen. And nothing would stop her from trying to keep her husband. Not even Mikael himself.

He stepped back from her. "Then you'll do this and continue to lie to me?"

"No lies," she snapped back. "I'm telling you right now—I *will* talk to him."

His eyes burned. "That's not going to happen."

Nine hells it wouldn't.

Mikael rumbled with anger, then turned and left their chamber in a storm.

Norah clenched her fists in frustration. She let herself fall back onto the bed and threw her arm over her face. She wanted to scream. It might make her feel better. But things wouldn't actually be better. No—she needed to find a way to get the vial back.

But when she sat up, she froze. Outside the window on her balcony sat a small bird on the railing. She rose and walked to the doors, opening them.

It was *him*.

Lucien.

She knew it was.

"Can you hear me too?" This wasn't a vision—he should be able to.

The bird cocked its head to the side.

"I need more blood," she said.

And it flew off into the sky.

Chapter Thirty-Eight

Norah sat in the dark. No one would find her in the hidden stairwell leading to the tunnels under the castle. The cold seeped through to her skin, and she tucked more of her skirts under her thighs. She should have brought her cloak, but no matter.

She held the vial of blood in her hand that she'd found on her terrace that morning. In the dim light of her lantern, it looked black as the night. Her heart beat heavily in her chest. She'd told Mikael she would speak to Lucien again. She hated to do it in secret, but she would do whatever it took to stop this war.

She pulled the top off the vial and smeared a streak across her palm, curling her fingers closed. And she let her eyelids fall shut.

He came immediately, as if he'd been waiting, and stood at the bottom of the short stairwell.

She couldn't see his face in the darkness of her mind, but she knew it was him.

"An interesting place to call me to," he said.

Norah couldn't help an amused smile. Perhaps she could have imagined a room in the castle, something more pleasant. She didn't put much thought into the space around her when she'd called him, she'd only imagined herself in her current surroundings.

"We won't be interrupted here," she told him.

He lit up the passageway around them, and she was able to see his face—harsh, but not unfriendly.

"I take it that's what happened before?" he asked. "Why you left so suddenly?"

"I'm sorry about that. But there's still so much more to talk about. I wanted to see you again. I hope you don't mind."

He gave her a small smile. "I don't mind."

The nervous racing of her heart eased.

"Will you walk with me?" he asked.

She nodded and stood and stepped down the remaining few stairs to the tunnels. The light grew brighter around them, bright as the outside day, and she glanced around to see tunnels no longer of stone but of wisteria and vining flowers. The cobbled walk under her feet turned to a pathway lined with ferns.

He motioned them forward. "Shall we?" he asked, and she fell in step beside him.

"I've been thinking, a lot, just about everything," she started.

He nodded. "I have too."

Promising. "I still have questions."

"Ask them."

It was a genuine invitation, but it didn't make it easier. "Why didn't you try to kill me again? Why only come after me once?"

"I came twice, actually."

She stopped. "What?"

"I came once before, when you traveled to marry the king of Aleon."

Her pulse beat faster.

"But by the time I arrived, someone had beaten me to you."

The tunnel of vining flowers fell away, and darkness surrounded them, but moonlight painted the scene. They stood in a travel camp off the road she had journeyed on her way to wed Phillip in Aleon. The remains of her army lay around them, all dead.

Yes, Mikael had reached her first. Her stomach twisted at the sight.

"It's when I found this," he said, opening his hand and revealing her mother's crown.

She gaped back at him. "You had my crown all that time?" Her mind swirled around her. If Mikael hadn't taken her, she still wouldn't have made it to Aleon.

"Then came news of your marriage to the Shadow King," he continued. "*That*... was a surprise."

It had been to her as well, she remembered.

Lucien looked back at the crown. Then he dropped his hand, and it vanished into the night. "It was never really about you, though, Norah. I wanted Alexander. I thought he'd accompany you to Aleon, and he didn't. But, when his blood touched your skin in the Shadowlands, I knew he was there with you. He was so close; I couldn't not come."

"So it was never *about* me, but you came to *kill* me?"

His eyes were harsh and piercing now. "I came to kill the both of you."

It still didn't make sense to her. Alexander, yes... "But why me?"

"Because Alexander was sworn to protect you, and I wanted to show him he had no power to do so. And you weren't innocent—you so willingly allied yourself with a monster, the Shadow King. To turn a blind eye to everything he's done, that makes you complicit!"

She quieted. She wouldn't deny that—she'd been guilted by it many times over. But she was working to change things. Mikael was changing.

"And the Shadow King loved you," he added.

Compelling reasons. He certainly had motive. "Why didn't you try again?" she asked.

He paused, and his anger seemed to fade. "Because... you were not as I'd expected. And... I didn't want to, after that."

His words left her speechless. The tone had shifted between them. She hadn't forgotten that he'd kissed her in the Free Cities. A far leap to make, from trying to kill her to kissing her. She'd get to that. Eventually.

"How did you get into Kharav?" she asked.

"You ask me my secrets?"

"Do they really still need to be secrets?"

He'd said he would tell her everything, and if he shared this with her, it could mean a budding trust and that they were on a path toward friendship. If they were on a path toward friendship, it was a path away from war.

The darkness of night around them brightened to day, and the scene of death faded and opened to a landscape of rolling rocky hills. A flock of birds flew overhead, and he lifted his eyes to them.

"They show me," he said.

She followed his gaze up to the birds.

"They show me the landscape, how to get through, if danger is near. They are my eyes."

His birds. "You control them with your blood?"

Lucien gave a small acknowledging smile.

"So, you just go around dripping blood on creatures, having them do your will?"

He chuckled. "Something like that."

"Does it hurt? You have to... cut yourself?"

He nodded. "It did, but I'm used to it now."

"I'm sorry," she said, softer. "That still sounds terrible." He had to hurt himself to give the blood. He had to cut himself to talk to her like they were now.

"You don't need to feel sorry for me." He pulled his dagger from his belt and drew the blade across his palm, opening the skin and spilling his blood to the floor.

She gasped. But before her eyes, the edges of the skin closed themselves, and the wound healed. Her mouth fell open. "You can heal yourself?"

He watched her a moment before saying, "No. I have a healer. A true healer."

"Your witch?"

"No. Another, not a witch."

The fact that he would tell her that surprised her. She was gaining his trust, and her heart leapt. Would he tell her more?

"How do you control someone's mind?" she asked him.

He hesitated, then said, "I can't. Humans are too intelligent, too strong."

"But the men you sent to kill me—"

"My people. They willingly yielded their minds to me."

"And died for you," she added.

"They're all willing to die for me, for our cause."

"And what cause is that?"

But he didn't answer. She blew out a breath. So much death. And for what? They continued their walk through the rocky hills, although the birds had disappeared.

She had so many more questions for him but was wary of it being too much, too soon. This was so much more progress than she'd expected, and she wanted to protect it.

"I should return, before I'm missed," she said.

The scene around them changed back to the tunnels of woven greenery and flowers. He walked her to the short stair that led back up to her dressing room.

"I'd like to talk again," she said.

The sharpness of his face softened, and he gave a small nod. "I'd like that too."

"Goodbye, Lucien."

She opened her eyes back to the darkness of the stairwell.

Winter chilled the long main hall of the castle, but the light of the sun made it seem not so cold. Still, Norah pulled her shawl tighter around her shoulders. As she neared Catherine's room, she slowed to see Soren coming from the opposite direction. What was he doing here? Only Catherine's chamber and the music room were in the far east wing, neither of which she expected Soren to be anywhere near.

Norah eyed him suspiciously, waiting for him to explain himself. He didn't. He simply eyed her back and said nothing as he passed. She scoffed as she looked back to Catherine's chamber, then back to Soren, who disappeared into an adjoining hall. What was going on?

Stepping into Catherine's chamber, she saw her grandmother propped up and sitting against the tufted headboard of her bed. A needlepoint hoop lay in her lap, although she wasn't working on it.

"Good morning," Norah said sweetly. "A few visitors already?"

Catherine drew in a breath and gave a proper smile. "Not particularly."

Norah narrowed her eyes. Did she just lie? "Hmmm." Norah sat down on the chair beside the bed. It was warm... from someone else. Recently. "Are you sure?"

"Stop beating around the bush, what are you getting at?"

"Was the lord commander sitting in this chair?"

"So what if he was?"

Norah gasped. "I knew it!"

Catherine puffed a breath. "What?"

"Are you two becoming friends?" she goaded with a mischievous smile.

Catherine's lip twitched. "Nothing of the sort."

Norah's smile widened.

Catherine gave a weak harrumph. "He says you're still trying to broker peace with this king Cyrus."

That was probably a nicer version of what Soren had actually said. "*Trying.*" And had he not told her Cyrus was Lucien? Apparently not by the way she was acting. Norah wouldn't tell her either. It would only upset her, and her health couldn't take it.

"You can't be afraid to fight, Norah."

"I'm not afraid to fight, but this war will bring tragedy and suffering, to all sides, and I need to stop it before it starts."

Catherine gave a small smile. "You're a strong queen, Norah. I know you'll do what you think is right and best." Catherine paused, her eyes tearing. "And everything you've done has all been right and best." She shifted slightly and winced, bringing her hand to her side.

Norah moved quickly to the bed and sat down on the edge. Catherine's pain had been growing worse.

"I don't have much time left," her grandmother said. "But I wanted you to know that even when I'm gone, I'll never be gone from you. I'll be with you always."

Norah nodded, her emotion keeping her from speaking.

"I have one thing left to ask of you, though."

Norah's heart was breaking—Catherine was preparing for her end, and Norah didn't think she could handle it. But she nodded again.

"Send Alexander to the gods."

Norah stilled. Then she looked down at the patterned quilt on the bed. She couldn't have this conversation now.

"I've told the fiend to hound you until you do," Catherine said. "He's promised me."

"So that was your conversation with Soren this morning?" Norah asked. No surprise.

"That and Sophia."

Norah frowned as she looked at the gray feline on the foot of the bed. "Your cat?"

"Mmm," Catherine pursed her lips in simple acknowledgement as she reached for her cup of tea on the bedside table.

Norah picked up the cup and handed it to her. "What about your cat?"

Catherine shrugged. "Nothing. I only want to make sure she's cared for after I'm gone."

Norah sat back, looking squarely at her grandmother. "Wait. You've asked the lord commander of a four-nation army to look after your cat?"

"Oh, Norah, he's the only one who pays her any mind at all."

Norah scoffed. "I do too!"

"When? You don't so much as look at her."

Because she was a *cat*. Norah wasn't too keen on cats, but she would have taken care of her grandmother's cat.

Catherine's eyes taunted her. "He pets her every time he comes in."

Norah wrinkled her face. "How many times has he come?"

"More than you!"

"I come here every day!"

"So does he, sometimes twice a day!"

Soren came regularly to see her grandmother? Well—"I'm running two kingdoms!"

"He's leading a four-nation army to war!"

Norah gasped. "You got that from me."

Catherine pursed her lips, looking quite pleased with herself.

Norah stood. She couldn't believe this. "Fine. I don't want your cat anyway."

"That's why I'm giving her to the Destroyer."

She wanted to scream. "Well, I hope you're *all* happy together!"

"*They* will be," her grandmother replied shortly. "*I'll* be dead!"

Norah turned and stalked out of the chamber, her mind fuming. What was even happening? When she reached the main hall, she stopped and sank down onto a side bench, covering her face in her hands.

"Salara," came Mikael's voice, and she looked up as he sat down beside her. "Are you all right? What's happened?"

She sat back against the bench and shook her head. "I'm losing my mind. I just"—she paused and took a breath—"I just got into an argument with my grandmother about not giving me her cat." She covered her face with her hands again. "I don't even want her cat."

He put his arm around her and pulled her to him. "You're under a lot of stress right now."

"We all are." She put her hand on his thigh. "Including you."

He covered her hand with his. "Are we all right?" he asked softly.

Oh, right. They were supposed to be angry at each other. But she didn't want to be angry at him anymore. She sighed. "Of course."

He pulled up her fingers to his lips to kiss them. "Good."

In the dimly lit stairwell, Norah held the vial of blood in her hand. She'd have to tell Mikael she was talking to Lucien eventually. But when? She sighed.

After she brokered peace, she told herself.

That was her purpose, after all, and she was close—she could feel it. She drew a deep breath and called Lucien back.

She knew he was there when the room changed around her. Her seat on the stair turned to a seat on a garden bench. It was summertime. A bird lighted on a fountain in front of her, and then flew away, and she felt his presence on the bench beside her. She still had so many questions. She hoped they might be able to pick up where they left off before.

She pulled the vial from her pocket. "So, your birds bring me these?"

He nodded. A good start.

"And my crown?"

"I have larger friends." From between the topiaries in the garden, two dogs emerged, but they weren't like any dogs she'd seen before. They were black dogs, large—almost as big as Cusco and Cavaatsa had been, except they had no ears and no tails.

Norah shuddered. "Did you do that to them?"

He shook his head. "No. With me, they have a very different life than the one they had before."

A different life than before… Lucien had had a different life too. Mikael had told her how he'd been a blood sport fighter and led the rebellion against the old king of Rael.

He watched her watching him. "You have more questions?"

She pulled her mind back; she did have more questions. "You said something, before, both the last time we spoke and when you came as the assassins. You knew Alexander's blood had touched my skin in Kharav. How?" It felt strange to be talking so casually about the attempt on her life with the one who had tried to claim it.

He nodded. "His blood allowed me to travel the same as my own. When it touched your skin, I saw you. And I knew he was with you."

"And that's how you came to me in the mortium after he died."

He sat for a time before speaking. "I knew something had happened. A searing pain came to me, greater than I'd ever felt before. When I woke, his weight—the weight I'd carried inside for my entire life—it was just gone. And his blood touched so many. So many minds, so loud—his blood was on all their skins. And I knew."

She could only watch him.

"All those years, I wanted him dead," he continued, "and then for him to be snuffed from me in an instant… I wasn't ready. I couldn't believe it."

Lucien paused. "I wanted him back," he whispered. "And so I searched, but the weight was gone. I sought his blood, reaching out to everyone it had touched. And it brought me to the mortium. To you." He paused, his eyes now staring through her. "I saw him," he whispered, "in your mind, for the first time in our adult lives."

Norah swallowed. All the pieces were falling into place.

He smiled sadly. "You saw me as I am, before I realized where I was, before I realized I was in *your* mind. It was too late to change my projection."

"The markings on your neck," she remembered.

He nodded.

Norah pressed her knuckles to her lips, trying to make sense of the chaos in her mind. "And then you came back; you came as Alexander."

He gave another nod, seemingly ashamed. "I wanted you to let me back in," he said. "You still had his blood on your skin, and so I returned. I could project everything: his dress, his hair"—he paused—"everything but his voice and his words."

"So, you came back for my secrets."

"I saw it as an opportunity against my enemy, yes," he admitted. He hesitated before saying, "But as I got to know you"—he stopped again—"it didn't make me happy to deceive you."

They sat in the quiet for a long time.

"And now?" she asked. "Now that you know things are different, that things have changed—"

"Nothing's changed."

She shook her head. "How can you say that? You would still move against Mercia?"

"Norah, Mercia was never the target of my wrath. Only those who've oppressed my people." He sighed. "For Alexander I felt a personal vengeance, yes, but you and I have never truly been enemies. And I'm sorry you've been caught in the middle."

And she believed him. Her hope grew. He was being completely open with her. This was exactly what she needed—what they all needed. "No one wants this war."

But his eyes blazed back at her. "I want this war."

His sudden change in demeanor rattled her, and she stumbled over her thoughts for a moment. She shook her head in confusion. "What? No—why?"

"Because that's what change requires. And that's the price owed."

He *wanted* war? "Lucien, thousands of people will die, your own people included."

"All of us are willing to sacrifice."

"For what?"

"For justice! The Shadowlands must pay." His eyes flamed with a frightening fury. And it was growing.

Where was all this hate coming from? She desperately searched her mind for anything to help ease the tension. "Kharav is not the only kingdom who has slaves."

"The Shadowlands fuel it. They sell the spoils of their wars; the slavers use Shadow rice to support their trade. There are others, it's true—Etreus, Persus, Elam, Lorys—and they will all pay. Every single one of them. But I'll take the Shadowlands first."

The tension was escalating, and not in the right direction. She needed to get them back to where they were before. But she wouldn't be able to do that now; she needed to let him calm.

She steadied her voice the best she could. "I think we're both tired and have a lot to think on. Can we talk more later?"

He rose from the bench. For a moment, she thought he might not answer. Then he nodded. The world fell away, and they stood where they had started, at the stairwell.

"You'll return to me?" she asked.

"When you call me." It was a small reassurance. It wasn't broken between them.

"Good night, Lucien."

"Good night," he said with a stiff bow of his head.

A new day came with the sun, one Norah was determined to make the most of. She swept into Catherine's room. "I've decided that I'm perfectly fine that you'd rather have the Destroyer of the Shadowlands, known for his brutality and complete unpleasantness, look after your beloved Sophia, instead of your one and only endearing granddaughter—your own flesh and blood."

Where she'd expected a snarky reply, there was none.

She'd take it as forgiveness. She walked to the window and pulled open the draperies.

Catherine was still sleeping on the bed. She was growing more and more tired. *Great*, now she was going to have to repeat that all over again when she woke.

"I never thought I'd see the day you'd sleep longer than me. Time to stir. Serene's bringing breakfast."

But her grandmother didn't move.

She slowed. "Grandmother?"

Silence.

She approached the bed. "Grandmother?" Her breath wavered. Catherine looked so pale. Why was she so pale? She swallowed. Ever so slowly, she drew closer.

"Grandmother," she whispered.

Norah reached out and took Catherine's hand. But it was cold, void of spirit.

Void of life.

She dropped it as she sucked in a breath. A cry escaped her lips, and she covered her mouth with her hand.

No, not yet. She wasn't ready.

She sank down onto the bed beside Catherine's body as sobs shook her.

She wasn't ready.

CHAPTER THIRTY-NINE

Norah lay across her bed, staring up at the ceiling. Three days had passed, but it felt like both an hour and a year. Time had fallen apart. That morning she'd watched as her grandmother was sealed in the Hall of Souls. As important as it was, everything was a blur. All she could remember was Catherine's face: pale and hollow, a shell of the spirit she'd been. How did one so strong just waste away? The image would haunt her.

She couldn't believe her grandmother was gone. Now what would she do? She couldn't be queen without her. She didn't want to be queen without her. And now what? How was she supposed to do everything on her own—look after Mercia, be salara of Kharav, stop this war...

She bolted up.

Lucien.

They left their last conversation on a somewhat uneasy note, and she hadn't called him since. In the chaos, she'd completely forgotten. He must think... What must he think? She jumped off the bed. She was in no mind for conversation, but she couldn't let all the progress with Lucien fall apart.

Down in the stairwell, she stopped a moment to catch her breath. *Calmly. Calmly.* She didn't want to show up to a conversation with Lucien unsettled, and she forced in a deep inhale before pushing it out of her lungs completely. She hadn't brought a lantern in her hurry, and she fumbled with the top of the vial. With shaky hands, she drew a smear of blood across her palm.

Be calm, she told herself again, and she clenched her fist closed.

Her mind was quiet.

"I thought you might not invite me again," came his voice all around her.

He didn't light the darkness, and she couldn't see him.

"I thought you might be angry," he said, "but now... I see. I see your sorrow."

She hadn't planned to tell him about Catherine, but she supposed she couldn't keep it from him. Not when he was inside her mind. Did he see everything?

The darkness faded, and he stood at the foot of the stair. "I'm sorry for your loss."

She felt sorry too, but for what? For her own sorrow? For the time it took to call him again? Her mind churned for words, and still she found herself without them.

He offered his hand. She stared at it for a moment, then took it and stepped down beside him. He didn't release her. Instead, he pulled her hand into the fold of his arm and led them down the darkness of the tunnel. The stone walls fell away, and they walked through a field in the night. Around them flashed the luminescence of fireflies.

He led her to a bench beside a bubbling stream. The dark gave way to light, like the dawn before the sun, and they sat.

Perhaps it was against the laws of nature to share one's sorrow with the enemy, but here, it felt... not wrong.

"I can't believe she's gone," she whispered.

Lucien looked at her, his eyes carrying a sorrow in return. He didn't reply.

"How cruel death is," she said, her voice shaking. "I spoke harshly to her before, over something... so *stupid*, and I didn't even get a chance to make it right." She sniffed. "Death took the chance to tell her I was sorry, the chance to tell her goodbye."

He sat quietly, simply listening.

"She looked so fragile in her bed," she told him. "And I tried to remember her as she was before, but even that seems to be taken from me." Everything was being taken from her.

"I can show her to you," he said softly. "As she was. I can help you remember."

"No." She shook her head. "I would know it would be you under her face."

"And if I stay right here?" he asked. "I can simply show her to you."

She stared at him. Could he really do that? "Like a vision, or a memory?"

"Something like that, yes."

Just the thought of seeing Catherine well again knotted a cry in her throat. She couldn't speak; she only nodded through her tears.

The sky brightened, and he looked past her shoulder.

Norah turned and followed his gaze. Her breath caught as she saw her grandmother standing by the stream. She glanced at Lucien in disbelief, then back to Catherine.

Her grandmother's face was bright, healthy. She held out her arms to Norah.

Norah glanced back at Lucien, her eyes wide. "It's not a memory, it's..." She looked back to Catherine. "It's like she's there."

"You can touch her," he said softly.

She gripped his hand tightly as she stared at him in astonishment. He gave her a nod, and Norah stumbled up from the bench and rushed to her. She cried as her grandmother's arms swept around her, and she buried her face into the softness of her fur-shouldered gown.

Warmth. She felt warmth.

This wasn't a normal vision. Yes, she could feel Lucien when he came to her, but not his warmth. Norah didn't understand how it was possible, but she didn't care. She only clung to Catherine.

Finally, her grandmother pulled her back, looking into her eyes. Norah wanted to remember her just like this—smiling, happy. Catherine wiped a tear from Norah's face and pushed her hair back over her shoulder. Ever so softly, she leaned forward and gave Norah a kiss on her cheek. With a final smile and soft squeeze of her hands, she slipped back into the light and was gone.

Norah wept, smiling through her tears. She stared at the light long after Catherine had left.

Finally, she turned back to Lucien, but something was wrong. Blood ran from his right nostril.

"Lucien!" she cried, and ran to him. She dropped down on the bench beside him and pulled his face so that he looked at her. "Lucien, are you all right?"

"I don't have the strength to stay with you much longer," he said weakly. "It's the seemingly simplest things that are sometimes the hardest."

"What do you mean?"

He gave a weak smile and squeezed her hand. Blood spilled now from his left nostril. It grew dark around them.

"Lucien! Whatever you're doing, you have to stop! Go. Rest."

"Will you call me back, Norah?" he asked, wavering.

His image faded, and her hand pushed through him as though he were only a shadow. She gasped. She could no longer feel him. He slumped to the side, barely able to keep himself up, but Norah couldn't help him.

"Yes, but go," she urged him. "You're hurting yourself."

He gave her another weak smile and faded until he was gone.

She sat alone in the darkness of the stairwell, her pulse racing. What had just happened? Showing Catherine to her had obviously done something to him, had hurt him somehow. Why had he done that, at his own expense?

Her racing heart warmed.

It was a kindness. He'd given her a kindness.

She was getting through to him.

Norah closed her eyes and brought back her grandmother's smiling face.

"Queen Norah?"

Norah snapped her head up at the sound of her name. Around the table in the judisaept, the eyes of her council stared back at her. Her mind had wandered again. Two times she had tried to call Lucien back since he'd showed her Catherine, but he hadn't come, and she was worried. But she tried to push that from her mind as she struggled to focus on her council.

She swallowed. "I'm sorry, what was the question?"

"What are your thoughts?" Lord Semaine asked.

Not helpful.

She looked at Mikael at the opposite end of the table. His brow quirked. He knew something was off with her.

"She thinks we should wait," Soren interjected. "As I said."

"Yes." She nodded. "I agree with the lord commander. We should wait." What were they talking about?

"If Rael attacks within the next two weeks, we run the risk of not having our forces in position in time," Lord Branton said.

And she realized—they were talking about when to move the Mercian army to the stronghold in Bahoul.

Norah liked Lord Branton. He'd been a field general under her father; he was a man adept at war. He was thoughtful and honest, and she didn't take his concerns lightly.

"But if we move them too soon," Soren said, "we won't be able to sustain them."

It was in Soren's interest to move sooner, for Phillip's sake. But he said to wait. He would choose what was best for Mercia and Kharav.

"We wait," she said.

The councilmen bowed their heads, and they all rose from the table. Her thoughts turned back to Lucien. She suspected he'd overexerted himself, as Alexander once had, but it had been two days, and he still hadn't come.

She didn't have much blood left, perhaps enough to call him one, maybe two more times.

Norah brushed the wrinkles from her gown as she stepped out of the judisaept. A warm hand caught her arm.

Mikael. She cursed herself. She should have waited for him before stepping out. Her mind was failing her.

"Are you all right?" he asked.

She forced a nod. "Yes. I'm sorry. There's just a lot on my mind."

His brow dipped in concern, and he brushed her cheek. "Are you sure?"

She nodded again. "Yes." She spied Soren waiting in the hall for Mikael to join him. "Soren's waiting. Go. I'm perfectly fine."

"All right," he said. Then he kissed her forehead and went to join Soren.

Norah watched them disappear down the adjoining walk, then she turned and quickly made her way toward her chamber. Not too quickly. Not quickly enough to draw notice, or the suspicion of her guard. They'd tell Bhastian, and Bhastian's attention was like Soren's: hawkeyed for anything amiss. She loved her Crest captain, but that didn't mean she wouldn't avoid him like the fever when she was trying to hide something.

Safely in the privacy of her chamber, she lit a lantern. Then she fumbled with the access door under the hastily thrown-back rug and ducked into the stairwell.

Sparingly, she drew the blood across her palm and closed her hand over it. She prayed as she waited.

A flutter touched her mind, and she let out a relieved breath.

"I was worried for you," she said. She couldn't see him, but she knew he was there.

A shadow in front of her appeared, and the tunnel lit around them until she could finally see him. His brow dipped. "You were worried?"

"Of course. Two times I called you and you didn't come. I thought something might have happened."

The faint trace of a smile crossed his lips. "My last visit pulled a lot of strength. My healer can only repair the flesh, so I had to recover the old-fashioned way—sleep."

She smiled. He was so open with her now, his defenses gone. He trusted her. And she was beginning to trust him. "Thank you," she said softly.

He gave a small nod.

"What happened to you?" she asked.

He offered her his arm, like a proper man of court. "Walk with me."

She slipped her arm underneath, and they started down the tunnel. As they went, the walls fell away to reveal a walk along a cliff overlooking the sea. She loved some of the places he took her.

"How did you show me my grandmother like that?" she asked. "That wasn't a memory, or a vision. I know it wasn't real, but how could I feel her warmth?"

"Don't break the magic," he told her.

"But it was difficult for you."

"It's the most difficult. More than anything else. As I said, it's the seemingly smallest of things."

"Well, thank you," she said softly. "For that." She watched him as they walked. "You're a very powerful traveler, aren't you?"

"I suppose."

"Are those staves on your neck?"

His brows drew together. "How do you know about staves?"

"All travelers have them." Well... all the travelers she knew. Which was two, now three. *Close enough.* "Are they?"

Slowly, he nodded.

"Can I see them?" She resisted the urge to pull down the neck of his tunic and look closer at them herself.

He paused a moment, then reached between his shoulders and pulled his tunic forward, over his head and off.

Oh, all right then. She hadn't expected he'd take the whole tunic off, but here they were.

Then he reached down and pulled off his boots. *Wait,* what was happening? He loosened the ties on his breeches and stripped down to his braies.

"Oh... uh... I didn't mean—"

But she stopped when she saw him. There were hundreds of them, all over his body—smaller staves grouped together to form even larger ones. He held his arms open, giving himself for her study. Then he turned and showed her his back.

All bashfulness forgotten, she stepped closer, mesmerized. The markings weren't the same as those the Kharavian warriors bore. Instinctively, she put her hand out to him, but stopped herself.

"You can touch them," he said.

She refrained.

"What do you know of staves?" he asked her.

She shrugged. "Not much. Only that they protect your body from the strain of your power. And that the more power you have, the more staves you need." She paused for a moment. "You have more than I've ever seen."

"Alexander didn't have them?"

She shook her head. "He didn't... use power like you do. It was more like... he was immune to others', or something. He didn't really need staves." Her mind drifted back to the pool of the Wild where Alexander had overexerted himself. Maybe he did, and he just didn't know about them. But whatever Alexander was, whatever power he had, she'd never know...

She looked up to see Lucien watching her. And looking at her the way that he was, he looked so much like Alexander...

"I could give him to you, Norah. I could give you Alexander."

Her heart stopped. *Alexander.* She could see him again. Be near him. She could hug him again, feel his warmth.

But Alexander was gone. Her chest tightened, and emotion rose in her throat. "It wouldn't be real," she whispered.

"You could let it be real."

She smiled sadly. "No, Lucien."

They stood quietly for a time.

"Would you let me see Adrian?" he asked. "Will you let him come to see me? I've looked at him in your mind, but... to see him in his person, in life. I'd like that."

She hesitated, searching for words. "Things are... complicated." She licked her lips. "I haven't even told him you're alive."

His eyes gave a flash of surprise, but he nodded. "I understand," he said softly.

"Can I think about things?"

"Yes, of course."

Her eyes moved back over his body. So many markings. Everything she asked, he so freely answered, so freely gave to her. "Thank you, for sharing this with me," she said. "For sharing everything with me."

He nodded.

"I should go."

"Do you have enough blood to call me back?"

She had enough for one more visit, and she nodded.

"Goodbye, Norah."

"Goodbye."

She opened her eyes to the darkness of the stairwell and wiped the blood from her palm with her handkerchief. She was about to step back up into her dressing chamber, but she paused and leaned against the railing, trying to get a hold of the sudden swell of emotion.

He could give her Alexander.

No. He couldn't.

Alexander was gone.

Gone.

She turned back toward the tunnels and took the right narrow passage to the end before turning left. The lantern provided little light, but she knew where she was going. She followed the tunnel to the end and pushed out the door to a small cobbled street outside the castle. She glanced around as she hurried to the cliffs, making sure she wasn't seen.

Norah lowered herself down the center crag and toward the cave. She hadn't visited for some time, but the nostalgia that settled over her as she stepped inside brought a wave of tears. She didn't try to hold them. She felt her way along the cave until she reached the caverns.

Clouds choked out the sky, but the opening above still provided enough light to fill the cavern. She sucked in a breath, simply letting the emotion come. All of it. The sorrow in losing Catherine, in missing Alexander, the crushing weight of threatening war—everything.

Everything.

And she wept.

She stumbled into the pool and let the water's warmth envelope her. Her skirts billowed up around her. She wanted them off, she wanted it all off, and she clawed at the lacing on her back. Fabric tore as she pushed the gown down and over her hips, but she didn't care. She needed to get out of it. She stripped it away, until she stood only in her shift in the pool.

And she sank deep into the water.

Its warmth took her in its arms, holding her, rocking her. The pool drank her tears, became her tears, and she emptied her sorrow into its depths.

And then there were no more tears. She floated on her back in the water, looking up at the clouded sky through the opening in the top of the cavern, and a ray of sun broke through. She closed her eyes, feeling its warmth on her face. She didn't move as the light kissed her skin.

Alexander had called this a magical place. And it was. She felt him here.

As she opened her eyes, she splashed up abruptly. There was something she needed to do.

She waded back to the edge of the pool and clambered out, not bothering with her dress, and wove back through the tunnel of the cave, up the crag, and toward the castle. As she strode through the courtyard, Bhastian came running to meet her, with Titus close behind.

"Salara," he said breathlessly. "What happened?"

Oh, right. She glanced down at herself. She supposed she did look a mess in her chemise and sopping hair in the snow. She hadn't even felt the cold.

"I just want to get back to my chamber," she said.

Titus handed Bhastian his cloak, and Bhastian swept it around her. "But are you all right? Where were you? What happened to you?"

"Bhastian, I'm fine. In fact, I'm better than I've been in a long while. Can you just see me back to my chamber?"

He nodded with his eyes still full of concern. "Of course."

Norah took a bite of meat from her plate as they sat quietly at the table in the dining hall. Mikael and Soren watched her closely. Neither brought up the fact she'd shown up to the castle soaking wet in her undergarments, although they were quite aware.

She took another bite, giving herself time to chew and swallow before setting down her fork.

Then she took a drink of her wine.

"I'm going to send Alexander to the gods," she said.

Mikael's eyes locked with hers, and Soren set down his knife.

"Are you sure?" Mikael asked her.

She nodded.

"You don't have to if you don't want to."

"But she *should*," Soren said, casting a hard eye at Mikael.

Mikael shot a daggered glance back at him.

"I'm sure," she said, bringing their attention back to her. "And I do want to."

Slowly, Mikael nodded.

"I need to tell Adrian," she said.

"Of course."

"About Alexander *and* about Lucien," she added.

Both Soren and Mikael leaned back in their chairs and cast worrisome glances at each other.

"I don't think that's a good idea," Soren said.

"I can't keep this from him. He deserves to know."

"What if he wants to see him?" Mikael asked.

"Then he'll see him," she said firmly.

The shadow under Mikael's brow grew darker, but he didn't argue.

CHAPTER FORTY

The pyre burned brightly. Heat tinged her face, but she didn't move. She only stood, hypnotized by the flame. Norah thought she'd been ready, but as Caspian had lit the base, it was all she could do not to stop him. She needed this, she reminded herself. They all needed this. Alexander too.

She also thought she'd have tears. The gods knew how much she missed him—how she would give almost anything in the world to have him back again. And her heart still hurt and grieved, but the tears didn't come. Maybe it was a sign she truly was ready. Or maybe it was because she knew she needed to be strong for Adrian, who stood beside her.

When she'd told him she was going to send Alexander to the gods, he hadn't said anything, hadn't objected. Perhaps he accepted it now too. That's what she hoped. This would help them both heal.

They stood silently, watching the pyre being consumed by the flame. She hadn't told him about Lucien yet. She wasn't sure whether to deliver the news all at once or separately. And how would she find the words?

Her eyes drifted to him as he watched the flame. His face was fixed, stoic. Normally so full of expression, so full of light, he wore a mask now. Norah reached out her hand and took his. He didn't look at her but tightened his fingers around hers.

And they stood.

They stood until the fire ebbed and faded. Until everyone finally took their leave to give them space. They stood until they were the last two, and then they stood some more.

She looked up at him, watching his unmoving sorrow.

"He was all I had left," he whispered when only embers remained.

Well, if she didn't take that as an opportunity, she was a fool. But her stomach still dipped in apprehension. "There's something else I have to tell you," she said softly.

Finally, he broke his gaze from what remained of the pyre and looked down at her by his side.

"Adrian, Lucien's alive."

His brow came down slightly, and he leaned back on his heel. Then he shook his head. "No, that's not possible. He died. A long time ago."

"No," she whispered. "He didn't. He lives."

He shook his head again. "Alexander wouldn't have lied to me."

"He didn't know."

His breaths came faster and shallower. "My mother wouldn't have lied to me. Or my father."

As lord justice, his father would have been occupied by the needs of the kingdom. He would have known whatever his wife had wanted him to know. And Adrian remembered his mother fondly—very differently from Lucien.

"He's dead," he said firmly. He nodded as he trembled. "He's dead."

"I've seen him."

He stepped back, pulling his hand from hers. "When? Where?" His breath became ragged.

"When I went to meet Cyrus."

Confusion flooded his face.

"He *is* Cyrus," she said.

He shook his head again, and his nostrils flared. "No, that's not possible."

"He was captured as a child and taken as a slave to Rael. As a man, he led a rebellion and overthrew the king. Then he took the kingdom of Serra from those who had put him into slavery."

"And now he marches against us? Against Mercia?"

She left out Lucien's quest for vengeance against Alexander. That wouldn't help anything. And it didn't really matter now. "He marches against Kharav. Mikael's father is the one who gave him to the Serran slavers."

"The Shadow King is dead," he argued.

"I know, but Lucien still holds Mikael accountable. Kharav still has slaves and is still a primary supporter of slave trade."

He shook his head again but said nothing as he looked back to the pyre. His eyes glistened.

"I told Lucien about you," she said softly. "He didn't know."

His head snapped back to her.

"All this time, he didn't know about you. He wants to meet you."

His breath faltered. "You talk to him?"

She nodded.

"Does Salar know? The lord commander?"

She bit the side of her cheek and shook her head.

His eyes blazed back at her. "You've been talking to him without Salar knowing?"

"I've been trying to broker peace and stop this war. Lucien—he has a heart in him. It's broken and damaged, but I think it's possible to get through to him."

Adrian looked back at the fading embers of the pyre, his breaths uneven. Nothing remained of Alexander now. Adrian wiped his face with his hand.

She reached out her hand to his arm, but he pulled away. "Adrian," she said.

He shook his head and didn't answer. Then he turned and started back toward the castle.

"Adrian," she called after him. But he didn't stop.

A new day came with the sun. Norah drew in a deep breath as she stepped out of her chamber and down the hall to the stairs. The night had been quiet. Mikael had lain silently, leaving space for her to talk if she wanted, but she didn't. She did want the comfort of his touch, though, and buried herself in his warmth and refuge.

He had risen with the morning and kissed her before leaving, lingering just long enough to make sure she didn't want him to stay—to make sure that she didn't need him, that she wasn't going to fall apart in delayed sorrow. The scars still remained, but time had healed the sharpest of her pain, and she really was doing better. She kissed him back and waved him off.

Norah hadn't talked to Adrian again after she'd sent Alexander to the gods. She wanted to give him time to absorb everything, time to think. She walked alone down the main hall and out through the courtyard, breathing in the winter air. As her eyes settled on Samuel's gallery, she paused. She hadn't seen the seer or his painted visions since she last went with Catherine, when Mikael's fate still remained—even after Alexander was gone.

Now she knew. They all knew. It wasn't Alexander.

And she froze. It had *never* been Alexander in the paintings with Mikael—what about the others? Were there others?

She found herself in front of the door, about to knock, but she stopped. Should she knock? Catherine never knocked. But just like with Soren, that wasn't indicative. She glanced back at Kiran and Titus. "Wait here," she told them.

Slowly, she pushed open the door. "Hello?" she called out.

No one answered.

She stepped inside. Paintings stacked in piles littered the gallery floor, just as they had before. But today she had a new eye, a new understanding. She moved through the piles, looking for images of Alexander.

"Queen Norah!"

She turned at the sound of her name as the old seer hobbled in from a back room. "Forgive me, I didn't know you were coming. Is there something I can help you with?"

"Yes, actually. I was wondering—could you show me all the paintings of Alexander?"

His face grew serious, and he hesitated.

"Is something wrong?" she asked.

The ball of his throat bobbed. "*All* of them?"

She opened her mouth, then stopped. Then she glanced around. Looking back at Samuel, she said, "How many are there?"

His throat bobbed again. Then he gave a jerky nod and waved her to follow him.

Norah stepped into the hall and followed the old seer to the back room. She'd been there with Catherine before, although she hadn't remembered a lot of paintings with Alexander then. In the room, he moved to the far wall and pulled away some of the larger paintings. Behind them sat a door, and he opened it.

Her pulse quickened.

It was a small door, perhaps for a storage closet, but as they ducked inside, she saw it opened into a room as large as the one before.

And all around them—paintings of Alexander.

She moved through them, her mouth open. "You saw all of these?" she asked.

"Yes, Regal High."

"How are there so many?"

He shrugged. "The life force that draws the attention of the Eye—it must be very powerful."

She wasn't exactly sure what that meant, but she got the idea. Lucien was powerful—that wasn't news. Her eyes traveled over the paintings, not looking for anything specific, just... looking.

She stopped on one.

Alexander stood, sword in hand, facing another man armed with two. *No*—not Alexander. *Lucien.* He had only a battle garb around his waist, no tunic. No markings showed on his skin. Was this an old vision? Maybe he hadn't gotten them yet? She stared at him. It was so easy to think this was Alexander. But it wasn't. She could see it now.

Her eyes swept the details around him: sand under his feet, and in the near distance, a curved wall with grated gates evenly spaced.

Where was this?

She moved on through the paintings, noting others that were similar, and more of the background for her to put together that he was in an arena. An arena in Rael? Mikael said Lucien had been a blood sport fighter before he'd led the rebellion. Is that what she was looking at now?

Another painting made her stop.

It was a sprawling landscape of blood and battle, with Lucien at its center. A flag lay on the ground, nearly trampled into the mud. Red and yellow—so familiar. Had she seen it before?

"What kingdom has these colors?" she asked.

"I don't know, Regal High. I'll have Rector Tusten research it."

Was this an old vision or was it yet to come? Her heart beat faster as she focused her attention back on Lucien. He rode a black horse, dressed in armor of black and blood. He had the markings on his neck in this one.

Norah moved to another painting, then another. She pulled back the canvases and looked at the ones underneath. Then she moved to the wall and flipped through the ones standing on their side.

Lucien—they were all Lucien. In fact, nothing she saw was Alexander. But Lucien was a seer, and seers couldn't be seen by other seers. None of this made sense. "Did Alexander ever see these?"

Samuel shrugged. "Some. Not all. Visions of the lord justice never came to be, so we stopped paying mind to them."

Because they were never Alexander. All this time, they were seeing Lucien, and they didn't even know.

The door to the room swung open, and she jumped.

"Hammel's hell," she said.

Adrian.

His eyes traveled around the room, and he stepped through the small doorway inside. He stopped when he saw the paintings. Norah only stood and waited. He made his way slowly, looking at each one, taking them in as she had done.

"It's him, isn't it?" he asked her. "Lucien?"

She nodded.

His gaze locked with hers. "I want to see him."

CHAPTER FORTY-ONE

A tent stood in the distance. Norah drew in a deep breath. She'd used the last of the blood to call Lucien, to tell him she was bringing Adrian to meet him. He'd been surprised. She'd surprised herself. But if there was one thing that might temper Lucien's thirst for vengeance, it might be a connection with his brother. Adrian held a deep respect for Mikael and Kharav, a belonging and love. Kharav was a part of him now, a part of who Adrian was, and if Lucien could see that...

She glanced at Adrian as he sat on his horse beside her. It had been easier than she'd thought to take the tunnels and slip out of the castle. After a couple wrong turns, they'd found themselves near a city bakery, but they'd quickly been able to find the stables and leave without drawing attention. Bhastian and Soren would be looking for her now. She tried to push it from her mind and focused on the tent in the distance. There was a singular horse outside.

"Looks like he's quite trusting," Adrian said.

She combed her eyes across the empty terrain. "Well, he's confirmed we've come alone too, no doubt." She glanced up at the sky for birds.

Adrian followed her eyes and looked at the sky. "And you're sure we can trust *him*?"

She had told him of Lucien's ability, and how she'd been able to communicate with him. She wasn't sure he believed her or not.

"I don't know." She wanted to believe they could. "I do think there's good in him, though. There's a lot of pain... but kindness too."

He nodded.

"Are you ready?" she asked.

"I think so," he whispered.

They made their way toward the tent. As they neared, two dogs stepped out from around the sides. They were the same dogs Lucien had shown her before—the dogs used in blood sport that he'd taken for his own. A low growl emanated from them.

Just then, Lucien ducked outside, and the dogs dropped back and disappeared once more behind the tent. Lucien paused when he saw Norah and Adrian, then he started toward them. There was no sign of his witch.

Adrian pulled up his horse, and Norah brought Sephir to a halt as well. He slid down, and she followed suit.

Lucien wore no armor. He was dressed simply in a dark fitted tunic and breeches. His hair had grown slightly since the last time she'd seen him in person—it was still short, but it was long enough to show a slight curl, like Alexander's.

When he saw them, he smiled. Except for the staves reaching up his neck above the top of his tunic, he looked more like Alexander than he ever had.

Norah glanced up at Adrian, who only stared at him. His eyes welled. No doubt he felt the same shock she had when she'd first seen Alexander's exact likeness.

Lucien's eyes stayed locked on Adrian as he neared. His smile faded as he was caught in his own emotion. While Adrian wasn't a twin, there was no denying the similarity, no denying the blood relation. Lucien stepped slowly in front of him. They could only stare at each other.

Adrian was slightly taller and more heavily built, as he had been compared with Alexander, but somehow, now, he seemed smaller. He reached up his hand, trembling, and touched Lucien's face. A tear escaped down his cheek.

Lucien stood motionless—patient, or perhaps caught in his own wonder.

Adrian drew his hand down to Lucien's shoulder, as if testing that he was real. Then he abruptly pulled Lucien to him in an embrace. Whether he was hugging Lucien or Alexander, she didn't know.

But Lucien hugged him back. They held one another.

Curse the gods. Tears came to her own eyes.

Finally, they broke and stared at each other for another moment.

Then Lucien cuffed Adrian's shoulder. "Come inside," he said, with a slight crack in his own voice, and led them toward the tent.

Norah and Adrian followed and ducked inside. It was bare, save a small seating roll, but it was warm, like a fire was near. It felt nice to be out of the cold.

Finally finding his voice, Adrian said, "Mother told me you'd died."

Lucien's eyes found Norah's, and her stomach twisted. Adrian remembered his mother differently. She prayed he wouldn't take that from him too. What their mother had done to Lucien, and what Lucien had done in return to their mother, was something she wanted to protect Adrian from.

Lucien said simply, "She thought I did. I was taken away."

She let out a silent breath of relief.

Adrian gave an uneasy nod. "Norah told me."

Lucien glanced again at Norah, then back to Adrian. "Then you know my story."

Part of it. She clenched her hands together.

Adrian nodded again. "You were taken as a slave, led a rebellion... and now you're a king."

The corner of Lucien's mouth turned up, and his eyes narrowed slightly. "And now I'm a king."

Adrian stood, still staring at him in disbelief—disbelief that he was still looking at his very-much-alive brother or that Lucien had risen to hold two kingdoms. Maybe both.

"Do you want to see?" Lucien asked. "I can show you."

And there was *that* too.

Adrian's brows dipped, and he drew in an air of hesitation, but he nodded.

Lucien pulled his dagger and slipped his thumb along the edge, drawing blood. "Close your eyes."

Adrian looked at Norah. Her heart raced, but she nodded. He closed his eyes. Lucien took Adrian's hand, pressing his blood to his skin, then closed his own eyes.

Norah's heart beat in her throat. She didn't dare breathe.

Adrian jerked in surprise but didn't open his eyes. His breath came faster. He moved his head, as if looking around, but kept his eyes closed. "Where is this?" he said aloud.

"Rael," Lucien answered. He opened his eyes and looked at Norah, then pulled his hand from Adrian's and held it out to her.

Adrian's eyes remained closed as he stood, completely enthralled. She couldn't deny she was curious herself. Slowly, she stepped forward.

He touched his blood to her skin as he took her hand and closed his eyes again. And she closed hers.

Norah gasped as the sight of a massive city lay before her. But she wasn't walking, she was... flying. Cobbled market streets full of people passed underneath her. The city sprawled as large as Valour in Aleon—larger even—and just as beautiful. It was different than she'd imagined. Tall buildings—sets of stacked sandstone adorned with carved apertures and intricately latticed partitions—lined narrow streets. The golden stone glowed in the light of the sun and held an ethereal beauty.

"You can fly?" Adrian asked Lucien as they all looked down on the Raelean city.

Lucien chuckled. "No. Now *that* would be power."

Norah found herself suddenly standing on the cobbled street, now empty of people, and looking up at the sky. A flock of birds flew overhead.

"I see it through them," he said.

Norah swallowed. His birds.

"You control them?" Adrian asked.

"I can."

Norah couldn't see Adrian in the vision, but she could hear him next to her.

"Can you control all animals?" he asked.

"Most, I can. With blood."

"Did Alexander have power?"

The vision faded to dark, and they all opened their eyes. Norah opened hers to find Lucien looking back at her.

"He had power, yes," he said, "but it was different. What it was—I don't know."

"You"—Adrian's words caught in his throat—"you look just like him." He could only stare. "Just like him."

A sympathetic line etched across Lucien's brow. "Norah said you two were close."

Adrian nodded, and his eyes welled again.

Lucien's gaze fell to the ground as the line of his lips tightened. "I like to think we would have been close."

Adrian shifted as he swallowed. "We could be."

Lucien smiled sadly. "If I had known... about you... things might have been very different. I'm sorry, Adrian."

"Things don't have to be this way," Norah said. "Mercia's not your enemy."

"I don't see Mercia as an enemy."

He'd already told her that, but she wanted him to remember. "And Kharav isn't the same kingdom as it was," she added.

But his face sobered, and he took a step back.

"The king you knew is dead," she told him. "Everything has changed."

"Does the Shadowlands still force people into slavery?" he challenged back. "Still buy them? Still sell them?"

The answer was damning, and she couldn't bring herself to answer.

"Then nothing has changed," he said with steel in his voice.

"Lucien, change takes time," she pleaded. "Mikael is a good king."

"A good king?" he snarled back. "I've been in his mind, seen his memories. You think he's innocent?"

Norah stopped. Mikael had called Lucien with the blood he took from her. *He hadn't come*, he'd told her. "He said you didn't come."

"I didn't show myself to him. That doesn't mean I didn't see."

Adrian stepped forward. "Then you would have seen the good as well, unless you chose not to."

Lucien's gaze darted to his brother, and the corners of his eyes creased. "You defend the Shadow King?"

"I defend *my* king," Adrian said firmly.

Lucien took another step back.

Adrian's face softened, and he took another step forward, extending his hand. "Brother, things aren't as they were, and they can be different still."

Lucien's eyes moved to Adrian's hand and the sword entitlement marking that extended out from under his sleeve. Disgust flashed across his face. "You're one of them?"

"Mercia and Kharav are united," Norah said.

Lucien's face twisted, and any likeness of Alexander vanished. "Then Mercia will share the same fate."

She could feel his anger building. "Lucien, change doesn't always require war. Mikael works for things to be different; he just needs time. Even as king, he has people that he's accountable to."

"I do too!" he thundered.

Norah startled at his burst of anger but held her ground.

The darkness around him ebbed ever so slightly. "Even if I didn't want to take the Shadowlands, I have no choice," he said.

"There is always a choice," she pressed.

"Then you'll just have to accept the fact that I want to." His eyes turned cold and cruel.

She didn't know this man. She needed to bring back the man she'd come to know over the past few weeks, and she reached out and took his arm. "Lucien, please. I beg you. Help me change fate. I can't lose him. I can't."

His expression changed, then changed again—from realization to surprise and a myriad in between. Thoughts swirled within him, she only wished she knew what they were.

"The Shadow King falls?" he asked.

"By your hand," Adrian said.

Lucien's head jerked toward him. "What?"

"All this time, we thought it was Alexander," Adrian explained, "but it's you who will kill Salar."

"Me?"

Adrian snorted. "You're a seer, and you haven't seen this?"

"I can't see myself." He looked back at Norah. "I kill the Shadow King?" Then he froze. "Wait, you *saw* me?" His face twisted in confusion. "I can be seen?"

Silently, she nodded.

Lucien shook his head. "You're not supposed to see me. I'm not supposed to be seen." He pulled away and ran a hand over his face. "I can be seen?" He turned away from them.

Norah glanced at Adrian, but his eyes were on Lucien. She turned back and watched as the Raelean king slowly paced the length of the tent, then turned back.

When he reached them again, he stopped. "So, you can see me in the visions. And I succeed?"

Adrian shot her a troubled eye. Her pulse quickened. "Lucien," she whispered, "I'm begging you to help me create a different future. You're the only one who can." She reached out and took his hand. "Lucien. Please."

His eyes saddened, and his shoulders sank. "I'm sorry, Norah. I can't."

She fought the emotion building in her chest. *No.* No, she couldn't accept that. Her fingers tightened around his. He had to help her. He cared about her, she knew. And there was good inside him. He had to help her.

But he shook his head. "It's fate, Norah. If it's been seen, there's nothing you can do. And that means this is my fate too."

"No. *No.* We can change it."

He shook his head again. "I don't want to change it. It's my fate. I have to do it."

"No," she gripped him tighter. "I won't let you."

"As I've said, there's nothing you can do."

Her lip trembled, and her eyes welled—not tears of sadness, but tears of anger. Tears of hopelessness.

Fate, he'd said.

Well, curse fate, and curse the gods, and curse this king who thought he could take Mikael from her.

Norah ripped her dagger from her waist and let out a cry as she plunged it forward, but he caught it and twisted her wrist outward, and she dropped the blade.

Adrian pulled his sword and lunged to her aid, but Lucien bared his teeth, and suddenly Adrian sank to his knees, screaming as he held his head in his hands.

Lucien was still in his mind. He couldn't control him, but he could make Adrian feel pain. Norah delivered a hard kick to Lucien's inside thigh, almost dropping him.

Adrian fell forward in relief and struggled to stand.

But Lucien still held her. She clawed at his eyes, and when he raised his arm to shield himself, she reached for the dagger at his waist. He stunned her with an elbow to her face, making her stumble back. As she lost her balance, he grabbed her again. He held her by the throat, but not tight enough to choke her.

Blood trickled from her lip, and the taste of metal filled her mouth.

"I don't want to hurt you," he said angrily.

"Then don't do this," she hissed.

"I don't have a choice," he snarled back. "Fate is fate, Norah."

"I won't let you," she said between her teeth.

"How will you stop me? With the Destroyer?" He looked at her curiously, and his expression changed. "No. He'll do nothing. Neither will your king." Then he kissed her.

She froze, too stunned to fight him. It wasn't the kiss of affection, or even dominance. It was... strangely transactional.

Lucien pulled back with her blood on his lips. Then he closed his eyes and whispered into the air. She felt light-headed, but it passed quickly. He released her.

Adrian staggered and picked up his sword.

Lucien spun. "You don't want to do that," he said.

Adrian bared his teeth. "Brother or not, I think I do," he spat.

Lucien stepped back from the both of them. Then he pulled the blade of his dagger from his waist and sliced it across his own hand.

A searing pain cut across Norah's palm, and it pulled a cry from her lips. She gaped down in horror to see Lucien's wound on her own hand.

"We're bound now, you and I," he said. "Tethered through blood. What happens to me also happens to you."

She looked at Adrian, and he stopped his advance. Horror set across his brow. He could do nothing now. She glared back at Lucien. *Bastard.* He sought to protect himself by linking them together.

But if he thought this would give him power over Mikael and Soren, he was wrong. She wouldn't let that happen. "I won't tell them. So, all you've done is made me share your fate."

He gave a cruel smile. "You might not"—he looked at Adrian—"but he will."

Adrian trembled in rage.

"Do your duty, brother," Lucien told Adrian. "Protect your queen."

Lucien looked back at Norah, and the smile dropped from his lips. "I'm sorry, Norah," he said, and stepped out of the tent, leaving them in the quiet of defeat.

CHAPTER FORTY-TWO

Norah sat on the edge of her bed, her eyes swollen from her tears, her cheek swollen from the blow of Lucien's elbow. She hated that she was crying. Why was she crying? The pain had ebbed—it wasn't enough to be emotional. She wasn't sad, just... angry. And overwhelmed. She cursed herself for being so *very* foolish.

She clutched her hands together, rubbing her thumb over her palm where Lucien had sliced his own flesh. It had healed on the return ride, no doubt from the help of his healer. If only she could get the same benefit to her face, but that wasn't a shared injury between them.

Adrian sat beside her. He took her chin gently and tilted her face up to the light, wincing as he eyed her.

"Is it bad?" she asked.

He grimaced. "No."

"Your face says it is."

"My face lies."

"Well, your face is the one I believe." She sighed. "I'm so stupid. I should have never gone."

"It's my fault. I wanted to see him."

She shook her head, but Adrian took her hand.

"I mean it," he said. "You gave me the choice, and I chose this. I'm so sorry."

"You didn't make me do anything I wouldn't have done eventually." She shook her head again as she let out an emotional breath. "I wanted so badly to believe I could stop this war." But she couldn't—just as Mikael had told her, just as Soren had. She couldn't bring herself to face them now, but she didn't have a choice as they barged through the door.

Adrian stood abruptly as they surged toward them.

"What happened?" Mikael demanded. His eyes traveled over her, and his face twisted in anger. And fear.

Her breath shook. "Mikael, I'm sorry."

"What happened?" he asked again, his voice deeper. "Where were you?"

Might as well get it out. "I went to go see Lucien."

Mikael's nostrils flared. "You did *what*?" he thundered.

"I told you I would!"

"What's the matter with you?"

Lots of things, at this point...

The lines of his jaw, bold even under the short cut of his beard, tightened. "Do you forget he tried to kill you?"

Yes, there was *that*.

"He deceived you, came to our bed under the guise of a ghost."

And that.

"He conspires to destroy me. And you go to him—unprotected and trusting."

Not her finest decision. She couldn't argue with any of it. Not anymore.

"It was my doing," Adrian interjected. "I wanted to go."

Mikael and Soren ripped their gazes to Adrian.

"I wanted to see my brother." He stood for their judgment.

"As I told him he could," Norah added, "if he wanted to."

Mikael turned back to Norah, and his shoulders sank. He sighed. Then he took her hand and pulled her up and held her to him. "You're an infuriating woman sometimes," he said as he held her tight. He turned her face up to get a better look at her. "I'll kill him for this," he said softly as he brushed the swelling on her cheek.

She bit her lip. *About that…*

"Are you all right otherwise?" Mikael asked.

Norah could only nod.

"Not exactly," Adrian said.

She cut him a daggered warning. "Adrian."

"I'm sorry, Norah." He looked back to Mikael and Soren. "He tethered himself to her."

Mikael shifted his stance, and his hold on her tightened. "What does that mean?"

"Whatever injury he suffers, she'll suffer the same. You can't kill him. You can't harm him at all." He nodded back at Norah. "Not unless you want the same to happen to her."

"Perhaps it's another trick," Soren said.

"I've seen it with my own eyes," Adrian told him.

Mikael forced her to look at him. "Is this true?"

She swallowed. "He did it to protect himself. From you and Soren."

Mikael bared his teeth with a growling curse and released her. Then he lumbered backward and sank down into the side chair. Defeat hung over him. He leaned forward with his elbows on his knees and rested his forehead against his fists, thinking.

They sat in silence.

"He's clever, isn't he?" he said finally.

"What do you want to do?" Soren asked him.

Mikael drew in a deep breath and let it out again. "The only thing I can do." He raised his head and looked at Soren. "He's not to be harmed. No one's to touch him."

Norah bolted upright in the darkness of the night with a sharp pain across her left hand. A scream ripped from her lips.

Mikael jumped up beside her. "What is it?"

She clenched her fist to her chest as blood ran down the length of her forearm to her elbow. What was happening?

The Crest burst through the chamber door.

She let out another scream as the pain attacked her right hand now.

Mikael grabbed her shoulders. "What is it!"

But she couldn't answer.

Bhastian held a torch that lit the room, making them all gasp. Norah sobbed as blood poured from her hands, staining her nightgown red.

Mikael gaped at her in horror, then he moved into action. "Salara," he said, grabbing her hands and holding them tightly. "Look at me."

But she could only stare at the blood. Her blood. *So much blood.*

"Look at me!" he commanded, and finally she lifted her eyes to his.

"You're going to be all right," he promised as he pressed his palms against hers. "Hold through the pain, you'll be all right." He turned back over his shoulder. "Get the healer!" he raged.

Dizziness caught her, and she wavered.

"Look at me," he called her back, and her tear-filled eyes met his again. "You're going to be all right."

Suddenly, the burn subsided, and she gasped as she looked back at her hands to see the flesh bonding back together, healing as if the wounds had never existed. The pain faded altogether.

Her sobs calmed, and she quieted. Mikael's brows drew together in confusion as he stared at her hands. He wiped back the blood and gaped at her flawless palms.

"What..." He stopped, his mouth slightly open. "What happened? How is this possible?"

Her heart slowed as her terror subsided. She ran her thumb over the flesh. "He has a healer," she finally managed to get out. "A special healer."

"He did this to himself?"

Then she knew. "He's drawing his blood. So he can use it."

The pounding echoed through the darkness. Norah stood beside Mikael as he beat his fist against the door of the row home on a cobbled side street. They were looking for Nemus, the Mercian traveler seer, to see if he knew how to break the tether.

Norah's breath shook as they waited.

"Are you sure this is the one?" Soren asked from behind them.

Mikael beat the door again, harder this time.

She bit her bottom lip. "Ummm... yes." *Maybe.* She'd only been here once with Catherine... in the dark... after being led through a maze of tunnels. But this door looked like the one from before.

"Really?" Adrian asked. "Because it looks like all the others."

She glanced down the street at the rest of the houses. It did look like every other door.

"Perhaps it's a different one?" Caspian asked.

She pursed her lips. There were too many men here with too many opinions. This was the door.

Just as Mikael was about to beat again, it opened.

Norah let out a sigh of relief as a familiar face looked back at them. Esther, Nemus's wife. Norah had first met her when Catherine had brought Norah to see if Nemus could unlock her memory.

But Norah's relief was short-lived. Esther stood horror stricken, her eyes red and swollen, her breaths short and gasping.

Something was wrong, and it wasn't their midnight visit.

"Esther, what's wrong?" she asked.

Esther stepped backward.

"Where's Nemus?" Norah asked.

The woman shook her head, still overcome with emotion.

"Esther, where's Nemus?" she asked again. Her stomach twisted. Something was *very* wrong.

Slowly, the woman pointed back into the house, her hand shaking.

Mikael and Soren pushed past, drawing their swords. Norah followed. Adrian reached and grabbed her hand, ready to pull her back, but she shook him off. She needed to find out what was happening.

They reached the back room where a modest bed was centered on the wall. But Nemus lay unnaturally on the floor in the corner of the chamber, unmoving. A cushion had been flung against the foot of the bedpost—the same kind of cushion he and Norah had sat on when he'd done the blood spell to enter her mind.

They approached slowly.

The old seer was the color of death, his mouth open in a silent scream, his eyes wide with horror but unseeing. Black veins spidered under the icy hue of his skin, stretching from his fingers up his arms.

Soren dropped down and reached out to his neck.

Norah jerked up her hand. "Don't—"

But Soren paid her no mind and brought his fingers to feel the old man's pulse. Nothing happened, but it didn't keep her heart from nearly beating out of her chest.

"He's dead," Soren said.

Norah glanced at Mikael, but his eyes were fixed on the dead seer.

"It was a serpent," came a shaking voice from behind them, and they turned to find Esther.

A serpent? Norah drew her brows together. "A what?"

"In the Aether. He screamed for it to be gone. I couldn't wake him from it." Tears streamed down her face as she gave a small sob. "I couldn't wake him."

Soren stood, looking at Mikael. "We should take Salara to Kharav, to our seer. He can help us understand what's going on here."

"No!" Esther cried. "The serpent in the Aether—it would have come for him too."

Serpent in the Aether? Norah's heart stopped.

Samuel. The Mercian seer. He wasn't a traveler like Nemus, but he still entered the Aether to see visions and create his paintings.

"Samuel! I have to get to Samuel!" she cried, and she fled from the small home and out into the night.

Mikael and Soren were quick to follow, with Caspian, Adrian and the Crest in tow. Her side stitched as she ran, but she didn't stop. Racing back across the bridge, she barreled through the courtyard to Samuel's gallery. She nearly collided with the door when she couldn't open it fast enough but managed to swing it clear and maneuvered through the narrow aisle of paintings, knocking some over as she went.

"Samuel!" she called.

The rooms were lit by dim candles, and they moved farther back. When they reached the far room, she gasped as she saw Samuel lying facedown on the floor.

"Samuel!"

Norah ran to his side and turned him over. Like Nemus, black veins showed from under his skin. His hands caught her eye, and she jumped. They were covered in blood.

No, not blood. Paint. Wet, red paint. As if he'd dipped them in a can of it. She stared at them. Why did he have paint on his hands?

"Salara," Mikael said, and she looked up. A canvas sat on the easel, still glistening with wet paint and a new image.

The image of a red serpent.

CHAPTER FORTY-THREE

Norah lay in the bed in her chamber, curled under the quilts with her legs folded to her chest and her hands around her knees. She waited the long, agonizing wait for the pain of when her hands would rip open again and blood would pour from her open flesh. It had been nearly two weeks since Lucien had placed the tether. The cuts came more often now, but irregularly and without warning. Sometimes it was only her hands, and sometimes, perhaps when a lot of blood was needed, her forearm would open—a long cut from the center of the arm to her wrist. Sometimes she would grow faint, the energy draining from her. But as soon as the wound closed, the pain would leave as quickly as it came, as if it had never happened.

Each time it took a piece of her, of her hope. The loss of control eroded her spirit and the resilience of her mind.

Now she could only wait.

A message from Phillip had arrived a week prior. Two of Aleon's three seers had mysteriously died. It was a short message—delivered by bird—and likely followed by a messenger that would soon arrive with a more detailed one, perhaps with assumptions about how they'd died. But she knew how.

Lucien.

The door to her chamber opened quietly, followed by the clinks of a tray being set on the side table. Even though it was midday, Serene didn't say anything to her, didn't disturb her. For the past four days, Norah woke to dress and minimally tend herself. Sometimes she'd eat, then give herself to the solitude of her bed. Mikael came often, checking on her, kissing her palms, and nuzzling her cheek, then he'd leave her to the quiet. He was gentle, sweet, but underneath she could feel his silent rage, his hating anger, and his own suffering that there was nothing he could do to help her.

Bells rang out. She wasn't entirely sure she wasn't dreaming.

"Regal High," Serene said.

Norah didn't move.

"Regal High," her maid said again.

Slowly, Norah turned to Serene, who was standing at the window and looking down into the courtyard.

"You might want to come," Serene said.

Norah pushed herself up and ambled from the bed. She blinked her eyes into focus as she stared down at the group of riders who had arrived. Who were they?

She squinted against the light. Why was it so bright? Didn't the sun know it was a time of darkness?

Norah focused again on the riders. A smaller man slid from his horse, hooded with an oversize cloak. Suddenly, her heart picked up. She recognized the bright red garb of the men surrounding him—guards of the seer's temple in Kharav. The seer had come to Mercia.

The Kharavian seer had left his temple. And had come to Mercia.

Finding a burst of energy, she turned on her heel and sprang for the door. She raced down the hall and the stairs with her guards Titus and Kiran picking up behind her.

When she reached the courtyard, Soren and Mikael were already there. They stood with the seer, their large frames towering over him.

"Bhasim!" she called as she raced toward them.

Mikael and Soren turned in surprise, and when she saw the seer, she stopped in her step.

He stood solemnly, his left hand holding the wrapped stub of where his right hand used to be.

She gaped at him. "Bhasim," she said with a gasp, and drew closer. "Are you all right? What happened?"

"This is best suited as a private conversation," he said weakly. "Do you mind if we go inside?"

"Of course," she said quickly.

A guard of the seer stepped beside the old man, and Bhasim took his arm to steady himself, then followed them into the castle.

They swept into the dining room, and Caspian and Adrian joined them as they took seats around the large table.

Norah waved in water and hot tea.

"I'm going to need something a little stronger," Bhasim said.

Despite the seriousness of the situation, the corners of her mouth turned up ever so slightly. "Wine," she called.

"What happened?" Mikael asked as the doors closed behind the departing servants.

"There resides a great evil in the Aether now," he said finally. "A dark-magic serpent, attacking those who step in to touch the Eye."

"The what?" Soren asked.

"What's the Eye?" Mikael added.

Norah frowned. All those visits to the seer and they'd never bothered to ask how the visions actually worked?

"The Eye," Bhasim said. Then he sighed. He'd been annoyed at Norah for knowing about the Eye when she went to see him at the temple. Now he seemed annoyed he had to explain its existence. "There exists the Aether—the space through which the energy from all beings flows. It's here that the Eye sits. This is how seers see the visions, by stepping into the Aether and touching the Eye."

Norah glanced around the table. Excellent, everyone was caught up. "So what's happening with it?" she prompted Bhasim for more.

"The Aether has been infected with dark magic. A serpent guards the Eye, seeking to poison anyone who steps inside. It attacked me." He motioned to his absent hand. "Bit me, but I was able to escape the Aether, and"—he paused and looked at his guard—"cut the poison off before it traveled to the rest of my body."

Norah glanced at his guard who held a bladed staff in his hand. He'd cut off Bhasim's arm before it could spread. She shuddered at the thought. "If it bites you in the Aether, then it harms you in this world?" she asked.

"As I said, it's dark magic."

She lifted her eyes to Mikael. "It's Lucien. Now that he knows he can be seen, he seeks to prevent others from using the Eye."

"Who is Lucien?" Bhasim asked.

"The King of Rael and Serra," she explained. "He's a traveler. He's tethered himself to me, so that if anything harms him, then it also harms me."

The old seer's eyes widened as he looked at Mikael and then back to Norah. "A traveler that can be seen?"

"It's him in your visions," Mikael said. "Not the Bear." He was quite for a moment, then he said softer, "It was never the Bear." His stare locked with Norah's, and he held it.

"A traveler that can be seen by the Eye," Bhasim echoed again, still surprised, forcing Norah's attention back. "But this serpent is not the work of a seer," he said. "Seers have the gift to touch the Eye, but not the gift of magic. They can't create tethers. Or infect the Aether."

"He has a witch," said Soren.

"He'd need more than a witch," Bhasim said. "He'd need an entire coven."

Mikael watched the seer as the old man took a long drink from his wine chalice. "What do we do to stop him and break the tether?"

Bhasim shook his head. "The serpent is too powerful. A seer can't even step into the Aether, much less try to break a tether."

"There was a seer that survived in Aleon as well," Soren said. "Perhaps he has an answer."

"I am the strongest of the four kingdoms!" Bhasim said angrily. "And you're not listening. No seer can enter the Aether now, not while the serpent is there. And you must understand, the one who tethers you does so through the Aether. Perhaps a mind worker not of the Aether can help you, can go into your mind and break the tether from the other side."

"Get into my mind without using the Aether?" Norah asked. "So not a seer?"

The traveler gave a single nod.

"But who else can get into my mind if not a seer?" she asked.

"The Wild," Mikael said.

Norah jerked her head to meet his gaze. "We can't go back to the Wild." They'd barely made it out the last time they went.

"Their mind magic works outside the realms of the Aether, it's true," Bhasim said.

Mikael looked at Soren. "We go to the Wild."

"You can't go back there," she told him. "Naavi said they won't show you mercy if you return."

"I'll go," Soren said.

She shook her head. "They like you even less."

Soren didn't seem bothered, he only looked at Mikael. "You stay here. We *are* at war, or about to be, and the North at least needs her king. I'll take Salara and return when we've broken the tether."

Mikael nodded.

"Soren," she persisted.

"He's taking you," Mikael said.

And that was final.

Chapter Forty-Four

The Wild was as Norah remembered—quite ordinary, but beautiful. Chilled wind whispered through the trees, billowing back the hood of her cloak. She glanced over at Soren riding beside her, who'd come with little more than a winter tunic even though it was freezing. *Idiot*.

"Let me do the talking," she told him. "I don't know how eager they'll be to help, considering how we left things last." Not that he remembered; Naavi had stripped him of his memories of the Wild, except the memory of him nearly being forced to kill Mikael. "It's important this goes well. They're the only ones who can help. I just hope they know how. They should. They have a magical pool that should be able to show them. And even if it can't, they have a great library of magic that might have other options."

He said nothing as his eyes combed the trees around them. She sighed—he wasn't even listening. She'd made him leave his weapons at the tree line. All of them. And he wasn't happy. A twitch in his eye told her his mind was turning in thought—no doubt with something very unpleasant, something she wouldn't like hearing, but she couldn't help herself.

"What are you thinking about?" she asked.

"How I'd kill myself without a weapon."

She knew it—something unpleasant. She rolled her eyes. "You could be thinking of how beautiful the forest is."

"Why would I be thinking about that?"

She scrunched her face at him. "Why would you be thinking about killing yourself?"

"Because if the Wild is to kill me, they'll make me do it myself. That's likely. So I'm thinking about it."

Well, she *didn't* want to think about it. She puffed a small breath through her lips; she shouldn't have asked.

"I think I'd rip out my throat," he said.

Norah gaped at him, her eyes wide. "Gods, what? *Why?*"

"Were you not listening?"

She sputtered formless words. What was wrong with this man? "I mean, why would you pick that? That's terrible!"

"It's not what I'd pick for myself. It's what I would pick if I were *them.*"

Norah shook her head, her mouth still open in silent disgust.

"What?" he asked with a shrug. "I couldn't choke myself. I'd pass out, continue breathing. I don't think I could rip out my heart." He looked down at his forearms. "I could probably open my veins, I'm not sure with what, though. This is why you should've at least let me keep the dagger. I could have killed myself quickly. Now you'll make me suffer."

"Can you stop? Gods, Soren." She shook her head again. "You're not going to rip out your throat, or open your veins, or whatever your twisted mind can come up with."

He gave her an annoyed scowl but said no more.

Something had changed in the forest around them. Even the wind seemed to disappear. Sephir shook her head.

"Soren," she said as her pulse quickened.

They brought their horses to a stop and slid down. She looked at him, and he tapped his fingers to his throat, as if placing a bet.

"Shut up," she whispered.

He chuckled.

But it wasn't funny.

"Norah," sung a voice from the forest, and Naavi stepped out from between the trees.

Norah smiled. "Naavi!" A wave of emotion hit her. She wanted to go to her, hug her, but that seemed... perhaps too forward. She was happy to see the Wild woman again, though.

As if in answer, Naavi swept forward and pulled her into an embrace. "I knew I'd see you again, but I didn't expect so soon." She pulled back with a smile, but that smile fell when she saw Soren. The Wild woman glared at him. "You weren't welcome to return."

He shrugged. "I get that a lot."

"Naavi, I need your help again," Norah said, trying to pull her attention off Soren. "I need to know how to break a tether."

Naavi's focus snapped to Norah, forgetting Soren. Her eyes widened. "You've been tethered?"

That reaction didn't seem promising. Norah swallowed and nodded.

"Your Northman did this?"

"Alexander..." She glanced down at the ground. "Alexander's dead. It was his brother."

Naavi drew in a breath. Her eyes swept their gaze from one side to another, unseeing. "He had a brother?"

Norah nodded. "Yes."

"Is this brother a twin?" her voice came more urgent now, more concerned.

Norah's heart beat faster. "Yes, why?"

"Of course," Naavi said breathlessly to herself. "Why didn't we see it?"

Norah glanced at Soren, and then back to the Wild woman. "What didn't you see?"

"It's so obvious," the Wild woman mumbled to herself.

Soren frowned. "It's the opposite of obvious."

Naavi grabbed Norah's hand and pulled her toward the forest. "Come with me. Quickly!"

Norah let out a surprised gasp, but she let herself be led, hurrying along with Soren close behind. "We have to stop him," Norah said as they went. "Not only has he tethered himself to me, but he's killing seers."

"What do you mean he's killing seers?"

"As in, they're dying," Soren said irritably.

Norah glared back at him.

"Yes, but how?" Naavi pressed, not breaking her stride.

Norah almost had to run to keep up with her. "He's put some kind of dark magic into the Aether, a serpent, and it attacks anyone who enters to touch the Eye." She couldn't deny the small bit of pride in properly recounting Bhasim's explanation.

"How did he put dark magic into the Aether?"

Soren snorted. "Aren't *you* supposed to know things?"

"This is how you get forced to rip out your throat," Norah whispered back at him.

"Why?" he cut back. "Isn't there supposed to be a magical library somewhere with all these answers?"

Naavi stopped abruptly, and Norah almost ran into her. "How do you know about our library?" she hissed at Soren.

"I might... have told him that," Norah said quickly. The one time she wished he hadn't been listening.

Soren looked at her. "You *did* tell me that. And that they have a magic pool."

She pursed her lips at him. "Can you just... hush?"

Naavi sighed and pulled Norah forward again. "Don't repeat that if you know what's good for you. I have to take you to Sana."

"At the pool?" Norah asked.

"Yes."

"Wait"—she pulled the Wild woman to pause—"can we use the door?"

Naavi gave an exasperated sigh. "Fine."

Norah glanced back at Soren. "You're welcome."

"For what?"

She rolled her eyes; he remembered nothing of this place. "Never mind."

Norah was no stranger to the Wild, but it took her breath away nonetheless. The forest cathedral was still one of the most beautiful sights she'd ever seen. The high walls of trees and woven medallions of vine and stained glass stood like dreams from the gods. Hanging stars floated above, kissing the rooms with their light.

"I've been here?" Soren asked.

She smiled at him. "You were a little grumpier back then. Didn't appreciate the full beauty of things. That, and you were also coming off almost killing Mikael, so..."

"That I remember."

And that reminded Norah—"Is Sana still... mad? About how we parted last?"

"Yes," Naavi answered shortly.

And... "Do you think she'll help me?"

"I don't know."

Well... that didn't inspire confidence.

As if on cue, Sana stepped into the hall. "You return," she said to Norah coldly. Then her eyes moved to Soren. "Very foolish."

"He's a twin," Naavi said, as if there was no underlying threat to Sana's comment. "The Northman has a twin."

Sana's scowl turned to surprise, and her lips parted slightly. "Of course."

Norah glanced at Soren and then back to the Wild women. "Can someone explain what that means?"

Naavi drew an uneasy breath. "Twin travelers are the most powerful of seers. One carries the sight, and one carries the shield. Their bodies individually are not burdened with both sight and shield, so they're able to grow the gift more, handle more of its power. Think of it as... double the power"—she shook her head—"more than double, it's exponential."

Norah nodded slowly, absorbing the information. "So that's why you couldn't see Alexander? Because he carried the shield?"

Naavi nodded. "And it explains why his shield was so strong. It was meant to cover them both."

"But Lucien was still seen in visions."

"If they were far apart... A shield is not infinite. At least not while both twins are alive."

"What does that mean?" Soren interjected.

Naavi sighed. "Together, they remain balanced, but when one twin dies, there is nothing to balance the power, and the remaining force will only grow."

"Grow to what?" Norah asked.

"There is only one record in our library of twin travelers. They lived a thousand years ago. The twin with the sight perished in a fire. The twin with the shield survived. His power grew, encompassing the earth, shielding all the world and blinding all seers for eleven years until his death."

That's what would have happened if Lucien had died and Alexander had lived. "But it's Lucien who lives, and he has the sight. What does that mean? What will happen?"

Naavi shook her head. "I don't know."

Soren snorted, but Norah shot him a daggered gaze, and he kept silent.

"Perhaps he might eventually become powerful enough to break the confines of the blood spell," Sana said, "travel into the minds of others without their consent. Take control of them, even."

Norah's mind drifted to the birds. "He already does this with animals. But he still needs the blood."

"Probably not for much longer. He needs to be stopped."

"Can't have him being like you?" Soren snarked.

"Our power is bound by the forest," Sana cut back. "Even *we* have limits. But he would not. He would have more power than any one man should hold. And if he has ill intent, there will be no one able to stand against him. You have to stop him before he reaches that point."

"How?"

"You have to kill him."

Norah looked at Soren in desperation. "Mikael will never let that happen while we're still tethered." She turned back to Sana. "Do you know how to break it?"

"I do."

She sighed in relief. *Thank the gods.* "How?"

"The same way Naavi broke the seers' ability to see you when your father brought you here."

Norah's heart caught in her throat. "I would lose my memories again?"

Naavi nodded. "Yes."

"You are tethered through the Aether," Sana said. "We would break your connection to the Aether again, and thus break the tether."

She needed to sit down, but there was no chair. Her lungs called for air, but there wasn't enough of it. She couldn't get a breath. To break the tether, she'd have to lose herself again. She'd lose everything. She shook her head. *No*, there had to be another way.

"There is no other way," Sana said.

Norah looked back to Soren. How could there be no other way?

He stepped closer to her. His voice came softly. "You probably wouldn't come to like me again, but I'd understand."

"What?" she breathed.

"But with Salar, you'd come to love him again. I know you would."

She shook her head. "No. Soren. No. I'm not losing my memories again. It's all I have left of those I've lost: my grandmother, Alexander, Vitalia. And my memories with Mikael, I won't have them taken from me."

He stepped closer. "You don't have a choice."

"Yes, I do."

"If Lucien dies, you'll die. And you know Salar won't let that happen. We need to kill him. This is the only way to stop him."

Norah shook her head again. No. She wouldn't. She couldn't. "I'll find another way."

"The only other way is if the traveler breaks the tether himself," Sana said.

"Then that's what I'll have to get Lucien to do."

"Have you lost your mind?" Soren asked her.

"He's not a bad person! He's just... wrong. And he's angry. But if I see him again, if I talk to him... I do think he cares about me."

"Salara, did you just hear them?" Soren asked. "We have to kill him. He's not going to help us do that, no matter how much you think he cares." He looked to Naavi and Sana. "Do it. Break the tether."

"No," Norah said, stepping back.

His eyes grew dark and serious, burning into the sisters. "A threat you described is a universal threat. You think he'll stop with the world of men? Do it!"

"No!" Norah cried. "Soren! I can't lose everything. I can't lose Alexander. Or Mikael. I can't lose you!"

"You won't lose us."

She turned to Naavi. "No," she begged.

"Do it," Soren demanded.

Naavi stared at Norah for a moment, and her eyes welled. "I can't," she said, shaking her head. "I can't if it's not what she wants. I can't do it again."

Soren let out a snarl. "As long as he's tethered to her, no one will kill him. And you know what will come. You have to stop him. Break it!"

Sana stepped forward. "Hold her."

Norah shook her head again. Fear coursed through her as Soren moved toward her. "Soren, no." She took a step backward, but her back hit the wall. "No," she begged. "Soren, please! No!"

He brought his hands to cup the sides of her face. "I'm sorry, Salara."

"Soren!" she sobbed.

The gentleness of his hands hardened, and he gripped her still. "Do it!" he said between his teeth.

"No!" Norah screamed as she clawed at him, but he held her. Panic flooded her, and she lashed out. This couldn't be happening. They couldn't do this to her. Not again.

His eyes welled. Still, he held her.

Sana put her hands atop Norah's head.

But Norah fought. With everything she had, she fought. Pain seared through her mind, melting her from the inside. It was unbearable. But still she fought.

Burning, ripping, tearing.

She fought.

It was agony. Claws of destruction mauled her mind, breaking her. Erasing her.

And then thunder boomed, and suddenly the pain stopped.

A cloak of darkness swept around her.

Soren's hands fell away. Cool soothed the burn. What was happening? Was it over? But she could still remember...

When she opened her eyes, she was still standing, but leaning against the wall, doubled over. Soren stood against the far wall, steadying himself and holding his head, and Sana lay a few paces away, picking herself up from the floor.

Naavi rushed to Sana's side. "What happened?"

"It's him," Sana panted. "He's fighting back."

Him? Lucien?

"How's that possible?" Naavi asked.

Sana stood and straightened, breathless. "I don't know. But I felt him breaking through into my own mind. I can't go back. He's too strong."

"How was he able to hit me?" Soren asked, still recovering. They stared at him.

"You felt him?" Sana asked.

"Like a bolt of lightning."

"The limits of the blood are weakening. He's growing more powerful."

"How did he know what we were doing?" Soren asked.

"If his pain hurts her, then her pain hurts him as well." Sana shook her head. "But I can't go back in. There's nothing else we can do."

Norah only stood, half listening. Never had she felt so betrayed, so violated.

Soren's eyes met hers. "Salara," he said softly. He stepped forward and reached for her.

"Don't touch me," she seethed.

She stumbled down the hall the way she had come. She needed to get out of this cursed Wild, and away from those who had almost stolen that which she held most dear.

They rode in silence, Norah on Sephir and Soren on his destrier beside her. Her anger had left her. All she felt now was hurt. She'd trusted Soren. She'd trusted him not to hurt her, and this was the worst kind of hurt—the hurt of betrayal. Of course, he thought he was protecting her, and protecting Mikael, and he didn't know what it was like to lose himself. Regardless, it would stay with her. For a long time.

Pain ripped across her left hand, and she sucked in the cold air through her teeth as she doubled over, clutching her palms together tightly. The other cut would soon follow... and it did.

Soren reined his horse closer. "Salara!"

"I'm fine," she panted. "It'll pass."

She'd come to appreciate that she didn't know when she'd be cut. At first, she thought it was a curse, and it stole her spirit, but then she'd come to believe it would have been worse to know when it was coming and wait each time for it. And to know the healing would come shortly, somehow that soothed her.

Norah stopped and slid off Sephir. She waited for the healing.

"Are you all right?" he asked.

She only nodded with her eyes closed. The sharp pain dulled to an ache, then disappeared altogether, and her palms became smooth again, as if nothing had ever happened. Finally. She straightened.

He offered her the waterskin for a drink, but she didn't take it. She didn't look at him. She couldn't.

He sighed. "What would you do if someone you loved was choosing to hurt themselves?"

She didn't respond to him.

"Look what this does to you! And Lucien has to die. You're choosing to die with him."

"It's my choice!" she cried. "You would have taken everything from me!"

"Your life is everything!"

"I'll die before I lose myself again."

"Then you'll let Salar die too. He won't raise a sword to Lucien if he thinks it will harm you. He won't even fight. And Lucien will kill him, as the seer has shown us."

She knew the vision. She'd seen it a thousand times over in her mind, lived it a thousand times, mourned it a thousand times. Lucien would kill Mikael. And Mikael would let him. Because of her.

"He doesn't even lift his sword," Soren said, his voice cracking.

"But you will," she told him.

His head jerked up, and she met his tormented eyes. He shook his head.

"You'll kill him, Soren. The opportunity will come, and you'll take it."

It was so quiet she could almost hear their hearts beating.

"No," he said softly. "I won't. I can't."

"You will. It's the last thing I'll ask of you."

He shook his head.

"I need you to do it."

His eyes welled.

"Swear to me," she said.

His breaths came uneven underneath his wrap.

"Swear to me, Soren. You'll kill him."

For a moment, she thought he might not.

"I swear," he said finally.

Relief washed over her. It was done. Her heart filled with sadness—not for her death, but for what she was asking her friend to do.

"It's okay if it hurts," she told him. She was getting used to pain.

"You won't feel a thing," he whispered.

And she believed him. Soren could be trusted with how to end a life.

CHAPTER FORTY-FIVE

The sound of metal and horses hung in the air as the Mercian army readied to depart. They would march to Bahoul to join part of the Kharavian army, in line with their battle plans. Then the forces from Bahoul, with Mikael and Soren, would be ready to help Phillip drive Rael and Japheth south into the Canyonlands where Katya and the remaining Kharavian army would be waiting.

Norah felt uneasy; timing was critical. They couldn't sustain a large army in Bahoul for long; moving too early could work against them. But not being positioned in time would leave them without a full force if they fell under attack. The question was—when to go?

Word had come from Osan, thanks to Phillip's new alliance, that no more ships had sailed between Rael and Japheth—they weren't moving more forces between the two kingdoms. But the Raelean army had sat just inside the Japheth border for weeks. So if they weren't moving more of their army, what were they waiting for? That had been the question for some time. Soren suspected something wasn't right and didn't want to wait any longer. He wanted to move now, and Mikael agreed.

Norah would accompany them as far as Sandor, a Mercian stronghold just north of the Tribelands. Mikael had wanted Norah to stay in Mercia, but there was no way she'd stay in the safety of the North while everyone she loved marched to war. He reluctantly agreed she could join them as far as Sandor and then return to Mercia while he continued on to Bahoul.

The ride to Sandor was shorter than she'd expected. It took five days moving with the army, as planned, but time was in short supply, and it felt like barely a day. They didn't talk about what had happened in the Wild. Norah had told Mikael they couldn't break the tether, and they left it at that. She didn't tell him about almost losing her memories again. It didn't matter—it hadn't worked anyway. And she wouldn't let the end to come haunt him like it haunted her.

She wished Adrian was still with her. She could have talked to him. Soren had sent him back to Phillip before they left for the Wild. He'd have arrived by now. She hoped he was doing well. Of course he was doing well. He was tasked with helping Aleon build up their defenses and prepare Phillip's army to drive Japheth and Rael to the Canyonlands. And he had been taught by the best.

They reached Sandor, and the gates of the stronghold opened. It was the first time she'd been to this fortress, or rather, the first time that she remembered. It was smaller than the castle of Mercia, and smaller than the stronghold in Bahoul, but it was surprisingly beautiful. There were trees all around and throughout, and a garden in the center. It was interesting to have something so serene in a place meant as a stronghold of war.

She found herself in the garden as Mikael and Soren worked through final plans with Caspian and sent messages to Phillip and Katya. She'd imagined things differently when she had thought about accompanying Mikael. She didn't know what—just not sitting to herself. She wouldn't complain; she'd take every moment she could get, just knowing Mikael was near.

Sorrow sat heavy in her heart. Each day took them closer to war, closer to Mikael's fate. The sorrow grew to desperation as she watched everyone working toward the future that had been foretold—Mikael's future. Everyone was so accepting. Had she become accepting too?

Soren had sworn he'd kill Lucien, no matter the cost. While she trusted him completely, trusted him to do everything in his power to save Mikael, not everything was within his power. She couldn't rely on his promise.

Snow covered the ground. Norah sat on the bench in the middle of the evergreen gardens with quiet all around her. It was a deceiving peace. A flutter caught her eye, and she paused as a butterfly danced through the air. In the middle of winter—*how beautifully strange.*

It floated closer, dipping and rising around her, and she held out her hand. With a flit of its wings, it landed on her palm. She couldn't help an amazed laugh. For a butterfly to land on her hand—

She stopped.

She'd been here before.

Her lip trembled as she looked at the butterfly, and the world stood still. Even the light froze.

She clenched her hand and crushed it.

Her mouth opened in a silent scream, but she didn't make a noise. Not a noise. She could only sit, with the crushed butterfly in her hand.

She had crushed it. Not let it fly off again. *Crushed it.*

Hopelessness fell away, and air filled her lungs, and for the first time in months... she could breathe.

Norah sprang from the bench and ran back through the gardens, still clutching the butterfly. She tore into the war office, where Mikael stood with Caspian over a series of maps. "Fate can be changed!" she cried. She held the crushed butterfly in her hand, breathless. "Look!"

Mikael stared at her. Caspian gave a polite nod and left to give them privacy. She didn't wait for Mikael to react.

"Look," she said again as she held the butterfly closer. "Bhasim showed me a vision, when I went to the temple, where I held a butterfly in my hand in the garden, and then it flew away. But I changed it."

He brought his hand under hers, pulling it up to look closer. But he said nothing.

"Don't you see what this means?" she said. "Fate can be changed!"

He reached and cupped her cheek, giving a sad smile. "You never give up."

She drew her brows together. "What does that mean?"

"I've tried to change my fate long enough to know what the seer says is true."

He didn't believe her, and her pulse raced faster. He had to. "It's not! Look!"

"The fate of a butterfly isn't the fate of a king."

"It doesn't matter. It *can* be changed. No matter how small it is, this proves that change can happen."

He nodded, but didn't seem to accept what she was saying.

"Mikael, please."

"What does this matter? Being able to change fate or not, what would you have me do differently now? Everything's been set in motion."

She didn't have an answer for him.

"It's too late, Salara."

"How is it too late? I literally changed this vision in the moment! We have to keep trying."

He frowned and swayed away from her, but she caught his arm.

"Mikael. Mikael, listen to me. Don't go to battle." Desperation filled her voice because it filled her heart. "Let these days pass. We can change it."

"You want me to... just not show up for my fate?"

"Yes! Yes, I do." That's exactly what she wanted.

"If it were only that simple. Would men not have done that already?" He paused and pulled her closer with a deep sigh. "The curse of fate isn't truly one's actual fate. The curse is being consumed with changing it. And I've wasted enough with this obsession." He smiled sadly.

She shook her head. He was accepting his fate. He couldn't. She wouldn't let him. "No. Mikael—"

"You're a strong queen, Salara. I know you'll stay strong, no matter what happens." He locked his eyes with hers. "I don't want to speak about fate again. Ever again. I want to take each day as it comes." He brought his lips to hers in a tender kiss. As he pulled back, he smiled. "I love you, Salara." Then he turned and followed after Caspian.

She stood alone, astonished. It was like he didn't believe her. He didn't even want to try. No—he wasn't allowed to do that. She wouldn't let him. She raced through halls, almost tripping, bumping into random people and not caring at all.

She finally found Soren in the armory. "Soren!" The poor soldier she interrupted gave a startled bow and backed away before leaving. "Soren! Fate can be changed!"

He turned toward her with a crease in his brow. "What?"

She held up the butterfly to him. By now, it was barely recognizable in her clammy hand.

His eyes moved to the crushed remains in her palm, and his brow creased more. "You killed a butterfly."

"No." She shook her head, stepping closer and clasping his arm as she held the dead creature nearer to his face. "I mean, yes, I did, but I saw it fly away."

He glanced at the butterfly again, and his eyes narrowed. "It doesn't look like it flew away."

She wanted to scream. Her conversation with Mikael had shaken her. She knew she wasn't making sense, but she couldn't get her words out. "No! In the temple of the seer, Bhasim showed me a vision. It was of me in the garden and a butterfly landing on my hand. And I let it fly away. But look!" She shoved the butterfly closer to his face. "I *changed* the vision."

He lifted his chin to avoid her smacking him with the dead insect. "Changing the fate of a butterfly doesn't mean you can change the fate of a king."

Did Soren and Mikael both inherit the same blindness? "Why not? Bhasim said visions can't be changed, but they can! If something small can be changed, why not something more significant?"

"It's not that simple."

"But what if it is?"

"If it were that easy, we would have changed it by now." Irritation grew in his voice. "But look at everything that's happened—everything has unfolded as it was seen. No matter what we've done to stop it."

"Because we didn't recognize the moments, or what they meant! My father couldn't stop my capture because he didn't know it was *Mikael* who would take me, not the senior Shadow King. Mikael didn't know that the vision of me on his throne was as his wife and not his enemy. We thought Lucien was Alexander. Don't you see? We couldn't stop them because of our ignorance, not because it was impossible. But this vision of Mikael's death, it's here now. I know it. And we have the chance to stop it."

"And how do you know that everything you do won't take us one step closer to that vision?"

"We have to remove Mikael. We have to get him away and let this moment pass. We can save him." It sounded weak, she knew, but it was the only thing left she could think of.

He shook his head. "I can't do that."

"Soren, why won't you even try?"

"Do you think I haven't given everything to trying!" His voice shook in anger. "Do you not think I've spent my life trying to find ways to save him? Fate is always one step ahead. And it toys with us, teases us, gives us hope when there is none."

"I don't believe there's no hope!" she cried. "I don't accept that." She wiped the smear of butterfly on her dress. "Soren," she begged, "please."

"Have you shown him this? Have you told him what you're telling me now?"

"Yes! But he refuses the idea."

"Then what would you have me do?"

"You can force him away. You control the army; you can force him to return to Mercia where he'll be safe."

"You would have me usurp his power?"

"Just until this is over."

He reached out and clasped both sides of her face and held her. "Do you hear what you're saying? You would have me take his choice?" He shook his head. "I've done that once, Salara, and you above all others should know what it takes from you. I won't do it again. It's his decision to stay. I stand by his side. And you can't change fate. It's shown us time and time again." He released her, and with a final look of sadness, he left her to the room alone.

The room they'd taken for their chamber was quiet. Mikael sat on the edge of the bed in the dim candlelight, his hair loose around his shoulders. He was beautiful. She tried to capture this image of him, tried to burn it into her mind to remember forever. In the morning, he'd be gone. So she just stood, looking at him.

He returned her gaze. "Can I see you, Salara?" he asked softly.

He wanted to see her, to remember her, the way she wanted to remember him. Slowly, she reached behind her and loosened the ties of her gown. She pulled the shoulders down, slipping one arm from its sleeve and then the other before pushing it over her hips and letting it fall to the floor. Her corset, her shift, the silks—she removed them one at a time and discarded them to the side until she stood naked in front of him. Her skin prickled in the cool air, but she stood as he looked at her. She let him take his time.

He held his hand out for her, and she took it. Slowly, he pulled her to him. She stood between his knees as his eyes traveled her face and then ran back and forth between hers. He didn't speak. He only reached up and flattened his hand against her chest. Her heart beat under his palm.

"Of all the things this life has given me, you're the most precious."

She took his face in her hands. "Come away with me," she begged.

"Where?"

"Anywhere. We'll go where no one knows us. We'll have nothing, but we'll have each other. I'll learn... how to cook, and you'll... do everything else."

He smiled. "I would even do the cooking."

She laughed, but her laugh turned to tears, and she couldn't keep them back. Because she knew she couldn't keep him back.

"No, no, no," he whispered. "Don't be sad."

"You can't leave me."

He shook his head. "I'll never leave you. If I should go anywhere, I only go to our eternal bed. And when you're tired of this world and ready for sleep, I'll be waiting."

"You won't wait long."

He clutched her tighter. "Don't say that. Don't ever say that."

"I don't want to be in this world without you," she whispered.

He smiled, but his eyes glistened. "Kiss me, wife."

And she did.

CHAPTER FORTY-SIX

It was almost morning. Norah stretched along Mikael's warmth. They'd spent the hours of darkness making love and drifting in and out of dreams—dreams she never wanted to leave. She let her hands travel over his skin, etching each line of his body, each curve of his muscle, into her memory. The way he moved. The way he wrapped himself around her. His taste, his smell. His touch. Everything about him.

A horn sounded outside. Footsteps in the hall and a bang at the door jarred them awake. Soren swung it open without giving a hair's width of time.

"A messenger," he said brusquely, and left as quickly as he had come. The door slammed closed behind him.

Mikael was up in an instant, pulling on his breeches, and Norah rose quickly.

"Do you think it's from Aleon?" Her heart raced. She wasn't ready. She wasn't ready to get up, or for this day. She wasn't ready for him to leave.

"Likely," he said as he pulled on his boots. "Meet us in the courtyard."

"Wait, I'm coming too." She pulled on a thick robe over her nightdress and her cloak over the top and stepped into her bed slippers—hardly proper attire, but it was still dark out, and she didn't care. She followed Mikael, her hand in his, down to the courtyard.

Soren and Caspian were already there, waiting impatiently as the iron gate of the stronghold was raised. A soldier on a horse swept in, and his mount skidded on the cobblestone as he came to a halt and slid down. Despite the mud coating his armor, hints of blue peeked from underneath—a soldier of Aleon. He bowed his head to Soren and held out a letter. "Japheth and Rael are marching on Eilor."

Eilor—the southernmost kingdom of Aleon and Catherine's home kingdom—where Phillip was with his army.

"What?" Norah gasped. They had been so sure Rael would move against Kharav first.

Bhastian stepped closer with a torchlight as Soren broke the seal and scanned the parchment.

"Japheth *and* Rael?" Mikael asked.

Soren nodded and handed him the letter. "It's what he writes."

Phillip.

"How long do they have?" Mikael asked.

The lord commander looked back to the messenger. "How long did it take you to get here?"

"Three days."

"Then Phillip has another day before they reach him, maybe two given the size of Rael's army and how slowly they'll be moving." He shook his head, and Norah watched as his concern built. "Even if I diverted the Northern army and took them now, I wouldn't get there in time." He cursed.

"Do it," Mikael told him. "Take them. He'll hold until you get there."

Soren pulled down his wrap, his face the palest Norah had ever seen. "Phillip can't stand against both Japheth *and* Rael."

"He has a hundred thousand men," Mikael assured him. "He can hold until you get there."

"You ride ahead," Caspian told Soren. "I'll follow as quickly as I can with the army, but you go now."

Soren looked at Mikael. "You need the Northmen in Bahoul."

Mikael shook his head. "They're needed in Aleon more now. Take the Northern army, join with Aleon, push Rael and Japheth down toward the Canyonlands. I'll be ready with the forces in Bahoul to join you." He clasped Soren's shoulder. "Now go get your Aleon king."

Soren reached out and gripped him, pulling their foreheads together. "You'll keep yourself well until we meet again."

"Until we meet again," Mikael said. "Goodbye, brother."

They broke, and Soren looked at Norah. He gave her the faintest of nods, then turned to leave.

"What was that?" she demanded.

Soren stopped. "It was... goodbye."

"That's not a proper goodbye." She crossed the space between them and threw her arms around him, gripping him fiercely. "Keep yourself well," she whispered.

For once, he returned her hug. "I'll come back."

"You'd better."

He nodded. Then he moved to get his horse, and Caspian followed after.

Mikael's face was somber as he looked at her, and their stares locked. The time had come. He had to leave. Wordlessly, he took her hand, and they walked back to their chamber.

Neither of them spoke as she helped him dress. She knew his departure was urgent, but she took her time, pulling each tie tight on his clothing, each strap straight on his armor. His eyes watched her as she worked. On the last vambrace, the last fastening, she stopped. She couldn't close it. Once it was fastened, he'd be ready.

But he couldn't be ready, because she wasn't ready. So, she stood, her fingers frozen.

Slowly, he put his hand over hers and pressed it closed. The click of the metal rang in her ears—a sound that would forever stay in her mind. He pulled her close and drew his eyes over her face before bringing his lips to hers. His kiss trailed from her lips to her cheeks, over each eye, to her forehead, and back to her lips again. She tried to capture each touch in her mind—to remember, to never forget.

"Stay strong, Salara," he said.

Then he turned and left for Bahoul.

Soren urged his mount relentlessly toward Aleon's southern kingdom of Eilor. He'd only taken Cohen with him, because the boy wouldn't slow him down, and Soren could use him. Caspian would follow behind with the Northern army.

They traveled quickly. Phillip could hold until he got there, he told himself. And if he couldn't, he'd fall back to the mountains of Songs—that was the plan. He cursed himself. The plan had been that Rael would attack Kharav. Now he had to shift, change the strategy. Aleon could fall because of his mistake. He couldn't let that happen.

They journeyed for what seemed like an eternity, stopping only to rest their horses. They could swap mounts in the Tribelands, but then he'd be left without a proper warhorse when he reached Eilor. He needed his destrier, Khalel al'Dakar, for the battle he would bring to this pretend Bear and the coward king of Japheth.

Cohen didn't speak, not even using his silent language. Soren knew he sensed his worry and chose to remain quiet. And Soren was grateful.

The lowlands turned into highlands, then to hills, and he pushed his destrier on. His body tired but his mind raged, and he pushed himself on. He had to get to Phillip.

Suddenly, Cohen reined his horse to a sliding stop. Soren didn't have time to snap his head to see before he was falling.

The ground quaked underneath him as he hit the earth. Pain shot up his back and into his neck, and the world spun around him. He groaned as he rolled onto his side, then struggled to his knees. A few paces back, his mount flailed in a hidden trench.

"Kal!" He staggered up and toward the animal as Cohen jumped down from his own horse. As Soren neared, the destrier managed to get back on its feet. He let out a pant of relief. Curse the North gods if he'd lost this horse.

A stir behind him made him spin around and reach for the short sword at his back.

He was met with a grinning face. Adrian chuckled from atop his horse. "Looks like you found our defenses."

Soren hissed out a breath but couldn't help a small smile. "Little Bear."

Adrian dropped down from his mount and reached for him. They clasped arms, cuffing each other on the shoulders.

"Where's the king?" Soren asked.

"Not far. He'll be glad to see you."

Soren exhaled the fear that had been consuming him. Phillip was all right. He could breathe again. He tightened his grip and jerked Adrian closer. "You almost hurt my horse."

Adrian still wore his grin. "Yeah, well, I didn't expect you to come tearing across the hills and get caught in our own traps. It was a good set, though, right?" He looked past Soren to Cohen. "Didn't drop *you*, though."

Soren glanced over his shoulder, and the boy smiled. Of course Cohen had seen it. He had an eye. And while Soren had admittedly been distracted, he couldn't deny the handiwork. "It was a good set." At least Aleon had some defenses now. *Wait*—"What's going on? Where is everyone?" He'd expected to arrive straight into a full-fledged battle.

"That's a good question," Adrian answered. "Japheth and Rael stopped just short of our borders. They wait."

That didn't make any sense. "For what?"

Adrian shook his head. "We don't know. Come on, I'll take you to King Phillip."

Soren and Cohen followed Adrian through the hills and across the river to the army camp of Aleon. Before they even reached Phillip, Soren could already see what Adrian had been talking about. Across the flatlands to the south, from horizon to horizon, spanned the largest army he'd ever seen. But they waited, just short of the border. The armies were split in two: part of the army, presumably Japheth, lay to the east, and Rael just to the west.

"Why are they split?" Soren asked.

Adrian shrugged. "We have suspicions. It's best to show you."

Interesting...

"This way." Adrian led him to a large center tent and ducked between the flaps.

Soren followed, and when he stepped inside, he stopped.

Phillip sat, pouring over letters. When he looked up, he stood in surprise, and a smile came to his face. That beautiful smile that made Soren's chest hurt—the smile he'd feared he wouldn't see again.

Phillip wore only a few pieces of armor. The lion surrounded by four stars, representing the four kingdoms of the empire, shone proudly on his breastplate. He stepped to Soren and stared at him for a moment. Then he reached up and clutched him by the shoulders and pulled him into a tight embrace.

Soren stiffened. Adrian and Cohen's presence ate into his mind. Soren wasn't one for affection, and certainly not so publicly, and not so openly with the Aleon king.

"I didn't think you'd come," Phillip said as he clutched him even tighter.

How could he think he wouldn't come? Soren forgot all thoughts of watching eyes. He leaned back and caught Phillip's eyes with his own. "You didn't think I'd come? I told you I would."

"I know where your duty lies."

Soren gripped the nape of Phillip's neck, holding him close. "I told you I'd come for you."

Phillip's eyes glistened, and Soren felt his own rush of emotion. Remembering himself, he stepped back and glanced at Adrian and Cohen, but they looked at him as though nothing were amiss, as if they hadn't just seen his heart in his hands. And he loved them all the more. The battle, he reminded himself. "Caspian follows with the Northern army; they're another day behind, maybe two."

Phillip smiled, emotion still in his eyes. "You bring the Mercian army?"

"Salar and Salara send them for you."

Phillip shook his head. "No, they send them for you. And I'm grateful."

Soren's own emotion still lingered. "I was so certain Rael would march on Kharav first. I'm sorry."

Phillip's hand gripped him reassuringly. "We need to show you something." He led Soren out of the tent to where the enemy armies spanned the horizon.

Adrian pointed to the far right of the Raelean army. "Look at that tent. The one with the large red banner."

Soren saw it. "All right."

"And now look at the one in the center. Look at their banners."

"All right." What was he looking for?

"Do you see how they move exactly the same with the wind?"

Banners flying in the wind. "All right?"

Adrian's brows creased. "Isn't that interesting?"

Was it?

"Keep following," Adrian said. He pointed back to the far right of the army. "Do you see that man, on the end, with a can-looking helm?"

Soren squinted. The army was far, and he could barely make out one man from another. Damn getting old. But then he spotted the man Adrian referred to. "Okay."

"Now look." Adrian swung his finger to the left a little.

It took Soren a moment, but then he spotted him. The same man. But standing in a different place.

Adrian pointed a little more to the left, at another. "And again."

And Soren saw the same man yet again.

"Pick another man," Phillip said, "any other Raelean man, and it's all the same. Replicated across."

Replicated across... Soren's mind turned. What did that mean? How was an army replicated—

"I think they're fake," Adrian said.

A fake army...

Why would Rael have a fake army?

Norah stood in the courtyard of the stronghold, eyeing Titus with frustration as she readied to depart. Mikael had made him swear to take her back to Mercia, even if he had to drag her. She promised to go, but she couldn't. She stalled for two days, until Titus wouldn't let her delay anymore and threatened to make good on his promise, and it infuriated her.

Calla sat on her horse quietly, which was out of character. It was better that way. Norah didn't need anything else fueling her fire. She was already two heartbeats away from knifing Titus in the heel and making a run for Bahoul, to Mikael. But what would she do after? She had nothing that would help him. In fact, she'd be a hindrance more than anything else. But she couldn't go back to Mercia.

A horn blew in the distance, and she turned.

"Messenger!" the watchman called, and her pulse quickened.

From where? Who would send a messenger?

The iron gate raised, and a messenger swept in on a heavily lathered horse, pulling it up abruptly. He'd driven the animal hard. "I've a message for King Mikael of Kharav," he announced.

Norah frowned. The title sounded strange to her ears. "He departed already," she said, "but I'm salara of Kharav and queen of Mercia. What's your message?"

He slid from his horse and held the letter for her with a bow. "From King Tagasi of Osan."

Why would King Tagasi be sending Mikael a letter? Yes, he was now allied with Phillip and had joined their cause, but she hadn't thought them friendly enough to be exchanging letters directly. Norah broke the red-and-yellow seal, then stopped suddenly.

Red and yellow. Red and yellow were the colors of Osan.

And the colors of the flag of the kingdom that had fallen to Lucien in the vision.

Her heart jumped to her throat, and she ripped open the parchment to find the words she feared.

"I thought the Aleon messenger brought word that Rael was marching to attack Eilor," she said to Bhastian, her voice shaking.

He nodded. "That's right. And your Northmen are headed there now."

She shook her head. "King Tagasi says that Rael just marched a path of destruction through Osan. Osan has fallen. Now Rael is headed toward Bahoul and will attack from the west." The opposite direction of Aleon.

She clutched the letter tightly in her hand, a horror washing over her. "Lucien's marching on Bahoul. And Mikael's all alone."

Bhastian shifted. "Salar only has a quarter of the Kharavian army in Bahoul. Katya holds the rest in the Canyonlands, waiting."

Her heart jumped to her throat. They'd been tricked. She swallowed as sickness filled her stomach. "Lucien *is* attacking Kharav first. And tricked us into leaving Mikael vulnerable."

"Bahoul is a fortress," Bhastian tried to assure her. "Salar can hold against a much larger army."

"Against the entire army of Rael?" For months escaped slaves from all kingdoms had been flocking to Rael. It was now the largest army in the world. Larger than Phillip's legendary hundred thousand.

He didn't need to say it. She saw her answer in his eyes.

"We need to get you to Mercia," Titus said.

Her eyes blazed. "I'm not going to Mercia. I'm going to get my army. Then I'm going get my husband."

Soren drew his brows together as he stood beside Phillip and Adrian and looked out across the waiting ranks of Japheth and Rael. "A fake army?"

"At least Rael's," Adrian said. "We haven't seen the same on the Japheth side."

Cohen stepped up beside him. *Something's not right about Rael*, he said.

Soren pulled down his wrap so the boy could read his mouth. "That's what we're talking about."

Adrian chuckled. "He's good. Took me two days before I noticed it."

Soren turned his eyes back to the horizon. A fake army? How was that possible? Adrian was a clever man—perhaps the cleverest he'd ever known. He wanted to trust him, but it just sounded like madness, like... *witchcraft*.

Soren stilled. "He has a witch."

Phillip's brows creased. "What?"

"The Blood King. He has a witch. That has to be how he's doing it."

Phillip stared back out at the armies. "Why would Rael show up with a fake army?"

"It would explain why they haven't attacked yet," Adrian said.

A worrisome thought came to Soren. "I'd show up with a fake army if I wanted to create a diversion." His worry pitted itself deeper. A diversion that would take him away from Mikael. His pulse quickened.

Phillip frowned. "Gregor's army seems real enough, though. And he'd never show up on his own against me with a fake ally."

"Unless he doesn't know," Adrian said. "Maybe that's why they're separate. Easier to keep the ruse."

Phillip lifted a brow and tipped his head to the side in agreement with the possibility.

Soren's heart beat faster. "If this is a diversion, I need to know *now*. It would mean Rael isn't here, and I'd need to get the Northern army back to Salar as quickly as I can."

"We could attack," Adrian said. "If it's witchery, and not real, it will only be Gregor. We could take Japheth. That could leave Rael to stand alone and us with more of an advantage."

Possibly—if they could make it back to Mikael in time for all their armies to stand together.

"And if the Raelean army *is* real?" Phillip asked.

They all knew what would happen if it was real and they attacked—even at a hundred thousand strong, Aleon would be decimated, especially since Caspian and the Northern army still hadn't arrived to join them.

But Soren couldn't wait for the Northern army to arrive to find out. That would be too late for Mikael—if it wasn't too late already. He turned to Adrian. "Do you think it's real?"

Adrian swept his eyes across the line that stretched horizon to horizon. He pursed his lips together, then shook his head. "No. I don't."

Soren looked at Cohen. "You?"

Cohen shook his head. *I don't think it's real*, he answered.

Soren didn't either, but was he sure enough to risk it all? If he didn't, he risked Mikael. "Today's a day for blood then."

It was just a matter of whose.

CHAPTER FORTY-SEVEN

The earth shook as Soren thundered forward with the Aleon army behind him. He'd always loved the charge to battle, but this battle was different. He'd always fought to take. Now he fought to keep, and he had more to lose than he ever had before.

If he'd decided wrong, if the Raelean forces *were* real, he'd be damning both Phillip and Mikael. The Aleon army would be overwhelmed and defeated. Then Rael and Japheth would rest a day or two and easily take the Northern army when they arrived late. And then Mikael would stand alone.

Mikael would fall alone.

But it was too late to turn back. Soren's eyes locked on the enemy as he led the charge; he had to push out the doubt. He had to focus on what he did best—killing. He'd kill as many as he could. And then he'd kill more.

Japheth's army reacted in surprise, with a delayed start of their return charge. *Unprepared.* Or cowards. Or both. Of course, it helped that they assumed only fools would attack their joint armies. But they finally did return the charge and drove their forces to meet the attack.

Rael waited, although its army seemed ready. The army waited with intention, but just what was the intention? Finally, the army of the

Blood King swept forward like an ocean wave—massive, with the speed of the tide. It would be Rael that met him first, and Soren welcomed it—fortune or foolishness, he would know now.

Cohen rode at his side, his sword drawn. Soren wasn't ashamed to wager the boy might claim more kills than he did. He was fast—faster than Soren—and precise. And Soren realized that other than Adrian, there wasn't a better man beside him in battle. He should have given him a proper place in the army. If they survived this, he would.

Three legions of the Aleon army followed closely behind him. He'd only led the army of Kharav into battle, never another, and he was sure the soldiers of Aleon had never followed a commander like him. For a brief moment, he smiled. They were about to find out exactly what it was like.

Adrian and Phillip took the left flank with the majority of the Aleon army, driving straight for Japheth and Gregor. If the decision to attack was wrong, Soren hoped Phillip would at least get his brother's head. With Adrian by his side, it was likely.

The armies came together like mountains colliding. Soren let go of Kal's reins—the destrier knew what to do—and he swung his battle-axe high above his head. The Raelean army rushed forward to meet him. He let out a raging roar and gave all of himself to the clash. His horse leapt high, kicking out its cleated ironclad hooves at the enemy as Soren brought his axe down to collect the first strike of heads.

And his blade cut through like it was an army of air.

No flesh.

No bone.

No blood.

The Raelean army was a false image—a ruse. Soren's destrier landed with a jerk, and he reached his hand down to steady the beast. Soren was a bit unnerved himself as the image of the army charged through him. The chaos threatened his senses. He gave his mind a moment to process the state around him and regain his balance. Then he twisted around to find Cohen. The boy was just behind him, with the Aleon legions. Even with the image still moving through them, they gave a ready signal.

Relief hit him, but only for a moment. Still the clash of battle rang in the air. Japheth's army was very much real, and the battle hadn't been won yet. Gregor still had a significant army, and not only that but if there was a witch on the battlefield, she could bring more trouble than just a ruse.

"Find the witch!" Soren bellowed, and he pushed his Aleon legions deeper into the sea of spirits. Even though the images didn't harm them, it was hard to find their way through the madness. They still used their weapons, not willing to take the risk of a threat being real. Soren drove his men deeper.

More spirits flooded through them, their numbers growing. He was getting closer, and the witch was throwing chaos at him. He pressed on. He could feel her desperation in the growing masses, and it gave him strength. Desperation meant fear. Fear meant victory.

Suddenly, the sky darkened and the spirits of men turned to spirits of monsters. Scaled-serpent bodies broke from the ground and shot into the sky, sprouting webbed wings and claws that threatened to snatch a man to the hells. They gained height and swooped back down toward the army, their mouths open for blood.

"They're not real!" Soren bellowed back to his men. "Press on!"

But the Aleon army wasn't the Kharavian army, and they wavered.

"Forward!" he ordered.

Waves of soldiers flung their shields up over them and ducked down. The horses panicked, throwing their riders. Cohen's mount reared but settled under the boy's hand. Soren's destrier held steady. The Aleon army's advance stopped. But they couldn't stop. Soren needed to find the witch, then lead his legions back to help Phillip take Gregor. He glanced at Cohen, and the boy drove his mount forward alone. Cohen was right—forget the army—and Soren pressed his destrier forward after him.

They ripped through the horror-filled void, ignoring the winged serpents that turned to writhing, rotting carcasses of terror dropping from the sky.

Suddenly, the ground split open in front of them, and their horses came to a grinding halt. Cohen's mount cut sideways, nearly throwing the boy to the ground, but he recovered. Total pandemonium surrounded them. Behind them, Aleon soldiers still swung their weapons at ghosts of the enemy; they still cowered at the monsters of the sky. It was like nothing he'd ever seen.

A low whistle sounded, and Soren threw his attention back to Cohen. The boy pointed his blade to the south, and Soren focused his eyes through the chaos to a small group of soldiers. Forty to fifty Raelean men stood defensively in a circle, and at their center Soren caught glimpses of a blonde-haired woman.

He glanced back at Cohen.

The witch, the boy said.

He saw her. Her eyes were closed, and her hands lifted as she breathed silent words into the air. It was a different woman from the one that had been with the Blood King before. *Curse the North gods.* How many witches did he have? It didn't matter. There would be one less. He looked back at Cohen, and the boy clutched his sword and gave him a ready nod.

Soren hated to rob him of a good charge, especially one that would give him a score of more kills, but it wasn't necessary. He held out his hand for Cohen to throw him his spear, and he did.

Soren circled his destrier. The witch was far, but he could hit farther. He coiled back, his eyes locking on his target, his body aligning to his intent. He ignored the turmoil around him and drowned out the sound of battle. Then he hurled the spear at the circle's center.

His aim was true. He knew it the moment the spear left his hand.

The witch's eyes flew open as she stopped abruptly, the spear protruding from her chest. She staggered backward. Her eyes met Soren's in surprise, and she pointed at him, but she couldn't speak before she collapsed to the ground.

The vast Raelean army evaporated into nothing, and the winged serpents disappeared from the sky. The soldiers that had surrounded the witch pulled the spear from her body and grabbed her from the ground. Then they leapt onto horses and retreated toward Japheth.

Soren's legions looked around, confused by the sudden absence of an enemy, but battle still rang in the air. Japheth remained—now alone against Phillip's hundred thousand men.

Soren turned his attention on them.

He pulled up his large battle-axe and circled his destrier back to his legions. Then, with a haunting call to battle, he led the charge to join Phillip against Gregor.

The second clash came like thunder; this time weapons met flesh and bone. Now attacked by both the north and west sides, the Japheth army fell back in surprise. Bellows rippled through them of Rael's disappearance. And realizing their situation, they started to flee.

Soren smiled. That was the problem with mercenary armies—they were the first to desert. He looked across the Aleon ranks and spotted Phillip in the distance—his Aleon-blue forces pushing back Japheth's sea of green. Soren could only watch him.

Phillip led his own men, deep in the front lines of battle. He wielded his sword like it was a part of his own body. He was fluid. Graceful. Beautiful. His armor gleamed under the sun as he moved. Soren usually hated armor, generally considering it protection for cowards. But Phillip didn't need protecting. And there was nothing about him Soren hated. Even his armor.

A death cry rang to his right, and he jerked as a sword came for his head. But Cohen's blade caught the man, dropping him to the ground.

Soren cursed. That had been close. Maybe *he* should start wearing armor. This distraction of an Aleon king was going to get him killed.

Cohen's eyes locked with his. *Pay attention*, the boy told him.

Soren snorted at Cohen's reprimand but snapped his attention back to the battle. They needed to find Gregor.

"Hold! Hold, you cowards!" a man's voice screamed from a distance. "Cyrus! You fucking traitor! Fucking coward!"

Soren chuckled. He thought it would've been harder. His eyes followed the screams of desperation to the rear of the dispersing Japheth army, where Gregor sat atop his horse. *The back of the army*. Who was the coward now?

Soren scanned the horizon and found Phillip's legions pressing in from the east, toward Gregor. He needed to bring around the west side and surround the Japheth king and trap him.

He drove his destrier back to realign his legions. "With me!" he bellowed to them. And they followed.

The remaining forces of Japheth fought with panic, and Soren cleaved a trail of blood to the king as he thundered through, mercilessly dropping men clad in green before they could scream. The Aleon army swarmed them. All one hundred thousand.

And then there was no Japheth army.

Gregor held a small force around him, a force already wavering. When he saw Soren, his eyes widened, rimmed with fear. He froze.

Soren smiled.

It was a good day to kill a king.

Soren pressed his mount toward him as the last of the Japheth king's forces were cut down.

"Come on!" Gregor screamed at him.

Oh, he was coming.

"And, Cyrus!" Gregor screamed out into the sky. "Fuck you and your witch, you coward! The gods will curse you!"

Soren's smile grew. Too bad Gregor couldn't see it underneath his wrap. He pulled it down. It was rare he wanted to show his face, but this king would see him as he died.

Gregor tried to rein his horse around to flee, and he struck its flank with the flat of his sword. But instead of jumping to a gallop back toward Japheth, the beast reared, dropping Gregor to the ground before taking flight.

Poetic.

When Soren reached him, he dropped down from his destrier. "Looks like even your horse abandoned you," he said to Gregor as he lumbered nearer. "Along with your ally."

Gregor stumbled to his feet and clutched his sword, holding it out, threatening. "I'm not afraid of you, Destroyer!"

Soren chuckled. "Yes, you are." And he swung and severed Gregor's sword arm.

Gregor screamed. He gaped in terror at Soren as he held the stump that had once been connected to his hand. Blood pulsed from the wound, feeding the battlefield. "Don't kill me!" he cried.

Soren delivered a sharp blow to Gregor's stomach, and the king fell to the ground. "I'm not going to kill you," he said as he knocked off Gregor's helmet. He grabbed the king by his thinning hair and pulled him to his knees, stepping behind him and holding him still. "I've saved that for someone who wants your head even more."

Phillip stepped in front of Gregor.

"You!" the Japheth king seethed with spittle around his mouth.

Phillip only stared at him. Soren knew that stare—the realization of a moment long dreamed.

"I'm the rightful king of Aleon!" Gregor spat at him. "You don't have what it takes to be the king of an empire!"

Phillip's eyes brimmed full of emotion. "I'll be the last king of Aleon. When I'm gone, I'll give the empire to democracy. But not before I erase you from history."

"You can't erase me!" Gregor screamed. "I'm the firstborn of Horath, and the rightful heir! Japheth, Hetahl, and Aleon are my birthright!"

Phillip said nothing. He only pulled his dagger and held it to Gregor's throat.

Gregor choked on a raging sob. "You would destroy the empire our family has worked so hard to build?"

Phillip's eyes met Soren's. His voice softened. "Sometimes those feared for destroying things... actually make them better." His eyes locked back on Gregor. "I'll make Aleon better. Greater than it ever was."

Gregor seethed under Soren's hold. "You think this war is done?" he snapped. He looked back at Soren over his shoulder. "Well, I'm not the only one fooled today. Ask yourself, where is Cyrus?"

Soren stared down at the pitiful excuse for a king. "He'll join you soon." He glanced back at Phillip and nodded.

Phillip drew the blade along Gregor's throat, spilling blood down the Japheth king's front. Gregor gurgled and sputtered, and Soren held him as he flailed weakly. Phillip only stood, watching him, clenching the bloodied dagger in his hand. When Gregor's body stilled, Soren pushed him forward to the ground.

And it was done.

Phillip stood frozen. Then his lip quivered. His lips parted in a silent cry, and his body shook. He started to sink. Soren surged forward over Gregor and caught him, stopping him from dropping to his knees. He gripped Phillip's face, pulling him to meet his eyes.

"Stand," Soren commanded. "High King."

It was a title that hadn't been used in thirteen years. Phillip wept.

"High King," Soren told him again, and he pulled him into a tight embrace.

Phillip held on to him, letting the emotion ripple through him. "It's over," he finally whispered. "Thirteen years, and it's finally over." He pulled back and looked up at Soren with tears in his eyes. Soren saw it—his release, the release that vengeance brought. The relief.

But Phillip was wrong, and Soren didn't share his relief. It wasn't over.

Phillip stilled, and his face sobered. "What's wrong?" he asked.

Soren's gut turned as his mind recovered from battle, seeding horror with his next question. "Gregor's right. He wasn't the only one fooled. This *was* a diversion. If that was Cyrus's fake army, where's his real one?"

Mikael walked the corridor of the mountain stronghold of Bahoul. He grazed his fingers along its stone walls, felt its foundation under his step. His bloodline had built this stronghold. Had lost it. And now he held it again. Being back in this place drew emotion from him that he wasn't accustomed to, and hadn't expected.

The last time he'd been here was with his father. The senior king had made sure he knew every defense, every strength, every weakness. Mikael ran through them now. He'd thought it likely not much had changed since he'd last been there. Of course, the Northmen had repaired the wall they'd crushed in taking it, and as much as he hated to admit it, they'd rebuilt it even stronger.

But he'd been wrong. A lot had changed.

The North was good at building things. Their isle capital had near impenetrable walls. They may not be a kingdom of warriors, for which he judged them harshly, but they were a kingdom of scholars. Their architectural calculations and tools made for the strongest of structures, and when reinforced with Mercian steel, no other kingdom could compare. Perhaps he should be happy Bahoul had fallen into their hands for a time. The structural improvements—improvements he would never have been able to make—weren't lost on him.

The double doors at the entry had been replaced and were now Mercian steel, as were the side doors and defensive gates. No man would get through there. The rock foundations had all been reinforced and sealed, and battlements added to the walls. Impressive, it was. Perhaps when all this was over, he'd invite more Northmen to Kharav.

Mikael smiled sadly to himself. He knew he wouldn't live to see that day. But still, it was nice to dream about. It was nice to dream about Salara—being with her. Happy. Their two kingdoms united, fortifying each other. Her dream had become his dream.

Salara.

He likely wouldn't see her again. The thought brought him to a stop, and he let himself lean back against the wall. It gutted him.

No. He wiped his hand over his face and tried to push the crushing weight off. The past three years of his life had been the best he'd ever had. Even if it was all that fate would give him, he considered himself fortunate.

Mikael pushed himself off the wall and continued on. He needed to focus on the plan. The Northern army had diverted from Bahoul to join Aleon, where they'd meet the armies of Japheth and Rael. With luck, they'd push them down and progress them toward Kharav. He held a quarter of his army in the mountains, and when Soren and Phillip drew close enough, he'd join them to push the enemy armies back into the Canyonlands, where the rest of the Kharavian army would finish them.

It was a solid plan, even though they'd miscalculated the offensive. He hadn't thought Rael would attack Aleon first. Neither had Soren. It had been a terrible time to be wrong, but hopefully they'd recover. Now he just needed to prepare. And wait. There wasn't much else he could do anyway with only a quarter of an army.

Bells rang, and he paused. A messenger must have arrived. He strode to the stairs and took them up, two at a time, to the wall. He squinted as he stepped into the light, temporarily blinded. A group of soldiers were gathered.

"What is it?" he asked. They looked at him with eyes wide, then motioned past the base of the mountains. He shielded his eyes as he looked out, then stopped.

There was movement on the horizon, not singular, not small. A wave, like an ocean wave, spanned from sky to sky. It was an army—the largest he'd ever seen—headed toward him. A warrior stepped beside him, and his eyes widened.

Kiran. He was supposed to be with Salara.

"What are you doing here?" Mikael demanded.

The guard of the Crest held out a rolled parchment. "From Salara."

Mikael glanced back at the sea of approaching men as he unrolled the message to find Salara's words inside. But he didn't need to read them to know her warning.

Rael wasn't east. Cyrus wasn't in Aleon. They came from the west to march on Bahoul.

Cyrus was coming for him.

Norah pressed the small group hard toward Aleon, after the Mercian army. She'd sent Kiran and the Crest to Mikael before leaving the stronghold, all except Bhastian and Titus, who'd flat out refused to leave her. Calla stayed with her as well, but everyone else she sent. With only a small portion of the Kharavian army, Mikael needed every man he could get, but she knew it wasn't enough. Rael's numbers threatened Aleon, Mercia, and Kharav combined. He couldn't possibly stand against Lucien by himself, but she tried not to let panic take over.

Focused now on catching up to her army, she'd intended to set a fast but sustainable pace, but as her mind turned, she pushed them even faster. Cuts marred her hands twice while they rode, but she kept linen wrapped tightly around her palms and continued on. As evening fell, Titus pulled them up. "We have to slow, Regal High. We're going to exhaust the horses."

She forgot sometimes; Sephir didn't tire as a normal horse. But they couldn't slow. Mikael only had days before Lucien reached him.

Norah sat at the fire, clutching her arms. Days, he had. If Lucien hadn't reached him already.

It could be days before they reached the Mercian army, and that meant even more days to bring them back. Her desperation grew. Mikael needed help. She couldn't lose him. Panic threatened again, but she pushed it down, inhaling deeply. She had to be smart.

What else could she do? She stilled, then turned to Bhastian. "You have to get to the eastern pass, where Katya waits, and tell her Mikael needs her in Bahoul. By the time he gets the messenger that we sent, then sends one of his own to her, he'll lose at least a day."

Bhastian looked uneasily at Titus. He'd already refused to leave her, but they had no choice. They needed Katya to bring the rest of the army to Bahoul. Reluctantly, he nodded. "I'll rest my horse another hour or so, and I'll go." He looked back to Titus. "But you'll stay. Regardless the task she tries to send you on."

Titus nodded. When Bhastian was appointed captain of the Crest, she wasn't sure how her Mercian guard would take answering to a Kharavian warrior. But the two held a mutual respect for each other and seemed to view managing her safety as more than a one-man job. When Bhastian was away, the Crest answered to Titus.

Her focus turned back to Mikael. It was only a small relief that Katya would bring the Kharavian army. He needed more. But Norah was at a loss for other options. The wheels of her mind turned as her desperation grew.

Her eyes landed on Sephir. That was it—

She jumped up and turned to Calla. "I need you to go to the Uru. To Tahla. The Kharavian army won't be enough, and I don't even know if they'll make it in time." She pulled the girl to the mare. "Take Sephir. You don't need to wait. Go now!"

"But you're the only one who can ride her," Calla protested.

"Get on!"

The girl looked at the mare with her eyes wide, but she obeyed, and Sephir stood quietly as she mounted.

Norah clutched Calla's knee. "Tell her to come and bring everything she has. Mikael needs her. I need her." Then she drew to the front of the horse and put her hands on each side of the mare's face, pressing their foreheads together. "Get her to Tahla. I beg you." The animal gave a snort. Norah released her, and the mare tossed her head. Then she kicked up in a gallop toward the western pass.

Norah turned back to Titus. "We keep going. Now." They pressed on after her army.

CHAPTER FORTY-EIGHT

Rael came like a curse of locusts, with more bodies than could be counted. They charged the stronghold of Bahoul. There were so many that Mikael couldn't see the ground underneath them. Fifteen thousand men he had in the fortress. A quarter of his army—fifteen thousand men. Rael's army had to be twenty times that size. At least.

And they swarmed.

But this wasn't a seasoned army. These men of Rael weren't soldiers. They'd been slaves, and now they were free. And while they fought with heart, heart wouldn't protect them. Heart wouldn't give them the experience they needed to survive.

They started their charge too early, and fatigue slowed them before they even reached the walls. His archers loosed arrows as they came into range, dropping them almost as quickly as they passed the threshold of reach. Mikael put the rest of his men along the walls to rain down arrows on those who got through. Not all his men were archers, but even the worst of them would hit a body down below in the masses.

The numbers kept coming. They reached the base of the fortress and started to lean ladders up against it. Mikael signaled the counter—another Mercian defense blessing. Large boulders with chains drilled through them were released off the battlements, swinging like a ball on a string. They arced across the stone face of the stronghold, sweeping anything clear from their path. Then they were hoisted back and released again. All along the wall these defenses were positioned. And his men could do this all day, and all night, as the bodies piled below.

But he wasn't encouraged. It was a cruel strategy, but a common one—use the weak forces first to drain the enemy—use up arrows, spears, and energy. Cyrus had blood sport fighters from the Raelean arenas, like Cyrus himself. They'd be his best warriors. He'd bring them in the end. But right now, they were nowhere in sight. Which meant the end was nowhere in sight.

Her pace felt slower without Sephir, but Norah pushed on. It was another day without the Mercian army on the horizon, and she was on the verge of breaking. Each day it took to reach them meant a day more in returning. Mikael didn't have that long.

And what had happened in Aleon? Adrian's message had said they were being attacked. But who was attacking if not Rael? Japheth? She prayed they fared all right.

Titus urged her to slow, to rest, but she couldn't. She hadn't slept since they left the stronghold. Two days? Three days? More? She didn't know what time was anymore. Her body ached, and she could barely feel her legs, but she drove them on. They couldn't stop. She had to get to her army. Mikael needed them.

They took a rocky ridge to the top, but when they dropped down the other side, her horse stumbled, dropping to its knees.

Norah jumped off, almost falling herself. "No! No, no, no," she begged. The horse moved to rise again, but its knees buckled, and it resigned to lie down. "No!" she pleaded.

"Regal High," Titus called to her, "we have to stop."

She ignored him, and petted the animal's face, trying to coax it up again. "Please get up!"

"Regal High."

"We have to keep going!" she snapped.

"Let's rest for just a few hours, then we can pick up again."

She couldn't just... pause. She didn't have time. Mikael didn't have time. She stumbled the rest of the way down the ridge, continuing on foot.

"Regal High!"

But she kept going. She had to keep going.

"Norah!"

Her legs were numb. She ignored them too. Another small ridge rose in front of her, and she charged up it.

Titus's arms came around her. "Norah!"

"No!" she cried. "We have to keep going. I have to get the army!"

"You have to stop!"

"Let me go!" she screamed.

"Stop!"

Norah threw back her elbow, catching him in the chin and dropping him to a knee, and he released her. She ripped away from him, but he caught her calf, and she fell forward. They moved slowly from exhaustion, but still she managed to kick him off and took the ridge again. She stumbled once, then again. Days of travel, days without sleep. Without much food. Her body was failing her, but still she pushed on.

"Norah!"

No! But she didn't have the energy to scream it back. She focused everything she had on just reaching the top. And as she did, she stopped.

And let out a cry.

Before her stretched the Mercian army—marching toward them.

Norah staggered down the ridge toward the army. She wanted to cry, to laugh, but the only thing she had energy for was keeping herself upright. She saw a rider break toward her, and she knew it was Soren. She cried in relief as she ran, not trusting herself not to fall, but not caring.

When he reached her, he dropped from his mount and caught her in his arms. "Salara!"

She clutched him. "Soren!"

He held her tightly. "What happened?"

Tears threatened, but she swallowed them back. *Stupid emotion*—not now! "Lucien's launching an attack from the west. Aleon was a trick!" She gasped between breaths. "We have to get the Mercian army to Bahoul."

He nodded. "I know—we're headed there now."

"We're not going to reach him in time. Osan's fallen. I've sent word to both Katya and Tahla to come, but it won't be enough."

"You called Katya and Tahla?"

She nodded.

"And you came to retrieve the North army to take back to Bahoul?"

Her brows dipped. "Of course I did."

The corners of his eyes smiled slightly.

She shook her head. Her mind wasn't even working to draw anything from what he was saying. "What?"

"You're a proper war queen now."

She'd be amused later. "We have to go to Bahoul. Right now."

"We're going," he assured her.

Relief flooded, and suddenly, she didn't have the strength to stand.

"Come on," he said, and scooped her up.

She let him carry her. She couldn't do anything else. "Where's Phillip?" she mumbled as her eyes grew heavy.

But she didn't hear his answer.

Enemy bodies continued to pile at the base of the stronghold walls, but Mikael urged his warriors on. They took shifts, using arrows less and less to conserve them and relying on the boulders to sweep the walls free of climbing men. He'd lost three hundred of his own to attacking arrows and spears between the battlements. He couldn't lose any more—he needed every man he had for when Cyrus launched his real attack.

But the first wave kept coming. Their bodies covered the ground. There were so many that it broke the fall of those cast down, only for them to be able to attack again. Mikael knew they couldn't sustain with these volumes. It was only a matter of time before they breached the walls.

"Salar," Rahim, one of his captains, called.

Mikael turned. "How many more have we lost?"

"A hundred and eighty-four."

Mikael swore. Fifteen thousand men sounded like a lot, but he couldn't lose one more.

"And they've calculated where the arcs of the boulders don't clear. We've had to move back to arrows for those areas."

Mikael swore again. They'd run out of arrows before Rael ran out of men.

"It's only a matter of time," the captain said.

Mikael wanted to grab him by the weapons strap fastened tight across his chest and shove him against the wall, but he couldn't be angry with the captain for saying what he'd been thinking only a moment earlier. And it was the truth. They couldn't hold for much longer.

"It's time to think of the tunnel," Rahim said.

The tunnel was a narrow passage under the stronghold that ran below the mountains and up into the hills toward the Canyonlands, coming out not far from the abandoned manor where Soren had grown up. It wasn't meant for more than a handful of men at a time; it was designed for a king to escape.

"The tunnel was sealed when the North took Bahoul," Mikael said. He knew. He'd tried to use it to retake the stronghold himself in the Great War.

"The Bear had it unsealed when Aleon came, so we had a way to sneak back in should the Aleon king prove to be untrustworthy."

Mikael stared at him, realizing. "That cunning bastard." He chuckled to himself. The Bear was still helping him beyond the grave. But it didn't matter. He had no plans to use the tunnel. "I can't leave, Rahim. I'll stay with the men and hold this fortress. Plus, my fate is with Cyrus."

The captain nodded. "We fight on, then."

"We fight on."

To the end. It wouldn't be a long wait.

CHAPTER FORTY-NINE

Her body ached, still steeped in exhaustion, and her muscles complained as she stirred awake. Wait—was she on a horse? Suddenly, Norah's mind came reeling back.

Mikael.

The Mercian army.

She startled awake at the unfamiliar arms wrapped around her and was about to push herself off the horse.

"Easy," Adrian calmed her as she twisted against him. "It's just me."

She let out a panting breath. "Hammel's hell." Despite the scare, she was happy to see him.

He chuckled. "I was beginning to wonder if you'd ever wake up."

She frowned. "How long have I been asleep?"

"All day," said Soren, riding beside them. "After sleeping all night."

"All night and all day!" She brought her fingertips to her head. She *had* been exhausted. She glanced back at Adrian, and he flashed her a grin. "Have you been carrying me this whole time?" she asked him.

Soren snorted.

"Uh, no," Adrian said. "I... we... just, uh—"

"We passed you around a bit," Soren finished.

If she wasn't awake before, she was now. "What?"

He shrugged. "You're heavy."

"Excuse me?"

"Just the lord commander and I," Adrian said. "Oh, and Caspian."

"Cohen," Soren added.

"Oh, right. Cohen. Titus, for a little while, although he fell asleep too, and you both almost fell off his horse. You didn't wake for any of it."

She rubbed her temples again. Gods, help her.

"She drooled on Phillip too," Soren added. "I almost forgot."

"Right, Phillip too. Okay, so a few."

Gods, take her now. She covered her face with her hands. "I drooled?"

"Well, you bled on me," Soren said.

The cuts. She looked at her hands. Dried blood stained her sleeves and parts of her shirt and breeches. She didn't even wake for that?

"You were really out of it," Adrian said. "How are you feeling now?"

"Better, actually. Hungry. Thirsty. But a lot better."

"Here." Soren held out a waterskin, and she took it and drank deeply until she coughed.

"How far are we from Bahoul?" she asked.

"Another day and a half yet."

Any relief she'd previously garnered quickly left her. Norah felt like she couldn't breathe. "Lucien's reached Mikael by now."

Soren's face was somber. "A small army can hold Bahoul."

She closed her eyes. She wished she could believe that.

"Salara."

She looked back at him.

"He'll hold till we get there."

So she prayed.

"We're out of arrows."

Mikael slowly nodded as one of his captains delivered the news. It had only been a matter of time. And still Rael came—unending waves of bodies.

"We'll keep using the boulders," Rahim said, "but we're down to hand-to-hand fighting to hold from a breach where the boulders don't reach."

"How many men have we lost?"

"Over a thousand now. We've taken nearly ten times that of the enemy, but it hasn't seemed to have fazed them."

Mikael searched his mind for additional options.

"Salar," Rahim said, "please. Take the tunnel, fall back. We'll hold them here, distract them."

Mikael reached out and clasped the captain's shoulder. "No. I stay. We kill as many as we can and give the lord commander the best chance to defeat them when he comes." He *would* come. Mikael didn't know what had happened with Aleon. But if Kharav fell, Soren and the Mercian army might be the only thing that remained between Rael and the North—between Cyrus and Salara. Mikael would give Soren the best chance he could.

A bell rang out.

A warning bell.

Something was wrong.

Mikael and Rahim ran along the walls of the stronghold, looking down at the attacking Raelean army. They were still coming strong but hadn't yet breached. Still the Kharavian soldiers held.

The bell came again, and Mikael looked at Rahim in confusion. "Where is it coming from? Rael hasn't breached the outside."

Rahim shook his head, then he stopped and his face paled. "Not an outside breach. One within."

Mikael's pulse thrummed. A breach within. Which could only mean... the tunnel. *Curse the North gods*, the Blood King's army had found the tunnel.

They raced down the stairs, deep into the stronghold, gathering men as they went. If the Raelean army breached through the tunnel, it would be over. Bahoul would be lost.

They reached the door of the tunnel where a half dozen Kharavian warriors stood with their blades drawn. Mikael pulled his own sword, ready. He cursed the North—the one door that hadn't been replaced with Mercian steel. The Bear had kept one way to break in.

Behind it—the scrape of metal, the sounds of an army. He waited. When they broke through the door, he would attack with everything he had. He'd kill as many as he could. They all would. His only consolation: he wouldn't die here. He'd seen the vision. He'd die outside. By Cyrus's hand.

Until then, he'd fight. He clutched his sword tighter.

But it wasn't the banging of a metal ram trying to break down the doors that they heard.

It was a key.

A key.

Mikael glanced at Rahim, and the captain glanced back at him, his own sword ready.

Then the door swung open.

It wasn't the Raelean army looking back at him.

It was the eyes of someone he hadn't expected to see again.

Katya.

"Salara sent a message, said you boys could use some help," she said wryly as she stepped aside and Kharavian warriors poured out of the tunnel and into the stronghold.

It took a moment for him to fully understand what was happening. Then Mikael straightened, giving a chuckle laced with relief, and he sheathed his sword. The captain's eyes smiled as she stepped in front of him. He reached out and clutched her shoulder, simply holding her. Grateful.

"Don't get emotional, Salar."

He laughed.

"I bring two thousand through the tunnel to help reinforce from within," she said. "The rest of the army will wait until the cover of night, then attack the enemy from the outside."

Mikael nodded. A fair approach. She wouldn't have been able to bring all forty-five thousand through the tunnel anyway. Warriors poured into the stronghold. Hundreds. "To the wall!" Katya ordered, and they raced to join their brothers-in-arms against the attack on the wall.

Mikael spotted Bhastian, captain of the Crest. He'd been with Salara, and now he stood beside Katya. "Salara sent you to get the army?" Mikael asked him.

Bhastian nodded. "Yes, Salar."

His heart nearly burst with pride. He was just grateful she was safe now. "And she's returned to Mercia?"

Bhastian stiffened. His hesitation sent a wave of dread through Mikael.

"She's returned to Mercia?" he asked again.

"No, Salar. She's gone to call the Northern army back to you."

Mikael's chest seized. He should be happy about the possibility of aid from the Northern army. But that meant Salara would be with them. Not in Mercia. Not away from the battle. Not safe.

No.

But before he could protest, shouting rang through the tunnel, and they all spun toward it.

"What's that?" Katya asked to no one in particular.

"Rael!" came shouts from the men in the tunnel.

Mikael ripped his sword from his scabbard again. "Rael's in the tunnel!" A weakness—the entry from the outside to the tunnel, while far from the stronghold, wasn't well hidden. It came out among the barren rocks in the low of the hills. Rael must have spotted them enter—two thousand men were hard to hide, even for the Shadowmen—and followed.

His blood pulsed hot, ready for the battle that was coming. His Kharavian warriors were still inside the tunnel, but instead of continuing into the stronghold, they turned back to face the enemy.

Katya scanned her eyes around the room, then back to the tunnel. "This door won't hold them out, even if we bar it." The darkness of worry filled her eyes. "If they get inside, Bahoul will fall."

"We have to collapse the tunnel," Bhastian said.

They snapped their gazes to him.

"Our men are still in there," Katya said.

"And they'll help me do it." Bhastian pulled up his battle-axe. "It's the only way. We can't let them through." He barreled back into the tunnel. Bhastian—Soren's trusted man.

"No!" Katya yelled as he raced to the thick wooden beam that framed the sides and swung his axe against it.

"Bring it down!" Bhastian bellowed. Another warrior with an axe struck another beam.

She tried to go after him, but Mikael grabbed her. As painful as it was, it was worth the lives of fifteen hundred men for Bahoul to remain strong. It was worth Bhastian's sacrifice. The rest of the Kharavian army still remained just beyond the battle and would attack at nightfall. They had to hold until then. It was these decisions that crushed him the most.

It took Bhastian four body swings for the beam to cave and fall. The warriors beside him took out two more beams. Some dirt and small rocks fell from the top. It wasn't enough.

"Bhastian!" Katya cried.

He moved to the next beam and swung with everything he had, again and again. Then he gave one last look back to them, his fist to his chest, before the rush of rock collapsed on top of him.

A tear streamed down Katya's cheek.

Mikael panted back the pain of the loss. They would all fall. Even him. And he accepted this. He had to make the most of the time he had left.

He had to focus on the battle. The war.

It would be a long day, and an even longer night.

Despite the exhaustion that still lingered, Norah couldn't sleep. How could she when Mikael was under attack? She knew Lucien would have made it to him by now. He would have reached Mikael days ago. How long could Mikael hold?

He had to hold.

They started their march again before dawn. The time it took to move an army was excruciatingly slow. It was all Norah could do to not break from them and race alone the rest of the way.

She rode with her hand wrapped around the hilt of her sword. Adrian had given the weapon to her, and being able to clutch it brought her an inkling of comfort. Soren had also strategically stowed a short sword and two additional daggers in the folds of her saddle. She carried a crossbow fastened to the back of her seat, although she'd always struggled with the strength it took to pull back the cord. Still, having it made her feel slightly better.

The Aleon army had come with them, aside from two legions that had stayed behind to finish the takeover of Japheth. The ranks traveled in file, Mercia in the front, led by Soren and Caspian, trailed by Aleon with Adrian and Phillip. As they drew nearer to the mountains, they moved to stretch across horizontally. Phillip and Adrian joined beside her.

They reached the final ridge, and the mountains of Bahoul came into view. They seemed darker now than they had before—her mind was playing tricks on her. She squinted, and a sickening chill went through her.

The mountains seemed darker because they were covered in men—the men of the Raelean army.

Had they taken the stronghold? Had Lucien gotten to Mikael?

The urgency now cut to her soul. "Soren!"

His horse quickened, but he said, "We can't start the charge from this far. We need to save strength for the battle."

The wave of their armies moved faster, but not fast enough. Rael's numbers were staggering. *So many*—there were so many men that she couldn't see the snow that blanketed the ground of the mountains. But—

They were fighting...

The Kharavian army was still fighting. Hope seeded inside her. They hadn't taken the stronghold yet.

Hold on, she begged Mikael. She couldn't breathe.

The time it took to bridge the gap felt longer than the entire journey, but their pace quickened as they neared.

"Fall to the back," Soren told Norah as they got closer.

As if he could make her...

Phillip pulled his sword as he rode beside her. The horses of the cavalry around them picked up to a trot, then a canter.

"Fall back!" Soren demanded of her.

But the army picked up more speed, and she pulled her own sword as she pushed her horse to a gallop. She wasn't here to fall back.

"Salara!"

Horns sounded from the enemy, and the Raelean army poured out to meet them.

Norah charged with Phillip riding beside her. Their men followed, bellowing their cries of attack. The ground shook underneath her. Time slowed in the thunder. She cast her eyes down the sweeping line of Mercia and Aleon. For as long as she could remember, she'd fought the notion of war. She'd rejected its violence, its death. But now she came for Mikael, and she'd bring death to save him.

The initial clash was deafening. Metal rang in her ears. Soren veered his destrier toward her, but she cut her horse left and away. She hadn't come to watch—she'd come to fight for what she loved. To the end. She screamed as she charged into the masses of black and blood.

Her blade met armor and bone, and she tore through with a fury, but no one tried to strike her back. As the enemy attacked her army, they only parted around her.

And she realized—she was linked to their king—they wouldn't hurt her.

That didn't mean she'd give them mercy.

Norah pushed her horse forward, toward the stronghold, striking down anyone that couldn't get out of the way of her blade. To her right, Soren swung his axe like he was skinning the earth, arcing blood through the air. He'd stopped yelling at her, understanding, too, why the Raelean army steered clear of her.

Phillip fought to her left, bellowing commands as they tried to push forward.

But they weren't moving forward. They were being pushed back. The armies of Mercia and Aleon were formidable, but as the sea of Rael swept through them, the realization hit her that it wouldn't be enough. Rael came in floods, and the northern kingdoms were now losing ground. She set her eyes on the stronghold in desperation. She had to make it to Mikael. Where was he?

She couldn't see through the battle; she only felt herself being driven backward. A Raelean soldier leapt at Adrian, and she caught him midair with her sword.

"That was luck!" Adrian shouted with the hint of a smile.

But she couldn't smile back. They needed more. They weren't enough. They needed the rest of the Kharavian army. "We have to hold until Katya gets here with the army!" she yelled over the deafening clash of battle.

"They're already here!" Adrian yelled back. "No one else is coming."

What? The rest of the Kharavian army was already there? She scanned the bloody scene around them. The Raelean forces were so many that Kharav seemed so few. But they were all here. They were all dying.

No one else was coming. That wasn't entirely true—Tahla hadn't reached them yet, but the forces of Rael were too overwhelming. The numbers of the Uru wouldn't matter.

She swept her eyes desperately around her. And she froze.

The north wall of the stronghold had crumbled. How had they brought down the wall? It was breached. Bahoul was *breached*. Rael was both outside and within.

Panic threatened. Where was Mikael?

A pain sliced through her hand—*no!* Not now! But it was just the left hand that bore the cut. The right didn't come.

She tried to ignore it and focus on the chaos around her. They were falling. Mercia and Aleon were falling to Rael.

She turned her mind to the only thing that mattered now. "Where's Mikael?" The stronghold was overrun. "Where's Mikael?" she screamed.

CHAPTER FIFTY

Mercia and Aleon were falling. Kharav was falling. Soren had been hit and knocked from his horse. He stood shoulder to shoulder with Adrian now, desperately trying to hold the line and keep Rael from driving them away from the stronghold—away from Mikael. Caspian worked on the north side to keep Rael from flanking them, and Phillip cut south with the Aleon army, but they were slowly losing ground.

Salara fought with a vengeance, striking down man after man. He realized they weren't trying to kill her. She did, too, and used it. Soren had thought he'd be focused on keeping her protected, but she'd saved even him a time or two. If they lived through this, he had every intention of dragging her to Salta Tau for the markings.

The Northmen loosed arrows as fast as they could draw them, but it merely dented the waves of Rael. The enemy numbers were staggering. Slaves had flocked to the army of the Blood King, but no one could have imagined how many. Most of them weren't warriors, but they didn't have to be. Their numbers alone were overwhelming.

Salara's scream stopped him cold, and he whirled to see her dragged off her horse by two Raelean soldiers. Soren snarled and tried to cut through the wave of men that had rushed between them, but a sharp pain sliced across his side, dropping him. He took the head of the man who did it before he paused to check himself. Blood poured from his side, but it looked worse than it was. It would make for a painful continuation, but he'd be all right.

Soren pushed forward and shaved the field with his battle-axe, showering the Raelean soldiers in their own blood. But it didn't stop them. They kept coming. He tried to push through to Salara, who had been dragged farther from him now. "Salara!" he bellowed. But he couldn't see her.

He swept his axe for blood again, only this time, it was met with the strength of steel—that had equal power behind it. Around him moved soldiers of Rael. Not slaves. He knew fighting men when he saw them. These were the blood sport fighters freed from the arenas of Rael, men who lived battle every day. The Blood King's trusted—his best, saved for the end.

Because the end was near.

His eyes flicked between them. Four, five, six. But one in particular caught his attention. A man with skin of night, not like the others, and almost as large as Soren. The way the other men's eyes flicked between him and Soren—he was clearly a man of authority. Their leader. A thumb's smear of dark crimson marked his forehead. *Blood.* Purposeful blood. Soren's mind turned. That was how the Blood King talked to him, how he coordinated his army. How many men bore the king's blood? How many men could send messages?

Soren dropped his axe and pulled his two short swords from his back. He bared his teeth. Well, he had a message for the Blood King.

Their dance was a battle within the battle, a tempest of steel and blood. All around him they swarmed. Just as he kicked one back, he had to spin to face another. Each of their blows carried the strength of death.

Another sting bit his thigh, almost sending him to the ground, but miraculously he stayed upright, fighting on. Soren dropped two of them, he wasn't sure how.

A blow hit his stomach, and he doubled over, only to catch a knee to the face. He blocked the second and sliced through his opponent's leg, severing it.

Behind him came another, and he spun again.

He almost didn't feel the blade as it pierced through the low of his left shoulder, just narrowly missing his heart.

Their leader.

The blood sport soldier pushed the sword through Soren all the way to the hilt. Face-to-face, they stopped, close enough to feel each other's breath. And they both looked down between them.

Soren's blades sat buried in the man's gut, to the hilt as well. Their eyes locked, the man's realization sinking in. In a final effort, with his final breaths, the blood sport fighter tried to twist his weapon in Soren's shoulder, but Soren butted his head forward, knocking him with a *crack*, and shoved the man off his swords. The fighter pulled his blade with him as he fell backward, and Soren bellowed in pain.

"Everan!" a man cried out.

The rest of the men were on him in an instant. A searing burn ripped across his arm, but he ignored it. Soren drove his exhausted body purely from muscle memory, from instinct. He let his rage fuel him. He didn't know where Salara was. He'd lost her. Adrian was missing from his side.

Had death claimed him? He forced it from his mind—he couldn't let his desperation take over.

Only two of the blood sport fighters were left now, but there was no relief. His left arm could no longer hold a weapon. Something struck him in the back of his head, and he fell to his knees. Another blow to his stomach took the wind from him, and he fell forward. He struggled to raise his head.

Was this how it ended?

Phillip's horse galloped by, riderless. He couldn't draw a breath.

All around him Rael swarmed, drowning him. Darkness closed around him.

He fought blindly now. Blood ran down his face. He wasn't sure if it was even his own, but it didn't matter—he'd fight until the life ran out of him.

And it was running out.

The earth shook underneath him. Was it coming to swallow him in eternal sleep? No—not yet. *Salara. Mikael. Phillip.* He couldn't leave them yet...

The vibration underneath him felt like thunder.

He wiped back the blood from his eyes, but it still clouded his vision. A sword came for his head, and he knocked it from the air—the sword and the arm that held it dropped to the ground. Screams rang around him.

The thunder—another Raelean wave of attack.

He wiped his face again and turned to meet the clash of battle he heard coming from behind. He turned to meet his end.

But it wasn't the rush of Rael.

A wave of Horsemen crashed into the sea of carnage.

They came in the thousands. More warriors than the Uru—so many. *So many Horsemen*. Not just the Uru, he realized. All of them. All the tribes. Some he recognized, some not. Some were friends of Kharav. Some weren't. But they all came and launched themselves against Rael.

And leading them—*Tahla*.

Riding Sephir.

Her sword gleamed under the blood-misted rays of the sun. She charged high in the saddle, her blade in the air, her lips peeled back in a snarling scream that he didn't need to hear to feel—the scream of battle.

Soren struggled to keep his footing as the masses rushed past him.

A distance away, he spotted Adrian. Emotion swept through him, but he managed a nod as their eyes met. Adrian gaped at the tidal wave of Horsemen sweeping around them and locked eyes back with Soren in disbelief.

With a newfound energy, Soren charged into action. He needed to find Salara. He cut down men as he went, but froze as his eyes caught a fallen body on the field.

No...

He raced to Cohen and dropped down beside the boy. Blood poured from his partially severed arm.

But the boy pushed him off. *No, I'm fine*, he said. *Go! Salara needs you!*

"Cohen!" Adrian yelled and was beside him in a moment. He stripped linen from his undertunic to bind his arm.

Cohen struck Soren in the shoulder. The injured one. Hard. *Go!*

"I've got him," Adrian said. "Go!"

Soren pushed on and dodged through the battle, looking for Salara. Where had they taken her? The small consolation he carried was that they wouldn't kill her. But it was a *very small* consolation.

He swept his eyes over the screams and sound of steel, but the battle raged around him, blocking his view. What direction had they taken her in? He couldn't see her through the fighting. He couldn't find her. Defeat washed over him.

He'd lost her. The one person he was supposed to protect, the one person he was supposed to keep. He'd lost her.

"Soren!" Her cry rang above the sound of battle, and he spun. Through the fighting, Salara rode toward him on his own horse. *Kal.* Phillip rode beside her.

He almost wept.

She reined his destrier up beside him, kicking her foot out of the stirrup so he could swing up behind her. "We have to find Mikael!"

He noticed her left hand dripping with blood, and he pulled it to look. Across her palm were two cuts. Deep.

"They're not healing," she said. "I think he's lost his healer."

A terrifying thought.

"It's fine," she said. "My right's fine. I don't know why, but he hasn't cut it."

Soren knew why—if he'd lost his healer, he wouldn't cut his sword hand.

Together they charged back through the Horsemen to where the Kharavian army was locked with Rael. The fortress was overrun, with all armies both inside and outside its walls.

Rael's numbers seemed less now. He looked across the Raelean forces and noticed some of them fleeing. Despite that, Rael still held strong, although the Horseman joining had turned the tide, and they started losing ground.

"There!" Salara cried.

And then he saw him.

Mikael fought from atop his horse surrounded by his Kharavian soldiers. They battled against a thick ring of the Raelean army around them. Soren was still too far to help him, and he drove his horse toward him.

His destrier plowed through, catching the enemy under his heavy hooves and driving forward. Salara fought as they went. She leaned far to reach as many heads as she could, even one handed, and Soren struggled to keep hold of her. The wind caught her winter mane, and it whipped him in the face. He cursed. Just what he needed—to be blinded by blood *and* hair.

And then they were falling.

Soren hit the ground with a force that tore his left shoulder from the socket. As if it didn't hurt enough. He staggered up. Salara slowly rose beside him. The wind had been knocked out of her, but she was seemingly unhurt. He looked back in horror to see his destrier felled with a spear to the chest.

Phillip rushed to beat back the enemy that swarmed them. Another horse leapt forward, and Soren's eye caught sight of his farm girl.

Calla loosed arrows at men as they rushed toward them, taking them down before they reached him and Salara. Not a single miss. Soren gritted his teeth and jerked his shoulder back into place. He looked back at Mikael, who was still battling.

"Soren!" Salara cried, and he snapped to see the Blood King bearing down on Mikael on a horse of night. But Soren was still too far to do anything.

"I'm out of arrows!" Calla cried.

Soren sliced through another Raelean soldier, and they raced toward Mikael on foot. Fear rippled through him. They weren't going to make it in time. They were too far.

Suddenly, an arrow wisped through the air and hit Mikael in the side.

"No!" Soren bellowed, and Salara screamed from behind him.

Mikael stayed for a moment, wavering in his saddle, then slowly dropped from his horse.

Soren barreled forward with a snarl, swinging his sword wide and laying a path of blood and destruction as he tried to bridge the eternity of space between them. He jerked up a spear from a fallen man as he went.

The Blood King stopped just short of reaching Mikael and slid down from his horse, sword in his right hand. Mikael dragged himself back. He didn't try to stand. He wouldn't. He wouldn't fight Cyrus, just like the vision.

"Soren!" Salara cried from behind him.

Soren stopped and coiled back with the spear in his hand. The Blood King was within range. He could hit him. He could kill him.

Cyrus struck Mikael's sword from his hand, and Mikael dragged himself farther backward, the arrow still protruding from his side.

Soren settled his sight on the Raelean king and steadied his breath to steady his hand.

"What are you waiting for?" she screamed from behind him.

He'd promised Salara he'd take the opportunity when he had it. And he had it. But he couldn't. He couldn't do it.

It gutted him.

"Stop him!" The terror in her voice was another dagger to his heart.

His hand burned to release the spear—the spear that would save his brother, the spear that would end it all. But it would also end Salara. He couldn't do it.

"Soren!" she screamed. "Do it!"

Cyrus swung his sword above his head, and Soren bared his teeth as he wept, but he still couldn't throw it. Anguish ripped from his throat.

Cyrus's sword gleamed, as if celebrating its want for blood—celebrating that it was about to take the head of a king.

The Blood King held it high.

But it didn't come down.

Cyrus wavered. Then he stumbled sideways, swaying.

Soren's brows dipped. What was happening?

Then the Blood King staggered backward as he let go of his raised sword, and it fell to the ground behind him. He clawed at his chest, looking down as blood poured from underneath his ribbed breastplate. But there was no weapon. Nothing had struck him.

Cyrus sank to his knees.

Soren could only stare as confusion flooded him. There was nothing—

His heart stopped, and he glanced back at Salara.

He gaped in horror.

She stood unsteadily, with her hand wrapped around the hilt of a dagger protruding from just below her breast.

"No," he mouthed as he dropped his spear and raced toward her. Then his voice broke with a thunder. "No!"

"Norah!" Phillip yelled, but he was still fighting back Raelean soldiers in the thick of the battle around them.

Soren reached her just as she fell forward to her knees, and he caught her in his arms. "Salara!"

Her mouth moved, but no words came out.

Stupid woman. Stupid, stupid woman. "What did you do!" he raged at her. "What did you fucking do?"

She frowned as tears stippled the corners of her eyes, and then she tried to smile. "I think you're getting blind as you age," she answered between gasps.

"I'm sorry," he begged. "I couldn't do it. I'm so sorry."

She shook her head. "I should have never asked you to."

Soren wept as he pulled her into his arms, ignoring the searing pain in his shoulder. He had to get her to Mikael.

"I'm sorry," she whispered.

He shook his head as he picked her up and rose to his feet, but he couldn't speak. He didn't want her apology. Not when it was for taking the most important person in the world from him, taking herself from Mikael and from Adrian. From everyone who loved her—everyone who needed her.

Her breaths came labored, and he moved faster.

"Salara!" Mikael's bellow rang out when he saw them. He struggled up and toward them, limping as he clasped the arrow in his side.

Soren laid her down on the ground as gently as he could. Mikael sank down on her other side, his hands shaking as he hovered them over the hilt of the dagger just under her breast.

Mikael's voice shook. "Salara."

She reached up and grazed his face with her fingertips. "I told you fate can be changed." She smiled weakly.

Mikael wept as he looked around them in desperation. The battle still waged as far as the eye could see, but then his eyes stopped, spotting something. Soren followed his gaze to Tahla in the far distance, still on top of Sephir and battling back the Raelean army.

"The Wild," he said.

Soren creased his brow. "What?"

Mikael reached up and palmed his scarred shoulder where Soren had once hit him with an arrow. "The Wild. How far are we from the Wild?"

What difference did that make? Soren shook his head. "Three days' ride? Likely more."

"We have to get her to the Wild. They can heal her."

Soren glanced down at Norah. Her eyelids fell. "We'll never make it in time. She won't last the hour." His words shook as he said them.

Mikael grabbed him. "Don't say that!" He looked back down at her as tears fell from his eyes. "We have to."

Picking up Salara carefully, Mikael moved to a nearby horse and mounted with her in his arms. Calla gave Soren her own mount, and grabbed another nearby for herself, and they urged the animals through the carnage and west.

To the Wild they'd never reach in time.

CHAPTER FIFTY-ONE

Adrian stepped through the bodies on the battlefield. Pockets of fighting still remained, but the army of Rael had largely scattered, retreating back as the news of their dead king rippled through. The Mercian soldiers had helped him with Cohen—his friend would lose his arm but keep his life.

He'd caught up to Phillip, who told him what had happened to Norah, and the high of victory came crashing down. He could do nothing—nothing but wait to see if they made it. But in his heart, he knew they wouldn't. The Wild was too far.

Adrian stumbled through the carnage, numb. In a way, he was glad Alexander had gone to the gods—that he wasn't there to suffer the loss of Norah. Again. Tears streamed down his face. Adrian would suffer it for the both of them.

There was a rustle to his right, and he looked to see Katya. She was checking the battlefield for survivors. When she saw him, she approached.

"You look like shit," she said when she reached him. She pulled down her wrap and took a swig of water from the goatskin at her hip.

He knew it was a jest, but he couldn't bring himself to smile. She offered him the water. He declined.

Her face sobered. "You fought well today."

"Not well enough."

She looked out across the battlefield. "Is it ever enough?"

No. No, it wasn't.

She sighed and looked back to him. "Will you be going back to the North?" she asked.

He shook his head. "No. To Kharav. I need to get back to Sevina and Theisen. They're... they're all I have left."

Her eyes glistened, and her lips parted slightly. She stepped closer to him. "Adrian... I need to tell you something..." She paused.

His brows dipped. She seemed nervous. He'd never seen Katya nervous before. They'd just finished a war for gods' sakes.

She only stared at him.

"Katya?"

She swallowed. "We're all your family," she said finally. "You have us all."

That wasn't... what he'd expected. He opened his mouth to speak, then closed it again. She clasped his shoulder and then continued her work across the battlefield looking for survivors.

Adrian turned his own attention back to the battlefield. The injured had been carried off, but Bahoul still looked like a mountain of bodies, and the hills around it a rolling sea of death. He recognized a Crest warrior half buried and hurried toward him. Dropping down beside him, he reached a hand to the man's neck to feel for a pulse.

He was gone.

Adrian stood again, his eyes still on the warrior. So many were gone—so many he knew, so many he loved.

He continued, sweeping side to side, searching.

Then, in the hallow of a hill, he saw something that made him stop. Lucien.

He lay on his back. Blood seeped from underneath the armor on his chest, down his sides and into the ground. His face was turned up toward the sky, staring blankly.

Adrian drew closer, and Lucien's hand moved ever so slightly.

He still lived.

He stepped even closer, his shadow falling over him, and Lucien's eyes found him.

"Adrian," he said weakly, so quiet he almost didn't hear.

Slowly, Adrian sank down beside him.

Lucien opened his mouth to speak, but no words came. He reached his bloodied hand along the ground toward him.

Adrian stared at it. If he took it, Lucien could come to him, enter his mind.

"Adrian," Lucien struggled again. Pleading.

Adrian's lip trembled as Alexander's face looked back at him—the face that tore his heart in two, the face that he missed more than anything in the world. He looked down at Lucien's outstretched hand, then took it and closed his eyes.

In the depths of his mind, they were still in the battlefield. But now, Lucien stood in front of him, whole and well.

"Brother," Lucien said.

Adrian looked at him warily.

"I broke the tether," Lucien told him.

"But it won't help her now, will it?" It wouldn't heal her.

Lucien's eyes tightened, as if filled with guilt. Did he feel guilty? He was. "I've sent someone to help her. A friend."

The faintest of hope flickered in him. "A healer?"

Lucien shook his head. "I lost my healer."

Adrian shifted. "Will this friend save her?" Did he dare to hope?

"I don't know if she can." Lucien swallowed. "I didn't mean to hurt Norah. I didn't think she'd sacrifice herself."

"Because you don't know her at all," he snapped back.

Lucien nodded, accepting the guilt, accepting Adrian's anger. "I don't have much time, but I wanted you to know that I wish things could have been different between us. I like to think they could have been, if we'd have lived in a different world, in a different time." He smiled sadly. "I don't dare ask your forgiveness, but I do want to give you something."

Lucien looked to his right, and Adrian followed his gaze to see Alexander walking toward them. He wore a warm smile.

Adrian trembled as his breath left him. "Is it really him?"

Lucien nodded.

"I don't understand. You can link with the dead?"

Slowly, Lucien nodded again. "Something like that."

But Adrian didn't really care how. He stumbled toward Alexander, and his brother held his arms wide. He fell into them with a sob. Alexander's arms came around him and embraced him tightly. Warmth from his body surrounded him. He was there. *He was really there.* Adrian clung to him.

He pulled back, blinking back his tears. "How are you here?"

But Alexander only smiled. Everything about him was as he remembered. His eyes, his face, his smile. He'd never gotten to see him one last time, to say goodbye. But now, he was here. And he could feel him—feel his warmth.

Adrian glanced back at Lucien. "Can he not speak?"

"I don't have enough power to let him speak, but he wants you to know that he loves you." His voice tightened in emotion. "He's proud of you and the man you've become. He says our father's proud."

"I love you, Alec," Adrian said through his tears. "I'll hold everything you taught me. I'll honor our father, and our family. I love you."

Alexander clasped the side of his neck and gripped him tightly. He nodded. With a final smile, he faded.

"Our time's come," Lucien told him.

Adrian looked back at him.

"Goodbye, brother," Lucien said softly, and Adrian's mind faded into darkness.

He opened his eyes. Lucien still lay in front of him. But he was gone. Blood trailed from his nose and down his cheeks. Adrian leaned over the body of his brother and wept.

Soren and Mikael drove their mounts hard, with Calla close behind them. The girl had picked up a few more arrow quivers that lay with fallen archers on the field, but they didn't need much now. They weren't met with resistance. Most of the Raelean army had begun to flee. Soren was grateful. He wasn't sure he could get another fight out of his body. He could barely hold his sword.

Mikael wasn't faring well either. He'd broken the arrow off in his side, unable to pull it out. He still carried Salara in his arms. Soren feared they'd already lost her. *No*—he couldn't think about that—it would break him.

Suddenly, their horses reared and skidded to a grinding halt as a woman appeared before them. She wore a cloak the color of burnt blood, with her long, dark curls loose down her front. She pulled back her hood. Although Soren hadn't seen her face the last time they'd met, he knew exactly who she was. "It's the Blood King's witch," he called to Mikael. He pulled his sword, having to use all his strength now to wield it.

She turned her eyes on him. "That didn't get you very far before, and it won't get you far now."

"Get out of our way," Mikael snarled between his teeth.

"My king has sent me to help the North Queen."

Soren snorted. "Your king is dead."

The faintest of emotion flashed across her face. Surprise? No. Blood marked her forehead. She knew he was dead. It was pain. "I'll still keep my promise," she said.

A promise to kill Salara, more likely. Soren clutched his sword tighter, ready to take her head.

"Are you a healer?" Mikael demanded.

"If you wanted a healer, your army shouldn't have killed the only one in this world," she snapped back.

"It's *your* king that started this war," Soren snarled.

"Enough," Mikael hissed at him. He turned back to the witch. "How can you help her?"

Soren looked at him in astonishment. "You can't be serious."

"I'm not a healer," she said, "but I can give you more time to get to someone who might be able to help you."

"Or you could kill her," Soren growled. "Kill us all."

The witch gave a cruel smile. "She's already dying. I needn't do anything. And yes, I brought down the wall of your mighty fortress. I could kill you. Right now."

Soren spat in frustration. Why didn't she, then?

"Make your decision quickly," she snapped as she looked at Norah. "She only has moments left."

Mikael slid down from his horse with Salara in his arms. Soren gaped at him. He couldn't believe he was trusting her. "Take caution, witch," Mikael warned.

Slowly, the woman looked over Norah and put a hand on her head. Then she reached out and touched Mikael, whispering words Soren didn't understand. He clutched his sword tighter. A slight wind swept over them, and then the air calmed.

"What did you do?" Mikael asked.

"This won't save her, but so long as she touches you, she can draw life from you, until you get to where you're going. Don't let her go—if you break the touch, you break the bond."

Mikael let out an emotional breath and nodded. "Why do you do this?"

"I already told you," she snapped. "For my king."

Why would the Blood King help Salara?

Mikael mounted his horse again, with Salara in his arms.

"This magic comes with a price," she warned. "It gives you time, yes, but it's limited. So long as the bond isn't broken, she'll draw life from you. But she'll draw it until she drains it all, and then both of you will die. So I suggest you get to wherever you're going quickly."

Death sat everywhere around him, death from every kingdom—Mercia, Kharav, Rael, and the Horsemen. So many were dead. Caspian stumbled through the sea of bodies.

They'd been victorious, although this didn't feel victorious. The fighting had stopped, and everyone who remained seemed to be collecting their wounded. Everyone except Rael, who'd fled. His eyes found a soldier in the carnage, carrying the body of another. They were covered in blood. He couldn't tell whether they were from Mercia or Aleon.

"Hang on, you're going to be all right," the soldier said to the man he carried as he staggered by. But his friend was already gone. Caspian could only watch as they faded into the fog of death.

His own weariness was on him now. He hadn't slept in two days, and he'd fought until his arms couldn't lift his sword. But he needed to turn his attention to anyone who might be alive. With the battle now over, he started sifting through the bodies of the fallen.

Caspian's eye caught movement, and he stooped down beside a soldier. It was a man of Rael. He was young, and his eyes were wide with fear.

"Please," the young man begged. "I don't want to die."

Caspian's eyes drifted to his blood-soaked midsection, where he'd taken a blade. There was no escaping death for this one. Caspian moved to stand.

"Please," the soldier said, his eyes filling with tears. "Don't leave me." He reached out, and Caspian dropped back down and took his hand. "Don't leave me," he begged again.

"I won't," Caspian said gently.

The man clung to his hand, pulling him closer. "I don't want to die," he pleaded again.

"You're going to be all right," he lied, echoing the soldier carrying his dead friend. But he could still see the man's fear. "What's your name?"

The soldier drew a labored breath. "Brandon."

"Brandon." Caspian looked at him. The man was young, too young to die. "I'm here with you, Brandon."

The soldier clasped his hand and seemed to calm. "I have a son," he said.

Caspian smiled sadly. "I do too."

"I haven't met him yet. I need to get home."

It was all Caspian could do to keep his emotion in. "You will."

Brandon nodded, but his eyes grew heavier, and his breathing became shallow.

"Rest awhile first," Caspian said softly. "Then you'll go home."

He nodded faintly. "All right. Maybe just a little while."

The soldier let his eyes close but kept hold of Caspian's hand. Then his grip relaxed, and the rise and fall of his chest slowed to a stop.

Caspian's lip trembled, and he wiped back the tears from his face. Curse the gods and curse this wretched fate. He released the soldier's hand and fell onto his back on the ground, looking up at the sky.

Curse this world. Was this all there was to life? Pain and death and heartbreak? And for what? It was all for nothing. Everything had been taken from him. Alexander. Norah. There was only one thing left that he wanted in this world—the one thing he couldn't have—Tahla and Katakah. He wanted them so badly he could almost see them as he looked up at the clouds. He could almost feel Tahla in his arms. He could almost hear her.

"Caspian," she seemed to call.

He clutched on to everything in his mind, everything he remembered of her—her touch, her taste, her sound. He closed his eyes. Maybe he'd rest awhile too.

"Caspian!" came her voice, and he opened his eyes. "Caspian!"

He bolted up to sit and looked out across the field of fallen battle.

"Caspian!"

It came from his right, and he jerked toward her sound. And there she was, running toward him.

Tahla.

He staggered to his feet just as she launched herself and threw her arms around him. He clung to her.

"I saw you," she cried. "I saw you, and..." She couldn't finish. She'd seen him on the ground.

"I'm all right," he assured her. "I'm all right."

She wept into his neck.

"I'm all right," he said again.

Finally, she pulled back to look at him, but still clutched him tightly. "I was so scared."

"I'm here," he assured her. Then he stopped. "*You're* here. Tahla, you saved us. You saved us all." He was still astonished at the sheer number of Horsemen that had come to their aid. "How did you get them all?"

"I called them with Savantahla. And they followed."

Norah's mare. The mare of the Wild.

This woman—this woman had united all the tribes of the Horsemen to turn the tide of war against Rael. He held her in his arms, then pulled her hands up to his lips and kissed them. Then he stopped. On her forefinger was a ring.

His ring.

His eyes locked with hers, and she smiled through her tears. "I put it on the night you gave it to me."

Tears came freely now, and he couldn't speak.

"I haven't told anyone what it means," she whispered.

"It's okay. It was only for you to know."

She smiled through her tears. "But now it's for you to know too. Husband."

He pulled her closer—his love, his wife.

Chapter Fifty-Two

The ride to the Wild was the longest Soren had ever known. Mikael carried Salara like he carried his heart in his arms, watching it fade. And he was fading with her. Soren worried neither of them would last the journey, but still they rode. They stopped only for a few hours each night to rest their horses before continuing. Then on they went—not eating, not speaking, just desperately riding.

They reached the tree line of the Wild on the third day, their horses staggering in exhaustion.

"You stay with the horses," Soren told Calla as he slid down from his mount. There was a chance no one would return from the Wild alive, and he didn't want her pulled into that.

Mikael dropped down from his horse, but he couldn't catch himself and fell to his knees. He tried to stand again but stumbled and dropped back to the ground.

Soren cursed. He was losing them both. He hooked an arm around Mikael and pulled him to stand, but Mikael was almost as large as he was, and almost as heavy. With his own injuries, Soren couldn't hold them both. Mikael fell again, and Soren spewed another slew of curses. They'd never make it.

"Let me carry her," he said.

"I have to stay connected."

"Hold her damned hand!" He pulled Salara from his arms, despite the nauseating pain in his shoulder, and gave Mikael a moment to get to his feet. "We have to go. Quickly."

They were anything but quick. Soren carried Salara, but slowly, so Mikael could hold on to her as they went. The pain in his shoulder was excruciating, but he ignored it. He was the least injured of them all. Blood soaked Mikael's side from the arrow still within—too much blood. Soren tried not to think of how close death was to them.

The forest fell quiet around them. Eerily quiet. Were the Wild women here?

"Naavi!" Soren bellowed. "Sana!" But neither of the sisters showed themselves.

Mikael stumbled. He fell to the ground and broke his hold from Salara. "No!" he cried.

Soren's breath caught. *No.* The bond, they had to get back the bond. He dropped to his knees beside Mikael, and Mikael clasped hold of her again.

"Salara!" Mikael called to her, holding her hand tightly. But her breath was fading. "No. No! Salara!" Mikael clutched her tightly. "I'm here. I'm here!"

But as she exhaled, she didn't draw in another breath.

Soren shook as he held her. *No*—they were so close. They were practically here. She couldn't leave them yet. But she didn't draw a breath. She had to breathe.

She had to *breathe.*

"Naavi!" Soren bellowed.

"What have you done?" a voice came behind them, and they spun to see the green Wild woman.

"Please," Mikael begged. "I know you have the power to heal. You have to heal her!"

Naavi's eyes widened as she looked over Norah, and she stepped to them. Her hands shook as she dropped down to brush Salara's cheek. She held her face. "No," the Wild woman whispered. Her lips pulled back in a silent sob, then she screamed, "Sana!"

A second Wild woman appeared from between the trees, and quickly came to them. No smart remarks about Mikael or Soren, just her eyes on Salara. She reached out and touched Salara's pale skin, and her face twisted. Then she looked at her sister with a great sadness in her eyes. "Sister," she whispered. "She's gone."

Soren's chest seized. She couldn't be gone.

"No," Naavi pleaded. "We have to try."

Sana's frown deepened. "Even with the power of the pool, you know we can't bring life back after it's completely gone."

"We have to try," Naavi pressed.

"But it's not possible."

"Try!" Mikael and Soren raged together. Soren would burn this forest to the ground if they didn't at least try to help her.

Sana looked at her sister, and then gave a reluctant nod. "Quickly, bring her to the pool."

Naavi scooped Salara from Soren's arms like she weighed nothing at all and followed her sister. Soren pulled Mikael to his feet and, with Mikael's arm wrapped around his shoulder, they followed after.

The Wild held all the beauty and amazement Soren remembered, but he didn't pay attention now. He only followed the sisters to the pool.

When they reached it, they splashed into the water. Soren and Mikael followed, surprisingly with no objections. The sisters weren't focused on Soren and Mikael—they were focused on Salara. They placed their hands on her and closed their eyes.

Soren locked eyes with Mikael. He could see his fear and felt his own fear swelling. If Salara died...

The women broke from their concentration and looked at each other, their eyes wide. "We don't have enough strength," Sana panted. "We need to pull more."

"Can you use me?" Soren asked. He considered himself pretty damned strong.

"You don't have power, you idiot," Sana snapped.

Soren didn't even know how to respond to that. He was about to argue that the witch had used power from Mikael, but a small, horned creature appeared and put her hand on Sana's shoulder, and his argument left him as he realized they were surrounded by creatures. So many of them—where had they come from?

Another creature followed suit, reaching out to Sana. All the creatures of the Wild around them drew forward, placing their hands on one another, linking their strength.

Naavi and Sana closed their eyes again. Sweat beaded on their brows. Everything was quiet. *Eternity in the quiet.*

Tears streamed down Naavi's face. That couldn't be good. Soren's heart pulsed faster. He looked at Mikael, whose own eyes were rimmed red.

And then they all stopped.

Warmth. Warmth flooded her senses.

Norah's eyes opened as she sucked in a breath. Was she in water? She focused her eyes to see Naavi looking back at her, smiling with tears in her eyes. She smiled back. *Naavi?*

And then Mikael pulled her to him, holding her tight. How was Mikael here? A splash sounded beside her, and Soren leaned closer. What was happening?

And then the memories flooded her.

The war.

The battle.

How she'd used the dagger on herself to stop Cyrus.

She twisted as she clutched her chest.

Mikael gripped her hand to calm her. "You're all right," he said through his tears. "You're all right."

She stopped, and her breaths started to calm. *He* was all right. And he was here, with her.

"You came back," he whispered.

"There was life still in her," Naavi said.

Norah reached up and touched his face. She couldn't take her eyes from him. He was alive, and with her. She smiled through her tears at him. "I was so scared," she whispered. "I thought you were going to die."

He held her tighter. "I thought you *had* died."

"She did," Naavi said. "But there was still life inside." The woman gestured to her stomach, smiling at Norah. "We used it to keep you."

Life inside. Norah looked at her stomach and then to Mikael, then back to Naavi. "What?" She didn't dare to hope their meaning.

"You carry a life inside you," Naavi said. "A child."

"A child?" Norah breathed, tears springing from her eyes. "I'm with child?" A sob rose in her throat. After all this time, after all the wanting and the disappointment and the heartache. Finally. *A child.*

Naavi nodded.

Norah let out a laugh through her sob. Mikael pulled her to him and shook as he buried his face in the fold of her neck. All she could do was hold on to him. *A child.* Mikael was all right, they were together, and they were going to have a child. Her heart was so happy it hurt.

Suddenly, Mikael pulled back and looked at the Wild women. "You used the child to save her?"

Naavi nodded again. "Yes."

His brow creased in worry. "Is he all right?"

"She." Naavi's smile widened. "She's perfectly fine."

Soren sat in wet clothes. He didn't care, but he still grumbled about it. It was the only thing that kept him from losing himself to the emotion he struggled so hard to keep down. He wished he had his wrap to hide his face, to hide the emotion brimming. He'd lost it somewhere on the ride to the Wild.

Salara had done it—she'd changed fate. Mikael was safe, and for that Soren wanted to cling on to her, hold her, hug her.

Then she'd almost died and, in doing so, had ripped his heart from his chest. This wretched woman, the thought had destroyed him. And now... she and Mikael had what they'd wanted for so long—a child. His heart swelled to near bursting.

A movement to his right caught his eye, and he turned to see the two Wild women approaching. Finally, something to be annoyed about to distract his mind from feelings.

"Destroyer," Sana said as they neared. They really liked calling him that, but he didn't mind too much. It reminded him of Salara's grandmother—feisty wench. Death didn't deserve her.

His attention shifted back to the women, and he stood. "Come to take my memories?" he said with an edge of challenge. Not that he could stop them, but he'd still give them the nine hells if they tried. They hadn't taken them the last time he was here with Salara—they had a lot to catch up for.

The Wild women stopped in front of him and stared at him for a moment.

He stood and shifted uncomfortably.

"We saw you in the water."

How observant. "Yes, I was in the water." Maybe he shouldn't have jumped in the pool—the magical pool—but he hadn't even cared. Salara was all he could think about.

"No, we *saw* you," Naavi said. "We saw who you are."

He raised a brow. "I've been here three times, and you're just now seeing?"

Sana rolled her eyes. "We didn't care before. And to be very clear, we don't care now. But the pool showed us regardless." She reached out and gripped his shoulder.

He stiffened, and a groan escaped him as pain shot through him. It almost brought him to his knees. When she pulled back her hand, he gaped down at his shoulder. The sword wound was stitched with an earthy binding. She'd healed him. He drew his fingers over it as he stared back at them in surprise.

"And we have something else we want to give you," Naavi said. "A gift."

Soren didn't like gifts. They were generally in poor taste and expected to be reciprocated. But he stilled as he saw two wolves step out from between the trees—large wolves, the largest he'd ever seen. Both wore coats of black, and their eyes burned a deep gold.

Naavi's eyes changed from green to bright gold, and she stepped in front him. Her hands reached up and cupped his cheeks, and she pulled his face down to hers. Ever so softly, she pushed herself up on her toes and planted a kiss on his forehead.

He gasped as visions rippled through him, and he realized—he was looking through the eyes of the wolves. His eyes flew open, and he stumbled backward, almost falling, but he managed to catch himself.

"You've made me a seer?"

Sana looked at Naavi. "He really is an idiot sometimes."

Naavi smiled. "No. Not a seer. But these wolves are bonded to you now. They're loyal to you, and they'll give you a greater power to do what you've always done."

He snorted. "Destroy?"

Naavi shook her head. "Protect."

He stilled and stood wordlessly. He looked at the wolves and then back at the sisters.

Naavi nodded to him.

Then he knelt down and willed the wolves to him. And they came, knowing his mind. His hands trembled as he reached out to run his fingers through their thick fur. They were beautiful beasts. Strong. Fearless. They would do nicely. He looked back at the sisters.

"Now get out of our forest," Sana said.

Soren smiled.

The morning air was frigid as they prepared to leave the Wild and head back to the North. The rising sun spilled its rays down on them, but they held no warmth. Soren scowled out at the snow-laden sky in the distance. It would turn colder as they traveled. He hated the cold.

The Wild women had offered them to stay longer, to wait out the small storm approaching, but Salara was eager to get back and show their people that their queen was alive and well—a little snow wouldn't keep her. Soren was eager too. He needed to return to what was left after the battle. Caspian and Adrian would be waiting for him.

Phillip would be waiting for him. The thought warmed him.

Soren sat on his horse, his wolves standing beside him, and rolled his eyes as he waited the eternity it took for Salara to say goodbye to the Wild women and mount up behind Mikael. Calla sat on her own horse, smiling. The girl was in a perky mood, which meant he'd have to listen to her incessant chatter all the way back. The journey already felt long, and they hadn't even started yet.

Soren glanced around impatiently and found Mikael looking back at him with a smile on his lips. Never had he seen his brother so happy.

Happy was different.

Many things would be different now. Their kingdoms were united with the new Aleon Empire. A lot would change. Kharav would change.

They were already abandoning their slaving norms, which had fallen apart through the course of the war. Salara would make sure it stayed that way.

The united kingdoms would no longer be constantly on the brink of battle. Soren wasn't quite sure what he'd do with himself. He thought of Phillip again. He'd figure it out.

Finally, to his relief, they started on their way, urging their mounts past the tree line of the Wild and north.

A stinging wind swept through with the faint beginnings of snow.

"Curse the North gods," he muttered.

Calla wrinkled her brow. "Why the North gods?"

"Because we don't have gods, so you curse the North ones."

"But... why the North ones? Elam has gods, and Persus. And Lorys."

Soren shot the girl an annoyed glance. "Because everything that makes your life hard comes from the North."

"Not me," Salara said sweetly as she leaned against Mikael's back with her arms wrapped around him.

Mikael chuckled.

Soren dipped his brow. "Especially you." He glanced at her belly and then rolled his eyes again. "And now there's going to be two of you."

"Ah, Soren," she teased him, "what are you going to do with another girl around?"

Soren snorted as he looked out at the rising sun. He'd do the only thing to be done with a girl—

Make her a warrior.

Acknowledgments

By the time this trilogy is published, it will have been over ten years in the making. There are so many people who've been a part of this journey, and I'm incredibly grateful to each and every one of them. However, I have to call out a few very special people.

I've written as a hobby since grade school and never intended to publish anything. Ever. I never even thought about it until one evening I was at dinner with a friend and colleague, Lisa Chung, who pressed me to consider publishing. And while I told her that publishing wasn't for me, it planted a seed. Five years later, here I am, putting my work out into the Wild for everyone to read. Lisa, without that conversation, I'd still be writing to myself.

Even though I've written all my life, I still had so many things to learn. Evolving a story is hard, and honestly, lonely sometimes. Critiques, especially harsh ones, can destroy a creative heart's fragile confidence. It's so easy to doubt yourself and want to abandon the effort. For those of you who gave me honest feedback with love, I can't even begin to describe how much your support means to me.

To all my early beta readers, you got the worst version of everything, and helped not only my story, but me personally. Kaylin Barlow and Kaylyn Nicole—you both have been my constants, with me since the very first book and every step of the way. Janete Lawson, Bruce Bendle, Noelle Rayne, Jacqueline Schimel, Cat Fletcher, Hunter Harrison—you all gave me the early encouragement and support to keep reworking and moving forward. While this story isn't the same as it was when you had it, it's certainly what it is today because of you.

To Kate Studer, Dev Editor Extraordinaire, your keen eye and brilliant feedback made this story even better.

For any fragments and one-word sentences you see through this trilogy, abjectivizing or verbizing nouns, know that my amazing editor, Hanna Richards, did her best to talk me out of them. I'd also like to acknowledge and thank Merriam-Webster for now recognizing *snuck* as a past tense of *sneak*. To my proofreader, Lauren Riebs, I'm so grateful for your polish and helping me turn this into a *real* book!

Landing on a cover design has been the most stressful part of this journey, and I've changed direction several times. I'd rather write another trilogy. Jupiter—thank you, thank you, thank you, for helping wrap these books in art that beautifully represents my story.

To my daughters, Allyriane, Everly, and Rosemary, who listened to me talk for countless hours about my books, gave me plot and name ideas, and gave it to me straight when I had bad ideas (thanks for keeping me humble)—I love you, my littles.

And last, because I always save the best for last—Shaun, Mr. Nicola Tyche. Without you, not only would this trilogy not have been published, it wouldn't have been written. As a mom of three working in a corporate job, it's already hard to balance things; to write in addition is near impossible. You run our house while working a full-time job yourself, you're dedicated to our kids, you make sure we're all fed and functioning and loved, and you create the time and space for me so I can keep dreaming up my stories. I couldn't have done any of this without you. I love you.

ABOUT THE AUTHOR

Nicola Tyche is an American fiction and fantasy author writing romantic fantasy, paranormal, urban fantasy, and other women's fiction. Suspenseful plot twists, strong heroines, relatable villains, and melt-your-insides anti-heroes are ingredients for every book, and Nicola is a sucker for a happily ever after.

She lives in Vancouver, Washington, with her husband and three daughters. When she isn't writing, she enjoys tacos, traveling, gardening, exploring the great outdoors, and other creative projects. Visit her website at www.nicolatyche.com, connect on the Nicola Tyche Facebook reader group, or the platforms below!

nicolatyche